Whitehwas my home, a kingdo... ...I believed in, I had a co... ...my life. Over the last y...

DISTANT FIRES

It was all I could offer. The only thing I had to give, now that everything was gone. Myself. Most likely I would die in the attempt. But I would leave a grievous mark upon them. They would remember me. I would never be forgotten again.

THE WEIGHT OF WATER

Combat—after months of hiding and banditry, real combat at last! His blood thrilled, eager to engage the enemy in a battle for the honor and glory of his homeland. He felt other Karrns close at hand, surging upwards with him, ready to take the battle to the cowardly Aundairians.

WAR MACHINES

"What will you do when it's over?" Spear's even tone made his words even more blunt.

"Over? You think it ends? We are machines of war. With or without the war, our job is slaughter."

CALL OF THE SILVER FLAME

"Of course there's no justice in a war like that. People . . . there's no justice among people at all. Everyone will shift sides if they've got a good enough reason. But this—this is different. This isn't people playing their war games."

ALL THIS AND MORE IN
TALES OF THE LAST WAR

THE DREAMING DARK TRILOGY
By Keith Baker

The City of Towers

The Shattered Land

The Gates of Night
(November 2006)

THE DRAGON BELOW TRILOGY
By Don Bassingthwaite

The Binding Stone

The Grieving Tree

The Killing Song
(December 2006)

THE TALES OF THE
LAST WAR

EDITED BY MARK SEHESTEDT

THE TALES OF THE LAST WAR
©2006 Wizards of the Coast, Inc.

All characters in this book are fictitious. Any resemblance to actual persons, living or dead, is purely coincidental.

This book is protected under the copyright laws of the United States of America. Any reproduction or unauthorized use of the material or artwork contained herein is prohibited without the express written permission of Wizards of the Coast, Inc.

Published by Wizards of the Coast, Inc. EBERRON, WIZARDS OF THE COAST, and their respective logos are trademarks of Wizards of the Coast, Inc., in the U.S.A. and other countries.

Printed in the U.S.A.

The sale of this book without its cover has not been authorized by the publisher. If you purchased this book without a cover, you should be aware that neither the author nor the publisher has received payment for this "stripped book."

Cover art by Dana Knutson
First Printing: April 2006
Library of Congress Catalog Card Number: 2005928124

9 8 7 6 5 4 3 2 1

ISBN-10: 0-7869-3986-9
ISBN-13: 978-0-7869-3986-2
620-95468740-001-EN

U.S., CANADA,	EUROPEAN HEADQUARTERS
ASIA, PACIFIC, & LATIN AMERICA	Hasbro UK Ltd
Wizards of the Coast, Inc.	Caswell Way
P.O. Box 707	Newport, Gwent NP9 0YH
Renton, WA 98057-0707	GREAT BRITAIN
+1-800-324-6496	Save this address for your records.

Visit our web site at www.wizards.com

INTRODUCTION: THE TALES OF THE LAST WAR 1

DEATH AT WHITEHEARTH 3
    Keith Baker

DEATH BEFORE DAWN 33
    Paul Crilley

THE BLADE OF THE FLAME 67
    Tim Waggoner

DISTANT FIRES 111
    Aaron Rosenberg

THE VEILED CHARGE 145
    David A. Page

THE WEIGHT OF WATER 181
    Edward Bolme

WAR MACHINES – 992 YK 219
    Ian Burton-Oakes

CALL OF THE SILVER FLAME 259
    James Wyatt

FLIGHT OF THE *RIGHTEOUS INDIGNATION* 303
    Ari Marmell

THE TALES OF THE LAST WAR

For almost nine hundred years, the kingdom of Galifar dominated the world of Eberron, bringing civilization from the Barren Sea in the west to the Lhazaar Sea in the east. With the unearthing of ancient magics and the discovery and development of new arcane inventions, the kingdom of Galifar brought new wonders to the world—great cities, wondrous monuments, weapons of war, and conveniences that eased the burdens of day-to-day living and made continental travel possible (for those who could afford it). The mastery of the arcane arts allowed for the founding and growth of cities, the size and majesty of which the world had never seen. Greatest of these was Sharn, the City of Towers, where the homes of the wealthy floated a mile or more above the squalid streets of the poor. Magic brought the rains in years of drought and assured days of sunshine so that crops and herds prospered like never before, making hunger a thing of the past for all but the most poverty-stricken within the kingdom.

THE TALES OF THE LAST WAR

Magic was the heart and soul of Eberron, and it was the foundation upon which the kings and queens of Galifar founded their magnificent kingdom.

All of that came to an end in the year 894 YK, when King Jarot, the last of the Galifar kings, died. Civil war broke his kingdom as his scions ignored tradition and instead fought for his crown. For over a hundred years, war shook the once-proud kingdom, and the artificers and arcane masters of the magic arts turned their efforts from building and creating to killing and destroying. Entire cities fell to flame and ruin, but the worst tragedy came in 994 YK, on a day forever afterward remembered as the Day of Mourning, when the nation of Cyre died in a magic cataclysm. The once glorious nation became a barren wasteland where horrors beyond imagining walked and preyed upon the unwary.

In 996 YK, the warring nations called off hostilities and signed the Treaty of Thronehold, thus ending over a century of warfare. In the following months, thanks in large part to the reporting of the *Korranberg Chronicle,* those years of fighting have become known as the "Last War," in hopes that it will be. Time will tell.

The following tales are accounts of only a few of the many adventures that occurred in the final days of the war or immediately thereafter. Herein you will visit the doomed nation of Cyre only weeks before its destruction, ride aboard the famed flying fortress of Argonth, see the dying days of a city as war tears it apart—and the vengeance wrought by its last defender, and witness the mission of soldiers in the dark continent of Xen'drik as they walk the fine line between wonder and terror. All this and more await you in the following pages, so settle in, for here are only a few Tales of the Last War. . . .

DEATH AT WHITEHEARTH

Keith Baker

We *returned to Whitehearth today. There was a time when I swore I'd never set foot in the Mournland again, that I'd never go back to the broken land I'd once called home. But I know all too well how simple it is to break a vow.*

As difficult as it was for any of us to return to the corpse of Cyre, the trip was hardest for Lei. I had trouble looking at some of the things we found, but some of these people had been her friends and family.

I'd only visited Whitehearth once before, but I could still see the faces of the people I'd met. Karizal. Halea. Dravot. When we found the hall filled with corpses, I wanted to find Karizal, just to know for certain. But there was a job to do and time was against us. As we searched, I could hear the voices from the past whispering in my mind. I found my thoughts slipping back four years, back to when I'd first seen the halls of Whitehearth. . . .

We'd been stationed in the Felmar Valley for almost a year. As wars went, it was almost civilized. We stayed to the north and the Brelanders stayed to the south. Neither side had the resources or the interest to try to take the enemy fortifications. It was a simple matter of patrolling the valley and maintaining that blue line on the map. For a while, I could even sleep at night.

Then the Valenar showed up. The Valenar *like* war. Some of them had been waiting for centuries for a chance to spill this much blood. Those damned elves are like cats—they like to toy with their prey. And they can see in the dark far better than you or I. The first we knew of them was when we woke one morning to find that every one of the night patrols had been—

Well, I'm sure you've seen it before.

I didn't get much sleep after that.

The Brelanders didn't even bother attacking in the day anymore. They were content to wait and let the elves do the dirty work. Occasionally the Valenar would launch a full cavalry raid, but usually they were ghosts in the night. We consolidated our patrols as much as possible, but we were there to guard the valley, and so guard we did, and each morning I'd find out how many we'd lost during the night. My requests for reinforcements were denied. To the north, every sword was dedicated to slowing the Karrnathi advance, and in the south the Queen's Council was more concerned with protecting Celyria than holding the Felmar line. We were ordered to hold our position and do our job. There were only a few dozen Valenar in the region, they said. Surely a mere handful of elves weren't enough to defeat a full regiment of the Queen's Guards. Eventually, it became clear that they were. But the council still couldn't spare men or magewrights to help, so they took another approach. One cold Therendor morning, I received orders to travel to a nearby forgehold of House Cannith. I didn't even know there *was* a Cannith forgehold nearby, but Lei d'Cannith, our artificer, knew the way. There I was to meet with the Forgehold director to discuss materiel aid.

And that's how we came to Whitehearth.

2

"Our nation is losing ground on all fronts. My regiment is engaged in a hopeless and suicidal defense. What better time for a jaunt in the woods?"

I was speaking rhetorically, but Pierce had never had a good ear for sarcasm.

"I am certain that the lord commander would not have ordered you from the valley unless he had good reason, Captain Daine." Pierce's voice was deep and calm, like slow water flowing across rocks. "While it seems unlikely that House Cannith will be willing to provide assistance without some form of compensation, the magical weapons developed by the House could prove most useful in our struggle."

"Yeah, good point," I said. "Always put your faith in the lord commander, right?"

I had to admire Pierce's dedication. Sometimes I wished I commanded an entire unit of warforged. They didn't eat, they didn't sleep, and they didn't leave as much of a mess when the Valenar were through with them. This last point had been driven home quite clearly over the last two weeks. I'd thought soldiers who don't sleep would be the best choice for night patrol. As a result of that little theory Pierce was the last warforged in our unit—not that flesh and blood would have fared any better. I am a tall man, but Pierce has a good three inches on me, and his longbow is at least seven feet from tip to tip. Compared to the bulky juggernauts you usually saw on the field, Pierce was lean and graceful. He—

—Yeah, I know warforged have no gender, but I can't think of a friend as "it"—

—could outrun any man and move as silently as any elf. Pierce was the only truly effective weapon we had against the Valenar.

Warforged are as heavy as a knight in full armor. Pierce rode an enormous gray charger, with Jode perched behind him. Small even for a halfling, Jode added little to the stallion's load.

"Personally, I see no reason to complain, Captain," he said. Jode had always been a free spirit, with only a loose bond to the hierarchy of his House. But his heritage was unmistakable. He was bald—rare among halflings—and his dragonmark spread across the top of his head, a complex labyrinth of vivid color. This mark allowed him to mend flesh and bone with a touch and a thought, and like most members of his House he'd had no trouble finding employment with the armies. "Would you really rather be trapped in that dank fortress when you could be out here enjoying the sun and wind?"

My orders were quite clear: I was to bring Pierce and Lady Lei to Whitehearth, and to tell no one else about the mission. But Jode was more than just a healer. He was also the cleverest person I'd ever met, with wits even sharper than my grandfather's sword. Jode's cunning had saved me more times than I cared to remember, and the Keeper could take the lord commander and his orders.

Lei had been silent for most of the journey and ignored the

banter. At first I thought she was intentionally ignoring us, then I saw her expression and realized that she was lost in another of her reveries. She was an artificer from the House of Making, which maintained the warforged and other arcane equipment assigned to the regiment. Lei's dragonmark was usually hidden from view, but there was no mistaking her heritage. House Cannith had been wealthy enough before the war began, and if anyone benefits from war it's the weaponsmith. No nation could afford to let an enemy gain an advantage, and so platinum flowed into the Cannith coffers. In all ways that mattered Lei was a princess, and even though she had chosen to serve with the army of Cyre, she carried herself with the proud bearing of a noblewoman. She had the pale complexion common to her house, along with coppery red hair—a trait of the Cyran Cannith that some called "the fire of the forge." Where Jode mended flesh and bone, Lei worked with magic and steel, and where he was lively, she was usually more distant, lost in her arcane schemes.

"Lei!" I barked.

She looked over, startled. "What?"

As a dragonmarked, Lei was not part of the hierarchy of the Queen's Guard of Cyre and was therefore not obliged to acknowledge my rank.

"We're almost at this forgehold. Before we get there, I want more information. Who is this Director Halea? What work are they doing here? And why was I ordered to bring Pierce, of all people?"

"I don't know," she replied, with a wry smile. I almost believed her. "I know where Whitehearth is, but I don't know what sort of work is being done there. I've never heard of an outsider being invited to a forgehold before. The order was relayed through the lord commander's office, so I assume it's part of an arrangement between the House and your queen."

Your queen. That still irked me. Here we were on Cyran soil, yet Lei felt no loyalty to the ruler of the land. In her eyes, her House was a power above mere kings and queens. Serving alongside Cyran soldiers, she felt no association with the cause. She was just taking care of the warforged, doing a job.

There was a part of me that understood how she felt. I had been raised the same way. But I'd chosen to leave that behind. I'd made mistakes along the way, given my faith too easily . . .

But Cyre was different. Cyre was the one nation that had held to the traditions of the old kingdom, the one nation that had not given in to greed and aggression. The horrors I'd seen had stripped away my faith in divine benevolence or the inherent goodness of the human soul. But I still believed in Cyre. We were under attack from all sides, but I knew we would prevail somehow, that ultimately the great kingdom of Galifar would be restored. Perhaps this was the next step on that path.

"Fine," I said. "Let's say I believe you. What I want to know is—"

I never finished the sentence. There was a blur of motion and fluid steel as six figures slipped out of the shadows. They were warforged scouts, each one scarcely larger than Jode. Each had a crossbow in place of its left hand and a long sword strapped across its back. Most curious of all was the metal of their armor. It seemed to be a mithral alloy, but the colors shifted and blurred, making the 'forged almost invisible in the shadows of the forest. They moved with an unnatural silence, as if they were leeching the sound out of their surroundings.

And those crossbows were rising up to point at us.

Before the lead 'forged had his crossbow fully aimed, my sword was out and I was spurring my horse forward. The tiny soldier rolled out of the way just before I struck him, and a quarrel buzzed past my head.

I heard Lei call out in a language I didn't recognize, and then she shouted, "Daine! Stop now! Drop your weapon!"

I brought Graymane up sharply. "Devourer's Teeth! What are you talking about?"

I turned and noticed that while the other five 'forged had their crossbows aimed at my head, none had fired. Not one.

"Just *do* it!" said Lei. "Quickly!"

I threw my grandfather's blade down on the dirt. The warforged didn't move, but they didn't fill me full of quarrels, and I suppose that said something.

Lei swung down from her horse. Holding her hands in front of her, palms down, she walked over to the nearest warforged. Kneeling, she held out her right hand—the hand bearing her house signet ring. There was a glimmer of light, as the seal of the house shimmered within the stone, confirming her status as an heir of Cannith. Lei said a few quiet words then returned and remounted her horse.

"They're Whitehearth guards. They'll escort us the rest of the way."

"And if we'd just been a random patrol of Cyran soldiers?"

Lei smiled. "Better not to ask."

3

The warforged patrol soon brought us to a hillside clearing. At the base of the slope, a tunnel reinforced with lumber braces bored into the hill. A man waited at the entrance. He looked to be in his forties, but he had a solid build and carried himself with confidence. His fair skin and red hair and mustache implied his House Cannith ancestry, and the blue-and-silver badge he wore over his heart confirmed it. He wore studded leather dyed a dark blue, and five black wands were tucked into his belt.

Lei looked surprised. "That's Dravot, one of the finest wands in the House," she whispered. "He led the bombardment of Golan Rath."

We dismounted, and Dravot bowed and went to one knee. "Lady Lei, you honor us with your presence." He stood and gave me a cold stare, one hand idly drifting to one of his wands. "Captain Daine, for a military man you seem to have a surprising amount of difficulty following simple orders. House Cannith has shown you a great honor by inviting you to Whitehearth, and you repay us by revealing the location of the forgehold to another dragonmarked family." He pointedly ignored Jode while his hand closed around a wand of polished darkwood marked with two red bands. "I'm afraid you have done your friend a great disservice."

Even as my hand dropped to my blade, Jode stepped forward. "Please! The last thing I want is trouble on my account. Dravot—it is Dravot, isn't it?—I recognize you from the songs I've heard sung about the siege of Golan Rath. What an honor it is to actually stand in the presence of a true hero!"

You'd think that it would be hard to say such a thing with a straight face, but Jode was a portrait of wide-eyed sincerity. Dravot kept his hand on his wand, but he didn't draw it out.

"Daine never told me anything about where we were going or why," said Jode. "If the captain and an important dragonmarked heir leave alone, it's just common sense to bring a healer along. I'm sure you understand. What if there was an accident? Or an ambush? Should he have put the Lady d'Cannith at such risk? I'm sure that if your tiny tin men hadn't forced the issue, Daine would have left me behind in some nearby clearing."

"Damned straight," I said. "Don't blame us for your mistake. And if you harm my healer, I'll be taking it straight to the queen herself. We're at war, remember? And with all your holdings on Cyran soil, I really don't think you want to make an enemy of the throne."

"What is this, Dravot?" Lei broke in. "Are we afraid of House *Jorasco* now?"

Jode cleared his throat and waved us aside. "Friends! I don't want any unpleasantness on my account. Sir Dravot, if you please, even if my House were interested in whatever you are up to here, I am not. I would be happy to be placed under guard so you can make sure I don't steal your terribly important secrets. As long as I'm here, surely you have some folk in need of healing?" He nodded toward the mouth of the shaft. "Underground living can be very unhealthy. Why you yourself have quite a sickly pallor. I think a daily infusion of teral root would do wonders for all of you, and—"

"Very well," Dravot said, his hand slipping away from the wand. "But the final decision will be up to Director Halea. Follow me."

4

Halea d'Cannith was a severe woman who wore her gray hair in a tight braid. Despite her age and rather emaciated frame, her eyes were sharp and calculating. She was accompanied by Karizal d'Cannith. Even I'd heard of Karizal. In addition to being one of the top arcanists in his House, he was famous for his work with the Grusanga kobolds. It was due to his diplomatic efforts that the forest tribes were now working as miners instead of raiding supply caravans. He was a handsome man near my age. His dark hair and eyes hinted at a trace of Karrnathi blood in his veins. His most obvious feature was his arm—or lack thereof. Like Lei, Karizal had spent a few years serving with the Cyran army, and he'd lost his left arm during a Karrnathi raid. From what I'd heard, he was one of the few heirs of Cannith who believed that the House had a duty to protect Cyre, its ancestral homeland. With all my misgivings about this assignment, I was glad to see him here.

Halea studied Jode as he repeated his story and his offer. In the end she agreed, and guards took him away. Karizal embraced Lei and then led her and Pierce away to catch up on family matters. Dravot relieved me of my weapons and left me with Halea, who was without question the fun one of the bunch. Looking at her, I couldn't help but wonder how many years it had been since she'd tried to smile. She led me through the halls of Whitehearth. Occasionally we'd pass an open door and I'd catch a glimpse of magewrights molding what appeared to be frozen flame or binding threads of light to bars of molten steel.

"Captain Daine," Halea said, her voice as cold as her eyes. "I understand that your regiment is in a difficult position. This is hardly surprising. The only reason Cyre still exists as a nation is because of House Cannith. Without our support—our warforged and our weapons—Cyre would have fallen long ago."

Not if you didn't sell weapons to every nation under the sun, I thought, but I said nothing.

We entered a conference room. At first glance it was quite a change from the bare stone of the forgehold. Light came from a beautiful crystal chandelier, each crystal enchanted to hold its own inner flame and reflect off the darkwood walls. An oval table dominated the center of the chamber, the seal of House Cannith engraved into the surface.

But when I followed Halea inside, I found that the only thing real was the table and the surrounding chairs. The walls, floor, and ceiling were translucent crystal, and the rest was an image in the glass. I was standing inside a giant crystal ball.

Halea noticed my surprise. "It's a scrying chamber," she said. She made a gesture over the table and our surroundings melted away. Suddenly we were a thousand feet above the Grusanga Forest, seemingly standing on thin air. She gestured again, and the image of the room returned. "There are a few of them in the forgehold. Besides allowing us to monitor the area around Whitehearth, they allow us to observe dangerous experiments. Unfortunately, it's a very expensive technique, and the range is limited." She sat down at the head of the table. "Now please, join me."

I walked over to the table. As beautiful as the Riedran carpet appeared to be, it was as hard and cold as walking on a mirror.

Once I was seated, Halea said, "Captain, indulge my curiosity. You were not born a citizen of Cyre, were you?" Her eyes were still cold, her expression as impassive as any warforged.

"That's correct," I said.

"You were born into House Deneith, which holds a virtual monopoly on the mercenary trade in Khorvaire. While you failed the test of Siberys and do not bear the dragonmark of your House, you showed excellent promise in your early service in the Deneith Guards. But when you were twenty-two you left your House, gave up your family name, and joined the army of Cyre. Why?"

"After House Cannith started making all those warforged, I wanted to find a little more job security." I wasn't about to tell her anything she didn't already know.

She nodded. "A wise observation, Daine. You have seen the future of war."

She made an intricate gesture and one of the walls faded away, replaced by a forest scene. It showed a patrol of warforged scouts like the ones we'd encountered earlier. The chameleon effect of their armor was fully active, and it was almost impossible to see them clearly. The vision followed the group as they hunted two warforged juggernauts.

"This is the Greenshadow," Halea said, "one of our latest models. It possesses the ability to absorb sound and divert light, rendering it very difficult to detect. It has perfect visual acuity at all levels of illumination—even mystical darkness. The embedded crossbow has a regenerating stockpile of bolts, and the soldier can choose to charge each bolt with fire or electricity. Like all warforged, each unit is immune to the effects of hunger, thirst, disease, exhaustion, and has no need of sleep. Once we have found a way to reduce the cost of creation, the human soldier will become obsolete."

I'd been making a joke, but she seemed serious. And I have to say, watching those little warriors, it didn't seem so far fetched. If they worked as well as she said, we could sure use a few of those scouts back in the valley. But I didn't think she'd brought me here to brag.

"And the point of all this?" I asked.

"The Treaty of Galifar established the dragonmarked Houses as standing outside all kingdoms. By the terms of the treaty, we are to hold no lands beyond our estates, hold no people as our subjects, and hold no influence in the courts of kings or princes. With the exception of House Deneith, we are not to maintain armies, mustering forces sufficient only to protect our own property."

I nodded. I'd heard all this before.

"But much has changed over the last thousand years," she said. "Our Houses have grown far beyond the simple guilds the first king brought to heel. Regardless of the law, we have land, and we certainly have influence. But we could have far more."

I did my best to keep all emotion off my face.

"The old kingdom of Galifar is gone, Daine. This war has been going on for over a century. The queen of Cyre isn't going to restore the old crown. No one will. But perhaps it is time to forge a new kingdom—one that better reflects the true balance of power in this world."

"If you're trying to forge an alliance with House Deneith, you've picked the wrong man to talk to, Director. I'm just a captain."

"Oh, this is all conjecture, Daine," she said, though her tone suggested otherwise. "Even if such a thing were to come to pass, you said it yourself: mercenaries are no longer necessary. Given a decade House Cannith could build its own army, and it would be a force like none ever seen in all the ages of the world." For a moment her eyes clouded over with that same faraway expression I'd seen on Lei's face so many times. "But for all the power of our warforged soldiers, they lack experience, and our House has a notable lack of capable military officers. So you see? Even if we did create such an army—a purely hypothetical thought—we would need to find people to lead it. I'd think that the perfect person would be someone who had served with both a dragonmarked House and an army of the crown, someone who understood both worlds but was smart enough to leave both behind for the right opportunity."

For a moment, our eyes locked.

"As fantasies go, that's an interesting one," I said. "If I find anyone like that—again, hypothetically—maybe I'll send him your way. Galifar's not dead yet. The queen is still the rightful heir to the throne of the old kingdom, and the war's far from over. It may not happen in my lifetime, but Cyre will prevail. Galifar will rise again."

Halea's eyes narrowed. "It may *not* happen in your lifetime, Captain." To my astonishment, she smiled. "Please. You're quite right, and I hope you will forgive an old woman her flights of fancy. Now, you were brought here for a reason. Let's get on with it." She produced a large sheaf of parchment from a rather small pouch on her belt and spread it across the table. "Now, captain. If your queen wishes to hold on to her throne—let alone reforge the crown of Galifar—she will need more than men and swords. She will need magic. She will need the power that only we can bestow."

Now we seemed to be back to the familiar tune, but the next verse was a surprise.

"I contacted your commander to offer my assistance. Even if the queen is not my sovereign, Cyre is still my home. I would like to provide you with a unit of Greenshadows to use as you see fit. These soldiers are already prepared, and you may leave as soon as you wish."

I frowned. I knew how expensive 'forged were. Cannith would never just give them away.

"What do you get in return, Director?"

She raised her hands in a placating gesture. "Do you have a monopoly on compassion, Captain?"

"Not a bit," I said. "But House Cannith doesn't give away prized soldiers for free."

"True. But your using the Greenshadows will have benefits for us. It will allow us to see how they perform in true combat conditions."

Could she be telling the truth? Did she just want a proving ground? If so, what did that say about the 'forged? Were they not as reliable as she said?

"There is one more thing, actually," she said. "A small favor, nothing more."

"Yes?"

"I believe that you have a warforged archer assigned to your task force. Unit 21."

"We call him Pierce."

"In exchange for the six Greenshadows, we would like to reclaim this . . . Pierce. Think of it as a trade. Obviously a very fair one, given all of the wear and tear I saw on 21 earlier."

I frowned. "Pierce isn't just a piece of furniture. He's been with the guard for longer than I have, and he's the best soldier in the unit—and that includes me. Besides, it's not my decision. He's the property of the Cyran Guard."

"That's where you're wrong," Halea said, tapping the sheaf of papers. "As its commanding officer, you are authorized to make any and all decisions regarding 21. If it is in the best interests of your regiment, you can certainly exchange the unit for goods or services. In this case, you will be exchanging one outdated warforged for six new and enhanced units. All I need is few signatures, and you can be on your way with your new soldiers."

I paused, considering. Certainly, those 'forged were just what we needed to deal with the Valenar. But whatever his legal status, Pierce wasn't just a tool to be bought and sold.

"I don't understand, Director Halea. If Pierce is so outdated, why do *you* want him?"

"I'm offering you an excellent deal, Captain." Her tone lost a little of its warmth. "Our interest in 21 is purely academic. It is one of the earliest units still in service, and we'd like to preserve it. As a memorial, if you will. A benchmark to measure the evolution of the warforged over the generations."

There was something going unsaid here. Even if she was telling the truth, I didn't like the thought of Pierce gathering dust in some sort of museum. I'd never known that he was one of the first warforged. Far from being obsolete, he seemed to be swifter and smarter than any other construct I'd had under my command. I didn't know how I was going to explain my decision to the Lord Commander, but I knew what that decision had to be.

"This is a very generous offer, Director—and I do hate to waste your time—but I'm afraid I must decline. Right now I can't afford to take any risks. I'd rather have one soldier I know I can count on than six I know nothing about. Perhaps your little green men are all you say." I stood up. "But I'll keep Pierce. Now, if you'll take me to my friends, I think we'd better be on our way."

She stood, all traces of warmth gone. "I'm sorry you feel that way, Captain. Please, sit. At least allow us to prepare you a meal, to give you an hour to consider our offer before you make another irreparable mistake."

A hot meal did sound better than the salted tribex I had in my saddlebags. I sat back down.

"Thank you," she said. "I'll see to it that Lady Lei and Unit 21 are brought here. We'll talk again, Captain Daine. Think carefully."

THE TALES OF THE LAST WAR

5

Time passed. I made random gestures over the center of the table to see if I could activate the scrying enchantment, but with no success. Eventually I tried the door and discovered, of course, that it was sealed. It hadn't been that long, so I decided not to panic.

Then the crystal walls went pitch black. The room had no windows, and the only illumination had been provided by the images in the walls. I couldn't see a thing.

Panicking suddenly seemed like a more reasonable option.

My hand went for my sword, but Dravot had confiscated my weapons when we arrived. The chairs and the table seemed to be fixed to the floor. So I set my back to the wall and slid over to the corner. The darkness seemed to stretch on forever. I have no idea how much time passed.

Then I heard it—the faintest sound of metal on glass. That was all that saved my life. Instincts honed by a decade of war took over. I threw myself to the side, and as I did a metal object smashed into the space where I'd been standing, showering me with fine shards of glass. I continued the roll and ended up in the opposite corner of the room.

I crouched, waiting, listening. At first I assumed that there was an archer in the center of the room, perhaps even one of those Greenshadows. But the attack came from the previous point of impact. I moved just in time, but even so a ribbon of razor-sharp steel tore across my back before striking the glass wall. I could hear it writhing on the floor, and I spun around to grapple with the source of the sound. I found what felt like a steel spear—until it moved. It seemed to be a serpent formed of steel. Both ends terminated in sharp blades. It was extremely strong and flexible, and I strained to keep those blades away from my face. Slowly, ever so slowly, I stretched it out into a straight line, as far from my face as possible. But if I'd learned one thing from working with warforged, it was that constructs never get tired. It was taking every ounce of my strength and will to hold the serpent at bay, and sooner or later my strength would fail.

While I knew defeat was inevitable, I wasn't prepared for what happened next. The coils of the serpent compressed and it flew to the left, tearing itself from my grip. Obviously this explosive flight was how it had been attacking me. I'd assumed that it needed a physical surface to brace against. Never assume.

I crouched low, listening for movement and ready to jump at the slightest sound. Then the door opened, and someone stepped inside.

"Daine?" It was Lei. The door slid shut, and the darkness returned.

"Lei?" Distracted by her voice, I almost missed the launch of the snake. I rolled forward just in time. "Watch out!"

I spun to the side and the serpent smashed into one of the chairs. Lei murmured a quick formula, and then there was light. She had a crystal sphere in her left hand, and it burned as bright as any torch. For a moment I was blinded by the unexpected illumination, and in that moment, the serpent struck my shoulder. It was a glancing blow, but the bladed tail came whipping around. I caught it just in time. The tip of the blade was slowly pressing down over my heart. Once again it was my strength against the steel serpent, but this time my arm was injured, and steel was overcoming flesh.

"Hold on, Daine!"

Dropping the ball of light, Lei leaped over the table. As the steel blade bit into my chest, she grabbed the center of the serpent and mouthed incantations. I felt a terrible pain as the blade pressed deeper—and then the serpent became dead weight in my arms.

Breathing heavily, I slid down against the wall and hurled the creature away. Ignoring my injuries, Lei immediately went over and picked up the serpent.

"I'm fine, thank you for asking," I said, gingerly probing my wounded shoulder. It wasn't bad, but I wished Jode were around.

"You're welcome," she said absently.

I knew better than to press the point, and she had just saved my life.

"What is it?" I asked.

"I've never seen anything quite like it before," she said. "It's more like one of the warforged than a true golem—created with enough intelligence to be able to adapt to evolving tactical situations." She tested the edge of a blade with one finger. "It's Cannith work."

"Shocking," I said. "Never would have expected that. It's not like we're in a House Cannith military forgehold."

She looked over at me, puzzled. "Why would anyone here want to kill you?"

"No time to explain. Can you get that door open? We need to get Pierce and Jode and get out of here."

"What do you mean get the door open?"

I pointed, and she blinked as she recognized the arcane seal. Her brow furrowed and she produced a small set of wands. In seconds she had broken the seal and opened the door.

"Where's Pierce?" I said.

"Karizal took him down to the lower level. He wanted to examine him."

I picked up the steel serpent. Lei had disrupted its enchantment, but it was a flexible length of steel with blades at both ends, and I could use it as a weapon if I had to.

"Someone here just tried to kill me. Probably Director Halea. She may have been acting on her own. If not, I suspect we'll find out when we open the door. Are you ready?"

She nodded, and we opened the door.

6

Karizal's workshop was on the lowest level. The forgehold was a strange place—a maze of workshops connected by a system of enormous rotating chambers. Without the proper keys, it would have been virtually impossible to penetrate the lower levels. Of course, Lei had the keys.

Much to my surprise, magewrights and artificers filled the halls, not arcane assassins. The one guard we saw approached and inquired about my wounds, but Lei managed to talk our way out of it. Everything was going so smoothly that I began to wonder if the assassination attempt hadn't been some sort of accident.

Karizal's hall was slightly darker than the other levels of Whitehearth. Karizal must have had a mystic alarm placed in the hall, for when we turned the corner he was already waiting for us outside the door of his workshop.

"Lei! Captain Daine!" he said, raising his hand in greeting. Like Jode, Karizal had an aura of infectious enthusiasm, and I found myself smiling as I shook his hand. His eyes widened at the sight of my torn clothing and blood. "What . . . what happened?"

"Someone tried to kill Daine," Lei said.

"So I see. Have you reported it?"

"No."

"Whyever not?"

"We came to get Pierce," I said.

Karizal looked shocked. "What are you talking about?"

"Someone sent this after me." I handed him the steel serpent." Any ideas who might have built it?"

He studied it closely. "No . . . no, the style is unfamiliar to me. But why would anyone want to kill you?"

"I believe it was Director Halea," I said. "She asked me to help conquer Khorvaire, and when I turned that down she demanded we give Pierce to her. Next thing I know, I'm fighting that thing."

Karizal frowned. "You'd better come with me. If Director Halea is indeed involved, you're both in danger. I'm surprised you made it this far."

He led us down the hallway to a portal that seemed to be filled with solid shadow. He stepped through it and vanished. I followed. It was a strange sensation, almost like walking through a thin layer of tar. The first thing I noticed upon reaching the other side was the heat. The second was the sound—half a dozen hammers all ringing out at once. This workshop was far larger than those I'd seen above. The left side of the room contained a full forge, and a dozen kobolds were scurrying about, working steel and stoking the furnaces. I sensed Lei enter behind me, and I looked down and saw that I was surrounded by what I'd first thought were kobolds. But these creatures were a strange patchwork of flesh and the composite materials of the warforged. Most had one or both of their arms and shoulders replaced by oversized warforged limbs. A few had both legs replaced, making them look like macabre stiltwalkers. Others had armored chest plating. The last thing

I noticed was the strange collar each kobold wore around his neck—dark metal engaving with intricate patterns, each collar bearing a small glowing crystal that pulsed through the full spectrum of color.

"Restrain them," Karizal said, and the mob of flesh and metal closed in.

7

We could have fought, I suppose. But at the time, I think both Lei and I were too stunned by this new betrayal to act. Before I could blink, iron hands were pinning my arms behind my back.

"What are you *doing*, Karizal?" Lei cried, her face flushed.

"Don't worry, cousin. This is for the best." He still had the same sunny tone in his voice. "Bring them."

I strained against the iron grip, to no avail. We were forced to follow Karizal past the forge and down a small hallway. We emerged into a smaller chamber. The dominant feature of the room was a massive crystal sphere mounted on a silver pedestal, etched with the same patterning as the collars. The orb was filled with a dizzying whirl of light and color, and the effect was almost hypnotic; it took some effort to tear my eyes away from it. Looking around, I saw a darkwood desk lined with notes and papers next to a workbench that held a few beautifully forged weapons—and a partially assembled metal snake, like the one that had attacked me. At first I thought that there was a window above the desk, and then I realized that it was a mirror—one that reflected the image of the conference room where I'd been attacked.

And finally, I saw Pierce, standing in the far corner.

"Pierce!" Lei and I said together. He didn't move, cold and impassive as any statue. That was when I noticed the collar around his neck.

"I'm afraid it can't respond," Karizal said, tossing the deactivated steel serpent on the workbench. "Those collars give me full control over their wearers. Unfortunately, I still haven't found a way to make them work on humans, but they've been most helpful in my dealings with the kobolds."

"What is this about, Karizal?" Next to me, Lei was studying Pierce.

"Ending the war, of course." He gestured toward the mirror. "I was listening to your conversation with Halea. Her dreams of conquest are just that, nothing more. Besides, she would just trade one form of chaos for another. This war is an abomination. I will put a stop to it. But the squabbling barons of the dragonmarked Houses are no better than kings and queens. My new world will be a place of perfect order, and everyone will work for the common good."

"Even if they have no choice?" said Lei.

Karizal ignored her comment and walked over to the workbench and picked up a beautiful adamantine dagger. "It's unfortunate that you won't live to see it, but I can't take any chances."

"Wait!" I said. "What is all of this? What are you doing with these kobolds? And by the Flame, why did you try to kill me before? I didn't know anything about this!"

Karizal shrugged. "The kobolds make excellent test subjects, pacified as they are. My work on prosthetics serves two purposes. The first should be obvious—" he glanced down where his own missing arm should have been. "The second: if we can create a soldier with the power or resilience of a warforged at a fraction of the cost, the benefits should be obvious. Unfortunately, the process tends to drive the subject mad, which is why I haven't taken advantage of it yet."

Could have fooled me, I thought.

"As for your death, there is more to your 'Pierce' than you know. It took some effort to convince Halea to have you bring it here, and I can't allow you to take it away now. I'm afraid there's no other alternative. Lei, I hate to throw away an artificer of your skills. If you want, you can join me in my work. I'd have to keep you imprisoned down here, but you'd have a chance to reshape a world. What do you say?"

She said nothing, her mouth tight.

"Well, I offered," he said. "Now, let's get this over with." He walked toward me, a dagger in his hand.

"I think not," said Pierce.

Pierce stepped up to the glowing crystal sphere. With a single motion of his armored fist, he smashed the orb. There was an explosion of glass, and a brilliant burst of color flooded the room. As the light faded from the shards, it also fell from the gems in the metal collars, and the kobolds pinning my arms let go. I leaped forward, kicked the dagger out of Karizal's hand, and caught it in the air. But before I could bring it to bear, a wave of kobolds struck us both.

Karizal was right. The kobolds were mindless berserkers intent on destroying anything in their path. Karizal went down in a mass of flesh and steel, his voice choked off by metal fists.

I barely managed to escape the mob. As they closed in I dove forward, using the massive metal shoulders of a particularly stocky kobold as a springboard to leap up and over the swarm. Spinning around, I struck the maddened creature in the back of the head with the bladed construct. The adamantine blade sliced through steel as if it were mere flesh. Kicking the kobold to dislodge it from the blade, I turned to Lei as my foe fell to the floor.

Unarmed and weary from her earlier mystical exertions, Lei was facing three of the malformed monsters. Even as I charged, one of them struck her with a vicious steel claw, leaving a red trail along her ribcage. She cried out but still managed to grab the metal wrist of the creature. Its scream echoed her own, and its steel arm went limp in her grasp. But even as it fell, the other two slammed into her, bearing her down to the ground. With a howl of triumph, the larger of the two raised a mace-like fist to smash her skull, but his cry was cut short; a single slash of my blade separated his head from his shoulders. Even as I gave thanks for adamantine, I had to throw myself to the side to avoid the sledgehammer blow of the remaining kobold. Within seconds Lei brought him to the ground with a kick to the knee and I finished him off with a single blow.

But for all that we were holding our own, the seven kobolds that had swarmed Karizal were beginning to lose interest in their fallen master.

"Pierce, we need to go *now!*" I cried as I hauled Lei to her feet.

Pierce was defending himself with the silver pedestal that had once held the crystal sphere.

"As you wish, Captain," he said calmly and scattered the two kobolds in front of him with a single sweeping blow. Swinging the pedestal before him, he charged for the hallway leading out of the chamber, knocking aside anything that got in his way.

Supporting Lei, I followed Pierce, slashing at the steel and scaled hands that reached out to grab me. We raced down the hall and into the large chamber holding the forge. I spun around the corner, ready to slash at the nearest beast. But there were no kobolds waiting us. Instead, there was a line of guards in

House Cannith livery, with Lord Dravot standing in the center. Each had a darkwood wand leveled in our direction, and it didn't take much imagination to imagine what powers might be unleashed at any moment.

I wondered if I could reach Dravot before I was electrocuted or burned to a crisp. Not likely.

"No offense, Lei," I said as I prepared to charge, "but I'm really starting to hate your family."

8

As it turned out, my fears were ungrounded. Dravot and his guards were simply responding to the energy released when Pierce had destroyed the orb, and they helped subdue the remaining half-kobold monsters. To my surprise, it appeared that Karizal had indeed been acting alone. It took time to confirm our story, but the evidence in Karizal's workshop was damning enough. Halea swore that she would never condone such experimentation on living creatures. She seemed truly contrite and even embarrassed as we were reunited with Jode and led to the exit. Not that she offered any help with the war.

"I'm sorry we couldn't come to an understanding, Captain," was all she said.

An hour later we were back on our horses and on the road to the Felmar Valley. While Jode tended to Lei's wounds, I made Pierce tell me what had happened. He said that the collar had suddenly stopped working when Karizal was about to kill me.

"Had it ever worked?" I asked. "Why did Karizal want you so badly, anyway?"

No one had an answer.

"You certainly had an easy time of it," I said to Jode. "Where were you when I was being attacked by half-'forged kobolds and metal snakes?"

"I spent the whole time carousing. I even managed to lure Halea and a few of the other administrators into a game of twelves. I know. Not hardly as heroic as your bold acts. On the other hand . . ." He rummaged around in the saddlebags and emerged with an old burlap sack. "Take a look at my winnings!"

We reined in the horses, and Jode upended the bag. Six small warforged soldiers came tumbling out, their armor instantly adjusting to blend with the shadows. They were followed by a bundle of wands, a small bag that appeared to be filled with *eyes of night*, and a small arsenal of glittering arms and armor. The six warforged turned in unison and saluted Jode. He grinned at me. "I think I've found your new night patrol, sir."

I laughed. The war was far from over. But at that moment, I believed we were going to win.

9

We've finally completed our investigation, and we're preparing for the long journey back to Sharn. I don't know if d'Cannith will be pleased with what we have to report, but we didn't do this for him. If we're going to move up from the depths of Sharn, we need the gold, and I'm tired of having to show my sword just to feel safe on the streets.

Whitehearth is a ruin and a mausoleum. I still don't know what happened to Karizal, but it's clear that the Forgehold was continuing the work he had begun. I can't help but wonder: Did anyone in the enclave survive the Day of Mourning? Were they all killed instantly, or did some live long enough to be burned to ashes by the sentient flames or devoured by the warforged wolves?

It's hard to believe that it's only been four years. Back then, this barren wasteland was my home. A kingdom I was willing to die to protect. I had a cause I believed in, I had a country, and I had three friends I could trust with my life. Over the last year, all of that has changed. Cyre is gone, and I'm selling my sword in the greatest city of my old enemies. And one of my friends is dead.

THE TALES OF THE LAST WAR

ABOUT THE AUTHOR

Keith Baker discovered *Dungeons & Dragons* in elementary school, and this was the beginning of a lifelong interest in games of all sorts. In 2002 he quit his day job to become a full-time freelance writer. Much to his surprise, in 2003 his world Eberron was selected as the finalist in the Wizards of the Coast Fantasy Setting Search. Keith currently lives in Boulder, Colorado with his lovely wife Ellen and a very bossy cow.

The City of Towers in 2005 was his first novel. *The Shattered Land* (2006) is the sequel.

Editor's Note

"Death at Whitehearth" originally appeared as a limited-edition promotions booklet that Wizards of the Coast included in the first Eberron roleplaying adventure *Shadows of the Last War*. It contains many of the unique iconic elements associating with the world of Eberron—the warforged, the practitioners of utilitarian magic called artificers, the dragonmarked Houses, and the Last War, which raged across the continent of Khorvaire for generations.

The story takes place in the final years of the Last War, in the doomed land of Cyre. It is a prequel to Keith Baker's trilogy, The Dreaming Dark, which began with *The City of Towers* in 2005, continued with *The Shattered Land*, and concludes in *The Gates of Night*.

DEATH BEFORE DAWN

Paul Crilley

Col closed his eyes and listened to the morning rain patter against his leather hood. He took a deep breath of the chill autumn air and released it, a slow exhalation of pent-up tension.

Trouble was coming.

He'd known it even before the messenger came for him this morning. He'd felt it building all week, a pressure that steadily increased as the Argonth traveled the achingly slow route from Thrane to Breland. He'd thought it had something to do with the Mournland, a constant wall of mist and madness off to their left, but they'd left that blasted landscape behind two days ago and still the uneasiness persisted. He could feel it even now. It thrummed through his body the way the vibrations from the Argonth's engines thrummed through the soles of his feet.

"Sergeant! Hoi!"

Col opened his eyes and squinted up into the rain. A balcony encircled the top of Cannith Tower. Lieutenant Selius was leaning over the railings. As soon as he saw Col look up he ducked back inside. Col sighed. Selius only called him by rank when he was in a foul mood. It didn't bode well for what awaited him inside.

Col was about to look away when something made him pause. The rainwater sluiced over the balcony and poured down in a solid sheet that separated into individual droplets halfway down the tower. But there was something not quite right about the runoff. The water looked . . . almost pink. No. Not pink, he thought. Darker. Much darker.

He frowned and looked down to where the water collected on the uneven cobbles at his feet.

The puddles were red.

Col shivered. Yes. Trouble was definitely coming.

2

It was called Cannith Tower. It even had a plaque outside the entrance that proclaimed it so, although the brass plate was now tarnished with a green patina of grime. The tower held the only good apartments in a city that hunched atop the back of the Argonth like barnacles attached to a decrepit old whale. Captain Alain usually used them, but he was forced to give them up when people more important than himself came onboard. It was a fact that irked the man intensely, if barroom talk was to be believed.

Two privates stood guard at the entrance. They were young

but already bore the mark of the King's Swords, the specially trained fighters of the King's Citadel.

"What kind of mood is he in?" asked Col, nodding in the direction of the stairs.

The two men looked at each other. "Um, he's cracking jokes," said one.

"And being sarcastic," said the other.

Col winced. Not good. Not good at all. He muttered his thanks to the privates and hurried into the tower, taking the thickly carpeted stairs two at a time. He passed the landings leading to the less well-appointed rooms and headed straight to the top. Most of the apartment doors were closed. All except four at the end of the corridor. There was movement coming from one of them.

Col straightened his clothing, strode purposefully into the room—

—and stopped as his boots sunk into the carpet with a soft *squish*.

"Tell me, Col," said the clipped, authoritative voice of Lieutenant Selius. "What do you get when the peace delegation from Thrane is murdered while they are under the protection of the King's Citadel, the *elite*—and I use the term loosely, you understand—special agents of the King of Breland?"

Col grimaced and looked up from inspecting the blood that coated his feet. He didn't answer straight away. His eyes roved the large room, taking in the five bodies slumped around the table, the horribly grinning wounds opening their throats to their spines.

And the blood. There was so much blood. It soaked into the carpet and trailed out onto the balcony where the last vestiges were even now being washed away by the rain. The room smelled like the meat warehouses on the south-side of the Argonth. The coppery smell of old blood was so strong he could taste it at the back of his throat.

"Well?"

Col looked away from the gruesome sight to one almost as unsettling. Selius paced back and forth across the blood-soaked carpet, his arms folded angrily in front of him. His passage left footprints in the carpet which slowly faded behind him as the blood rose back through the weave. His gray hair stuck up in an untidy ruff that bespoke the fact that he had also been called from his bed.

"I don't know, Lieutenant," he said.

"You get *war*, Col. Or at least, the *continuation* of war. Someone doesn't want the Thrane delegation to meet with King Boranel to discuss the peace treaty. It seems the events in Cyre were not enough to disavow these people of the notion that fighting to the bitter end is the best thing for all." Selius clapped his hands together. "Now what do you propose we do about it? And stop standing there with your mouth hanging open like a youth in a whorehouse. Come inside and do your job. You *are* a member of the King's Dark Lanterns, are you not?"

"Yes, Lieutenant," said Col, stepping into the room.

"Well done, Sergeant. I'm glad you've finally faced up to the fact. Now—"

The sound of raised voices in the hallway outside the room interrupted Selius. He frowned at the interruption. Col turned and saw Sir Valin Kelain climbing the stairs with one of the privates from downstairs scrabbling before him in an attempt to stop the paladin of the Silver Flame. He really had no chance. Valin was a seven-foot-tall monster of a man, and at fifty-five years of age his body was corded with muscles that steadfastly refused to give in to old age.

He was also wearing his armor, which added quite a bit more to his size. He grunted in irritation and swatted at the private as he would an annoying fly. His arm struck against the private's breastplate with a clash of metal that sent the young man sprawling to the floor. Valin didn't even spare him a glance. He stepped over him and bore down on Col like an unstoppable rockslide. He would have simply brushed him aside as well if Col hadn't held out his hand at chest height and braced himself in the doorway. He heard Selius chuckle behind him.

Valin Kelain kept coming, but when he saw that Col was not about to scramble out of his way, it threw his stride. He slowed, then quickened his pace again, then slowed once more as he tried to figure out what to do. He chose the least complicated option and simply stopped. He blinked and stared down at Col's gloved hand as if he would like nothing more than to reach out and break it.

"You will let me pass," said Valin.

"I apologize, sir, but I cannot," said Col. "This is a crime scene. Members of the Thrane peace delegation have been murdered and we need to seal the area in case the killer left behind any evidence."

"Don't be absurd," said Valin, "I'm sure your people would have been more careful than that."

"Sir?"

"Come now," said the knight. "Five members of the Council of Cardinals and their knight protectors, all slain aboard a military vessel owned by the King of Breland. And this happens while there is a war between the two nations? Draw your own conclusions, Sergeant—or don't. The Dark Lanterns deem intelligence a prerequisite for entry into their ranks, do they not?"

"I'm not sure I like what you are implying."

"Like it or not, there it is."

Col stared up at the knight. "I can't help but notice that you seem to have survived the assassination," he said. "Would you mind telling me where you were last night?"

"What?" roared Valin. "How dare you! Members of my order lie dead in these rooms and you stand there and accuse me? I'll have your skin, you jumped up latrine-cleaner!"

"Enough, Col," said a tired voice behind him. "Let Sir Valin through."

Col stepped aside to let the huge knight inside, not once breaking eye contact.

"A wise decision, Lieutenant Selius," said another voice.

Col turned in surprise and saw that Cardinal Domnel had been standing behind Valin all this time. Domnel was the head of the Church of the Silver Flame templars and represented the order on the Council of Cardinals. Col had never liked the man. Too quiet by half.

The man brushed past Col. He surveyed the room, his lips pressed into white lines of anger. "To answer your question, Sergeant," said Domnel, glancing briefly over his shoulder. "I was having dinner with Captain ir'Ranek last night. Obviously, my protector was there as well. We were the ones who discovered the bodies and raised the alarm. Perhaps you should make sure you gather all the facts before you throw around wild accusations."

Col flushed and decided to keep his mouth shut. He glanced around the carpet, trying to find a relatively dry path to the balcony. The stench of blood was starting to get to him. He stepped over the worst of the patches then hopped to the double doors leading out into the fresh air.

There was a muffled crack from beneath his feet.

Frowning, he bent over to examine the carpet. He had stepped on glass of some kind. There was a small pile of it ground into the carpet. He picked up the largest sliver—a piece no longer than his small finger—and examined it. The glass was stained a yellowish color. He brought it to his nose and sniffed. He sneezed abruptly. It had a terrible smell to it—an acidic, cloying scent that hit him hard in the back of the throat and made him gag.

"Something Sergeant?"

Col glanced up and saw all three men staring at him. He straightened. "No, nothing." He didn't know what the glass was, but he wasn't about to say anything in front of Valin and Domnel.

He stepped outside onto the balcony. The city sprawled below him, an uneasy mix of rusted metal and stone. The fortress wasn't even that old and already it seemed to be falling into disrepair. It was all the damp they traveled through. It got into everything. He shivered and listened to the conversation behind him.

"Obviously, the treaty was no more than a ruse to get us aboard this vessel with our guard down," said Domnel. "We will tell Captain ir'Ranek to drop us at the nearest town so we can gain passage back to Thrane and report this outrage to the Keeper of the Flame. King Boranel will regret this treachery."

Col shook his head. King Boranel was one of the main proponents of the peace treaty to end the Last War. There was no way he could have had anything to do with this. But if the real killers were not found before Domnel left the Argonth, none of that would matter.

The war might go on for another hundred years.

3

Col remembered the first time he had seen the Argonth. He and Selius had been waiting at one of the city's frequent stop-offs to take on supplies. The vast bulk of the mobile city had loomed out of the rain, a solid shadow that towered above them like a hulking beast out of a childhood nightmare. When it finally came to a stop in front of them it looked like the massive prow of a ship that had somehow beached itself on the vast grasslands. Steam and smoke billowed from chimneys, roiling together and merging with the lowering rain clouds. Rust and corrosion had spread and leaked over every surface, making it look like the metal and stonework had melded together into the same mud-colored material.

He had been surprised to find that although the Argonth was a military vessel, her population was one-tenth civilian. After some thought, he supposed it was logical. Soldiers still needed to eat, to drink, to relax, and they needed people to supply those services to them. The town that occupied the back half of the fortress was like the camp that follows after an army on the move, full of services and items the soldiers didn't have the time to seek out. Every time the Argonth stopped at a village or town, these civilians would get their official passes and head landward to restock on whatever provisions they needed.

Of course, what they brought back was not always legal. Checks were carried out, but when some of the contraband was used by the soldiers themselves, it was difficult to catch everything.

The Dark Lanterns knew all this. One of Col's first jobs when they boarded the Argonth had been to put together files on potential troublemakers. He knew who did what, who supplied what, and to whom. Selius always liked to have that kind of information for what he called the fallow periods.

Unfortunately, Col now had to show their hand in the game. He needed information, and that information could only come from a specialist.

4

Col crossed the rain-soaked street and pushed open the door of the Cat's Whiskers tavern. It stuck on the damp floorboards, but a hard shove jerked it open with a loud scrape. A disgusting combination of smells wafted over him—urine and vomit, stale beer and cold ashes. Col wrinkled his nose and surveyed the taproom by the gray light that filtered in behind him. Even at midmorning people were propping up the bar, although he wasn't sure if they were newly arrived or had been there since last night.

The man he had come to find, Martigen, sat behind the bar, asleep on a stool with his head leaning against the wall. It looked like his favorite spot, as the dull paint was stained by whatever he used to plaster his hair so tightly to his head.

Col walked to the bar and slammed his hands onto the worktop as hard as he could. Martigen jerked and banged his head against the wall. Someone off to his left yelped and fell from his stool, but he couldn't muster the effort to get up again, so he simply curled up where he was and went back to sleep.

Martigen rubbed his head and glared at Col. "Whaddya do that for? I was just resting my eyes."

"Rest them some other time," said Col. "And before we get into the whole witty back and forth bit with the accusations and the evasions, let's get a few things straight. Have you heard of the King's Dark Lanterns?"

"Of course I have."

"Good. That simplifies things. I am a member of the Lanterns, and we know all about what you get up to here—" Col held up his hand to cut off Martigen's protestations. "I said I didn't want to get into that. I'm here for a different reason." He fished inside a pocket and pulled out the piece of glass. He handed it to the now nervous-looking Martigen. "Tell me what this is."

Martigen held it up to what little light there was and turned it in his fingers.

"And if you say 'a piece of glass,' I'll have your head right here."

"I wasn't going to say that," he protested sulkily.

"Glad to hear it. Now, what is it?"

Martigen slid from his stool and leaned over the bar. He sniffed the glass, grimaced, then opened his mouth and touched it delicately with his tongue. Col winced. It looked like a sickly grey slug emerging from a dank cave.

"What you've got here," said Martigen, "is a combination of two substances."

"Which ones?"

"Well, that's the thing you see. One of them, I've got in the back room here. Very common. It's a depressive, you see. People use it to sober up. But the other—now that's the tricky bit." He grimaced and handed the glass back to Col. "This drug, was it used as a gas? Perhaps to render someone unconscious?"

"Possibly."

Martigen nodded. "Thought so. See, when the depressive is mixed with a specific soporofic—that's the funny smell, right?—it'll make this gas."

"Do you have the soporofic?"

"No way. There's no demand for it, and I only supply to demand. I'm a businessman you see. Besides, you can't get hold of it unless you've got permits. It's *very* heavily regulated."

"Who regulates it?" asked Col.

"You should ask some of your friends that."

"Which friends?" asked Col. "I have so many, you see."

Martigen grinned, showing yellow and brown teeth. "The healers and doctors in the army, that's who I mean. They're the only ones allowed to dispense such strong soporofics."

Col stared hard at the man then turned to leave. "By the way," he called over his shoulder. "You've got one day."

"One day for what?"

"One day before I come back here with a full squad to make sure you've disposed of any illegal substances. And don't even think you can just move them somewhere else. Someone will be watching."

"What am I supposed to do with it all?" shouted Martigen, but Col had already stepped outside.

5

He headed over to the medical dispensary, which turned out to be nothing more than a locked room fronted by a small office. It was a waste of time though, as the retired captain whose job it was to make sure everything was signed for had no way of knowing if the numbers on the requisition forms matched the numbers actually needed for the patients.

Col returned to the barracks at the end of the day frustrated by his lack of progress. What he needed now was sleep. He would report to Selius in the morning, give him all the details, and see where they would go from there. He headed into the building. The duty sergeant wasn't behind his desk.

Strange, thought Col. Someone was always there. He looked into the dormitories that opened off from the hall. All of them were dark. Not a candle or everbright lantern anywhere. That was *definitely* strange. At this time of night, the barracks should be full of soldiers coming off duty.

Col stood still in the center of the entrance hall and loosened his sword. He wasn't sure what for, but it was best to be ready. He walked down a corridor that branched off from the entrance hall. His dormitory lay at the end, looking out over the training yards behind the barracks. Col pushed open the door. Darkness greeted him.

He stepped inside and waited for his eyes to adjust. It was at that moment that he realized that something was wrong.

And he was standing framed in the light, a perfect target. He swung the door closed, plunging the room into darkness, and quickly ducked into a crouch. He heard the whoosh of air as something swung through the point where his head had been.

Col dived to the left and hit his shoulder against a bed. He dropped flat and rolled beneath it just as the club cracked down into the floorboards. He kept rolling, moving beneath as many beds as he could. He stopped himself before he reached the wall, not wanting to risk being cornered. He slowed his breathing, straining to hear anything that would help him.

The silence stretched. He could hear quiet shuffling sounds from all over the room. How many were there?

"You might as well come out, turncoat," said a voice.

Col frowned. The speaker sounded familiar. Where had he heard that voice before?

"We'll get you in the end, Col. The whole city is searching for you."

Searching for him? Why? He slid his body along the floor to look out from beneath the bed. His eyes had adjusted to the darkness, but he still couldn't make much out.

"Why did you do it? That's what I want to know. Were you paid? Did you do it for yourself? What?"

Col remembered where he'd heard the voice. This morning. Outside Cannith Tower. His heart sank into his stomach. It was the King's Swords who were out to get him. His own people.

"These talks were meant to end the war, Col. How many more will die because of what you did?"

Realization dawned. They thought he killed the Thrane peace delegation. He frowned in confusion. Why would they think that?

He felt a rush of air as the bed above him was thrown away. Hands grabbed him and yanked him to his feet as the bed crashed to the floor. Voices erupted from all sides, shouting, questioning. Col lashed out blindly, feeling his hands connect with flesh. He struggled, kicking out in front of him. He heard breath explode from someone in a rush of air. Arms grabbed him around the chest. He jerked back as hard as he could, gritting his teeth in pain as the back of his head connected with a nose. Warm blood gushed down his neck. The arms loosened and he squirmed around and shoved at his invisible assailant. He heard footsteps running. The door was flung open, letting in a stream of light. Col blinked, but he didn't waste time counting how many there were. He scrambled over the beds, slipping once and banging his shin hard against a wooden frame. He righted himself and fixed his eyes on his only means of escape. He leaped straight into the window, arms held protectively in front of him. Glass shattered all around him.

As he fell through the air he heard the solid *thunk* of a crossbow bolt hitting the window frame, then his knees were driven hard into his chest. He pushed off from the ground, rolling to the side. He scrabbled to his feet and sprinted out into the night-time streets, leaving the confusion and madness behind him.

6

Col peeled his sleeve back to inspect the damage caused to his arm by the breaking glass. It wasn't too bad. It should really have stitches, but it would heal without them. He winced and patted the blood-soaked cloth back against the wound, letting it stick there as a temporary bandage.

He looked around the refuse-strewn alley. Rats scuttled through the rubbish piled against the walls, searching for something to eat. He needed to figure out what was going on. Someone had obviously framed him. The question was, who? He thought back over the events of the day. He hadn't mentioned anything about why he was nosing around the medicine dispensary. He hadn't found anything out anyway. He'd irritated the knight Valin, but he would have no reason to frame him. Unless he was in on it? Col thought about the possibility then shook his head. Valin didn't seem the type. He was too earnest.

He stared up at the night sky. The rain had stopped, though clouds still skittered across the moons. He watched as a thick bank of clouds once more swallowed up the silver light, and it was then that realization dawned.

Martigen. It had to be. He must have lied about the drugs.

He had them—or he supplied them. Either way, he'd reported to his employer that Col was asking lots of questions and that employer had gotten nervous.

The more he thought about it, the more he reckoned he was on the right track.

He slid out of the alley, hugging the shadows cast by the wall of an apartment block. He glanced around, eyeing the entrance to the street and the windows above him, making sure no one was looking. Then he pushed off and headed to the Cat's Whiskers for the second time that day.

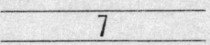

7

The only sign of life at the tavern was a flickering light in a second floor window. Col waited in the recessed doorway of a butcher shop. He'd been watching the inn for the past half hour and there had been no sign of movement. It seemed to be closed for business.

Why tonight, though? Could it have something to do with what had happened? What if the Swords were waiting for him inside? He didn't think that likely, though. They had meant to intercept him back at the barracks and they would have been confident of catching their prey. Arrogance was a common trait among the Citadel agents. He'd suffered from it himself on more than one occasion.

No, he didn't think they were waiting for him. But they might turn up later when they failed to find him elsewhere.

He crossed the road and crouched down before the tavern door. He tried the latch, but the door didn't budge. It wasn't even a lock he could pick. It must have been bolted from the inside. Typical. It was never easy. He moved along the tavern wall, hoping to find an alley down the side of the building, but again he was out of luck. The tavern stood flush with the shop next door. He looked up. A rickety overhang sheltered the front of the tavern. He rose from the ground and took hold of one of its wooden support poles. He gave it a slight shake, not at all comforted by the creaking that accompanied the movement.

He sighed again. Nothing else for it. He reached up as high as he could and pulled himself up the pole. He reached up and grabbed the lip of the overhang. A loose slate came away in his hand. He half slid to the ground but managed to catch the tile before it fell to the ground and smashed. He took a slow breath and carefully tucked it into his jerkin.

He gingerly felt around above him, making sure there were no other surprises waiting. He took a deep breath and pulled himself up. The structure swayed alarmingly. Col froze where he lay until the movement stopped. Orange light illuminated the overhanging roof. He craned his neck back and saw the window right above him.

He rose to a crouch and lifted the window. It rose smoothly, his first piece of luck that night. Breathing a sigh of relief he studied the room beyond. There wasn't much to look at. An unmade bed. A cracked mirror and a lantern sitting on a bedside table made from an empty ale barrel.

Col slipped into the room. There was the faint smell of unwashed laundry. He wrinkled his nose and took a more careful look around, but nothing new presented itself.

He unlatched the door and opened it slowly in case the hinges creaked. He usually carried a small vial of oil for these types of jobs. He hated being caught unprepared.

The door opened onto darkness. Col stayed in the room

and moved to the side of the doorframe, waiting for his eyes to adjust to the blackness beyond.

"Looking for someone?" said a low voice.

Valin Kelain stepped around the doorframe and into the light of the lantern. He grabbed hold of Col before he could react and threw him back into the room. He hit the bedposts and fell over backward, landing on his back. His head thudded solidly against the floorboards.

Sovereigns, he thought as small white flashes blinked before his vision. How many more times was he going to walk into a trap tonight? Anyone would think he was a civilian the way he was acting. He pushed himself back against the wall, trying to stop his head for spinning.

"I didn't kill them," he said. "I don't know what's going on, but I had nothing to do with it!"

Valin walked into the room and closed the door. He moved to the window to block Col's escape, the lantern light lending a soft glow to the burnished silver of his armor.

He stared down at Col. "Funny, but I thought that as well. I thought, 'That annoying *boy* would not have the intelligence to plan such a thing.' But then one of your Dark Lanterns tells us that in pursuing his investigations he came across this drugmaker named Martigen and the man said that you paid him to manufacture the gas. Still I thought, 'No, he couldn't do it. He is too stupid.' But I looked around the drugmaker's place while everyone else was out looking for you, and who should turn up at the drugmaker's home? Sergeant Col. Our chief suspect. Please, explain this coincidence to me. I am intrigued."

"It *is* a coincidence. I approached Martigen because I found evidence that some kind of gas was used back at the tower. I *knew* Martigen was involved with drugs. Everyone does. We have *files* on him. But he denied having anything to do with it.

He sent me on a dead trail. The next thing I know I'm being attacked by my own people. I came back here to find out who he spoke to."

Valin was silent as he mused over his words. Col shook his head, trying to clear the cobwebs.

"An interesting story," said Valin.

"It's not a story. Take me to Martigen and we can clear this up."

"I cannot."

"Why?"

"He escaped. He is nowhere to be found."

"How convenient," spat Col.

"Regardless, you will come with me now. I want you alive to stand trial in Thrane. If you are not guilty, you have nothing to fear."

"Are you really that naïve?" asked Col. "Don't you see? I'm a scapegoat. Someone has set me up. If you take me into custody I won't last ten minutes. They want me *dead!*"

"That is not my problem. Justice must serve its course."

There won't *be* any justice! Col thought. "Wait," he said. "I have something here that may prove my innocence."

Col sat up and smoothed his jerkin over his body. "See? No hidden knives or anything. I'm going to reach in and pull out a sheet of parchment. Is that all right?"

Valin nodded. Col reached inside his shirt. He hoped the bad light would be enough to give him the split second he needed. His fingers wrapped around the slate he pulled from the roof. He drew it out.

"If you look at the writing—"

Before Valin could react Col turned the slate on its side and flicked his wrist. The slate spun through the air. But Valin was quick. His arm came up, the slate hitting his gauntlet and shattering. But the broken shards still spun into his face. He cried out and turned his face to the side. Col was already moving. He leaped to his feet and bounded across the bed. There was no time for finesse. He dived through the window. Valin snagged his foot, but he kicked out hard and felt the paladin's fingers loosen.

Col belly-flopped onto the overhang. He knew there was no way it would take his weight. The supports splintered with echoing *cracks!* and the roof plummeted to the ground. Col landed flat on his stomach, the air exploding from his lungs. He lay where he was and gasped for breath like a landed fish. Dust settled slowly around him.

Then he heard the loud footfalls of Valin running down the stairs. Col winced and pushed himself to his feet. He staggered into the night, gingerly prodding his ribs. Nothing felt broken. Another bit of luck.

8

He'd been going about this the wrong way. He shouldn't be wasting time trying to find out *who* was responsible. His first priority was to figure out what was actually going on. *Why* were the emissaries murdered? If he could solve that, then all the rest should fall into place.

But first he needed to convince Selius he was innocent. He needed the man on his side if he was to investigate this. He hoped that wouldn't be too hard. They'd known each other for three years after all. Selius was the one who'd recommended his promotion into the Dark Lanterns.

The only good thing about being the most wanted man

on the Argonth was that the barracks were almost completely deserted. Col climbed the walls of the training yard and dropped silently to the hard-packed earth. He crouched motionless until he was sure no one was about then skirted the perimeter and entered the building through the back door.

A dimly lit passage stretched before him. The kitchens were off to his left. He could hear the clink of dishes and the low hum of conversation. He moved into the front entrance hall. Everything was as it had been earlier that night. Deserted. He leaned around the corner to check out his dormitory. The door still hung open.

He took the stairs to the second floor of the barracks, where the officers had their apartments. He moved quietly down the corridor and up another, shorter flight of stairs that led straight to Selius's apartments. His rooms occupied a tower that jutted from the side of the building. He'd once said to Col that he liked the height, that it gave him an excuse to look down on everyone else.

Col knocked softly on the door, but there was no answer. He tried the handle. Locked. Obviously. He took a folded piece of leather from his pocket, opened it, picked two slim pieces of metal, and inserted them into the lock. One he used to hold the mechanism open, the other he used to probe the lock until he managed to engage the tumblers. He put the tools away and entered Selius's rooms.

Darkness greeted him, but he'd been here often enough to know the layout. He moved carefully to the long desk that curved halfway around the wall. He felt around until he felt the cold metal of the everbright lantern, opening the shutter just enough so that he could see his surroundings. No sense in announcing his presence.

Now what? Wait, he supposed. Nothing much else he *could*

do. He slumped into the tattered armchair Selius loved so much, groaning as the knocks and beatings he had taken all vied for his attention at the same time. At least being constantly on the move had distracted him from his aches and pains.

He yawned and closed his eyes. He hoped Selius turned up soon. He didn't know how much time he had.

He must have dropped off to sleep, because the next thing he knew he was looking at a very surprised Selius standing in the doorway. He closed the door behind him and dropped a large sack he was carrying over his shoulder.

"Col, what have you gotten yourself into?" he demanded, striding forward.

Col struggled to shake off the vestiges of interrupted sleep. "Nothing," he muttered. He rubbed his face and sat up. "Nothing," he said again. "Why do you think I'm here? Selius, you *know* I had nothing to do with their deaths."

"Of course I do. What do you think I've been doing since the word got out? Trying to clear your name."

"How did they even manage to implicate me?"

"Vials of the gas were found among your possessions. And a shirt covered with blood." Selius grinned. "Imaginative, weren't they? If only our real criminals were so stupid as to keep evidence in their personal belongings." He shook his head. "Regardless, they're convinced you did it. They need someone to blame and you're that person, I'm afraid."

"But what will happen now? The treaty . . . ?"

"The treaty won't be signed. Not after this. And I'd watch your back if I were you. Whoever did this needs you dead so you can't say *anything*. They'll kill you and say you were working under the orders of the King."

Col pushed himself up and paced the floor. "But this is absurd! We just need to prove this was the work of one person, not a royal conspiracy! That way the treaty can still go ahead."

Selius shook his head. "The Thranes won't accept that. They'll say we framed some poor bastard to cover up the conspiracy. However this was supposed to work out, Col, the effect is the same. Domnel has locked himself in his room and dismissed all our guards. Says he doesn't trust them. He'll only come out when we reach Starilaskur, which will be in two days. From there he and Valin will catch the lightning rail back to Thrane."

"There must be something we can do!"

"Possibly," mused Selius. "I came back here for money to loosen some tongues I know. I may have good news for you when I get back."

"I want to come, Selius. I need to *do* something."

"Col, if we're caught together, then *both* of us will be implicated. I can't help you if I'm locked in a cell. Or dead." He opened a drawer and withdrew a pouch. It clinked quietly as he tied it to his belt. "I'll be two hours, no more. Try and relax."

Col nodded and watched the door close behind Selius. He slumped back into the chair and muttered a curse.

He couldn't relax, no matter how hard he tried. He got to his feet and wandered around the room, picking up books and briefly examining them before putting them down again. He opened the door to the bedroom and poked his head through. A simple bed and a wardrobe. That was it. He sighed and closed the door.

He eventually climbed the tight spiral staircase that led up to a tiny lookout room. Col couldn't even stand upright, the room was so small. He knelt on the wooden boards to look out the windows, his head brushing against the peaked roof. Selius's apartments were close to the edge of the city, so he could see the blackness of the landscape drifting by, lit every now and then as the moons flashed from behind the clouds. He couldn't see where they were though. Just vague outlines of trees and fields.

Col was just about to climb back down the staircase when something caught his eye and made him pause. He stared at a spot just below the building. He was sure he'd seen movement down there, something dark moving amidst the shadows. He held his breath and waited.

Nothing.

He let his breath out in a shaky sigh. He was just seeing things. It was to be expected, he supposed. Lack of sleep and all the stress were bound to confuse his mind.

He shifted backward and put one foot on the spiral staircase, still staring out into the city.

So he was perfectly positioned to see the shadows come alive and give birth to wave after wave of armed soldiers.

Col stared in horror. There must be a hundred of them. He looked over his shoulder, saw more coming from the rear. Hundreds, then. He turned back and saw that they were already at the entrance to the barracks. He swore and scrabbled back down the staircase, slipping the last few feet. He sprinted into the bedroom, looking for a place to hide. They'd caught his scent somehow, but maybe he could still evade them. He yanked open the cupboard. It was filled with boxes and clothes. No room for him in there.

He caught sight of another door, half hidden by the curtains. He bounded across the room and pulled it open. It was a small storage closet, but he couldn't see much in the dim light. He reached in and felt around. His hand hit something soft and sticky. He gently prodded it, wondering what it was.

He pulled his hand out and studied it in the half-light

coming through the door and window. His skin was coated with something black. He brought it closer to his face and realized it was blood.

He looked up just as the body fell forward and hit him in the chest. Col stumbled back, letting it hit the floor face first.

He caught his breath, staring down at the corpse. He stepped forward and rolled the body over.

Martigen.

The man had been stabbed through the chin and up into the brain.

Martigen . . .

Why was Martigen here? That meant . . .

"Selius." He whispered the word, and almost as if giving voice to the name brought realization home, everything else fell into place. It had been Selius all the time. He organized the gas. He killed the members of the delegation. And when Col went off on his own to investigate, it was Selius who framed him—after disposing of the loose end that was Martigen, of course.

His surroundings faded to a muted haze of sight and sound. All he could do was stare at the body of Martigen. All he could think was how he had been betrayed by the one man he thought he could trust.

Move, said a voice in his head. *You have to move. They're coming.*

Col blinked. He looked around. Yes. He had to get out of here. He couldn't be caught like this.

He ran to the front door and wrenched it open. He looked down into the upturned faces of soldiers, their mouths round "oh's" of surprise. Selius was there as well. He lounged against the wall at the bottom of the stairs, his arms folded before him as he grinned up at Col.

Col slammed the door and ran back into the bedroom. He pushed open the window and looked out. The roof was about ten feet below him. He climbed out backward, hearing the door crash open as he did so. He dangled down from the ledge and let go, hitting the roof with a loud thump. He got up and ran along the peak, sending loose tiles crashing to the ground with every step. He heard shouts behind him and risked a glance over his shoulder to see a soldier hanging out the window behind him.

His foot caught a loose tile and slid out from under him. He fell onto his side with a cry of pain and started rolling down the incline. He tried to catch hold of something to slow his descent but only managed to rip the skin from his fingertips. Digging in with his heels he managed to slow himself, but by then it was too late. He felt himself weightless, floating in air. He looked beneath him and saw the roof of the stables coming toward him.

He hit hard, but at least he didn't slide. He dragged himself to the edge and dropped off. He fell exhausted onto his backside, trying to catch his breath. Shouts and running feet echoed all around him.

He pushed himself up and opened the stable doors, limping inside. Shuffling and snorting surrounded him as he roused the horses from their sleep. Col opened the first stable and was met by the disinterested stare of a pitch-black gelding.

Col grabbed him by the mane before he could do anything and pulled himself onto his back, keeping his head low so he wouldn't hit the ceiling. "Sorry, friend," he muttered. "If I'm not getting any sleep, I don't see why anyone else should."

The horse laid his ears back and tried to bite his leg, but Col dug his heels in. The horse lurched into the open air, almost running over a group of soldiers running around the corner.

They dived out of the way and Col smacked the horse's flank, coaxing more speed from the beast.

They burst through the gates and into the street, scattering soldiers as they went. Arrows flew past his head. He ducked low, the musty smell of horse and hay filling his nostrils. The beast clattered way from the barracks and turned a corner, cutting them off from the line of fire.

Col breathed a sigh of relief and loosened his grip on the mane, letting the horse gallop away at its own pace.

9

Hours later, Col watched the sun rise over a miniature cityscape of brass chimneys and copper piping. The rays hit the metal, occasionally throwing up flashes of gold as they found new dimples and dents for the moment untarnished by the grime and smoke.

Col had let the horse take him out of the central city and into the areas that housed the Argonth's outer areas. That suited Col. All he could do was lay low, now that he knew who was after him. He was no match for Selius. The man had taught Col everything he knew. How could he hope to match wits with him? He'd been one step ahead of Col the whole time.

No. Better to lay low and leave the Argonth when they arrived at Starilaskur the next day.

And what then? he asked himself bitterly. He would be a deserter. Worse, a deserter in a time of war. He would be an outlaw.

But what choice did he have?

He leaned his head back against a pipe. Sovereigns, he hurt. His whole body was one big bruise, especially his hip bone, where he'd fallen on the roof. His ankle was swollen as well. He wasn't even sure when that had happened. He took a deep, careful breath, wincing at the sharp pain. He reckoned he'd cracked a rib when the overhang collapsed back at the inn. Every time he moved it brought on more pain.

Why had Selius done it? That nagged at him. Not knowing why. If the war continued, how many thousands upon thousands would die? And all because of the actions of one man.

Would he ever be able to live with himself, knowing he was partially responsible? Oh, not directly, he knew. But by doing nothing to expose Selius, or at least try, was he guilty of being an accomplice? He didn't know. He didn't want to think about it right now.

A small lizard scurried past his feet. It looked like it was newly-hatched. It scuttled to a pipe and was just about to climb up when a spider about the size of Col's palm dropped in front of it. The lizard didn't stand a chance.

But the little creature refused to back down. It scurried around as the spider came for it, both of them going in circles as they looked for openings. The lizard refused to run.

"Brave little bugger," mumbled Col, watching as the spider managed to back it into a corner. As soon as it tried to climb the pipe, the spider would have it. They froze where they were, facing each other.

The spider moved—

Col reached forward and brushed it away. It flew to the side then scampered into the shadows. Col watched as the lizard bolted up the pipe and disappeared.

Col closed his eyes. He thought about what he had just seen.

After a moment, he opened them again and smirked at the empty pipe. "Taught a lesson by a baby lizard. Col, my friend, you *are* going mad."

10

That evening, as the invisible sun set behind the newly returned rain clouds, Col sat in an empty apartment and watched Cannith Tower through a grimy window. He had dumped his uniform and was now dressed in a simple leather shirt with black trousers and a short black cloak over the top. He'd smeared ash into his hair at the temples, aging his face by a few years. It wouldn't stand up to close inspection, but he didn't plan on letting anyone get that close.

He'd been sitting here for the past hour. It was the perfect vantage point to watch the entrance to the building in case Selius came back to finish the job. Col wasn't sure if he would, though. It might be better for him to let Domnel and Valin leave to tell their story. On the other hand, if his plan had been to kill the whole delegation, he might try and go through with it. One of Selius's main faults was his inflexibility.

And if he was going to do anything it would have to be tonight. The Argonth reached Starilaskur in the morning.

Col made himself comfortable and settled in to wait.

About two hours after midnight, Selius returned. He was wearing a heavy waterproof cloak to keep the rain off, but Col knew it was him. He could tell by the familiar swagger in his walk.

He watched as the lieutenant paused by a wall and checked out the plaza before the tower. Apparently satisfied, he hurried across the empty space and disappeared through the door. Col stared at the black doorway. What was he doing? Surely the guards would stop him.

That was when Col remembered that there *were* no guards. Domnel had barred himself in his room and spurned all offers of Breland protection. Domnel was on his own in the tower.

Col sprinted from the room and down the stairs of the tenement. Cold rain gusted into his face as he emerged onto the street. He ran across the square, paused before the doorway, and peered inside. Everbright lanterns illuminated the staircase. There was no sign of Selius.

He was about to slip inside when a voice shouted behind him. Col turned to see Valin and a squad of Breland soldiers running toward him. He debated simply waiting and trying to tell Valin what was going on, but he didn't think the knight would believe him—or if he did it would be far too late to save Domnel. Col turned and ran, trying to ignore the pain in his ankle. He ducked around the back of the tower and took the first street he came to. It carried him past a restaurant. He skidded to a stop and pulled open the door, slipping inside. He couldn't outrun them, not with his injuries.

Col watched as the soldiers thundered past, led by Valin. He waited a moment, then stepped outside and limped back to Cannith Tower. This time he didn't hesitate. He ran up the stairs straight to the top floor. He paused there, trying to calm his breathing so it didn't hurt his rib. Selius was nowhere to be seen. He hurried down the landing to the room he knew Domnel was using and put his ear to the door. Nothing. Was he already too late?

Col drew his sword and stepped back. He braced himself then kicked at the door with his uninjured foot. The door caved open, slamming against the wall with a loud crash. Col rushed inside, his sword held level before him.

Selius was walking across the carpet to where Domnel stood with his back to him, staring out over the balcony. Both men turned at the noise.

Col took advantage of his brief moment of surprise, rushing forward to grab hold of Selius. He placed the point of his sword against his mentor's throat.

"I won't let you do it, Selius. I won't let you finish what you started."

Selius frowned at him. "Whatever do you mean?"

"Don't play games, Selius. I'm not in the mood. Tell him." He jerked his head in the direction of Domnel. "Tell him the truth about what happened."

Selius raised his hands in the air. "Very well. You outwitted me fair and square. It was I, Domnel. It was I who used the gas and killed your people. It was I who set up young Col here when he got too close to the truth. It was all me. Me alone."

Col stared at Selius in amazement.

Then a voice right next to his ear said, "Well, I wouldn't go *that* far, Selius. Not *quite* alone."

Col felt a sharp pain and a bloom of warmth in his side. He looked down and saw a long dagger sticking between his ribs. Blood gushed down his leg. He staggered, then caught himself and looked up at Domnel. The Cardinal was frowning as he tried to wipe blood from his hands with a silk kerchief.

"I hate blood," he muttered.

Selius pried the sword from Col's fingers and tossed it aside. Then he swung his fist and hit Col in the face, snapping his head back and sending him reeling onto his back.

Col blinked and stared at the ceiling in a daze. He wasn't sure what was going on. Everything had gone wrong. Everything . . .

Selius appeared above him. "You see, Col, *we* don't want the war to end. It's that simple. Domnel here has too much going on the side. If the war ends, so do his profits. Me, I just don't want to be made obsolete. The war keeps me busy, you see."

"But . . . all those people. They'll die—"

"They'll die anyway. Wars just give their deaths meaning."

Col shook his head. As he did so he thought he saw movement in the hallway. "You're insane," he said.

Selius knelt beside him and grabbed his hair. "Not insane. I make sense out of chaos. I make order where there is none. That is not insanity. Fighting me, now *that's* insane."

"Oh, just kill him and be done with it, Selius," said Domnel. "We'll say he came back to finish the job but I fought him off."

Selius pulled a dagger from his belt. "Too bad my boy," he said. "You had potential." He put one knee on his chest and pressed the dagger to Col's throat. Col tried to twist away, but the weight on his chest was too much. The dagger pierced his flesh—

Then he felt a sudden lightness as Selius flew backward through the air. Col lifted his head and saw Valin bounding over the lieutenant and heading straight for Domnel. The Cardinal let out a squeal of fear and ran into the bedroom. Bellowing in anger, Valin followed.

Col looked at Selius. He was sitting up. He glanced over his shoulder, frowning in anger, then he turned back to Col. "Complications, complications, complications," he said, shaking his head. "But let's at least get you out of the way, hmm?"

He picked up his dagger and started to rise. Col knew this was his last chance. He grasped hold of the blade in his side and gritted his teeth. He pulled it out, screaming in pain, then pushed himself to his feet just as Selius realized what he was doing. Col stumbled forward, grabbing hold of Selius's arm. He looked into his eyes and thrust the dagger up through his ribs and into his heart.

Col watched the confusion register, then the pain.

Then came the anger. Selius pulled his lips back in a sneer of hatred. Blood boiled from his mouth.

"You . . . die," he whispered. He tightened his grip on Col and staggered toward the balcony.

Col realized what he was doing and tried to free himself, but Selius's grip was too strong. They stumbled outside and bumped up against the balcony. Selius leaned back as far as he could. Col tried to grab hold of something with his feet, but there was nothing to latch onto. Selius started to slip back over the rail, still grasping hold of Col's arms, the dagger still plunged hilt-deep into his chest. Col felt one foot lift from the ground.

He was going to die, he realized. There was no way out of this. He couldn't break Selius's grip.

At least he'd stopped him though. Valin must have heard everything. If one of their own was involved the incident would be hushed up. The treaty would go ahead.

Col smiled.

When Selius saw him smile he screamed in rage and pulled harder. They were both slipping now. Col was bent over the balcony. The only thing preventing them both from falling were the fingers of one hand pushed behind the small of Selius's back.

One by one, the fingers slipped. Selius grinned in triumph, showing bloody teeth.

A gauntleted hand reached past Col and grabbed hold of Selius's hand. Col heard the loud cracks as his fingers were yanked back and broken. Selius's grin turned to a scream of pain as he let go of Col's arm. He managed to hold on a moment longer, then his other hand slipped and he tumbled over the balcony. Col watched him spin slowly through the air until he hit the cobbles below with a muted thump.

Valin yanked Col back and dumped him to the floor. Col groaned in pain. Valin knelt down to examine his wound, then pushed Col's hand against the puncture.

"Hold the pressure. Help is coming."

Col looked him in the eyes. "It wasn't me," he whispered.

"I know, boy."

Col's eyes widened. "You're the giant hand."

Valin frowned. "What?"

"The giant hand that saves the lizard from the spider."

"What are you raving about?" snapped Valin.

Col let out a wheezy laugh. "Nothing. Nothing at all. Thank you, Valin. And good night."

With that, Col closed his eyes and gratefully let unconsciousness sweep him into oblivion.

PAUL CRILLEY

ABOUT THE AUTHOR

Paul Crilley is a Scot currently living in South Africa with his partner, his daughter, seven cats, and two dogs. He recently turned thirty, and much to his surprise the world did not, in fact, come to an end.

He is a writer on a prime time sitcom due for broadcast on South African television next year. He came to the attention of the Eberron editors through the War-Torn open call. "Death Before Dawn" is his first Eberron story, and he thoroughly enjoyed exploring this small part of the world.

Feel free to visit Paul at www.paulcrilley.com.

THE BLADE OF THE FLAME

Tim Waggoner

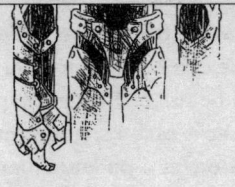

1

"What is your name, child?"

The young woman who lay on the straw-filled mattress looked up at Diran, but her only reply was a slow, sly smile.

"I told you, her name is Yalene." The woman who spoke was older than the one on the bed, though no less comely. She had long, curly red hair and her dress, while far from new, was in good repair, with only a few patches marring the fabric. Diran assumed the woman used a charm or two to accentuate her physical beauty, but then she was the owner of the Little Rose—the only house of pleasure in Kartan—and thus had to look her best.

Diran glanced over his shoulder at the red-haired woman, who stood next to the door beside a scowling half-orc.

"Lady Onelle, if you would kindly allow me to proceed in

own fashion . . ." Diran tried to keep the irritation he felt out of his voice, but was only partially successful.

The half-orc's scowl deepened, accenting the more monstrous side of his heritage—prominent brow ridge, broad flat nose, pointed ears, and pronounced lower canines jutting up over his bottom lip. His black hair and sideburns were a wild, tangled thatch, as was the thin strip of beard running down the center of his chin. He carried an iron hand axe tucked beneath his leather belt, and he reached for its haft now.

Diran made no move save a slight narrowing of his eyes as he sized up the half-orc as a potential opponent. Tall, broad-shouldered, well-muscled, obviously short-tempered—which wasn't uncommon for his kind. He had the beginnings of a paunch around his middle, however, and Diran guessed him to be a soldier or mercenary who hadn't seen much, if any, action since the Last War and was starting to lose his edge. He wore a scuffed, dented breastplate over a tunic of brown cloth, a souvenir of his soldiering days, Diran guessed. His only other clothing was his belt, trousers, and a worn pair of black leather boots.

In the old days, Diran would've already buried a pair of daggers in the half-orc's eye sockets with two swift, graceful flicks of his wrists. But though the tips of his fingers itched to draw blades from any of the numerous places they were concealed about his person, he resisted. He was a different person now—or at least he was trying to be.

Lady Onelle lay a slender hand on the half-orc's forearm to stop him from drawing his axe.

"Relax, Ghaji. This man has come here to help us, to help poor Yalene."

The air in the room was cold despite the tropical climate outside, and curls of mist accompanied the woman's words. The half-orc glared at Diran for another moment before removing his hand from the handle of his axe. But Ghaji didn't stop scowling.

Let him scowl, Diran thought, as long as he does nothing to interfere with my work.

As near as Diran could tell, the half-orc worked as guard for the Little Rose, although Onelle treated him more like a friend than an employee. Diran supposed the particulars of their relationship didn't matter, but in his former . . . occupation, Diran had always paid attention to details, no matter how minor or inconsequential. It was often such unimportant details that meant the difference between success and failure, life and death.

Diran broke eye contact with Ghaji, gave Onelle a nod of acknowledgement, then returned his attention to Yalene. The girl couldn't have been more than twenty and quite likely was several years younger. She was garbed in a simple white blouse that while clean was frayed at both cuffs and collar. Her skirt was a patchwork made from bits and pieces of other garments, burlap, and sackcloth. Diran had seen similar makeshift clothing on many others since coming to Kartan, but as this was a frontier village nestled amidst the wilds of Q'barra—and inhabited primarily by Cyran refugees displaced during the Last War—such frugality was a necessity.

Yalene lay atop the bed without a blanket to cover her. Her pale skin held a bluish cast, doubtless from constant exposure to the room's cold, though she didn't shiver. According to Onelle, she and some of the other girls had tried several times to place a blanket over Yalene to warm her, but none would remain on the girl's body. Every time someone attempted to cover Yalene, the blanket would jerk off her body and fly across the room as if yanked by an unseen string. The last time they'd attempted to put a blanket on her, the coverlet flew off Yalene, landed in a corner, and burst into the flame. The small pile of black ashes lying in the corner was testament to Onelle's story.

The girl's hands were clasped on her stomach, the knuckles white as if she were keeping her grip at tight as possible, almost as if her body was fighting some sort of battle with itself. But her facial expression showed no sign of discomfort or tension. Her features were relaxed and calm. Her smile, however, held more than a hint of mockery and her eyes shone with a cold, cruel gleam that Diran had seen before but hadn't quite gotten used to. He wondered if he ever would.

The moment you become comfortable in the presence of evil, Diran, is the moment you are lost. These were the words of Tusya, priest of the Silver Flame and exorcist, Diran's friend, mentor, and above all, savior. And as usual with Tusya's words, they were wise ones.

"Is it true?" Diran asked the girl. "Is your name Yalene?"

The girl's nails dug into the flesh of her hands and blood welled forth from her wounds.

"Do you take me for a fool, priest?" Her voice was clear, but completely devoid of human emotion. "You're fishing for my true name—and in a most obvious and clumsy manner, I might add. I'm almost insulted."

Diran knew better than to allow himself to be baited. "I prefer to think of myself as direct."

He was tall, lean, and gaunt of face, with long black hair that was starting to gray at the temples. He was garbed entirely in black—black shirt, black pants, black boots—and the leather armor vest he wore over his shirt was black as well. He had on a simple traveler's cloak (black, of course) which he wore with the hood down. The only weapons he carried—at least, the only ones visible—were a pair of daggers tucked into sheaths on either side of his belt. His clothing was dusty and worn and had obviously seen much hard use. When he moved, he did so with grace and precision, and without wasted motion, and when he stood still, he seemed completely motionless, not blinking or even breathing. His most striking feature, however, were his eyes. Crystal-blue and cold as ice, they seemed to contain fathomless arctic depths, and if one stared into those eyes too long, he or she would begin to feel cold settle into their bones and be forced to look away. Those eyes had served Diran well over the years, almost as well as his blades.

Diran glanced around the room. Aside from the bed, the only furniture was a crude nightstand, a wooden chair, and an old chest of drawers that looked as if it would fall apart if one of the drawers were closed too hard.

"Lady Onelle, I'll need this furniture removed, lest it be used as a weapon against me. Could you please have your . . . servant take it out?"

"You could ask me yourself," the half-orc said in a voice close to a snarl. "And I have a name, and it's not *servant*."

Diran considered for a moment before inclining his head. "My apologies, Ghaji. Would you be so kind as to remove the furniture for me?"

The half-orc glared at Diran as if trying to decide whether or not the priest was making fun of him. Finally, he shrugged and said, "Of course."

But before the half-orc could begin, Yalene—or rather the fiend that had usurped her body—laughed.

"So you intend to perform an exorcism, priest?" Another laugh. "Look at you. Despite all your training, your past still shows in your face and eyes, and in the way you dress and carry yourself. You're no priest, Diran Bastiaan. You remain what you've always been. A killer."

Diran barely succeeded in keeping the shock he felt from registering on his face.

"Your hands are trembling, Diran," the fiend said.

"It's the cold," he replied, knowing it was a lie and knowing the thing that had stolen Yalene's body wouldn't be fooled by it.

Still smiling, the girl took her lower lip between her teeth and bit down hard. Blood gushed, but she displayed no reaction to the pain she must've felt. She sucked blood into her mouth, leaned forward, and spat a crimson gob at Diran. The priest made no move to duck or step aside. His right hand became a blur as it drew a dagger from his belt and swept the blade in a narrow arc. He held the dagger out so that the entity in possession of Yalene's body could see that he'd caught the bloody spittle on the flat of his blade. With a flick of his wrist, he cast the blood onto the wooden floor before wiping the dagger clean on the edge of his cloak. He replaced the blade in its sheath. His hands no longer trembled.

"Still fast as ever, I see," the fiend said. Blood from Yalene's wounded lip trickled down her chin and spattered onto her neck where it began to pool in the hollow of her throat. "Is that the first blood your steel has tasted since you took to your current path? I'll wager it's not."

Diran stared at the girl, his jaw muscles bunching as he clenched his teeth. There were so many things he might've said in reply, but none of them would've done him—or Yalene—any good, so he kept his mouth shut.

Diran turned to Onelle and Ghaji. "See that the furniture is removed. I must . . . meditate to prepare myself."

Without waiting for either the woman or the half-orc to respond, Diran walked out the door. Behind him, Yalene laughed and the room seemed to grow colder.

THE TALES OF THE LAST WAR

"Take your time, Diran. I'll be waiting!"
More dark laughter followed Diran.

2

The village of Kartan lay in the center of a region called, optimistically enough, Hope. Located on the Q'barran peninsula and surrounded by dense jungles filled with hostile lizardfolk, marauding kobolds, and vicious giant reptiles, Hope was home to a mixture of criminals, deserters, homesteaders, and refugees from the Last War. While the inhabitants nominally accepted the rule of the New Galifar nobles, the truth was these were lawless frontier settlements, in their own way as wild and savage as the jungle around them. The "village" of Kartan was one of the more recent settlements, primarily a cluster of wooden buildings surrounded by a sea of refugee tents.

Kartan's tavern was so new it didn't have a name yet, but as it was the only one in the village, a name wasn't necessary. There were a number of tables outside which, given the warm climate and the fact that the tavern itself was little more than a small wooden shack, made good business sense. Diran sat at one of these outside tables, his back to the tavern's outer wall, nursing a clay mug of ale, thinking, and sweating.

Though it was midafternoon, the atmosphere remained hot and humid, and every breath felt as if he were trying to draw in air through a mouthful of wet cloth. Diran could feel lines of sweat rolling down his chest and back, and he wished he were wearing something lighter than his current clothing, especially the leather armor and traveling cloak. But the vest's protection and the cloak's storage capabilities—he had numerous daggers concealed in its hidden pockets—were too useful for Diran to forego easily. He'd been uncomfortable before; he'd manage, though he could have done with a breeze. At least the tavern-owner had cast insect-repellent charms on his tables; sigils burned into the wooden tabletops glowed softly, their magic keeping jungle pests of the smaller variety at bay.

Diran wasn't the tavern's only customer. Although the tavern's clientele was primarily human—traders and vagabonds for the most part—there were a few representatives of other races present. Among their number was a warforged who was missing his left arm. Just one more individual who'd been marked by the Last War, Diran figured, and who evidently didn't have the coin to pay for an artificer to attach a new arm. It was hardly uncommon to see someone who'd been maimed in the Last War, but warforged were artificial constructs imbued with life and sentience and thus didn't think or feel in the same manner other beings did. Diran wondered if the one-armed warforged felt the same about losing a limb as a human soldier would, or if the loss was of no more moment to the creature than the discarding of nail clippings would've been to Diran. He supposed he'd never know, and he wasn't about to go over and ask.

A female shifter sat at a table next to the warforged, her back to the construct, sipping ale and eating dried dates. She wore a short tan leather vest that left her arms and midriff bare, and a short leather skirt that barely covered what needed covering. She carried a sword belted to her waist, and Diran guessed her to be either a wilderness guide or another mercenary looking for work. Hope was full of them. Shifters were humanoid descendants of the all-but-extinct lycanthropes, a race that Diran's order had nearly wiped off the face of Khorvaire.

Shifters in and of themselves weren't evil, despite what some of the more fanatical members of the Church of the Silver Flame believed, but Diran had never been quite comfortable around shifters, even before becoming a priest. They tended to be wild and unpredictable, and you never knew when the more savage side of their nature might come to the fore.

A few tables over from the shifter, a pair of halfling traders were arguing more or less good-naturedly over what appeared to Diran to be a handful of animal bones spread out on the table before them. Diran assumed the bones—tiny, polished things that couldn't have belonged to any creature larger than a mouse—possessed some sort of value, to the halflings if no one else.

Diran looked away from the halflings and directed his gaze upward. The sky was a clear blue, the clouds so white they almost seemed to glow. Diran had heard that glidewings often flew over the village, but he had yet to see one of the flying lizards. As he gazed up at the sky, his thoughts drifted toward the past.

"Are you ready, Diran?"

Diran lay on hard earth, wrists and ankles bound by leather thongs tied to stakes driven into the soil. He was bare-chested, his black pants his only clothing. He looked up at the wizened old man garbed in gray robes. Tusya was bald, but with a scraggly white thatch of beard. His eyes, which usually shone with kindness touched with the merest hint of sorrow, were now cold and hard as steel.

Diran's throat was dry, and at first words wouldn't come, but he swallowed once, twice, and then managed to croak, "I am."

"This isn't going to be easy, my son. You've played host to the entity inside you for quite some time. It isn't going to let itself be evicted without a fight."

"I know."

Summer sun beat down on Diran, but that wasn't the reason he was sweating. He knew far better than Tusya just how hard the spirit that shared his body intended to fight to remain on this plane, and Diran, who feared nothing on the face of Eberron, including his own death, dreaded what was to come next.

Tusya nodded. "Very well. We begin."

The old priest held up his hand and a silver flame blazed into existence in his palm. The flame's purifying light washed over Diran's body, penetrated his flesh to illuminate the very core of his being. Diran screamed with two separate voices.

"Is this what your order considers meditating?"

Diran looked up to see the half-orc guard from the Little Rose standing before him. He didn't recognize Ghaji at first, still lost in the fog of memory. But the fog quickly burned away, and Diran smiled and gestured for the half-orc to join him. After a moment's hesitation, Ghaji did so. Diran drained what remained of his ale then set the mug down on the table.

He gave the half-orc a smile. "There are as many ways to meditate as there are reasons for doing so."

"Onelle sent me to find you. I removed the furniture from Yalene's room as you requested, and Onelle wants to know if there's anything else you'd like us—and by us, she means *me*—to do."

Diran chuckled. "No. Removing the furniture is enough. I assume you left the bed, though."

Ghaji blinked in surprise. "Of course. Should I have taken it?"

"No. Yalene, or at least her body, needs to be as comfortable as possible. But if the fiend that's taken possession of her wields enough power, even a simple pallet may become deadly in its hands."

The tavern's sole server—a young girl who was barely more than a child and most likely the owner's daughter—walked by, and Diran caught her attention and held up two fingers. The girl nodded and scurried inside the tiny shack.

"What's this *fiend* going to do with a pallet?" Ghaji asked. "Throw straw at you?"

"Exactly. And if they're hurled with enough force and velocity, their strike can be as deadly at that of any blade."

Ghaji looked doubtful, but he did not dispute Diran's claim. The serving girl returned with two clay mugs of ale and set one down in front of Diran and the other in front of Ghaji. She passed her hands over the mugs and muttered a charm to cool the ale. Diran paid the girl. She thanked him then hurried off to attend to the shifter, who had finished off her dates and evidently wanted more.

"My thanks," Ghaji said, "but I thought priests took vows of poverty."

"Depends on the priest." Diran took a drink of satisfyingly cool ale, then wiped foam off his lips with the back of his hand. "It's true that I have renounced earthly treasures, but I find a few coins in my purse come in handy now and again."

Ghaji grinned and took a sip of his ale. "I think I like you, priest. When you showed up at the Little Rose, waving your little silver arrowhead—"

"It's the symbol of the Church," Diran said, a trifle stiffly.

If Ghaji noticed Diran's displeasure, he ignored it. "I thought you would turn out to be some sanctimonious do-gooder—or worse, a fraud who was hoping to perform a 'holy' service for us in turn for a free session with one of the girls. But you're sincere, aren't you?" The half-orc said this last sentence with a mixture of doubt and what sounded to Diran like hope.

"I am."

"And you just happened to wander into Hope?"

"Not exactly. I'm making my way—though admittedly in a somewhat leisurely fashion—to the Lhazaar Principalities. I grew up there, and it's been many years since I've been home."

The two men fell silent for a time as they contemplated their own thoughts. Finally, Diran asked, "Has there been any change in Yalene's condition since I left?"

"Still the same," Ghaji said. "She didn't say anything as I carried out the furniture, just kept looking at me and smiling, as if she found the situation funny. Her smile was . . . unsettling." Despite the tropical heat, the half-orc shuddered. "Poor Yalene. It must be awful, having another spirit inside your body."

"It can be," Diran said. "But it can also have its advantages and its . . . pleasures. That's what makes some people susceptible to possession. It can be quite seductive in its own way." He paused for a moment, remembering, but then continued on. "When I first arrived in Kartan, I came here for something to drink. I overhead two men talking about the Little Rose, and how their favorite girl had taken ill, and wasn't it a shame. The serving girl overheard as well, and she came over to their table and told them she had heard that Yalene was possessed by a demon, and that it was safest to avoid the Little Rose entirely. I thought at first it was just talk. After all, few folk are conversant with the signs of true demonic possession and often mistake those who suffer from various forms of mental enfeeblement and nervous conditions as possessed. Still, I am a priest of the Silver Flame, and so I was duty-bound to investigate. But a physical examination is only one part of an investigation. I have some additional questions, and since you are here and the opportunity presents itself . . ."

Ghaji took another drink of ale then shrugged. "I just work there, though Onelle treats me well." The half-orc's lower lip curled down to expose his over-sized bottom incisors. "Not like some." He glanced around and some of the tavern's other patrons, who'd been staring at the half-orc and priest and whispering, quickly looked away. Ghaji faced Diran once more. "I don't know what I can do to help you, but I'll try."

Diran nodded in appreciation of the half-orc's willingness to help. "When did Yalene first display signs of her current affliction?"

"Almost two weeks ago. She'd been with a man named Laris, a customer she'd seen several times before and was fond of. He was a former soldier, I figured, given the way he dressed and the scars on his hands."

Diran understood. Ghaji had more than a few such scars, as did Diran himself.

The half-orc continued. "Laris was middle-aged, though he seemed in good health. Nevertheless, while he was . . . *with* Yalene, he died." Ghaji shrugged. "It's not common, but it happens more often than you might think. A man's heart gets to racing, and it's not as strong as he thinks . . ."

"There are worse ways to go." Diran said this without a trace of humor, for he well knew it to be true.

"Yalene ran out of her room to tell Onelle what had happened, and in turn Onelle summoned me to remove the body and haul it to the undertaker's. That was the last customer Yalene had, for within a few hours, she became as you saw her today."

"I see. What is Yalene normally like?"

Ghaji finished off his ale while he thought.

"Good-natured. Friendly. Well liked by Orelle and the other women who work at the Rose. She has a number of regular customers. She's one of the more popular girls, but the others don't seem to be jealous of her. As I said, she's well liked."

Diran was about to ask another question when Ghaji added, "She sometimes tells stories about her childhood. Her mother and father were fortunetellers with a traveling caravan of entertainers—acrobats, jugglers, and the like. They traveled quite widely, despite the dangers of wartime, before finally running afoul of raiders in Droaam. Most of the caravan members were slain, including Yalene's parents. A few managed to escape, and Yalene was among them. The survivors eventually settled in Hope, and Yalene came to work at the Rose."

Diran nodded. "How very interesting. Thank you, Ghaji." Diran had ignored his ale while Ghaji spoke, and now he drank half of it down in several swallows. "And what of you? I'd say you were a former soldier yourself, judging from the use your axe and armor have seen. How did you end up working as a guard in a brothel?"

Ghaji's eyes narrowed. "How did you end up as a priest?"

Diran smiled. "I asked you first."

Ghaji looked at Diran another moment before finally letting out a snort. "Nothing special about being an ex-soldier. Khorvaire's lousy with them. Still, I can handle myself well enough in a fight. I probably could've found work as a mercenary or justicar if I'd wanted."

"But you didn't want."

Ghaji was silent for a time after that, and Diran began to think he wasn't going to continue. The priest glanced around at the other tables. The two halflings had evidently come to an agreement of some sort, for they touched their fists together three times, quickly divided up the bones between them, then rose from their table and went their separate ways. The shifter had turned her chair about and was now talking to the one-armed warforged. Diran couldn't hear what they were saying, and the back of the shifter's head was to him, so he couldn't read her lips, and the warforged had no lips to read. He supposed it didn't matter what they were discussing, but he'd spent a lifetime paying attention to everything that went on around him, and old habits died hard, if indeed they ever truly died at all.

Diran almost started when the half-orc began talking once more.

"No, I didn't." He fixed Diran with an appraising gaze. "You have the look of someone who's spent some time in the soldiering trade. I mean, given the way you used your dagger when Yalene spat at you. I don't remember ever seeing anyone move so fast."

Diran made no comment.

"So you know what it's like to fight and kill day after day," Ghaji continued. "After a while, you're not even sure why you're doing it anymore. Your superiors give you orders and you carry them out. Besides, you're too damn busy staying alive to worry about the reasons you're fighting. And if you're lucky enough to survive, one day the fighting's over and you don't have to kill anymore. Not unless you want to, and I didn't want to. I'd had enough of meaningless slaughter to last me any number of lifetimes. So when the War ended, I decided to find a place where I could retire in peace. A place where I wouldn't have to do anything I didn't want to do, where I wouldn't be asked to kill or die for some abstract sense of values I'm not sure I understand, let alone believe in."

"So you came to Hope and took a job as a guard."

Ghaji shrugged. "I already had the axe, and most folks believe half-orcs are barely one step above animals anyway. If anyone gets out of line, all I have to do is scowl, bare my teeth, and reach for my axe. That's usually enough to make most customers behave."

"And what about the ones that still refuse to behave?" Diran asked.

Ghaji grinned, more prominently displaying his pointed lower incisors. "I can handle myself."

Before Diran could respond, he noticed the one-armed warforged rise from his table and begin heading toward them.

"I hope so," Diran said, "for it appears we may have one on our hands soon enough."

The warforged stopped when he reached their table. Missing arm aside, he looked much the same as any other warforged Diran had encountered—metal body, face a simplistic replica of a human's, with crystals set in dark eye slits and a crude gash of a mouth. He carried a large warhammer, though strapped to his back and not in his hand. But that didn't mean the warforged was harmless. Quite often his kind were weapons in and of themselves.

"Are you a priest?" The warforged's voice was devoid of emotion and came out as a metallic echo, as if it were produced deep within his artificial form.

"Assuming that you're speaking to me and not my companion, I am indeed. Diran Bastiaan, priest of the Silver Flame, at your service."

Diran made no move stand, but he shifted in his seat so that his hands were closer to his belt daggers. Out of the corner of his eye, Diran noticed Ghaji shift slightly so that he was in a better position to draw his axe.

"Tell me, my friend, how did you guess my vocation?" Diran asked. "I display no outward signs of my office."

The warforged hesitated before answering, not long, but long enough for Diran to notice. "I heard the two of you talking."

It was possible. Though the warforged hadn't been sitting that close to them, Diran had no idea how sharp the construct's hearing might be. Still, the warforged's answer didn't sit right with Diran, but the priest maintained a friendly smile as he asked, "What might I do for you?"

"Do you truly believe in the gods?" the warforged asked. His voice was still cold and inhuman, but Diran thought he detected a hint of anger now.

"A disarmingly simple question," Diran said, purposefully emphasizing *disarmingly* to see if the warforged would react. It was always good to keep an opponent—even a potential one—off-balance if you could. But if the warforged noted Diran's gibe, he gave no indication. He just stood there, waiting for an answer, as still as only the warforged could be.

"The simple answer is that I have seen and done much since taking my vows. Too much not to believe that there are powers beyond this sphere, both good and evil."

"In that case, where were you and your gods during the Last War?" There was more than a hint of anger in the construct's voice this time. "Where were you when my people were used as killing machines and then discarded after the fighting was done, left to find our own purpose in the world? Does your Silver Flame burn for our kind as well as yours?"

Despite himself, Diran's jaw muscles tightened as he listened to the warforged. Though he hadn't been a priest for long, this wasn't the first time he'd had to listen to similar accusations, and he doubted it would be the last. The Last War had devastated Khorvaire in so many ways, but perhaps the deepest mark it had left was on the souls of the survivors. So many questioned how the gods could've allowed such widespread destruction to occur. Indeed, many even questioned whether the gods existed at all.

Ghaji's lips curled back from his teeth. "Are you missing a brain as well as an arm? Why don't you be a good little toy soldier and march out of here? The priest and I have important business to attend to, and it doesn't include mollycoddling an emotionally disturbed warforged."

Though Diran sympathized with Ghaji, he didn't want the situation to get out of hand. He gave the warforged his best caring priest expression and spoke in a calm, kind voice. "I understand your confusion, my friend, and I—"

The warforged raised his one hand high over his head, made a fist and shook it, as if in defiance of the heavens and all they contained. "You understand nothing! Nothing!"

As Ghaji started to rise from his chair, reaching for his axe in the process, Diran grabbed hold of both his belt daggers and pulled them from their sheaths in a single fluid motion. Fast as a pair of striking snakes, his hands hurled the daggers, but the blades flew not at the warforged, but rather toward the pair of daggerstars that were flying at Diran from the direction of the shifter. The daggers struck the throwing stars with a pair of metallic clangs, knocking them off course.

By this time Ghaji had gotten to his feet and drawn his axe. The warforged, instead of attacking, was backing up, but the construct didn't get very far. Ghaji knelt and hooked the head of his axe head behind the warforged's right foot, took hold of the axe handle with both hands, and yanked hard. The warforged's feet flew out from under him, and he fell onto his right side. Without an arm on that side to catch himself, the warforged hit the ground hard.

Diran, trusting Ghaji to deal with the warforged, jumped out of his seat and ran for the shifter, drawing a fresh pair of daggers from hidden pockets in his cloak as he went. He ran crouched low to present a smaller target, but the shifter—who stood facing Diran, feet planted far apart, features now more lupine than human—didn't need much of a target. She hurled another pair of daggerstars, and as they left her clawed, fur-covered hands, Diran saw they were smeared with a glistening, greasy substance that he recognized as a fast-acting and extremely deadly poison. He should know; he'd used it often enough in the past.

Diran swept both his hands outward and deflected the projectiles with his daggers. He didn't stop running but rather increased his speed. He jumped up onto a table—causing the pair of traders who sat there to cry out in alarm and throw themselves back—and then launched himself into the air. His black cloak billowed out behind him like the ebon wings of some great predatory bird, and he threw his daggers. But the shifter had evidently realized her plan had gone bad, for she was already in the process of turning to flee as Diran's blades streaked toward her. One of the daggers missed and struck the ground, sinking up to the hilt. But the other hit the woman on the meaty part of her right shoulder, eliciting a howl of pain. As she started to run, she reached back and pulled the dagger free in a spray of blood. She dropped the blade to the ground and loped off, running with the swiftness of her kind.

She was already yards away by the time Diran's boots came in contact with the ground once more. He drew yet another pair of daggers from his cloak, but he didn't throw them. The shifter was already out of range, and Diran, though fleet of foot for a human, knew he couldn't hope to match the shifter's speed. He watched the woman flee down the dirt road, pedestrians quickly giving way before her, and soon she was lost to his sight. Diran glanced around to see if anyone had been struck by the daggerstars he'd deflected. Satisfied that no one had been injured during the brief battle, Diran turned to see how Ghaji was doing.

The half-orc knelt atop the warforged's prone form, axe blade pressed firmly against the construct's throat. Diran walked calmly back to his table, his daggers disappearing into the folds of his cloak as he walked. To anyone watching, it would've seemed as if the blades simply vanished from his hands, so swiftly did he return them to their hidden pockets. Diran stopped when he reached Ghaji and the downed warforged.

"I'd offer my assistance, but you obviously don't require it," Diran said.

"This oversized toy's a pushover," Ghaji said. "His joints are so worn it's a wonder he doesn't shake to pieces when he walks. One good shove of my axe—" Ghaji leaned his weight against the blade to demonstrate— "and our friend's head will pop off like a daisy's bloom."

"Please!" the warforged pleaded. "I have no quarrel with you. The shifter paid me to come over and distract you. I wouldn't have done it, but I've been trying to save up enough to pay for repairs."

"So you helped her try to kill us for a few measly coins?" Ghaji pressed harder and there came the sound of metal grinding against metal. The warforged cried out in fear, the sound almost human.

Diran laid a hand on Ghaji's shoulder. "That's enough, my friend. Taking vengeance on this creature won't change what happened."

"Maybe not, but it'd sure feel good." Still, the half-orc removed his axe blade from the warforged's throat and stepped off his chest. The construct sat up, but he made no move to stand.

"Did the shifter tell you her name?" Diran asked.

The warforged shook his head, the motion making his neck creak. "She did not."

Diran considered this, then he reached for his money purse and removed it from his belt. "Here." He tossed the coins to the warforged, and the construct caught the purse easily with his one hand. "A donation to your repair fund. Now go."

The warforged looked at Diran, his inhuman features unreadable. "My thanks." He rose to his feet, gave the priest a nod, turned, and walked way.

"How could you let him go without questioning him further?" Ghaji demanded. "Don't you want to know why that shifter wants you dead? And why in all the gods' names did you give One-Arm your money?"

"I gave the warforged money so that he might not be tempted to perform another evil deed in the future. As for further questioning, it wasn't necessary. I already know why the woman wants to kill me."

3

Diran and Ghaji made their way back toward the Little Rose, walking past crude shacks, stalls, tents, and lean-to's. Kartan was very much still a work in progress.

"When you were examining Yalene . . ." Ghaji began.

"Yes?" Diran had a feeling he knew what the half-orc was going to say, but he waited for him to get around to it in his own way.

"Well . . . you were talking with the spirit or demon or whatever it is inside her, and it . . . it said some things. Things that made it sound almost as if . . . as if you two knew each other."

Diran didn't respond right away, and now it was Ghaji's turn to wait patiently.

"I once suffered a similar affliction to Yalene's," Diran said. "I was . . . cured by a priest of the Silver Flame. He was a wise and strong warrior, and it was he who inspired me to became a priest."

"So this dark spirit in Yalene is the same one that was cast out of you?"

"I suppose it's possible, and I'm certain that's what the entity wants me to believe—to keep me off-balance, if nothing else. But I doubt it. I believe it more likely that the entity somehow read my mind and was able to sift through my memories in order to find a most painful one to use as a weapon against me."

At least, that's what Diran hoped.

They walked in silence for a few moments after that before Ghaji spoke once more.

"Do you think the shifter will try again?" he asked.

"Undoubtedly, though she's lost the advantage of surprise."

"You know her?"

Diran shook his head.

"Then how do you know why she wants to kill you?"

"The same reason anyone else wants to kill me. There's a price on my head. Quite a high one, too."

"Why would anyone pay to have a priest killed? What did you do, mispronounce a word while saying a prayer?"

Diran smiled. "I wasn't always a priest."

Ghaji snorted. "So I gathered."

"You guessed earlier that I was a soldier, and in a manner of speaking, I suppose I was. I was an assassin."

"Ah. Well, that explains your skill with daggers. Who did you fight for?"

"Whoever paid the most money."

"I see."

Diran could tell Ghaji was trying to keep the disgust he felt out of his voice, but Diran could hear it anyway. Perhaps because he felt the same disgust himself.

"My master was a mercenary warlord named Emon Gorsedd. He raised me from childhood, taught me how to wield a dagger, taught me how to kill, swiftly, efficiently, and without emotion. Emon caused me to become host to a dark spirit, so that he might be able to control me more easily. I would've continued to kill for him the rest of my life, if not for the priest I told you of. His name was Tusya, and after he freed me from the spirit, I decided to join the Church of the Silver Flame, in whose service I now employ the skills Emon taught me for good rather than evil." There was more to the tale than that, much more, but that was all Diran felt Ghaji needed to hear at the moment.

"That's quite a story," Ghaji said, "and I bet I can guess the ending. Emon wasn't too happy about losing his star pupil, so he put out a bounty on you."

Diran nodded. "Emon never forgives and he never forgets. And he never gives up. Neither do those who work for him. That's how I know the shifter will make another attempt on my life before long."

"So what are you going to do? Track her down and kill her before she kills you?"

Diran shook his head. "I will fight in self-defense and in defense of others, but I will never hunt another being as long as I live."

"That might not be long," Ghaji said.

Diran smiled. "Well, then my struggle will be over."

"So what *are* you going to do?" Ghaji insisted.

"I'm going to do what I intended when I first knocked on the Little Rose's door. I'm going to free Yalene from the dark force that has taken control of her. You said Yalene lost her family during an attack by raiders."

"That's right. At least, that's what she told me."

"And she was a child at the time, correct?"

"No more than ten, I believe. Maybe younger."

"Losing loved ones in such violent fashion is usually quite traumatic." Diran thought for a moment. "Does Yalene ever suffer from nightmares?"

Ghaji looked at Diran in surprise. "She does. Sometimes they're so bad she wakes up screaming in the middle of the night. It happens maybe two, three times a month. More if she's worried about something."

"And what does she dream about? The death of her family?"

"What else?"

"You say her nightmares are more frequent when she's worried. What could so concern a young woman liked Yalene?"

"She worries about all of us at the Rose—the other girls, Onelle, even me. She once told me we're all the family she has now. She's like a young mother hen, checking to make sure we're feeling well, that we get enough food and rest. And when someone takes ill, Yalene's the one who stays by their side and nurses them back to health."

"I see," Diran said. "Most interesting." He fell silent, pondering Ghaji's words as two men continued to make their way back to the Little Rose.

4

Volante crouched within a tent pitched at the edge of the village, cursing the name of Diran Bastiaan as she worked on bandaging her shoulder. Her features had lost their wolfish aspect, though her aspect seemed no less savage.

The tent flap parted with a quiet rustle and a large metal being bereft of one arm entered.

Volante glared at the warforged. "Tell me something, Akrit. Does your kind keep their brains in their arms?"

The warforged looked at her without expression—which was the only way he *could* look—before answering, "No."

"Are you certain? It seems the loss of your arm has left you a complete imbecile."

Another pause, then Akrit said, "You are upset."

"Of course I'm upset!" Volante tried to keep her voice down, though it wasn't easy, angry as she was. While many of the refugees who lived in the surrounding tents believed that minding one's business was an important survival skill, just as many saw the accumulation of coin as even more important and would run to Bastiaan and reveal Volante's location—for a price—should they discover who she was and why she'd come to Kartan.

"You were supposed to distract Dir—" She stopped, then finished, "The target."

"I thought I performed adequately." Akrit's voice remained steady and even, as warforged voices were wont to do, but Volante had worked with Akrit long enough to become sensitive to its subtle inflections. Right now she detected a hint of pouting.

"Did he look distracted to you?" Volante checked the dressing she'd placed over her shoulder wound. The cloth was already stained with blood and would have to be changed soon. Shifters were a hardier race than humans, and she would heal before long, but most likely not before she would have to hunt again. Bastiaan was aware of her now and on guard. She'd have to strike swiftly and soon, before he had much chance to prepare for her next attack.

"The priest is not the type who distracts easily," Akrit said. "In which case, the fault lies not with my acting skills but with your intelligence-gathering. If you'd been aware of all his capabilities—"

"Are you implying that what happened at the tavern was *my* fault?" As a shifter, Volante could be blunt at times, but that didn't mean she enjoyed others being blunt with *her*.

"I'm not implying anything," Akrit said. "I'm stating it directly."

Red fury flashed through Volante, and if Akrit had been a human, she would've attacked and slain him on the spot. But while warforged could be killed—or perhaps *destroyed* was a better word for their kind—it wasn't easy and took some doing. Volante didn't feel like breaking her claws or teeth on the construct's metal hide, so she restrained herself.

The most galling thing about it all was that Akrit was right, though she'd sooner slit both her own wrists with a dull blade than admit it to him. When she'd taken on the assignment to track down Diran Bastiaan and slay him, she had arrogantly assumed that her shifter skills—including a powerful sense of smell that helped her track anyone or anything in Khorvaire—would be all she'd need to get the job done. Bastiaan might have been a deadly assassin once, but in the years since the Last War, he'd studied with the order of the Silver Flame and become a priest. Volante had expected Bastiaan to have lost his fighting edge. On the whole, Volante favored simple plans to locate and dispatch targets—confronting them in a dark alley, slaying them while they slept . . . But in deference to Bastiaan's past reputation, she'd decided to go with a somewhat more elaborate plan this time. She'd sent Akrit to engage Bastiaan in an argument long enough for her to hurl a pair of poisoned daggerstars at him. But Diran had been too wily. Not only hadn't she slain the assassin-turned-priest, she'd nearly lost her own life to those damn knives of his.

She was tempted to give up and leave Kartan, but the money Gorsedd offered was too good, and she'd tracked Bastiaan too long and too far to abandon the hunt now. Besides, Gorsedd wasn't one to forgive failure. Look how many years he'd been trying to kill Bastiaan, one way or another. If she didn't want the warlord to put a price on *her* head, she had to bring him Bastiaan's—and soon. And that meant coming up with a new plan.

The tent flap rustled again and a pair of halflings entered. Though the two showed no obvious signs of relation other than the basic traits of their race—Drosen was stout and dark-haired, Sverrel lean and fair—Volante could tell they were brothers by their scent.

"Interesting technique you've got, Volante," Drosen said.

"Especially the part where you flee in terror while your target remains alive," Sverrel added.

Volante ground her teeth. The halfling brothers shared an irritating sense of humor that made Volante want to take a pair of her poison-coated daggerstars and shove them straight up their—

"But we have good news for you," Drosen said, and Volante decided to keep her daggerstars in reserve . . . for now.

"We followed the priest and the half-orc to see where they'd go," Sverrel said.

"They didn't see us," Drosen added.

"No one does," Sverrel agreed, "not unless we want them to."

Despite herself, Volante couldn't help but grin at this news, which was good indeed. "Where did they go?"

5

"The last of the girls are gone," Onelle said. "Now what?"

Diran and Ghaji sat in the downstairs parlor, where the Little Rose's customers waited until it was time for their appointments. Onelle stood in the doorway, looking half irritated at the thought of all the business she was losing by sending her girls away and half frightened by what was to happen next.

"It would be best if you departed as well," Diran said. "An exorcism is an unpleasant thing to witness, and there are certain special features to Yalene's situation that may well make the rite more . . . intense than usual."

Onelle put her hands on her hips. "I don't scare easy."

"It's not your emotional well-being I'm concerned with so much as your physical safety," Diran said. "This exorcism will likely be a dangerous one, for me as well as any bystanders. And to be frank, I stand a greater chance of success if I don't have to worry about protecting you."

The owner of the Little Rose frowned, but finally nodded. She was obviously unhappy, but she would do as Diran asked. She turned to Ghaji and said, "Ready to go?"

"If you don't mind, I'd rather stay," the half-orc said. He looked at Diran. "If things are going to get as dangerous as you say, someone should remain here to help you."

Diran looked at Ghaji for a moment before speaking. "Didn't you tell me that you originally came to Hope because you wanted to find a place where you wouldn't have to . . . how did you put it? 'Kill or die for some abstract sense of values that I'm not sure I understand, let alone believe in?' "

The half-orc scowled. "I don't remember saying anything like that. I think you need to cast a healing spell on your ears, priest."

Diran smiled.

6

Onelle left soon after that, and Diran and Ghaji were alone in the Little Rose with Yalene and whatever foul creature had invaded her body. Diran sat on the parlor floor, eyes closed, breathing slowly and deeply, truly meditating this time, while Ghaji sat in a chair sharpening his axe with a whetstone. At first, Diran had found the *shh-shh-shh* of Ghaji's whetstone distracting, but the regular rhythm soon became a comforting counterpoint to his meditation. In fact, it felt right to hear it, as if he'd been missing a vital component in his meditations and had never realized it until now.

After a bit, Ghaji spoke, though he continued honing his axe blade. "You told Onelle that this exorcism is going to be particularly dangerous. Why?"

Diran didn't open his eyes. "Despite the more lurid folktales you hear, possession occurs in very specific ways under very specific conditions. The signs Yalene has been exhibiting—the frigid atmosphere of her room, the ability to move solid objects without touching them, the capability of reading another's thoughts in order to taunt them—these are the stuff of superstition and myth, the sort of thing a child might believe."

"Are you saying a demon is incapable of performing such feats?" Ghaji kept at his work. *Shh-shh-shh.*

"Not at all. But the point of possession is to gain a foothold in the physical world. Why would an extra-planar entity go to all the trouble of coming to our dimension and entering a host body, only to announce its presence to one and all, alerting every priest within a hundred leagues? It wouldn't, of course. It would seek to remain hidden as long as possible."

"Makes sense." *Shh-shh-shh.* "But then why is Yalene's demon not hiding?"

"It's very simple." Diran opened his eyes and looked at Ghaji. "Yalene isn't possessed."

The *shh-shh-shh* stopped. "What do you mean? You saw her—that voice, those eyes, the cold. If she isn't possessed . . ."

"What I meant was that Yalene's body isn't host to an extra-planar entity. There is no demon inside her. At least, not in the usual sense."

Ghaji frowned. "I don't understand."

"Do you remember when I told you that true possession is rare, that supposed cases of it are in truth poor souls who suffer from a malady of the mind?"

"Yes, but that can't be Yalene. I've *felt* the cold in her room, I've *seen* blankets fly off of her body, watched one burst into flame and be reduced to ashes!"

"You told me that Yalene's parents were fortunetellers."

"So?"

"So I believe that they were more than just entertainers in a traveling caravan. I believe they truly had mental powers of some sort and that they passed those powers on to their daughter."

"But Yalene's never shown any sign of having such powers. And if she did have them, why would she work in the Little Rose when she could making a living telling fortunes herself?"

"Perhaps her abilities were latent ones," Diran suggested, "her powers an unrealized potential."

"You mean she had the powers but didn't *know* she had them?"

"Something like that. I believe that the trauma of losing her parents affected Yalene deeply, and she's never fully recovered from its effects. This is why she's always so concerned for the welfare of her friends, why she worries so when they're sick. She has a terrible fear of death—not her own, but rather the deaths of those she loves."

Ghaji's eyes widened. "So when Laris died while he and Yalene were together . . ."

"You said she was fond of him. When he died in her arms, it was too much for her to bear, and her mind retreated from the horror. This created a void within her, a void that was filled by a personality who is stronger than Yalene, who can wield her mental abilities to protect her from ever letting anyone get close to her again. I believe that's how she knew about my past experience with possession. She used her mental powers to read my mind and then used the knowledge she gained as a weapon against me. And this other personality will continue to use Yalene's powers to keep everyone away, for if no one gets close to her . . ."

"She won't have to be afraid of losing them," Ghaji finished.

"Exactly. I have seen cases where the mind turns inward due to trauma—from causes both natural and unnatural—but I've never seen anything to this degree before." Diran shook his head. "To be honest, I fear that I will be unable to help her."

"But you're a priest of the Silver Flame!" Ghaji protested. "Casting out spirits and healing the sick and injured is what you do."

"Yes, but the only spirit within Yalene is the one she was born with. As for healing her condition . . . the trauma she suffered occurred long ago. So long that it's become an integral part of her being. It may be too entrenched to heal in any traditional sense."

"So there's nothing you can do for her?"

"I didn't say that. Perhaps there's an *un*traditional way we can help Yalene. Provided you're willing to assist me, that is."

Ghaji's jaw was set in a determined line. "I'll do whatever it takes."

Diran walked over to the half-orc and clapped him on the shoulder. "Good man! Now, let me tell you what I have in mind. I'm sure you noticed the two halflings that were spying on us as we walked back from the tavern."

"Huh? Oh yeah, of course I did. No halfling's sneaky enough to keep *me* from noticing him."

Diran smiled and told Ghaji of his plan.

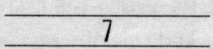

7

"There's no one else in the place. Just the priest and the half-orc."

"Are you certain?"

Drosen looked offended, and Volante decided not to pursue the matter further. Both Drosen and Sverrel were two of the best scouts she'd ever worked with. Despite how many hunts she'd been on and how many times she'd successfully brought down her quarry, she'd never faced anyone like Diran Bastiaan. As if in response to her thinking his name, her shoulder wound began to throb.

"I managed to strike up a conversation with one of the girls who works there," Sverrel said. "She told me that the priest ordered everyone to evacuate the building so that no one would be harmed while he performs his exorcism."

The four of them—Volante, the two halflings, and Akrit—stood in an alley across the street and cattycorner from the Little Rose. All wore traveler's cloaks with the hoods up, though Volante knew that Diran would mark them in an instant if he saw them, as would the half-orc, most likely. The assassins were hidden well enough here, but nevertheless, Volante hoped Diran would be too busy preparing for the exorcism to look out the window.

"I bet that isn't all she told you, brother," Drosen said with a broad leer and exaggerated wink.

"Well . . . she *did* tell me she liked her men short. I'm to meet with her after sundown—provided we've finished off the priest by then, of course."

"I knew it!" Drosen exclaimed. "My brother's always had an eye for the ladies and they for him."

Volante didn't find Sverrel all that attractive, but there was no accounting for taste.

"If the priest has sent everyone else away, why does the half-orc remain?" Akrit asked in his emotionless voice.

"Perhaps the lady who runs the house doesn't wish to leave one of her employees unguarded while Diran goes about his work," Volante suggested. "Or perhaps he's simply taking an extra precaution and the half-orc has remained to guard *him* in case there's another attempt on his life."

Akrit cocked his head to the side, a gesture Volante had

come to interpret as one of confusion. "But *we* are going to attempt to slay the priest again, aren't we?"

"Yes," Volante said, trying to keep exasperation she felt out of her voice. Warforged—or at least this particular one—could be somewhat slow at times. "Diran knows only that I tried to kill him earlier. He doesn't know the four of us are working together. A single half-orc, no matter how good a fighter, could never hope to stand against all of us. All we have to do is wait for Diran to begin the rite of exorcism, then we attack. While he's distracted, we'll slay the half-orc and then slay Diran."

"And what of the possessed girl?" Akrit asked.

Volante shrugged, then winced as the motion made her shoulder wound throb anew. "We kill her, too. If Diran hasn't exorcised the spirit before we slay him, then at least the girl will be free. And if he has . . ." Volante grinned, displaying teeth that were too long and sharp to be human. "Well, it would be sloppy of us to leave a witness behind, wouldn't it?"

Drosen and Sverrel chuckled, but Akrit made no response. Volante had never heard the warforged laugh. She had no idea whether his kind even *could* laugh.

She turned to the halflings. "Both of you move closer to the Little Rose. Climb up to the second story, if you have to. When you hear Diran begin the rite, signal us."

The loud sound of splintering wood crashed through the air. The four assassins hurried to the mouth of the alley just in time to see a chest of drawers smash onto the ground. Stockings, nightgowns, and frilly underwear spilled out as the chest was reduced to kindling. Volante looked up and saw the wooden shutters that had been closed over one of the Rose's upstairs windows had been nearly torn from their hinges.

Both Drosen and Sverrel looked at Volante and gave her a thumbs-up sign.

"They are giving us the signal you requested," Akrit said without a trace of humor.

"I'd like to give *you* something, you thick-headed—" Volante growled deep in her throat. "Nevermind. Let's go."

Volante loped out of the alley, the halfling brothers following close behind. Akrit hesitated, and Volante heard him say, "Give me what?" before he too finally followed.

8

"Best you get to your position on the stairs," Diran said.

Ghaji nodded, rubbing his left shoulder as he headed for the door. "First I have to haul the chest out of the room, then I have to bring it back and heave it out the window. Who knew a lady's undergarments could be so heavy?"

Still muttering, Ghaji went into the hallway and closed the door behind him.

Yalene, who'd been silently watching the two of them since they'd entered the room, gave Diran a puzzled look. "What are you up to?" she asked.

"Just playing a little game," Diran said. He concentrated on maintaining a mental shield around his thoughts so Yalene's other self couldn't read them. He supposed she might've already read Ghaji's thoughts. If so she was already aware of their plan.

Yalene smiled. "Can I play, too?"

Diran gave her a grim smile in return. "I'm counting on it."

9

"The door's not locked," Drosen said.

Volante considered this. Kartan was a small settlement, not even really a village. There probably wasn't enough crime here yet for people to worry about locking their doors—if they even *had* locks.

"Thinking it's a trap?" Sverrel asked.

"Perhaps," Volante said. "But if it is, it's a trap set up for a lone shifter, not for a team of assassins. Let's go."

Drosen and Sverrel exchanged looks but made no further comment. Drosen opened the door a crack, peered inside, then opened the door wider and gestured for his brother to go inside. Sverrel drew a long knife from his belt, which was big enough to be a sword in his small hand, and then stepped across the threshold of the Little Rose. Drosen followed, long knife in hand, followed by Volante and Akrit.

They found themselves in a parlor, though it didn't look like much: several wooden chairs and a crude couch most likely stuffed with rushes. On the far side of the parlor was an open doorway—the only exit out of the room. Volante nodded to the halfling brothers. They crossed the room swiftly and silently then paused at the doorway. They listened for a moment then peered around both sides of the doorway, Drosen on the right, Sverrel the left. Satisfied, they looked back at Volante and Akrit and gave them thumbs-up once more.

Volante shucked off her cloak and stuffed it under the couch. Her three partners did the same. Volante drew a pair of daggerstars from her belt pouch and indicated that Akrit should arm himself. The warforged released the leather straps binding the warhammer to his back and took hold of his weapon with his single hand. They were ready.

Volante gestured for her team to move forward. With the halflings once again leading, they passed through the door into a hallway and came across a set of stairs. Halfway up them stood the half-orc, gripping a hand-axe.

He grinned. "What took you so long?"

10

Diran was standing next to Yalene's bed when Ghaji crashed through the door. The half-orc quickly rose to his feet and moved back as a warforged carrying an iron hammer stomped into the room, followed by two halflings and the shifter who had tried to kill him at the tavern. Diran had already known that the halflings were working with the shifter, and he'd suspected the same about the warforged. Now his suspicions were confirmed.

Diran no longer wore his cloak or his belt. In fact, the only clothing he had on was a breechcloth. He raised his hands to show that they were empty. None of the assassins attacked right away. They stopped and stared at Diran in confusion.

"What trick is this?" the shifter demanded. Prepared to kill, she'd taken on the bestial aspect of a wolf-woman.

"No trick," Diran said, though that wasn't precisely true. "I am unarmed. My daggers lie over in the corner with my clothing." Diran nodded to a corner of the room where his cloak, shirt, leather vest, pants, boots, and belt were arranged neatly.

"Are you a master of unarmed combat?' the warforged asked.

"I can give a good enough account of myself if I have to,"

Diran said. "But I'd hardly classify myself as a master. Even so, I have no intention of fighting any of you."

The shifter frowned. "Tiger's blood! What are you talking about?" She held a number of daggerstars in each hand, but she made no move to throw them—yet.

Before Diran could respond, Yalene turned to face the four newcomers.

"The priest is a fool. He believes that if he pretends to offer himself as a sacrifice to you, he will rouse my other self from the inner lair in which she's taken refuge, and that she shall use our mental power to protect him. But we are aware of his plan and shall do nothing to save him. Slay him if you will." Yalene turned away from the assassins and settled her head back on her pillow. "His death means nothing to us."

"Uh, Diran," Ghaji said. "It might be time for a change in strategy."

Diran ignored his companion and trained his gaze on Yalene. "Though I'd hoped you wouldn't read our minds, I knew you probably would and that you'd discover my true intentions behind allowing these assassins to reach me."

"Allowing?" the shifter said, sounding mortally insulted.

"Of course," Diran said without talking his gaze off Yalene. "Do you truly imagine I wasn't aware that you'd make another attempt to kill me, or that Ghaji would fall before you so easily? We wanted you to reach us."

"You've only sealed your doom, priest," Yalene said.

"You may think that you're calling my bluff, Yalene," Diran said, "but if you've read my mind you know I'm not bluffing. I am prepared to die if that's the price I must pay for restoring your sanity."

"And what if you die and we remain as we are?" Yalene challenged.

Diran shrugged. "Then I die. But if there's even a chance that I can help you, then I must take it, regardless of the consequences to me."

Yalene sneered. "Why? Because that's what your order would have you do?"

"No," Diran said softly. "Because once a young girl named Yalene suffered a terrible loss that left her with an intense fear of death, a fear that's kept her from living fully, and it's past time she was free of it."

Yalene stared at Diran, her expression unreadable.

Diran turned to face the shifter and her fellow assassins. He spread his arms wide, offering himself to them. "Do what you came here for. I shall not attempt to stop you, and neither will my friend."

"Diran . . ." Ghaji said, tightening his grip on his axe.

"You heard me, Ghaji. Please do as I ask."

Ghaji said nothing at first, but then he nodded and lowered his axe. He looked miserable, but Diran was confident he'd honor his wishes. He smiled at the shifter.

"Go ahead," said Diran.

The shifter hesitated a moment, as if she couldn't quite bring herself to believe what was happening. But finally she grinned, baring her lupine teeth, and with a swift, fluid motion, she hurled her daggerstars straight at Diran's bare chest and throat.

Diran didn't close his eyes, didn't tense his muscles in anticipation of the impact to come. He merely stood and waited, ready to accept his fate, whatever it might be.

The daggerstars—six in all, and every one coated with deadly fast-acting poison—halted in the air mere inches from Diran's flesh. They remained that way for several seconds, still spinning, and then Yalene turned to look at the four assassins who'd invaded her bedchamber.

"Uh-oh," the shifter said, and the daggerstars reversed course.

11

Yalene was sitting up in bed, sipping warm broth, a blanket drawn up to her waist. The furniture had been returned to her room, but while Ghaji had done his best to rebuild her chest of drawers, it leaned to one side and looked as if it might collapse any moment. Onelle sat in a chair next to Yalene's bed, chatting with the girl and making sure she took enough broth.

Diran entered the room. Once more the priest was fully dressed in his leather vest and black clothing, and he'd donned his dark cloak as well. A traveler's pack was slung over one shoulder, a bow and quiver of arrows over the other,

"You're leaving us," Yalene said. It wasn't a question.

Diran smiled. "Reading my mind again?"

Yalene blushed. "No. At least, not on purpose."

"No need to worry, child. You'll gain more control of your abilities with time. And I've taken the liberty of writing a letter to an old friend of mine explaining your situation. I'm sure he'll be able to find someone who can tutor you in the usage of your powers. I affixed my seal to the letter and gave it to Lady Onelle. She'll see that it's delivered."

In his long career serving the cause of the Silver Flame, Tusya had made many friends and allies across Khorvaire. Diran had no doubt the old priest would find a perfect teacher for Yalene.

"Thank you, Diran," Yalene said. "But I can't afford to pay a tutor."

"No payment will be necessary," Diran said. And even if it was, Tusya would take care of it.

"Speaking of payment," Onelle said, "how can we ever hope to repay you? You've saved my business—and far more importantly, you've save the mind of my sweet Yalene." The older woman reached out and squeezed the younger's hand.

"I do what I do because it's right," Diran said. A small smile played about his lips. "But thanks to Yalene, there are four fewer assassins hunting me, and for that you have *my* gratitude."

The poison in the daggerstars had been more than enough to finish off the shifter and the two halflings. As for the one-armed warforged, while he might have been immune to poison, he hadn't been able to withstand a swarm of flying metal stars slicing away at the wooden joints that held him together. Diran had seen that his parts were buried along with the bodies of his companions, paying for the burials with the money he'd found on their dead bodies. While the assassins hadn't been rich, they'd had more than enough between them to cover the cost of their interment, leaving a little left over for Diran to add to his purse, along with the money he'd given the warforged to buy a new arm. As always, and in more ways than one, doing good was its own reward.

"I must go," he said.

"Of course," Yalene said. "I understand."

Diran locked gazes with the young woman, and he knew that she, perhaps even more than he himself, truly did understand.

He gave Yalene and Onelle a last smile before turning and walking out of the bedchamber.

12

Diran stepped onto the street and started walking. Before long he became aware of someone following him. Near the edge of town, that someone caught up to Diran and fell in step alongside him.

"I wondered where you were," Diran said. He looked at Ghaji and saw the half-orc wore a green traveler's cloak and carried a large backpack.

"I said my goodbyes. I didn't see any point in prolonging things."

Diran nodded and the two men walked in silence for a time.

After a bit Ghaji asked, "Still headed for the Lhazaar Principalities?"

"Yes. No telling how it'll take me to get there, though." Diran gave Ghaji a smile. "I have a tendency to get sidetracked."

"So I've noticed."

"How about you?" Diran asked. "Where are you bound?"

"Nowhere in particular. I thought I'd tag along with you for a while." Ghaji gave Diran a sideways glance. "That is, if you don't mind."

"Not at all. I could use the company. But if I may ask—?"

"Why do I want to come with you?"

Diran nodded.

Ghaji didn't answer right away. After a moment's thought, he said, "I may not have found something to fight for, but I believe I've found someone to fight alongside."

Together the priest and the half-orc continued on their way, heading in whatever direction the road might take them.

THE TALES OF THE LAST WAR

ABOUT THE AUTHOR

Tim Waggoner's novels include *Pandora Drive* and *Like Death* (Leisure Books), *A Nightmare on Elm Street: Protégé* (Black Flame), *Godfire: The Orchard of Dreams*, *Godfire: Heart's Wound*, *Necropolis* (Five Star), *Exalted: A Shadow Over Heaven's Eye*, *Dark Ages: Gangrel* (White Wolf), *Defender: Hyperswarm* (I-Books), and *The Harmony Society* (Prime Books). He is also the author of the short story collection *All Too Surreal* (Prime Books). He is the author of two books in the DRAGONLANCE: THE NEW ADVENTURES series, *Temple of the Dragonslayer* and *Return of the Sorceress* (Wizards of the Coast), as well as many novels and short stories for teens and adults. He's published close to eighty short stories of horror and fantasy, and his articles on writing have appeared in *Writer's Digest*, *Writers' Journal*, and other publications. He teaches creative writing at Sinclair Community College in Dayton, Ohio. Visit him on the web at www.timwaggoner.com.

Tim's first trilogy set in Eberron premieres in May 2006 with *The Thieves of Blood*.

DISTANT FIRES

Aaron Rosenberg

I

Darkness gave way to light. Slowly, sights leaked in around the edges.

I blinked once, twice, then forced my eyes open and looked around.

Gray and black. Stone and . . . ash? Soot? For an instant I thought I had been tossed into some massive fireplace. Everything within sight was blackened, charred. But no, there was a window, and there stairs. Simply a gray stone room, then, marred by flame.

My eyes focused. My body awoke. And protested loudly. Everything ached. My head throbbed, particularly once I lifted it off the flagstones of the floor. My chest and arms felt like the flesh had been peeled from them, and I saw that everywhere I was raw and red. And it was everywhere, for I was unclothed.

Dark spatters around me spoke of blood, and there was more caked on me as well—some on the arms, some on my chest, some on my legs. Angrier red patches around wrist and ankles. What had happened?

I sat up, groaning from the effort, and cupped my head in both hands to make it stop pounding. My fingertips came away wet. More blood, then, and I gingerly felt it along my scalp. That was not difficult, since I had no hair. Had I had hair, once? I couldn't remember. And the chill that shook me then had nothing to do with sitting naked in a stone room.

I could not remember.

Anything.

Where was I? *Who* was I? What had happened? I had no idea. None.

Oh, this was not good. I thought about shutting my eyes again, letting the dark that lingered at the fringes of my mind sweep back down and carry me off. At least if I were unconscious I would not worry. But no, I was awake, and passing out would only delay the matter. I would have to deal with the situation.

There was a chair behind me—or what was left of one. It looked like it had been good thick wood once, before whatever fire consumed this place had danced across it. In several places I saw patches that were not singed—on the seat and along the back and down along the front legs. Righting the chair and holding it steady, my hands shook. I studied the chair. Those spots . . . where someone had sat? I checked the backs of my legs and saw that I had no soot in a straight line down each. Right where the chair legs would have been. My flesh had preserved that wood from harm. The fire had washed over me and around me, sparing the chair where it touched my skin. I had been here when the flames had consumed this place.

I had a faint image of a blinding burst of light, a wave of immense heat. But that was all. I had no idea how I had survived whatever had caused this.

Well, sitting here was doing me no good, and it was cold on the stones—whatever heat had enveloped them was long since gone. I stood, using the chair's remains for support. A bit shaky, but I could manage. Good. Glancing around, I saw something else I had not remembered and could not fathom. I was not alone in this room. Bodies were strewn about. At least five, possibly more. It was hard to tell. Their blackened bones mingled so easily with shattered wood from more furniture. But clearly they had not endured the fire as as I had. The bodies were large, my height or taller and broader by half, with long arms and bowed legs. I could not make out features, of course, but I suspected they were not human.

Was I?

I made my wobbly way over to the stairs. Climbing them took effort, and I could only manage two before I had to lean against the wall for support. My breath was short, quick, and shallow, and my lungs felt bruised. Everything felt bruised. Once my eyes had stopped blurring so severely and my hands were only slightly shaky, I renewed the ascent.

The first door I found was also blackened, but still on its hinges. It was ajar, and I pushed past it into a large chamber. The fire had rushed through here as well, but not as severely, and the items strewn about were not completely destroyed, though none were whole either. And they were definitely strewn about—it looked as if someone had been searching through them in a great hurry. I pulled a tattered shirt from the corner of what might have been a bookcase once, and I pulled it over my head. It was torn away in parts, but it covered most of my back and half of my stomach and the upper portion of one arm.

Better than nothing. I could not tell its color in the dim light from the room's one narrow window. Not that I cared.

Kicking aside debris, I found trousers as well. Most of one leg was gone, and the rest had a large hole that exposed my knee and the flesh around it as well, but again it was an improvement from being unclothed. Nothing else seemed salvageable.

I returned to the stairway. Should I proceed farther up? The stairs kept on, curving with the wall. But I was near the end of my strength already. And I had clothing. Perhaps it was best to leave things at that.

The descent was much easier. I let gravity tug me down, and the wall kept me upright as I stumbled from step to step. I only had to pause once before reaching the bottom floor again.

There was a door here. I hadn't noticed it before. It was large, heavy, and though blackened it was still firmly within its frame. It had only an iron ring on this side, with no latch. I had not seen any other entrances to this room, aside from the stairs—the window was too high and too small. This, then, was my way out. I tugged on the ring. Nothing. I wrapped my other hand around it as well and tried again. Slowly the door shifted. My muscles protested, my ears rang, and my head pounded, but the door slid open, leaving a curving black trail where its burned lower edge scraped along the floor. When the gap was wide enough I dropped the ring and squeezed through.

The sun shone down on me, warming me through my ragged clothes. Instantly I felt better. I could see trees beyond, their green the first real color I'd witnessed since I'd awakened, and a faint breeze carried the scent of pine and oak and gave welcome respite from the heat. It felt like the building behind me was a mere dream, a wash of grey haze, compared to those trees. The door had several wide steps leading up to it, and I tripped down them, never taking my eyes from the distant foliage—

—which is why I ran into someone as my foot touched solid ground again.

"What've we here?" The voice was deep, guttural, and the words were harsh. Did I sound like that? I had not tried to speak—I was not sure I could, in fact—but I doubted it. I suspected my throat could not make those same rough-edged sounds.

I backed up, my mouth opening to apologize. A hand grasped me. Its thick fingers closed completely around my upper arm. The hand was encased in leather and metal, a gauntlet covered in scales and plates and small spikes, and I could feel it through the thin fabric of my shirt. Looking up, I followed the hand up to a thick arm, also wrapped in mail, and from there to an equally powerful body, then across the massive shoulders to a large, heavy head. Small, close-set eyes peered down at me under a heavy brow. The small, flat nose was wrinkled, perhaps in concern or amusement. And the wide, thick-lipped mouth was curved into an unpleasant smile. Tusks like those of a boar poked up along the sides. Bristly red hair jutted along the weak chin and atop the head.

Hobgoblin!

How I knew that I was not sure. I could not remember my own name, but I was sure I was right. A hobgoblin. And the bodies back in the building—those were also hobgoblins.

In fact, now that I glanced behind my captor, I realized that more goblinoids milled about. Most were of the same stature, though here and there I saw a few smaller specimens and one who appeared to tower over all the others. Several were looking at me. If I had glanced down when I'd stepped through the door, I would have realized that the small tree-lined clearing before the building was filled with the brutes.

While I had been taking stock, the hobgoblin holding my arm had appraised me as well. Now he turned away and swung me easily by my arm, tossing me to another hobgoblin standing nearby.

"Another for the slave pit!" the first one shouted, then marched away.

The second hobgoblin caught me, squeezing my arm so tightly that my hand went numb, and dragged me to one side of the clearing. A pit had been dug there, wide and deep, and I could see people huddled within it. A third goblinoid, this one of the smaller variety, stepped up, something in his hands, and then I heard a clink and felt cold metal about my ankles. Someone shoved me, and I pitched forward. My feet stepped reflexively, but something halted the right in midair, and I toppled, off-balance, into the pit.

2

"You hurt?"

As hard as the darkness strove to keep me, light kept drilling through, stabbing at me through closed lids. I gave up the fight and opened them.

A man was looking down at me. Strong, square features, short grizzled beard, powerful build. He seemed . . . familiar. My heart leaped. Was this someone I knew? But I could not put a name to the face, or anything beyond that vague sense of distant recollection. And he was not regarding me with particular warmth, though he showed no anger either. Simply the concern one might show a stranger in need.

"I—"

This was the first I had tried to speak since the gray room, and I was pleased when I opened my mouth and that first sound emerged. I was not mute, then.

"I think so," I managed, and sat up, discovering as I did that I had been lying in a heap on the ground. "Where am I?"

"Trapped in the same nightmare as the rest of us," the man replied bitterly. He offered me a hand up, and I noticed that his arms were as brawny as the hobgoblin who had captured me. Once I was standing I saw that he towered over me, and I knew somehow that I was not considered small myself. Perhaps he had some ogre or orc blood in him. Not that I cared about such things.

"Bennett's the name," he said then, holding his hand out again. It engulfed my own. When his brow started to drop into a scowl I realized he expected me to speak.

I nodded but could not offer a name in return. "I . . . I don't know my name. I'd hoped you might." Then, since he was still scowling and his grip was still tight, I added, "I hurt my head."

His expression cleared. "Ah, right. Sorry." Bennett released my hand and waved behind him. "These are the others. Some of them don't remember their names, either."

I saw now that we were far from alone in this pit. At least two dozen others were here, some standing, some leaning, some sitting or sprawling or curled up as I had been. All of us had those manacles about our ankles. All of us had blood on our clothes and on our flesh, and I was fairly certain it was all ours.

"What are they doing with us?" I asked Bennett, who had dropped to an easy crouch, arms bent and hands resting across his knees.

"Slaves," he said, biting down on the word.

I nodded. What else could be said after that?

I glanced around, studying the pit itself. It was not deep, perhaps twelve feet high—too far to jump, but shallow enough that a man could be boosted up. He saw my gaze, read it correctly, and shook his head.

"Don't try it," he warned. "These things"—he shook the manacles on his own ankles—"don't have much play. You can hobble, but that's it. They've got guards posted. Not right over us, but they don't have to be. Wearing these, a lame dog could catch up to you."

I frowned at my own restraints. Smart, these goblinoids. Too smart. They hadn't bound my hands. Why bother? The leg chains were all they needed. And Bennett was right. They could be twenty paces away and still catch me easily, as long as I was hobbled. Like a horse.

"No," I said, imagining the lives they had planned for us. I tugged at the right manacle, but it was solid iron, hard and heavy and cold about my flesh. It did not give. "No," I said again, tugging harder.

My fingers dropped the manacle and flexed about it, as if searching for openings, weaknesses, anything. I did not realize I was muttering until I heard myself, but I was not saying anything, not in real words. The strange sounds falling from my lips seemed merely an outward expression of my inner declarations, for I was telling myself over and over that I would not be penned like some animal and sold off like a beast. I would not!

Clink!

The sound was sharp, and in this sullen pit it carried. From the corner of my eye, I saw Bennett glance toward me. I was as curious as he was. With trembling fingers I pushed at the manacle again. With a dull clatter it slid open and fell to the ground. It had come loose.

"What the—?" Bennett stopped himself and simply watched as I nudged the other manacle. It slid open as well, and this one I caught before it fell free, setting it gently on the dirt and taking care that the chain between the two manacles did not clink either.

I was free!

Bennett glanced at the manacles lying there, then at me, then back at them. "Must not have tightened them," he muttered. "Too much of a hurry. Your lucky day, to be sure."

Others had seen them as well, and several hands clutched at me.

"Free me!" someone called out.

"No, me!" another argued.

"Me! Me!" cried a third.

All of them grabbed at me, pleaded with me, begged me to help them next.

Bennett stepped in front of me. "Enough!" he shouted, soft enough that it did not carry to the guards but loud enough that the rest of us heard him clearly. "D'ya think he gnawed his way through the irons? He cannot free you! Any of you!" He turned back to me then. "Get out of here. While you still can. Get far away."

"I could get help," I offered, though I had no idea where I might find such an elusive beast. "Surely someone—"

Bennett shook his head. "No. There's no help here." He sighed then looked me in the eye. "Though if you see Drosten, tell him he's needed."

"Who?" The name sent a shiver down my spine. Or perhaps that was the look he gave me then, as if he were shocked I could stand upright.

"Drosten," he repeated. "The wizard. Him we could use. If he'd been here . . ." He trailed off, then shook his head.

"Enough of that. Doesn't do any good, anyway. Let's get you out of here."

Bennett stepped back over to the nearest wall, slowly to avoid the chains jerking him short, and then turned, putting his back to it. He laced his hands together, palms upright, and waited. I knew what he intended. Stepping forward and enjoying the lack of those chains, I stepped up with my right foot and thrust it heel first into the saddle of his hands. Then I thrust up, uncoiling my body upward like a whip at the same time Bennett heaved up with his arms. The force of his push propelled me into the air, and my hands flew up, fingers grasping. They passed over the edge of the pit, followed by my arms and then my head and even my shoulders. My arc ended then, and I dropped back down, but my hands had found a root and caught it, and it held when my weight fell against it. My arms were on the ground up to the elbows, and I dug in with them, using my feet and knees to climb the rest of the way out.

"Hey!"

Two goblinoids had been standing on the other side of the pit, and now they turned toward me as I scrambled to my feet.

"Come back here!" one of them shouted, drawing his sword, but I was off and running before they took a single step. The trees, the same ones I had seen earlier from the steps, beckoned to me, and I dashed toward the safety they offered. The goblinoids took off behind me.

I could run! The realization burst upon me, almost making me stumble, for this was not the discovery of an infant discovering that he could move faster than a walk. I could actually run! As I moved I could feel my arms settling into an even rhythm, counterpoint to my legs, and my breathing slowed and steadied. I knew how to run—or at least my body did.

Exhilaration flowed through me, delight at my speed, at the ease with which I sidestepped rocks and small dips without slowing down, the sheer joy of running with the wind in my hair. That thought almost made me stumble, for I had no hair. My scalp, I had learned earlier, was bare. But it had not always been so.

For an instant I had a flash—a dim memory, perhaps. I was running, as I was now, but the clothes I wore were whole and clean and my hair flowed freely and the wind ruffled my beard. I could not see myself, but I knew this was a true memory. The running had triggered it, because I had always loved running. I loved it even now, when I was running for my life.

I reached the trees, the guards still behind me but the gap widening with every stride. Darting around tree trunks and over or around bushes, I put more distance between us until I could no longer hear the heavy pounding of their feet. Then I stopped as suddenly as I could and dove to one side. The bushes were thick here, and I squirmed beneath one, breathing slowly and deeply to prevent myself from gulping air. The thick branches above allowed only thin shafts of sunlight, and where I lay I was swathed in shadow and half-buried by loose leaves already turning autumn shades.

After a moment like this, I heard the footsteps again. And then they burst upon the scene—from my hiding place I could see only their unshod feet and brief glimpses of their arms and chests. They too slowed to a halt.

"Where'd he go?" the voice was every bit as deep as the one who'd shown me to the pit. He had stopped and was looking around. He was also sniffing with that wide, flat nose, nostrils distended, and I slunk lower, wishing I had thought to rub dirt upon myself. Could he smell my sweat?

"Gone," the other said, shaking its head. This one's voice

was not as gravelly, and I suspected he was a smaller goblin. "So what? What's one slave when we have the whole city to loot?"

"Hunh." The first hobgoblin snorted, but I could hear them turning around. "Guess so. Wish I was down there, 'stead of here guarding the pit. No chance for loot up here."

"Just our luck," his partner said as they walked away. "Maybe tomorrow we'll get to raid with Krachnaach's band. I hear they . . ."

I waited until I was sure they were gone before crawling back out, then I stood and stretched. I was free, but where should I go? They had said something about a city. Was there one near here? That felt right somehow. A city would have more people, defenders, food, and shelter. At the thought of food my stomach informed me that it too had survived the fire and had demands to be met. Perhaps they would feed me in exchange for information about the goblins. Yes, I was sure they would.

I looked around, trying to get my bearings. I found the direction from which I'd run, which meant the burned building was that way. So the city could have been anywhere else. The clearing had opened onto a narrow dirt road, I remembered, but I could not tell from that one glimpse which way it ran. I looked for clues of any sort but saw nothing. The trees here were tall enough and close enough to block out anything below the sky itself. There was no trail, no lanterns, nothing to guide me. And the sun was starting to set.

Well, I decided, one direction was as good as another here. I had come from that direction back there, so the easiest method would be to walk directly away from it. At least I would be putting more distance between myself and that pit, if nothing else.

So I started walking.

THE TALES OF THE LAST WAR

3

By evening my feet were bloody and my legs leaden, but I stood upon a small hill and looked down upon a large, handsome city. Or what was left of it.

Goblinoids were everywhere. I had dodged two patrols on the way to this place. The first had been in a hurry and had marched right on by. The second had been busy pursuing someone else. I had climbed a small tree and huddled atop one of its branches, pressing my back into the trunk, while several of the goblins and hobgoblins stalked across the leaf-strewn ground below, circling their prey. She had not been that young or that pretty, but they obviously did not care. She was human and alive, and that was enough. I hated myself for not helping her, though I knew that it would have meant my death and no change in her fate. When they caught her I thanked whatever powers existed that they did not do so directly beneath my hiding place, and then cursed myself again for thinking such things. It was some time later, after the last echo of her screams had long since stilled, before I could bring myself to descend and continue on my way.

From where I stood, peering around a stolid old tree, I could see the goblinoids writhing through the city like a breed of hairy ants. They swarmed in through doors and out through windows, engulfing porches and walkways and devouring everything in their path. Already a dozen fires raged among the wood and stone buildings, and several of the finer homes had been torn down with hooks and poles, their dignified slate roofs no longer gracing the skyline. The many trees and fountains were gone as well.

I knew this city. When I closed my eyes I could see the skyline as it had been instead of the scarred remnant I saw now. What she was called I could not say, nor how well we were acquainted, but this city and I were not strangers.

That cheered me despite the carnage, for it meant that before me was a link to my past, my history, and my identity. Somewhere down there might be someone who knew me or something that had belonged to me. Anything that could help me recall who I was and what I was doing here.

I pushed away from the tree and started down the hill, peering inside my own mind for any other information I could find about this place before me. I was still dredging my memories when I passed the outermost buildings. They had been hit hard during the first attacks and were little more than shattered bits of stone and wood. No one had lived in them for years, yet as I passed one of them a hand shot out from deep shadow and caught me by the wrist.

"Inside, quickly!" a voice hissed. "If you want to live."

I did want to live, so I did not protest when a small, dirty man in loose rags appeared in the ruins next to me. He released my wrist and gestured back to the shadows. "Come on!" he whispered. "Hurry!"

I followed him under fallen beams and over shattered blocks. A corner of one house had survived, and a portion of the wall above it had toppled but not crumbled, creating a leaning roof whose far corner tapped the ground. It was to this shelter that my new friend led me.

"You'd have run into a patrol if you'd gone another block," he said after we were crouching beneath the overhang, our backs against the remaining walls.

"Thank you," I told him.

He nodded. I could see even in the fading light and the shadows that he was a small, round man, red-faced and almost as bald as I. His clothes were dusty and torn but in far better shape than my own, and they had once been fine.

"Grandon's the name," he said, extending a hand. I shook it gladly.

"I don't know mine," I replied, and gestured toward my head. "I was hurt."

"Ah." Grandon nodded and glanced at my scalp. "Yeah, looks like a nasty cut there." Then he leaned back and studied me. "Well, you do look familiar. But I don't think you live here."

My hopes shattered. "Are you sure?"

"Absolutely," he replied. "I know everybody here. I'm the mayor. Was the mayor. And I don't know you." He frowned and continued to stare. "But I've seen you before—or maybe you look like somebody I know, somebody who does live here. Did live here."

My hopes rose again. A relative! I was visiting a relative! But the elation gave way to panic and pain. The city had been attacked. I had been injured. What if my relative was hurt, captured—or dead? My eyes grew misty at the thought of my unknown cousin, aunt, or sibling lying dead somewhere, and me here unable to even recall their name for a eulogy.

"Who?" I asked. "Who do I look like?"

Grandon studied me again then shook his head. "Don't know. It'll come to me eventually. Always does." He sighed then and rested his head back against the wall. "Bad time to visit, though."

"I guess so." I shifted my legs, trying to get more comfortable amid the shards and splinters.

"Shame you weren't here before," Grandon continued. His eyes were shut now. "Seen it the way it looked before all this." One hand waved idly in the direction of the rubble, the rest of the city, the destruction in general. "One of the prettiest towns in Cyre."

Cyre! That name sent a jolt through me, like lightning coursing through my blood. We were in Cyre! I had a sudden image, then, of rolling fields, wide open plains, fruit trees, row upon row of grain, neat houses in pleasant little communities. Cyre. I knew this land. I was from this land. Of this land. I was a Cyran.

It was but one piece of the puzzle my past had become and perhaps not the most crucial, but still it was a piece, and others would fit around it. I knew my homeland now. I belonged somewhere. I felt a surge of irrational rage when I thought of the goblinoids who were raiding the nation of my birth. They had not changed from that instant to this. But I had.

Grandon was shaking his head. "We thought we were safe, with our walls and gates and Drosten standing guard."

I had been musing myself, hearing but not listening, but that name brought me back with a shiver. "Who?" I demanded, leaning forward, and my host's eyes opened as he felt my position shift.

"The wizard," he told me then. "Hara Drosten. 'Winged Flame,' he's called in some parts. You never heard of him?"

"I . . . I think I have," I admitted. "It sounds familiar." I did not mention the shiver. Did the name bother me? Had I had a run-in with the wizard? I could not be sure, but that did not feel right. The shiver was not one of dread.

Grandon chuckled. "Not surprised. He's famous all through Cyre. And probably beyond. Coulda been a high court wizard working for the king, but he didn't like all the politics, they say. So he settled here at Saerun instead."

Saerun! If the name "Cyre" had thrilled me, this name was almost painful in the intensity of my reaction. Energy soared through me, sending great jagged waves into my brain, and I was surprised that light was not leaking out my eyes. Saerun!

I knew this city! I loved this city. How could I have forgotten her name, when it sang in my heart so clearly? Wherever I was from, it was this city that I held dear, here where all my hopes and dreams were stored. Now I could see her clearly again, her fountains and tree-lined walks, her graceful stone arches, her wrought-iron fences and railings. Saerun!

Grandon had not noticed my discomfort, for he was still speaking. ". . . lot of good it did us," he was grumbling, slapping at the dirt on his pants as if they were the source of his anger. "No sign of him at all."

"No sign of who?"

He glared at me. "Drosten! He's gone! Aren't you listening? Supposed to be our protector, that one, and last night these goblins and hobgoblins and orcs come pouring down out of the hills and he's nowhere in sight. Where'd he go, that's what I'd like to know."

I didn't know. I couldn't even picture the man, though his name still sparked through me. But my host did seem to be waiting for an answer, and there was no one else to provide it. "Maybe he's fighting the goblins somewhere else," I suggested. "Trying to stop worse from getting through."

That mollified him. "Aye, perhaps," he admitted. "He can't have run off, not and leave us here. Cared too much about Saerun, he did. But you're right—if this's just an edge of some horde, he might be dealing with the bulk of them." The idea seemed to cheer him immensely. "I didn't think he'd leave us open, not him." He seemed to have forgotten that the city was crawling with goblinoids. No matter what the wizard had intended, Saerun was already overrun.

"Well, we can't stay here," Grandon said at last, slapping his knee one last time and levering himself to his feet. "Goblins roaming about, looking for more loot and more slaves."

He spat to one side to show what he thought of them and their desires. "Best to get out of the city, into the hills for the night. Come on."

He ducked back out of the shelter. I scrambled to my feet and followed, rubbing at my legs where they had gone numb from sitting.

"Why were you here at all?" I asked as we picked our way around the house's remains and into a narrow alleyway that had once been bracketed by walls but was now open to the night sky.

"Looking for survivors," he whispered over his shoulder, glancing left and right. "Figured somebody had to, and I was the mayor. Lucky for you, eh?"

"Very." I shuddered to think what might have happened on my third run-in with goblinoids. I had survived the first two, but I doubted my luck would continue to hold.

Nor did it.

4

We had gone only a short distance, perhaps two blocks, though it was hard to gauge amid the rubble, when a pack of hobgoblins spied us.

"You there! Halt!"

I saw five of them, each as large as the one who had captured me before and each as heavily armed and armored. Metal bristled from them like spines, in hands and along shoulders, arms, and heads. I did not have time for more detailed inspection, for Grandon turned and fled and I followed.

Short though he was, desperation lent the mayor speed,

and he moved quickly between shattered beams and scattered stones. I was right behind him, and though my stride was longer I could not move as easily through the rubble, so I hovered just behind his right shoulder. We both heard the sound of the hobgoblins behind us, giving chase. Judging from the clatter, they were not bothering to sidestep wreckage, trusting in their mail and their heavy boots to see them through safely.

One of the hobgoblins must have had a crossbow, for I felt the air part beside me, and saw something long and slender shatter against the remains of an arch. It had missed me by perhaps a hand's width, and Grandon by half that. We sped up.

The second bolt came a moment later. This one was a full foot from me when it shot by—and planted itself in my friend's back.

Grandon cried out and fell. I almost fell as well, skidding to a halt, and only the jagged lower half of a door, jutting up from an intact doorframe, kept me from toppling headfirst. I was at his side in an instant, trying to pull him to his feet.

"Leave me!" Grandon said, gasping. He wrenched his arm free of my grip, despite the sigh of pain it caused him. I could see that the bolt had gone deep. Blood was oozing out around it. In the dim light it was hard to tell, but I thought I could make out a small protrusion in front, the material of his shirt tenting around the head where it had pierced his chest. I knew at once that there was no saving him. The look in his eye said he knew it as well.

"Save yourself," he begged me. His voice had already grown weak, and the fingers that tugged at my arm had no strength in them. Then his eyes rolled back and a deep sigh burst from between his blood-stained lips. He fell limp to the ground.

"Good aim!"

I had all but forgotten our pursuers, but now I realized that their heavy footsteps had not ceased, and had only grown louder. The one who had just spoken was perhaps a body's length away, axe in hand. His packmates fanned out around him. One of them was loading his crossbow as he ran.

"Waste, though," one of the others said. "Might have made a good slave. Now we've only got the one."

I stood and faced them. Anger and grief wiped away my fear. Grandon had been a good man and had tried to save me. Instead he had lost his own to these animals. And now they were discussing him—and me—as if I were not even here, as if I were the beast and they my owners to prod me and inspect me and sell or slaughter me at a whim. It was unacceptable.

"Filth!" I shouted, and my vehemence made several of them falter and step back. "Scum! You are not fit to lick this man's boots!"

"Nasty tongue, this one," one of the hobgoblins muttered, recovering and stepping forward again. "Might have to remove it."

"And a few other bits," another added, also closing in. "Teach it some manners."

"I am not an 'it,' " I snapped at that one. "I am a man, which is more than I can say for you. You are nothing, a mere infestation upon the land. You are vermin. Your kind is not fit to walk this earth!"

My body felt flushed, my head light, and I was still shaking with rage. My ears rang from my own shouts, which seemed to echo endlessly among the rubble, growing louder with each return. My would-be captors heard it as well and staggered, hands flying up to cover their ears. But the sound pierced through them despite such efforts, and I watched as three of the hobgoblins crumpled to the ground in agony.

Somehow, in my rage, that did not seem unusual. I raised one fist and shook it at the creatures before me. "Cyre herself writhes at your touch!" I yelled. "Your very presence offends her, and she shifts to avoid contact with your unclean flesh!"

I did know why my words had echoed so, but if it stunned them I could at least escape with my life. And then Grandon's death would not have been wholly in vain.

The echoes intensified. I staggered and caught myself against a small pile of shattered stone, the sound beating against me in palpable waves. The hobgoblins were not so lucky. The three on the ground were still twitching weakly but either unconscious or dead. The two still standing were writhing as well, struggling to reach me, but first one and then the other finally collapsed from the vocal onslaught.

And then the echoes faded. A moment later they were gone, and the silence was overwhelming. I was alone, strangely tired, and still trying to catch my breath. Grandon lay two paces away, blood pooling beneath him. The hobgoblins lay scattered about, unmoving.

I took several deep breaths. My heart was racing, and I willed it to slow. Sounds might crash through the ruins again, but for now the danger seemed past. I needed to take advantage of the lull and escape to the hills as Grandon had intended.

One task beckoned, however. I bent down and closed Grandon's eyes with one hand, then arranged his limbs about him as if he were sleeping. The crossbow bolt I could not dislodge. I took the partial door and several other wood fragments, and laid them over him. This way his body was covered, and perhaps it would escape the goblinoids' notice. I hoped so.

"Good-bye," I told him before I lay the last piece down. "Thank you." *You gave me back my homeland,* I added silently. *I am sorry I could give you nothing in return.*

I turned and walked away.

My luck was better this time. I covered four whole blocks before I was captured again.

5

This time it was only a pair of goblins, but they were smarter than the previous pack. They must have seen me coming. Still numb from Grandon's death, I was not making any attempt to hide or even to move quickly. They had ample time to prepare. As I passed between two ruined buildings, a hand snagged me and pulled me off-balance, yanking me forward. Another hand grabbed one wrist and then the other, tugging my hands behind my back and holding them painfully tight.

"Gotcha!" one of the goblins shouted, shoving his face so close to my own that I could feel his hot breath on my cheek. "All mine!"

"Ours," his partner growled, shoving him back. "All ours, Ritna. We split him."

"Right, right," Ritna said, straightening up and rubbing his shoulder. "Ours, Srell."

The second goblin—Srell, I gathered—pulled me around so he could stare at me. "Looks healthy enough," he said. "Should fetch a decent price."

"Should we sell him here or bring him back ourselves?" Ritna asked, and earned a scowl and another shove.

"Here? What? To Krachnaach? And get all of two dragons for him? He'll fetch five times that, we take him in ourselves. Why let Krachnaach make all the money?"

I had not said a word. The tugging had shaken me and I was still catching my breath. But they did seem motivated by greed. Perhaps I could offer them something to release me? Tell them I had a hidden treasure I would give them in return for my freedom? They might believe me, at least enough to relax their grip.

My thoughts were interrupted by the arrival of a hobgoblin. This one had a tattered cape slung about his broad shoulders, and a fancy sword at his side—its golden handle looked far too small for his massive hands, but a nasty axe hung from the other side of his belt.

"Ritna! Srell! Get moving! Everyone to the square!"

"We're going!" Srell snapped back and turned, tugging me by the wrists. The movement caught the newcomer's attention.

"What you got there?"

"Slave."

The hobgoblin grunted and grinned in reply, then he moved away to bark orders at some other goblins, and my two apparent owners marched toward the center of town, dragging me behind them.

6

They led me through the town, past burning houses and broken fountains. Bodies littered the streets. I closed my eyes and let my captors lead me until we came to a sudden stop.

Not long ago, this had been the town square. Handsome stone walkways traversed the grassy expanse, and fruit trees lined the edges, pleasant little benches set beneath them.

Saerun's residents came here to talk, to sing and dance and play instruments, to tell stories and look up at the stars. This was where children played, where lovers escaped for a moment's privacy, where merchants sometimes conducted business. It was where families gathered, and on rare occasions where the entire city congregated to discuss matters of great import. It was the heart and soul of the city.

The trees had been hacked down, their ragged stumps protruding like rotten teeth in some giant's gaping maw. The grass had been trampled flat, the stones smeared with mud, and the benches shattered and fed to the fires that smoked in the corners. And everywhere were goblinoids. I had never seen so many of them—hundreds stomping about, crouching here and there, eating and drinking and shouting. I saw a few other humans, each one in rags and chains with a goblin or hobgoblin close by. Was that what I looked like as well?

Near the center of the square was a small covered platform where the mayor would announce the start of holiday festivities or grant honors to various upstanding citizens. I remembered seeing some of those events. In my fragmented recollections I seemed too close to the event, and the angle wrong, as if I had been under that peaked roof myself, and I wondered now why I had not recognized Grandon when clearly I had seen him before. The roof of the platform had been torn away, leaving only the raised surface itself and a few loose beams still jutting up around it. A handful of goblinds stood there, and I could tell as Ritna and Srell pulled me toward it that these figures were bigger and more heavily ornamented than the rest. The leaders of the invasion, evidently.

One of them in particular drew my attention. He was not as tall or as broad as the other four—an orc, my memory whispered—and rather than full mail he wore a heavy robe with armor across the shoulders and chest. His scalp was bare save for a ridge of black hair down the center, and from his chin grew a tuft of equally dark hair. Golden hoops and gems adorned his ears, and more hung from his wrists and encircled his fingers. At his waist a leather belt held a large pouch, a small dagger, and a slender piece of wood that reminded me of the crossbow bolt. Something about him awoke a rage deep within me. He was holding something in his hands, but I could not see what it was. Neither could my captors, apparently.

"What you got there, Traark?" one of them shouted—Srell, I think.

The robed orc looked up, saw him and smiled, but did not reply, nor did he move his hands to reveal their contents.

One of the other goblinoids on the platform stepped to the front. This one was also an orc, but tall and burly, and various horned and fanged skulls decorated his armor. His helm was a single vast skull of some beast whose fangs ran from the goblin's brow down along his cheeks. Its eye sockets had been filled with brass so that they shone red in the light of the torches scattered here and there about the crowd. He carried a massive sword in one hand, its blade jagged and barbed, and an equally large and twisted axe in the other, and he raised them over his head and slammed them together. The resulting shriek of metal drew the horde's attention, and all other sounds stilled.

"My warriors," the skull-festooned orc shouted, "this city is ours!"

A cheer went up, so loud that my head throbbed again, and I raised my hands to cover my ears. Srell had released his grip on my wrists, since there was clearly no way I could escape now, and I was able to block out some of the noise, though I could still hear the goblinoid leader clearly.

"We have crushed their feeble little fighters," he continued, and the goblinoids cheered a second time, "laid waste to their walls," another cheer, "and pounded their homes into rubble!"

I was gasping for air to hold back the darkness that threatened to take me with each wave of sound.

"When we set forth, I heard fear from some of you," he continued, and there were only snorts at this one, for which my head was thankful. "Fear of their fighters. Fear of their defenses. Most of all, fear of their wizard."

Some actually muttered agreement, which was quickly followed by the sounds of metal on flesh as others beat them to silence.

"Yes, you were afraid of this Winged Flame," the leader shouted. "You thought his magic would destroy us. But we are here in the city! It is ours! And where is he?"

The crowd shouted again, though to my covered, ringing ears it sounded more quizzical than boisterous this time. Perhaps they knew as little about it as Grandon had?

The leader turned to one of his companions, the robed orc I had spotted before. "Our own wizard, Traark, has the answer," he said, and waved the other forward.

Traark stepped up, and I could see now that whatever he held was long and slender, longer than the wand at his belt and probably thicker as well.

"Do not fear the Winged Flame," he announced. His voice was thinner than the leader's, and raspy as if he had shouted himself hoarse long ago and never recovered. "He will not trouble us. I have bested him, and stolen from him that which he valued most. His greatest relic, the source of his power. Behold—the Firefacet!" With that he thrust his hands before him, holding high the object they contained, and I saw that it was a staff. Not of wood, this staff, but of some gleaming crystal, clear with swirls of red even in the dim light, and tapering smoothly to a small sphere at one end and an inverted teardrop at the other.

Firefacet. The wizard's staff. But that was not its true name.

And, in that instant of sight and recognition, I remembered.

All of it.

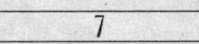

7

I had been upstairs, poring over another scroll. This one had been found deep within a swamp, protected from the ravages of time and moisture by an airtight tube of ivory encased in buoyant cork and silk around that. The scroll spoke of a wizard from days long ago, his sanity eaten away by his lust for knowledge and the spell he had created, so fearsome that even he had never dared use it.

I do not know how they got past my wards. Those alerted me when anyone approached within one hundred feet, and without the incantation of release held them a full fifty feet from my door. Their wizard must have breached them or somehow hidden himself and his companions from detection. However he did it, the wards did not bar their passage, and the first I knew of their presence was when the blow of a heavy axe shattered the door of my tower.

Gathering my robes about me and taking my staff from its stand, I had leaped down the stairs. But fast as I was, they were quicker, and before I had reached the first floor two hobgoblins were on the stairs and charging me, weapons at the ready. I struck one down, but the second had time to stab his sword at my stomach. I blocked it with my staff and batted him aside, but a third had joined him and was now close enough to grab me by the collar. This one did not bother to draw a weapon. He merely swung me into the wall, and the impact left me stunned. The staff fell from my hands, and I would have dropped to the floor myself if he had not hauled me toward him instead.

By the time I regained my senses, they had stripped me and bound me to one of my own chairs. Four of them stood around me, weapons drawn, while two more guarded the front door. I could hear several more tromping around upstairs, no doubt digging through my chambers for anything of value. But the one who concerned me was the robed one standing before me. He had a wand at his belt but was holding my staff instead.

"So, the great and mighty Hara Drosten," the orc wizard said. "The defender of the land, and scourge of evil! So terrible in your power, so awesome in your skill, so absolute in your mastery." He laughed and poked me in the chest with my own staff. "And yet here you are, defenseless, while I hold your power in my hands!"

"I am impressed that you slid past my wards," I replied, "but it will not help you. Leave now before I grow angry."

In truth I was stalling. My hands had been bound too tightly to move, which prevented me from casting my most powerful spells. And they had no doubt stripped me to take away any weapons or components I had at hand. I did have one weapon but I hesitated to use it until utterly necessary. I was hoping something else would present itself.

My captor sensed my thoughts, however, and grinned, showing his gold-capped fangs. "No help will come," he said, stroking my staff as if it were a new pet. I knew he was right. I had chosen to build my tower beyond the city's limits in the hopes that this would let me evade the city's politics as well. But it meant that, once the city's gates shut at dusk, I was alone beyond the walls until dawn. I could not expect any aid.

The hobgoblins returned from the upstairs while I was searching for a reply. They saluted the wizard. "Nothing," they said, and I almost laughed. All my books and scrolls were upstairs, but my magic concealed them from others' eyes. I could tell that the wizard was angered by this news, and he turned to me again.

"Where are your books?" he demanded. "Your scrolls? All your spells?"

"I do not need such tools," I replied, doing my best to sneer as if they were beneath me. "I have the Firefacet. That is all I require."

As I'd hoped, that spoke directly to his greed and distracted him. "But I have it now," he replied with a laugh, and spun it around so it caught the light. Then he straightened and stepped away. "If this is all you had, I have no further need of you." He nodded to the others, and they grouped around him. Despite his low tones I heard every word he said to them, though perhaps he intended it that way.

"Kill him slowly," he told them. "Feel free to toy with him first." And then, taking two hobgoblins with him, he left.

The remaining six clustered about me, leering. They scraped the hair from my head and chin with dull knives, they carved obscene symbols into my flesh, but these were just the preludes. I resisted as long as I could, in the hopes that some other option would appear, but when they started heating a poker to remove my eyes and a knife to remove my tongue, I knew I had to act.

The scroll I had been reading had contained the spell of that mad wizard. It was dangerously simple. I had no access to components, but this spell only required an open flame and the hearthfire would surely suffice for that. Nor did I require gestures for it, only the words and the will and the power.

I possessed all three.

One of the hobgoblins approached with his heated knife, the glow from the heated metal catching in his eyes.

I shouted the incantation.

The world burst asunder in a flash of light and heat. The spell itself partially shielded me, and my own wards protected me further, but not fully. The hobgoblin with the knife died first, and the blade flew from his disintegrating hand. Its red-hot blade seared across my forehead, cutting deep into my flesh, and the darkness took me.

8

And now I had awakened. I knew once more who I was. Hara Drosten, the Winged Flame, wizard of Saerun. Once her defender. Too late for that. It left me with one choice. I had failed as her defender. Now I would be her avenger.

"Chirith bulkh!" I shouted, one hand outstretched.

My staff flew to me. The instant it touched my flesh, the red swirls within burst into crimson glory, light and fire spilling forth until I held a spire of living flame in my hand.

Goblins fell away from me, cowering from the heat. A wave of my hand and a few muttered words transformed my clothes into my customary flame-embroidered robe. Another simple spell and my head no longer appeared raw and bare, as my hair returned to its familiar red mane and my beard covered my chin again.

The orc wizard stared at me in shock, and I could not help but laugh. "Fool," I said. "Did you really think I would surrender my power so easily? Or give you a name by which to bind it? What sort of madman would name his staff Firefacet? Only a dullard could have fallen for such a lie."

He reached for his wand, but a single gesture and a soft word froze him in place. "No, I think not," I told him. "You had your moment, back in my tower. This one belongs to me."

I spun on my heel, looking out over the horde around me. "Hear me!" I called out, knowing that my voice would carry easily across the square. "You have invaded my home. You have destroyed my city. Saerun demands blood in return, and you must pay."

When I had cast the mad wizard's spell before, I had already been weakened, and it destroyed my tormentors and the interior of my home but left the walls unharmed. This time I had my staff in hand, bolstering my own strength, and I fed the spell my rage. The golden fires that burst forth spanned the square and the first row of buildings beyond, turning even stone to ash. Goblinoids writhed as they were consumed, but they had no defense against these fires that melted metal as easily as flesh. Most died before they could even scream, long before they could feel pain, and a part of me was disappointed by that. Within moments the square was empty, nothing but a blackened plain sprinkled with gray ash. Only I remained.

I looked out over what had been my city's square, its very soul, and I wept for its loss, and my own.

9

The two guards at the pit were dispatched easily, a mystic circle appearing around them and killing them both in the time it took them to blink in surprise. A few simple gestures—the same I had so unknowingly used when here before—unlocked the slaves' manacles. A short phrase and another gesture produced a ladder. Bennett was the first to climb out.

"About time," he said when he saw me. "The goblins—"

"—are gone," I told him. "I have dealt with them. All of them."

"All of them?" He looked around, saw the bodies of the two guards, and nodded. "Right, then. Where's everyone else?"

I could not stop the sigh. "You are all that remains."

"What?"

Both of us looked at the pit, and the people crawling out of it. Perhaps two dozen in all.

"But—"

"Dead," I said. "Most of them. Some may have run away or were already carried into the hills." I looked toward the city again, because I could not bring myself to meet his eyes. "I will go after them."

"That's suicide," Bennett argued, stepping toward me, but I waved him away.

"It is my responsibility," I pointed out. "I should have stopped this from happening. Now I must make amends."

He must have realized that he could not talk me out of it. "What do you want us to do?" he asked.

"Get to safety," I told him. "Head north toward the capital. Do not look back."

Bennett looked like he wanted to say more, but he didn't. Instead, he turned away and, calling the others together, led them away. He glanced back once. I could feel his eyes upon me, though I did not look up—and then they were gone.

I waited until I was sure I was alone before looking around. Most of the goblinoids had been in the town square. These two had been left behind to guard the pit. But this horde was only part of the larger army. This leader had answered to a warlord, and that warlord and all his warriors were as much to blame as the ones who had actually struck Saerun. As much to blame as I was.

I could not save you, I admitted, looking toward the city. My city. I failed you and your people. My people. But I will avenge you.

With one last glance at my former home, I turned toward the hills. Holding my staff under one arm, I ran, picking up speed, my hair streaming behind me. From a distance, I knew that I must look like a fast-moving flame, darting between trees and around boulders, leaping through the high grass. Perhaps the goblinoids would see me coming, but it would not save them. Their darkness would fall before my light, until they swallowed me up.

It was all I could offer. The only thing I had to give, now that everything was gone.

Myself.

Most likely I would die in the attempt. But I would leave a grievous mark upon them. They would remember me.

I would never be forgotten again.

AARON ROSENBERG

ABOUT THE AUTHOR

Aaron Rosenberg was born in New Jersey, grew up in New Orleans, and went to school in Kansas, where he earned a B.A. degree in English and Creative Writing and an M.A. in English Literature. He has been writing roleplaying games for over ten years and has worked for most of the major publishers in the industry, including Wizards of the Coast, White Wolf, Decipher, and Pinnacle. He won an Origins Award for his work on *Gamemastering Secrets*. Aaron also writes novels for the STAR TREK: STARFLEET CORPS OF ENGINEERS series, for White Wolf's EXALTED and for WARHAMMER. He taught college-level English, including writing, for several years before going into publishing. Aaron has also worked in corporate graphics and runs his own roleplaying game publishing company. He lives and works in New York City.

THE VEILED CHARGE

David A. Page

1

A breeze stirred the cool air around Alrek, tickling his nose with the perfumed scent of flowers. He breathed in the pleasant fragrances and allowed himself a slight smile as he looked up from the field at the massive stadium around him. The throng of onlookers crowded into all twenty tiers of the huge, oval shaped arena. Their adoring shouts for their king and his most honored warriors reverberated so loudly that the very ground shook. Atop the stadium's walls, red and black pennants fluttered in the wind.

As one of twenty captains in the elite guard, he stood in a place of honor among the assembled warriors. Men, women, elves, and dwarves formed ranks around him, standing straight and proud in their polished, darkleaf armor. Emblazoned boldly in the center of every breastplate, a gold crown silhouetted against a green field—Cyre's coat of arms—broke up the sea of living night.

The silvery peal of trumpets drew his attention as heralds blew their golden horns from a large stone platform below the king's balconies. To either side of them, three golden-haired half-elf maidens stood proudly. Eloquent dresses spun from vibrant green leaves shimmered across their willowy forms. Their exotic, angular features, large almond-shaped green eyes, and graceful lines gave them a unique beauty that Alrek found captivating. He drank in the sight of them as they raised their supple arms and drew handfuls of red rose petals from woven baskets. They cast the flowers into the air. The breeze stirred by their command, wafting the fragile petals across the arena. They multiplied as if by magic again and again until they blotted out the cerulean sky. They drifted toward Alrek like crimson snowflakes, filling the air around him and his fellow soldiers.

The crowds roared even louder, clearly awed by the display.

Alrek looked up again and saw the flags collapse against their poles as if dead. The air grew warm and brittle, making it difficult to draw breath. He gasped. The crowd's cheering became a worried murmur.

"Something's wrong." Carena's voice was calm.

Turning to his right, Alrek saw that his second-in-command's face had paled slightly. She frowned, though it did little to detract from her beauty. It was not often that he saw her without the dirt and grime of hard traveling or the spattered blood of combat. He liked this rare glimpse of her.

"Yes, but what?" He met her fierce blue eyes, offering her the comforts of his own steady gaze. As usual, the depth he saw there drew him in and he had to restrain himself.

"The air feels . . . tortured," she answered slowly.

The rattling of swords and shields echoed around them as the elite guard held its collective breath and waited.

"These roses . . ." Carena held out her hand and let several petals land on her palm. The instant they touched, they turned black and fell to ash. "By the Five Kingdoms!" She brushed the dust away.

"I don't understand," Alrek said, studying her intently.

Several scarlet petals caressed her face. Without cause or reason, they blackened and turned to ash. Her flawless skin turned a frightening blue, hardening and cracking like worn marble. Her eyes widened and she opened her mouth to speak, but only a shattered moan emerged. She clutched her throat as the dark webbing spread swiftly across her features.

"Carena!"

Soldiers around them gasped and dropped to their knees. The commotion of the citizens died away, replaced by a loud rasping as their breath was ripped from them.

Carena's body convulsed as she collapsed into his arms. He lowered her to the ground, kneeling next to her and cradling her head against him as if she were a child. He had been here before, had seen this before, yet each time the anguish of it raped his soul, stripping him of his last shred of joy and hope.

"I should have been here with you . . ." The taste of ash and death was a bitter draught in his mouth. "I'm so sorry."

Her wrecked face contorted into a hideous grin. Her blue eyes turned a fierce yellow and burned with hatred.

"What?" Alrek blinked. This was new. Something was very wrong.

"I am coming for him!" The voice was a dark, twisted parody of Carena's.

"Who are you?" Alrek demanded as he held her.

Her mouth stretched open, wider than was possible. She

cackled, her malevolent laughter bringing thick black vomit with it. It oozed from her lips, sizzling as it streaked down her bluish, cracked skin.

"Stop this!" Alrek roared. *"Stop!"*

Carena's eyes faded to her natural cerulean as her body went rigid and her breathing ceased. Alrek heard a solemn crackling like leaves crumbling beneath booted feet. Her clothing, armor, and beautiful form turned to ash, dissolving before him. A soft breeze whipped the ash into tiny cyclones, brushed against him in a final caress.

"What's happening?" Tears stung his face, but he wiped them away as a new dread cooled his blood. Something was coming . . . something with black hatred for a heart and driven for vengeance.

"Alrek," a tiny voice hissed.

"Who's there?" Alrek spun around.

"Wake up, you brainless yak!"

Jagged lines ripped through the very air around him and the world shattered.

2

"Wake up!"

"Carena!"

Alrek opened his eyes and wiped the sweat from his forehead with the back of his hand. His heart hammered against the inside of his ribcage, as if seeking to escape from his body, but he managed to slow its frantic pace and focus. He found himself lying on his back between several stacks of wooden crates on the slanted floor of the lightning rail's fifth cargo cart.

"Nightmares again?" Aliana stood over him, her dainty halfling brow furrowed in genuine concern. Her black locks fell forward, dangling in front of her like ribbons of shadow.

"Yes." Alrek nodded to his diminutive companion as he sat up, bringing his head level with hers, despite the fact that she was standing.

"Who's Carena?" She arched a dark eyebrow in question.

"No one."

Alrek turned away. For over a year, the same nightmare had plagued him as guilt gnawed at his soul. He had survived while his friends had died . . . while she had died. Tears pooled within his eyes, but he forced them back. Something had changed within that nightmare this time, subverting the memory of Carena to mock and threaten him. The image of her cracked lips stretched open across dying flesh burned in his mind. A sea of angry flame churned his emotions, crashing over his sorrow in waves.

"Don't get angry at me." Aliana's breath was a white mist against the brisk air. She held up her small hands as if to deflect an attack. "I was only trying to help."

"I'm sorry. It's not you." He closed his eyes for a moment, turning inward to douse the angry inferno with the water of necessity. If a creature of the darkest evil were truly coming for them, then he would need to remain centered. Guilt would not help. He breathed in the cool air and listened to the sounds of the wind whipping past the lightning rail. There was no indication that anything out of the ordinary was happening. He glanced around the cart.

The floor of their spacious room sloped sharply down to the back as the lightning rail climbed steadily into the Ironroot Mountains. Fortunately, heavy ropes attached to metal rings in the floor anchored the cargo securely in place. Unlike the plush, house-like coaches in which the wealthy rode, or even the modest accommodations of the regular passenger coaches, this section was without a magical heat source or even a stove. The four walls and a thatched roof did little to hold in their meager body heat or protect them from the elements. Even with his heavy black cloak and his thick gloves, the cold still bit into his flesh. Beside him, his gold lantern provided light but little heat. Its wick flickered, causing ominous shadows to dance on the walls.

"Hello?" Aliana waved a hand past his face. "You hurt?"

Faded emotions stirred in his heart at her surprising concern, but he shrugged them off, chiding himself for momentarily letting down his guard. Friendship was a luxury he could not afford and did not want. The people he cared about were dead.

"How long did I sleep?" he asked.

"A couple of hours."

"Then we're a little more than halfway to Krona Peak." He rose slowly. He decided not to mention his dreams. He had no proof that anything was wrong. He pondered their destination instead. He wasn't sure exactly what he would find among the dwarf clans, but perhaps being so far from his former home would give him some peace.

"Yes." Aliana's child-like lips turned down in a frown and she shivered.

"It's going to get colder." The rail would continue to climb toward the pass for several more hours.

She hugged her arms to her chest. "We'll be fine."

Alrek doubted the halfling's cape or armor offered much in the way of protection. She traveled light, never wanting to be over burdened when they came upon something worth stealing. He dropped his hand to his belt pouch.

"I saw that!" she protested.

"I'm just making sure that my property is still attached to my hip." He had only been traveling with her for several days, hardly enough time to develop trust with her.

"Are you going to inventory your backpack, too?" She glowered at him.

"I don't need to. What few items of value I possess would never fit into that sack of yours."

"I saved you from those thugs, didn't I?" She put her hands on her hips and glared at him.

"I supposed you did." She *had* helped him escape from that tavern in Vedykar.

"That's right." Aliana poked at his stomach with one small finger.

Her passionate indignation struck him as comical. It had been so long since anything had gotten such a reaction out of him. The feeling took him by surprise. He smiled.

"Wow." Aliana blinked. "I haven't seen you do that yet. I must be hilarious!" Her little rosebud mouth split into a grin.

"Yes." He sobered up after a moment. "Thank you for that."

"You're welcome. Now"—she crossed her arms—"can we please figure out a way to stay warm?"

"Oh, so you are cold?" Alrek smirked, another expression that had become foreign to him.

"Of course I'm cold, you brainless yak!" There was a fire in her eyes that belied her height. "I'm gonna start opening crates. There must be a blanket somewhere." She stormed toward the other side of the cart.

She'd just bent to the first one when several loud cracks pierced the drone of the storm. Terrified screams mingled with the cacophony of splintering wood to form a twisted harmony of pain. The cart lurched violently, wood groaned, and the ropes round the crates snapped like broken bowstrings.

The force hurled Alrek forward into the heavy wooden door at the front of the cart. A cloud of red dropped over his vision. He cried out as he slid to the floor, momentarily dazed. He blinked.

Boxes crashed together, crates turned over, and barrels rolled into one another, some of them shattering on impact with the floor or with one another as the lightning rail came to a sudden stop.

"Alrek!" Aliana yelled somewhere from within the chaos of shifting cargo.

His lantern had slid across the floor and remained in a small area free of debris. They were lucky that it had not spilled flaming oil all over the cart. He blinked, thinking that his vision had gone blurry, but he quickly realized that a thick cloud of flour hung in the air over the scattered and broken crates.

I'm coming for him. The words from his nightmare flitted through his mind, but he did not have time to contemplate them. His instincts took over and he forced the pain away, focusing instead on what he had to do. The rail's forward momentum had stopped, but it continued to bob up and down on its magical cushion like a buoy on the stormy sea.

"Aliana!" His concern for her overrode his own danger. She was tiny, fragile, and somehow she had fallen under his protection. He had to find her, had to help her.

"Alrek!" Her voice was muffled but close.

"I'm here. Keep talking!" He lifted several brown sacks from where they had fallen against one of the larger crates. He heaved them out of the way and found Aliana wedged among stacks of smaller boxes. She was covered in a thin coating of flour from head to toe.

"Ugh, I smell like a pastry." She sat up and wiped her face.

"Are you hurt?" Alrek offered her his hand and pulled her to her feet.

"I'll live." She allowed him to pull her to her feet. She glanced around the cart. "What happened?"

"I don't know." Alrek released her.

"You don't think someone's after the cargo, do you?" She pulled her cloak around her, but Alrek did not think it was because of the cold.

"I'm not sure."

"We probably hit a snowbank or something," Aliana said, her voice uncertain as if she were trying to convince herself.

"Perhaps. But we must know for certain. We need to check out the front of the lightning rail."

"We're in the middle of a blizzard!" Aliana dropped her sack and shook her head like a petulant child. "And I'm short. I can't walk through deep snow."

"The path should be clear," he said. "The magic of the conductor stones will have thrown off any snow."

The car lurched back and forth and then bounced violently up and down. Alrek gripped a nearby crate and managed to remain standing this time. A wave of nausea crashed through him and bile clawed its way up his throat.

"Oof!" Aliana fell on her rear-end.

A distant crack split the air, followed by a muffled explosion.

"What's happening?" Aliana's voice shook.

"We're under attack!" Alrek's hand dropped to his sword.

The faint shouts of passengers echoed past, their voices

drowned by distance and the moaning storm, leaving little doubt that what had happened to the rail had not been natural. After a moment, their screams were silenced until only the faint memory of their terror remained. The cart jerked and then slowly started to move along its path again. For an instant, a spark of relief flared within Alrek, but it was quickly doused as he realized that something about the smooth motion was not quite right. A barely perceptible force pulled him forward, as if gravity had shifted.

"We're moving again!" Aliana cried joyfully, but her expression darkened as she too realized that all was not as it should be.

"Backward!" Alrek navigated through the wrecked crates to the front door of the cart. He had not noticed it before, but the frame of the door had cracked as boards from the next cart had driven through it in four separate places, wedging it shut.

"Maybe the driver is backing us out of a snowbank?" Desperation clung to Aliana's voice, and she clutched the nearest box to steady herself.

The feel of the cart changed again as its rate of speed increased.

"We wouldn't be going this swiftly." The fist in Alrek's chest squeezed his heart tighter than before. They continued to go faster with each passing second. "We're rolling. We've either been severed from the other carts or the elemental has died."

"If the elemental died, then why are we still floating?" Aliana yelled over the increasingly loud roar coming from outside.

"The elemental propels us forward, but it doesn't make us levitate. The stones do that on their own." He spun toward the rear door, but even from the other side of the cart, he could see that it was in a similar state, smashed beyond their ability to repair, sealed tight.

"What about the cargo door?" Aliana pointed frantically toward the large sliding door on the portside wall.

"It's a two-thousand-foot step if we go that way!" Alrek moved to the back of the car.

"What are we supposed to do?" Aliana looked around with the wild eyes of a frightened deer.

The shriek of tearing wood jarred Alrek before he could answer. The back door burst from its hinges and fell inwards. A short, broad-shouldered man in a green tunic stood in the entryway with a taller human man in studded leather armor a step behind. On each of their chests, the White Unicorn of House Orien, the dragonmarked house that ran the lightning rail, was clearly visible.

The stocky man pounded inside, a plain-looking wand in his right hand and an axe in his left. He stopped short as he spotted them. The taller man, really barely more than a boy, fumbled for a heavy crossbow, finally managing to grab it and aim in Alrek's direction.

"Who are you?" the leader demanded.

At first, Alrek took the man for a gnome, but he stood nearly as high as his chest and his muscular frame and shoulders were nearly as wide as Alrek's. His next guess was a short human, but the middle-aged man's nose was just a little too bulbous for that. Understanding dawned on him and he realized the man was a beardless dwarf! In all Alrek's years moving through the various kingdoms as a member of the Elite Guard, he had never seen a dwarf shave his face.

"My name is Alrek. And this"—he motioned to the halfling— "is Aliana. We're passengers."

The cart bounced violently, lifting them off the ground and jostling them about.

"Passengers in a cargo cart?" The dwarf narrowed his eyes

and raised his wand higher. "I'm very sorry about this, but there's no time! Hrod!"

Alrek's sword rang as he pulled it clear of its scabbard, but he stayed his hand as he realized that the wand had done nothing to harm them.

The young man took a step forward, sighting down his crossbow.

"Stop! There's no evil here." The dwarf's gruff voice carried easily through the cart, strong and commanding. The crossbowman allowed his weapon to dip.

"The name's Ravik." The dwarf slipped his wand into a pocket in his tunic without waiting for Alrek to disarm himself and then looked up at him. "I'm the rail artificer. This is Jorn. If you want to live, put that pig sticker away and help me. We've got to get off of this cart now!"

"How do we know we can trust you?" Alrek kept his sword at ready.

"Listen to me, lad. The lightning rail is headed directly for the last switchback we passed. When it gets there, it'll crash and we'll die. So decide now whether you're going to help or hinder." Ravik turned away and looked at the floor as if searching for something.

"I agree." Alrek sheathed his blade.

"I thought you might." Ravik crossed the cart. "Right here, lads!" He threw his shoulder into a rather large crate.

Jorn allowed his crossbow to hang from his side and ran to help the dwarf push it out of the way. Their efforts revealed the square outline of a trapdoor in the floor. An indentation housed a thick metal ring. Ravik grabbed it. Alrek joined them and took the massive circle in a two-handed grip.

"Now heave!" the dwarf ordered.

Alrek strained his muscles, pulling with all his might.

The heavy door rose slowly. A fierce surge of brittle air blasted them, whipping through his short Alrek's with icy fingers. He shuddered as he looked into the opening. The conductor stones sped past as they floated over them. Bluish electric bolts danced along the surfaces of the stones, arcing up to be deflected by the stones fitted to the bottom of the cart. Their crackling mixed with a loud sound like the raging of a river.

"What do we do now?" Aliana appeared at his elbow, shouting over the din of the storm.

"We lower you into the hole." Ravik pulled a ring off of one finger. "This will protect you from the lightning." He grabbed her hand and put the ring on her finger. It shrank to fit her.

"Lightning?" She put her hands up as if to deflect a blow. "I don't think this is such a good idea!"

Ravik ignored her, instead turning to Alrek. "There's no time for me to infuse anything else with protective magic. You and I must endure the pain."

"You're serious about this?" Alrek looked warily at the blurring track below. Even standing where he was, the magical energy made his skin crawl as if an army of insects roved over his body.

"It's either that or die." Ravik spun toward Jorn. "You first, lad. Hurry!"

Jorn slung his crossbow and kneeled in front of the hole.

The dwarf grabbed the man's forearms. "Hold onto my hands until I say to let go!"

Jorn leaned forward until he was almost lying face down against the floor of the cart.

"Here we go." Ravik lowered him into the gap.

As Jorn's feet scrapped against the stones, a ring, similar to the one Ravik had given to Aliana, glowed on his left index finger. The dwarf nodded solemnly and then released him.

And Jorn was gone from sight.

Ravik spun to Aliana. "You're next, little lady."

She backed away, looking at Alrek imploringly.

"It's the only way. It'll be all right," Alrek said. "Now go!"

She swallowed and stepped in front of the hole. She took Ravik's hands and leaned forward.

"You'll do fine." Ravik lowered her down.

She flashed Alrek a wide-eyed, panicked look and dropped into the hole. She hit the ground with the clanging of metal cups and was lost.

The cart tilted sideways, hurling Alrek away from the hole and into the corner of a crate, sending shoots of pain through his back.

"We're nearing the turn!" Ravik cried. "Hurry!"

Alrek rushed into position in front of the hole. He clasped Ravik by the forearms, nodded, and slid back into the hole. As the blurring stones rose toward his face, he wondered absently who had attacked them. And then his feet skidded against the stones and lightning seared his body as it arced through him. Of their own accord, his hands released their grip on the dwarf. He fell hard, wrapped in a blanket of electric agony.

A white flash swallowed the world.

3

"Alrek." Carena's voice had a strange distortion to it, as if several other voices spoke within it.

Alrek opened his eyes and found himself lying in the middle of Metrol's stadium and looking up at an eerily black, starless sky. Rose petals floated around him, never seeming to touch the ground, as if frozen in the moment. He sat up and realized that he was completely alone. The enormous and familiar stadium surrounded him like an empty tomb. The dream had changed. Again.

"Not completely alone."

"Carena?" He whirled around.

She stood a dozen feet away, a green silk dress clinging to the feminine curves of her lithe muscled form. Her light brown hair cascaded in waves over her bare shoulders, almost reaching the long emerald-colored gloves that flowed up her arms.

He blinked. He had never realized how soft her pale skin could look, nor had he realized that her bare neck was so graceful.

"Guess again." Her eyes burned with yellow passion. Her skin darkened to a deep blue and hardened until it was covered with angular scales.

"You." Alrek's heart plunged into a well of despair, but it did not remain there. Instead, anger ruptured his sorrow, exploding into him with violent force. "Who are you? How dare you take her form!"

"Your threats are hollow and weak." Her violet lips split into a hideous grin revealing gleaming fangs. "I have come for the Noldrun."

Her large, yellow eyes sparkled. Despite their bright glow, dark shadows stretched away from her as if draped over her body. She stepped toward him, her scales sliding against one another like blades on stone. The frozen rose petals turned to ash and fell to the ground as she passed through them, clearing a path for her.

Although Alrek was certain he still dreamed, it was possible that this creature could still do him harm. He lowered his hand, searching for the hilt of his sword only to find that his weapon was missing. Stepping back, he reached around his waist and discovered that his dagger was gone as well.

"There is nowhere to run, Alrek, Captain of Cyre." Her legs elongated like stretching tentacles, allowing her to slide swiftly across the distance. An odor reminiscent of rotten meat consumed the air around her.

"Carena, I'm sorry!" Alrek brought up his fists, ready to defend himself, but she lashed out, caught his forearms in her clawed hands and squeezed so tightly that he gasped in pain. Her thick stench made breathing difficult, as if the air itself had become poisoned by her presence.

"This will be easier than leaving your friends to die," she crooned. "You do not even know this Noldrun."

"It was not my fault!" He struggled to break free of her iron grip even as he gasped for breath, but to no avail. "I will not yield to your threats!"

"But you will, if you value the lives of those around you." She licked her fangs with a forked tongue, and her smiled widened. "Bring him to me." She squeezed tighter, the intense stabbing pain in his forearms driving him to his knees.

"I don't know who or what a Noldrun is!" he protested, struggling in vain to break free.

"Oh, but you do. Come to the fore of the lightning rail or I will be very displeased." Her smiled faded. "If you defy me, I will tear open your ribs and feast."

She jerked her hands, and pain ripped through his arms as his bones snapped.

The night sky dropped onto them like a heavy veil.

THE TALES OF THE LAST WAR

4

Alrek opened his eyes to see Ravik looming over him.

"Easy, lad. You've been unconscious a good while."

Alrek found himself seated on the cold conductor stones in the middle of the empty rail path. The dwarf stood over him. His green tunic was torn in places, but he seemed uninjured. Alrek understood why as he spotted the empty potion vial on the ground next to him.

"Are you hurt?" Aliana moved into his field of vision from behind. Still covered in flour, she nearly blended in with the snow swirling around her but appeared no worse for wear. Ravik's ring had apparently protected her. She had her thin cloak pulled tightly around her, but she shivered so much that Alrek wondered if she might bounce down the trail.

"I don't think so." His body ached in a few spots and he was conscious of crusted blood on his scalp where it had apparently impacted with the stones. "Thanks for the healing potion."

"Don't thank me." Ravik inclined his head towards Aliana and then helped Alrek to his feet.

"I didn't realize you had any potions." Alrek looked at the halfling. "Where did you get it?"

"In Vedykar." Her cheeks reddened.

"Thank you."

"You're welcome." She smiled sheepishly.

Alrek wondered why she had become shy but quickly dismissed it, instead focusing on getting his bearings. He spied the shattered wood and twisted metal of several cargo carts spread out over a considerable area and disappearing into the churning storm at the edges of his visibility. They had barely escaped with their lives.

"What do we do now?" Jorn asked from behind him.

Alrek spotted the young man pacing back and forth several yards up the track. He clutched his crossbow as if it were a raft in a stormy sea and his gaze was everywhere as if he expected attack from any quarter. Fortunately for them all, Alrek's assessment of the conductor stones had been accurate. The snow evaporated before it could reach them, leaving their path clear.

"First things first." Ravik looked up at Alrek. "Why were you on my lightning rail and what does it have to do with this attack?" He crossed his muscular arms and waited, seemingly oblivious to the snowflakes battering his face.

"We had a bit of a disagreement with some of the locals back in Vedykar," Alrek explained.

"A disagreement over what?"

"Over the fact that they wanted me dead." Alrek frowned. "I don't know why. In any case, they were local riffraff and could never have managed something like this."

"Maybe bandits attacked the rail." Aliana spoke slowly in what Alrek assumed to be an attempt to prevent her teeth from chattering.

"If true, they wouldn't have destroyed the cargo carts," Ravik pointed out. "They're after something else."

"Not something . . . someone." Alrek was uncertain how much to tell them, but he had to tell them something.

"What do you know?" Ravik's hand dropped to the handle of his axe.

"Twice in as many hours, a demon has spoken to me through my dreams." He let his hands hang freely at his sides far enough away from his weapons so as not to appear threatening—but still close enough for him to arm himself swiftly if needed. The creature might appear from out of the storm at any moment.

"A demon?" Ravik's brow furrowed and he tilted his head skeptically. "What did this creature say?"

"It is after someone or something called a Noldrun." He paused as he saw Ravik's eyes widen.

"What's a Noldrun?" Aliana asked.

"It's the forgotten clan of dwarves." Jorn moved closer to them. "Destroyed a hundred years ago."

"There's a forgotten clan?" Aliana swiveled to face Jorn. "How do you know?"

"Because he knows me," Ravik interrupted. "My grandfather was among the few Noldrun who was away from the clan hold when it was wiped from existence." He rubbed his smooth-shaven jaw and a wistful expression crossed his face as if he missed his beard.

"Then this demon is after you," Alrek said. "Why?"

"Tell me everything it said," Ravik ordered.

Alrek proceeded to repeat every detail of his last two dreams. Ravik listened intently, his frown deepening. He nodded from time to time but did not interrupt.

"We should flee." Aliana was trembling, but Alrek gathered it was not just from the cold.

"I'm not running away." Ravik hefted his axe. "This is my mess to clean up."

"Not yours alone," Alrek said. "The demon seems worried that I might aid you—so that's exactly what I intend to do." He drew his sword.

"Did I mention the fleeing?" Aliana yelled over the howling wind.

"I'm with you," said Jorn. He brought his crossbow to a ready position.

Alrek turned toward the halfling. "If we run, the cold will kill us. And there are people who need our help."

"But I'm really good at fleeing!" Aliana flailed her arms in emphasis. "I can take care of you!"

"Alrek's right, lass. We wouldn't last an hour in this storm. And I'm an employee of House Orien and I'm the artificer of this line." Ravik held his chin high. "No one attacks my lightning rail or its passengers!"

"Facing danger is always preferable to hiding from it," Alrek said. He had not been able to help his friends or his family at the end, but he could help Ravik.

"I like to face danger from behind." Aliana made a stabbing motion with her hand and then pulled her cape open to reveal the short sword and dagger hanging from her small belt.

"You might get that chance, lass," Ravik told her.

"We're wasting time." Alrek pointed his sword ahead of them, turned and squinted into the storm, but the blinding whiteout refused to reveal the secrets of what lay beyond.

"Wait." Ravik took a few steps towards Alrek. "You move with the grace of a true warrior and your blade is a masterwork, but you'll need an even greater edge if you are to be our champion."

"Champion?" Alrek paused.

"Aye, give me your sword." He pointed to Alrek's hand. "And I'll take that ring as well."

Alrek looked at the plain silver ring on his left index finger and understanding dawned on him. An artificer's skill lay in imbuing items with magic, making them valuable members of any party. He removed it and handed it to Ravik as commanded. Next, he offered up his sword, hilt first.

Ravik sat cross-legged and put the blade across his knees. He held the ring in the palm of his left hand, closed his eyes, and hummed. The pitch changed several times as if he searched for the proper tone. The ring glowed white for a moment and then returned to its normal color. He set it down on the conductor stones and then pressed his palms to the blade of Alrek's sword. Light flashed from his hands. He opened his eyes and held up the sword.

"There now. I've enhanced your blade."

Alrek took the sword. It did not feel any different, though he did not doubt Ravik's word.

Ravik offered the ring to him. "I've imbued this with an enchantment that will increase your strength. Put it on."

Alrek slid it back onto his index finger. Bright energy flowed into his muscles. He had always been strong, but as the magic filled him, his armor and pack felt lighter. He breathed deeply, sensing the new strength that flowed through his charged body.

"I've little else to offer at the moment." The dwarf retrieved his axe. "It's time we were going."

"I'll lead." Alrek turned into the storm.

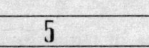

"There." Ravik pointed through the storm toward the wide area before them.

Alrek followed his gesture, searching the near-blinding conditions for any signs of danger. The trail of conductor stones split into three separate paths. One continued straight, while two others veered gently to the right into an open area. Ravik had explained that these provided an area for the rail to pull off in the event that another group of coaches traveled in the opposite direction. At the moment, the extra spaces were empty.

Their lightning rail had come to a violent halt on the through-path, just at the edge of visibility. Four of the tavern-sized coaches lay smashed together with beams jutting out like broken bones. Their doors and window shutters hung off of them like flesh clinging to a carcass. Flames engulfed the rearmost coach while its connecting rod had been torn in half, its metal bent open like the petals of a flower.

An armored man, his body pierced by broken glass and bits of wood, hung out of a window of the next coach, a longbow still clutched in his dead hands. The broken bodies of soldiers, each displaying the white unicorn of House Orien on their leather armor, lay strewn about the area as if someone had picked them up and scattered them like a farmer tossing down seeds. A muscular barbarian, his ribcage completely concave, sat where he had died against the lip of the second track. Next to him, the vacant-eyed corpse of a middle-aged woman in a brown robe sprawled on her back at an gut-wrenching angle, as if she had been folded in half.

"Sovereign Host!" Aliana hissed, peering out from behind Alrek.

"I knew every one of those guards." Jorn's face was ashen. "They were my friends."

"Aye." Ravik bowed his head somberly and then looked up with fierce hatred burning behind his eyes. "Whoever did this will meet my axe."

"I see only the bodies of defenders." Alrek gave the dead a casual glance before returning his attention to the area around them. Who or whatever had done this was most likely not far . . . especially in light of whom they were after.

"Whoever killed these people is probably farther up the path now," Aliana took a step back. "I think I'll just stay here and wait for a rescue."

"As you wish." Alrek strode toward the wreck. Ravik drew up to flank him on the right, while Jorn took up position on his left. Together, they moved slowly forward, careful not to slip on the slick stones. The magic of the track might be enough to prevent snow from building up, but it could do nothing about blood. The dark fluid oozed over the rock, slipping between the stones to form rivulets of gore.

"These bodies are still warm." Ravik pointed to the corpse of an elf. "Be on your guard."

Alrek wiped the snow from his face and glanced down to see steam rising from the dead elf's shattered body. Ravik was right. In this cold, bodies would not retain their heat very long. Their enemy was near. He reached up and undid the clasp on his cloak, allowing it to slip from his shoulders.

"Cyre Elite Guard!" Ravik stared with wide eyes at the gold crown silhouetted against the green field on Alrek's breastplate.

"I thought they were all dead." Jorn's voice was filled with tragic reverence.

"I am the only survivor." Alrek could not keep the bitterness from his voice.

"I'm sorry, lad. I know what it's like to be one of the last." Ravik gripped his arm. "I am glad you are with us."

"As am I," Jorn added, his voice regaining some of its strength.

Alrek wished he could feel blessed for having survived, but his guilt rose within him like bile. He should have died with his men, with her. He looked down and met the dead-eyed stare of a slain human woman. Shame flushed his face at his own weakness. He had survived and his newfound friends needed him here and now. Perhaps, he had been spared for this reason and this reason alone. Perhaps it didn't matter.

Holding his blade before him like a talisman, Alrek stepped cautiously through the field of the dead. The flame-engulfed coach blasted him with hot air, offering a welcome respite from the cold, despite the dark message it carried with it. He passed the remaining coaches, straining to detect any signs of life but hearing only the howling of the snowstorm and the hungry cackle of the flames.

The dim outline of a much larger coach became visible through the storm. It hovered alone a good distance ahead of the others and looked much like the two-story homes of Metrol's merchant quarter had looked before the Day of Mourning. The shutters on both floors had been sealed and probably barred from the inside. The door on the closer end, however, was a splintered mess. A dim flickering light cause dark shadows to dance around the interior of the coach.

"Where's the rest of the lightning rail?" Aliana asked behind him.

Before Alrek could speculate on her question, a low moaning uttered from within the coach.

"Someone's alive!" Ravik broke into a run.

"Wait!" Alrek sprinted after him, slowing only as they neared the opening.

The dwarf paused near the entrance stairs and waited for him. As Alrek moved closer, he could see part of the interior.

The front area of what had clearly been one of the tavern coaches was a mass of cracked tables and broken chairs. Dark humanoid forms lay where they had fallen, their outlines visible in the paltry light cast by the dying fire in the stone hearth beyond. A low creaking ebbed and flowed as the coach rocked gently over the stones and Alrek could see dim shapes hanging from what might be wooden chandeliers.

A long, oaken bar stood opposite the fireplace. Its proximity to the meager light allowed Alrek to see that its polished surface had been scorched by fire in a dozen places. Several patrons lay slumped across it, their bodies pinned by swords. Behind the bar, broken bottles and mugs lay strewn about the few shelves that had not collapsed. Past the bar area, he could see only darkness. He wished he still had his lantern.

The moaning came again, this time louder and clearly from a woman.

Alrek's blood cooled as if he had leapt into an icy lake, shocking his body but intensifying his readiness for anything that might follow. He leaped onto the small platform, pressed his back to the doorframe, and peered inside for a closer look.

"Hello?" he asked. "Can you hear me?"

The croaking voice uttered a string of deep, unintelligible gibberish that was reminiscent of chanting. The fire crackled, causing the light to jump and the shadows to writhe as if in pain. As Alrek's eyes adjusted, the corpses of men and women, several armored, one in priestly robes, and the others in the clothing of commoners, became clearly visible. Their blood smeared the walls. Normally, the small balcony ringing the interior of the coach created a more private dining or drinking accommodation. Now, it offered the dead a better view. Men and women lay draped over the balcony, some of them reaching for the floor, others dangling legs over the edge. Dark red fluid dripped from several places, creating small pools on the floor below. The air inside the coach was thick with the smell of blood and fear.

Alrek stepped inside. His foot slipped on the wet floorboards and he stumbled. He reached out to catch the wall, but his hand closed around something warm and fleshy. "By the Five

Kingdoms!" He managed to use the bloodied limb to steady himself as he spun around, and then released it. He discovered that he had grabbed the arm of a battered elf whose lifeless black eyes stared at him accusingly.

"Foul deeds!" Ravik's broad form was framed in the doorway. He held his axe in a two handed grip and stood with mouth agape. "Only something as vile as a demon could have wrought such slaughter."

"Yes." Alrek wiped the blood from his hand and drew his dirk. "Tread carefully."

"Aye." Ravik stepped shoulder to shoulder with him.

"Can you see any movement?" Alrek asked. Because of their long history of dwelling beneath the surface, Dwarves had developed keen eyesight. To Ravik, it probably looked as bright as day.

"I see death, misery. . . ." Ravik's voice shook.

The moaning issued again from the opposite side of the coach.

"There!" Ravik pointed to the back corner.

The familiar putrid odor of rank meat burned his nostrils as a large, dark shape detached from the underside of the balcony near him with the recognizable scraping of scales. He stepped back, frantically slashing upward with his sword as he caught his foot on an overturned chair. An ebony blade cut through the inky blackness, meeting his weapon and drawing a shower of sparks as he fell sideways. Yellow eyes blinked above him with a familiar malevolent hatred. The demon from his nightmares loomed above him.

Alrek pushed off the ground with his feet and threw his weight forward in a desperate attempt to control his fall. The room rotated as he soared over the corpse of a human woman. He thrust his dagger into the center of the dark beast's outline, but the creature slid to the side as if floating on the very air.

"You'll not harm us!" Ravik yelled.

Alrek rolled into an open space, came back into a crouch and spun to their enemy just in time to see Ravik leap toward it, axe swinging. Shadows churned around the demon as it flowed toward the dwarf.

"I've been seeking you, Noldrun. Why don't you just wait for me?" The demon spoke in a deep parody of Carena's voice as it had in Alrek's dreams. It batted Ravik's axe aside with one blue-scaled, clawed hand and then punched him hard. The dwarf flew over the bar and crashed down on the other side with a loud thump.

"Ravik!" Alrek leaped forward, sword ready.

As the demon whirled to meet his attack, its features were illuminated by the dim firelight. Despite its massive form, azure scales and clawed hands, the curves of its body were clearly feminine. Her pointed ears flattened back against her hairless skull as she regarded him with amusement through a mask of shadow.

"Leave the dwarf, Captain of Cyre," she cackled, swinging her ebony blade at him.

The large weapon crashed against his smaller sword with such force that a shock of pain went through his arm and he nearly dropped his blade.

Her free arm blurred as she backhanded him, and even though Alrek tried to dodge, the strike connected with the side of his face. White-hot pain ripped through him, the room tilted, and he fell onto the remains of a table, its wood jabbing him in the back. The breath expelled from his lungs and light danced across his vision.

A bowstring twanged and a crossbow bolt embedded itself into the demon's shoulder.

A hideous grin split the demon's sapphire colored face as she swiveled her head toward the entrance through which they had come. She mumbled a short sentence in her strange language and the darkness of a nightmare dropped onto them like a shroud. Alrek could still feel the fire, but could see nothing.

He heard movement, felt the air shifting around him and brought up his sword as he pushed off the ground to recover his footing.

Jorn's crossbow twanged again.

"Here is the first of your friends to die," Carena's twisted voice snarled from the darkness.

"Jorn, run!" Alrek pushed through the debris of tables, chairs, and the bodies in the direction of their voices, using his anger at the creature's mockery to spur him on.

There was a soft squishing sound as if someone had just stepped in thick mud . . . or plunged a blade through a man.

Jorn's scream echoed through the blackness.

The crossbow twanged again and then there was silence.

Alrek emerged from the zone of darkness into the dusky light to witness the demon pull its sword from Jorn's chest. Frantic emotions screamed within him as he sprinted forward.

The dark horror—her massive, muscled form silhouetted against the light beyond the entrance, swiveled to face him. She held the bleeding Jorn with one hand and her massive blade in the other. A second bolt had lodged in the splint mail armor that wrapped her broad torso. Jorn's attacks had not even slowed her down.

"Release him, demon!" Alrek charged through a table, kicked it aside, and swung his sword as he came within range.

"I am not demon!" She dropped Jorn to the floor as if he was a forgotten doll.

The crossbowman hit the ground with a muffled thud and did not move.

"I am Lucatia, daughter of the great demon Mordritch and Lady Suronnin, his human concubine!" She stepped in to engage him, parrying his blade and counterattacking.

"An outcast plagued by halfbreed weakness," Alrek said as he danced around her. "No wonder you fear me."

"The blood of the Noldrun will change that." She slashed diagonally down. "It will purge me of my weakness and the Five Kingdoms will bow down to me!" Her words lent proof to Alrek's barb.

"Your weakness is in your soul, not your lineage." Alrek blocked her attack, spun around, and thrust his blade at her chest. "No ritual can alter that!"

She moved to parry and unwittingly opening up her lower body to attack. He drew his hand back and drove his dagger into her muscular thigh, drawing a stream of green blood.

"Your attacks are meaningless! You cannot harm me!" She cackled, ignoring the wound and swiping at him with her free hand.

Alrek dodged to the left and slashed sideways.

She caught his blade and pushed it aside as she chanted and stepped into him. Her fist glowed with a soft azure light as it impacted with his chest, sending a jolt of agony crackling through him. The force of her blow dented his armor inward, cracked two of his ribs, and hurled him backward. His flesh burned from the magical energy. He sank to the floor, hitting the ground hard. His eyes teared as his aching body strained the limits of his endurance.

"You could not save her and you cannot save this Noldrun," Carena's voice whispered in his ear as if she were next to him, despite her being across the room.

The half-fiend floated off the ground and flew swiftly toward him, blade held in front of her like a lance, ready to skewer him.

Alrek tried to respond but could only gasp against the bands of agony squeezed his chest. Time slowed and his mind cleared of its chaos. This creature, Lucatia, had used Carena's voice to throw him off balance. His own guilt had allowed the tactic to work against him just as it had driven him away from the remains of his homeland and its survivors. Carena's death had not been his fault. He had followed the order of his king as he had sworn to do. There was no way he could have known that Cyre would be destroyed. Those misplaced feelings had stripped the meaning from his life as he had wandered without purpose since the fall of Cyre. As he lay there gasping for air, he realized that he did have purpose now, and that purpose was to save Ravik from this fiend and to protect his friends.

Lucatia descended upon him, her eyes bright with frightful glee.

"Let him alone!" Ravik emerged from the zone of darkness atop the bar, sprinted to its end and leaped at her.

The demon spun toward him. He collided with her in midair, knocking her back into the wall with several audible cracks. They plummeted to the floor in a jumbled mass.

Alrek did his best to ignore his injuries and pushed himself to his feet. He grew immediately faint and had to fight against nausea. Feeling only pain was a welcome relief. He squeezed his sword tightly. Ravik had probably saved his life. He would return the favor.

Lucatia roared as she got up. Ravik rolled onto his feet bringing his head level with hers. He had dropped his axe, so he punched her in her leathery face with both hands.

"If I did not need your precious blood, you would already

be dead, dwarf!" She caught his arms by the wrists and held him fast, positioning herself so that he was between she and Alrek.

"Dwarves make the best shields!" the demon taunted him. "You cannot attack me without harming your friend!"

"I can." Aliana stepped from the shadows and thrust her short blade beneath the slats in the demon's armor and up into her back.

Lucatia shrieked and stumbled, but she did not lessen her grip on the dwarf. Reacting swiftly, she slammed her head into Ravik's skull. It impacted with a crack, the dwarf's eyes rolled up into his head, and then she hurled him at Alrek.

Alrek dropped his sword and reached out, catching the dwarf's heavy form and lowering him to the ground.

Lucatia whipped around, swiping at Aliana. The halfling dropped into a crouch and the demon batted at air. The demon brought up her limb, catching Aliana in the shoulder with a sickening crunch of bones.

Aliana cried out and collapsed forward onto the floor.

Lucatia reared to her full height and raised her massive fist for a killing blow.

"Coward!" Alrek bellowed his defiance.

"Are you still here?" To his surprise, the demon squared off to face him, ignoring the wounded halfling, and smiled again.

"More than you know." Alrek retrieved his sword and leaped toward her.

The demon held out one hand. Her sword lifted from the ground and returned to her grasp. She stepped in to meet his onslaught.

Alrek struck high, deliberately allowing her to parry his attack. She moved slower now as thick, emerald-colored blood oozed from where Aliana's sword still stuck in her back. It did not, however, weaken the strength of her blows, and Alrek's arm soon felt numb from the force. He could not last long against her sheer power.

Turning his strike toward the ground at the last instant, he deftly reversed his attack bringing the pommel of his weapon up. He was rewarded with a satisfying crack as the haft of his sword caught her jaw, slamming her fang-filled mouth together.

"Your efforts are pathetic, human!" Her mocking tone wavered as she staggered back. She lashed outward and grabbed the wrist of his sword arm. She squeezed and sharp pain flared through his arm as bones snapped.

He chocked back a scream and his sword dropped from his nerveless fingers. Tears distorted his vision as the room swirled around him, growing darker as the shadows closed in. His time was almost up.

He looked about, desperate for aid and blinked as he spied his dirk, still embedded in Lucatia's thigh. With desperate precision, he grabbed the hilt with his free hand, yanked it from her leg, turned it up, and thrust it into her throat.

Her jaws parted as if to release a scream, but uttered only as a rasping gurgle as blood burst from the wound. She released Alrek from her damaging grip and pressed her hands to her neck, grasping desperately around the blade, frantic to prevent the loss of her life's blood.

Alrek staggered back, clutching his wounded arm.

"No . . ." Lucatia said in a new, gravelly voice. She blinked at him and her once bright eyes faded to a dull milky color as they darted wildly from right to left.

"Yes," Alrek said, and then fell into the darkly comforting arms of unconsciousness . . .

THE TALES OF THE LAST WAR

6

. . . and found himself standing on the field in the Metrol Stadium.

"You've killed me, Alrek."

He turned at the sound of Carena's accusing voice and saw her stumble through the floating rose-petals towards him. One hand clutched her throat in a vain attempt to staunch the flow of the jade-colored blood that spewed forth to stain her gossamer gown.

"You're not her." Alrek made no move to help her. "She's dead and soon you will be, as well."

"Perhaps we are both already dead." She choked on the thick fluid oozing from her neck.

"If that were true you would not be bleeding." Alrek nodded grimly. "You will die and suffer for the evil you wrought." And for Jorn's death, he thought, heat rising to his face.

She opened her mouth to answer, but only a gargling sound emerged before she dropped to her knees. Her eyelids closed over her beautiful blue eyes. When she opened them again, Lucatia's hateful yellow gaze locked onto him. She collapsed forward and as she brushed the brittle brown grass, shadows grew and contorted around her. Her form shifted inside the pocket of darkness until finally she kneeled before him in her true shape. Her scaled face looked up at him and she gnashed her fangs as if by will alone she could kill him.

"Your time on Eberron has ended, fiend." Alrek clenched his fists as he wondered how he might speed along her demise.

A harsh blast of fetid air drew his attention. He turned quickly and had to shield his eyes from a blinding light as a portal ripped open the dream. Within, an angry crimson sky hovered over a vast desert. Small horned figures twisted in an undulating dance across the sandy surface, the flash of blades visible in their hands.

"What sorcery is this?" Alrek wished for a weapon.

Foul laughter answered him.

Looking back, he saw Lucatia stand, her dream-flesh fully healed. He tensed, ready to fight her with his bare hands if necessary to prevent her escape.

She tossed back her head and laughed.

"It would seem that I am more demon than not. I have been called home by he who sired me." She walked toward the opening.

"You cannot leave this place alive." Alrek stepped in front of her and sank into a fighting stance.

"This place exists only in our minds, Alrek. You cannot harm me any more than I could harm you." She waved one hand dismissively. "However . . ."

An invisible force clamped over him, pinning his arms to his side. He struggled against it in vain, unable to even turn his head.

"Release me!"

"Spare me your demands, Alrek. You have won. The Noldrun and your halfling are alive. You have slain my physical body and I am banished." She stepped past him.

"So you return to the the demon who spawned you." Alrek attempted to distract her as he searched his memories for anything that might help him escape the mental bonds.

"So it would seem." She paused near the portal and swiveled her hideous visage toward him. She smiled, revealing the glint of her fangs. "But you will see me again . . . just as you will see her."

"What do you mean?" Alrek's chest compressed at the reference to Carena. "Answer me!"

Lucatia laughed again and stepped into the nightmare realm beyond. The doorway shrunk to a point and winked out. The force holding Alrek vanished. He ran forward, stopping where the doorway had been, knowing that it was pointless. Her soul had escaped. Although she would be trapped on whatever plane she'd gone to, he new he should heed her warning. Creatures banished to the nether realms did not always remain there. He thought about the deaths of Jorn and the others and vowed to be ready for her should she reappear.

He examined her words in his mind.

. . . you will see me again . . . just as you will see her.

He sighed and shook his head sadly, not daring to allow even a spark of hope to germinate within his core. Lucatia had left him with that final lie. There was no possiblility of Carena or any of his friends having survived the Day of Mourning. He turned to gather the emptiness of the stadium around him. Every time he closed his eyes, every time he dreamed, he had returned to this place, but he had never been alone.

He searched that newfound solitude, hoping, wishing that Carena would be there again. But she had abandoned his dreams with the rest of the ghosts. He would see none of them again. His soul screamed inside him and tears awoke from their long slumber. He wept openly.

As his first tear struck the earth, the air shifted and the rose petals fluttered to ground.

DAVID A. PAGE

ABOUT THE AUTHOR

David Page has been writing his own *Dungeons & Dragons* adventures and stories since he was twelve years old. He has learned over the years that gaming is a fantastic method for developing plots and fleshing out his characters in his various literary endeavors and has used it for that purpose. Although most of his current writing is set in an independent universe of his own creation, he finds it thrilling to be able to craft a story set in the world of Eberron.

Currently Page lives in the Pacific Northwest with his wife and daughter, where he collaborates on film scripts, spins tales about vampires, and derives inspiration from old rail beds and the drama of volcanic mountain ranges.

THE WEIGHT OF WATER

Edward Bolme

1

"How did it come to this?" Cimozjen muttered.

"Sir?" asked his aide.

Cimozjen slapped the telescope against his palm in irritation. "Nothing, Rembil," he said, handing the telescope over with a sigh.

Rembil peered through the ground-glass scope. "I make it at six wagons, captain. They look heavily laden." He handed back the telescope and nodded in satisfaction. "It'll be a good haul."

Cimozjen raised the glass to his eye once more. A half dozen wagons lumbered down the dirt path that escorted the lightning rail stones out of the Starpeaks and through the woods west of Thaliost. Four pitifully armored guards tended the caravan, two at the van and two to the rear, carrying only spears and small bows. Another dozen peasants tended to the animals and helped usher the ponderous wagons over difficult bumps and the like. "Predictable as ever," Cimozjen grumbled.

"Aundair must be hard-pressed not to be sending a military escort," said Rembil.

"Or they haven't yet noticed. All the same, let's get the pickets out now. It may be a trap, or the garrison at Thaliost might be withdrawing to meet this caravan."

"Of course, sir. But I think there's no need to worry. We'll handle this."

"How did it come to this, Rembil?" snapped Cimozjen.

"I don't understand your question, captain," said the aide, concern smoothing his voice with a touch of satin.

"I am an avowed paladin of Dol Dorn, sworn to protect the innocent and serve the right. I have followed my vows without fail. I serve my god and my king, and yet . . . here I am, on a hill in Aundair, and . . ." He raised his head to the sky and held up his hands in supplication. "How is it, Rembil, that I am raising my sword against defenseless peasants? How is it that—" He turned about in his consternation and found himself facing the priestess. She approached him sedately, a squad of four Karrnathi zombies lurching in her wake. The sight of her and her undead retinue stilled his tongue.

"Captain, we're protecting our land and our king—"

"Enough," Cimozjen said, turning his back upon the approaching cleric.

"But sir," persisted Rembil.

"I said enough! Not another word of this. May I never have spoken those words."

The priestess walked up to stand beside Cimozjen. A second after her arrival, the stink of the zombies washed over the group. Cimozjen stifled a cough.

"I understand another supply caravan has been spotted?" said the priestess.

Cimozjen nodded. Then he closed his eyes and prayed silently.

Dol Dorn, he prayed, *if I have found any favor in your eyes for my vows and service, save me from this torment that my obedience has led me to. I will submit myself to any other test or humiliation, but I cannot abide standing alongside the undead to command the slaughter of peasants.*

"This will be fun," purred the priestess. "I love to hear the enemy squeal and die like fattened animals."

Cimozjen turned and looked at the priestess, but the older woman did not notice the predatory gleam in the paladin's eye.

2

Commander Vargonne ir'Lain strode into the War Hall in the Castle of Fairhaven, his boots tapping crisply across the polished darkwood floor. The hall soared over his head, pillars curving in graceful arcs toward the vaulted ceiling. A huge table stood in the center of the hallway, well lit by a shaft of magically enhanced sunlight that descended from above.

Several figures stood gathered about the table, and it was to there that Vargonne walked. As he drew near, the figures stirred; Queen Aurala and the field marshals and master strategists of her senior war council turned to face him.

Vargonne stopped, clicked his heels and bowed deeply, his right fist held to his heart. "With my heart and sword I serve," he said.

"Attend us, Vargonne," said Jandeuse in a dusty voice. Utterly enfeebled by age, Jandeuse was a man most definitely too fragile for field services. Vargonne was nonetheless honored to be in his presence; he had written the seminal textbooks that had served to train the Galifar military, and since the outbreak of the Succession War ninety years ago the royal house of Aundair had used every arcane method at their disposal to preserve his masterful mind. His new tactics and creative concepts had been instrumental in keeping Aundair in the war while the country was beset by the powerful nations to the east and the wilderness rebels to the west.

Vargonne stepped to the table. A three-dimensional map of Aundair and surrounding environs covered the twenty-foot-square platform. So exquisite was the detail that Vargonne was unsure whether or not it was the work of a master modeler or simply a magical illusion mirroring the current state of the land (though the lack of clouds across the map's surface made him think the former more likely). Vargonne stood with his hands clasped behind his back and studied the map.

"We're having some difficulty near Scions Sound," said Jandeuse, and one of the other officers present gestured to the peninsula that stood closest to Karrnath.

"Trouble, m'lord?" asked Vargonne. "I'd thought the garrison at Thaliost has been more than adequate to secure the area."

Jandeuse slowly turned his wobbly head to face Vargonne. "It is true, commander, that there's been no easy way to cross the mouth of the sound since the destruction of the White Arch Bridge, yet we must not put it past our enemies to develop a clever new stratagem."

"Yes, m'lord. I apologize for my impertinence. What difficulty have we been having there?"

Jandeuse's head slowly dropped back to its original hanging position as he continued. "It concerns our forces at Thaliost. The skyriders there have a large aviary of dragonhawks to carry out aerial patrols. We send them regular caravans of supplies to keep the 'hawks in good health and the footsoldiers ready for action. However, the last several caravans have vanished. Mounted scouts sent along the route have failed to find any evidence concerning their fate."

"Raiders, then," said Vargonne, "with some sort of aerial ability or magical augmentation. Are we missing any elemental airships?"

"No, we are not," said Jandeuse, "at least none that are unaccounted for."

"Understood," said Vargonne. "Then it's most likely not freebooters, but Karrns or Cyrans. I take it you'd like me to escort the next few caravans until we catch our foes?"

"Not at all," said Jandeuse, wagging his head slightly.

"M'lord, I don't understand."

"The jackal does not attack the wolf, but the lamb. If you escort every caravan, the raiders will not attack. We will lose none but we will also lose the services of your troops, and the threat of the raiders will remain. Instead, we need to locate the enemy and use your troops to destroy them."

"Yes, m'lord. What is your plan?"

"You will follow the next caravan at a distance of ten miles. We doubt that the raiders will have scouts that far afield from their main body, yet you will be close enough that you could counterattack the raiders within a few hours of their attack. Your eyes will be this young man here."

A young man dressed in plain clothing stepped out of the shadows on the far side of the table and bowed politely. He stood barely to Vargonne's shoulder. He wore his dark hair cropped very short, and had not a touch of facial hair.

"Shouldn't we leave the scouting to someone more . . . seasoned?" asked Vargonne with concern.

"This is Teron," said Jandeuse. "He comes to us from the Monastery of Pastoral Solitude. I am assured that he has training and experience beyond his years."

"Of course, m'lord," said Vargonne bowing.

"You sound unconvinced," croaked Jandeuse with a smile. He coughed. "If you would, Teron, please tell commander Vargonne how you would kill him right now."

Teron, his hands placidly folded in front of him, did not hesitate an eyeblink before answering. "I would not engage him directly; the large table between us would negate the element of surprise. However, I note that the commander carries a hand-and-a-half sword, which, while fearsome, is difficult to draw. While drawing, the elbow must be raised, thus exposing the armpit. I would therefore strike at the neck of this gentleman to my right to cause alarm and to neutralize him as a threat. I would snatch the long dagger from his belt and feint towards the queen. Being a man of valor, Vargonne would move toward the queen, drawing his sword to defend her. I would then throw the dagger at the commander, at the moment that his armpit is most exposed and his upraised elbow blocks the greatest portion of his sight. If the blade did not pierce the heart itself, I should at the least sever the artery in the arm and puncture a lung. That done, I would remain in the room to maintain the perceived threat against the crown. The others would either pursue me or evacuate the queen, leaving Vargonne to die of blood loss."

Commander Vargonne stood silently for a moment, one eyebrow raised in grudging respect. "And . . . but how would you escape?"

"Survival was not given as a goal of the exercise," said Teron.

Vargonne stood quiet for a moment longer, then broke into a loud laugh. "Let's be clear about one thing, then, Teron: part of this assignment is for you to survive long enough to tell me where the raiders are hiding."

Teron blinked languidly, a slight smile gracing his face. "That will not be a problem, commander," he said with a nod.

3

Roglan hunkered down as the Aundairian caravan crawled into view. He had an ideal location within a dead stump that smelled of dry rot; it was largely hollowed out, with only a curved shield of wood left to it. The stump gave him excellent concealment, yet a long crack in what was left of the wood allowed him to peer through and watch the progress of the enemy.

Two bored soldiers trudged along at the front of the soon-to-be-funeral procession. Their heads were downcast in the summer heat. The first held his spear across his shoulders and draped his arms over the shaft; he looked like a criminal being led to execution. The straggler used her spear as a walking stick, and let her bow dangle listlessly from her fingers.

The wagons followed, each being pulled by tired mules. They were stacked with precious supplies. Peasants, unarmed save for skinning knives or some other equally useless tools, tramped alongside, occasionally lending their shoulder to help one of the large wagon wheels cross a small obstacle.

After several wagons passed Roglan's position, two more dismal soldiers brought up the rear. He raised his crossbow and took careful aim at the last of the two soldiers through the narrow split in the trunk. When the soldier was even with Roglan, he let his bolt fly.

The crack of his crossbow served as a signal to his fellow soldiers. He watched as his own iron-tipped quarrel struck the unsuspecting soldier in the temple just as the clatter of the other soldiers' deadly volley broke the stillness of the day.

Per plan, he dropped his crossbow, grabbed his mace and charged the survivors.

His job was to ensure that none fled the caravan to the rear, so he assaulted the other soldier, who struggled with a quarrel that had pierced his ribs. The hapless soldier had dropped his weapon in surprise when the missile had hit him, and Roglan grinned mockingly as he struck the unarmed Aundairian in the belly, doubling him over. Pulling his mace back, he followed up with a brutal strike on the back of the head; helmet or no, he knew the Aundairian was dead.

Roglan looked around for other potential escapees, and saw an elf pursuing a panicked peasant who was trying to make it to the dense brush on the far side of the road. With a quick glance, the elf wordlessly urged Roglan to join him lest the peasant get away.

Roglan spared another few seconds to ensure that the rest of the caravan was under control, then bounded after the elf.

He heard a strangled, burbling cry on the other side of the tall, thick bushes, and with a growl of disappointment he slowed his pace to an apathetic trot. He rounded the bushes, idly swinging his mace and looking around hopefully for another wounded Aundairian to kill, but he could see none.

Then he saw the elf.

He was face down on the ground, in a position almost like he was dreadfully sick after drinking too much, but a long blade of sharpened steel rose from his back, dripping with fresh blood.

Panic surging in his heart, Roglan turned to fetch help, but his foot caught in the tangled roots of a tree. He glanced back just in time to see a blur of motion as someone sprung forward and kicked him solidly in the midsection. He fell to the ground, and felt the unmistakable twang as his ankle snapped against the immovable roots.

He rose onto his elbow to call for help, but before he could cry out, he felt someone grab his chin.

He heard another crack, then he felt nothing but a dull tingling all through his body as he stared helplessly at the dirt.

4

In the brush, someone moved. Small, lithe, and robed in simple peasant's garb, he circled the caravan to get a better view of the happenings.

Years of training at the Monastery of Pastoral Solitude had imbued Teron with the ability to propel himself quickly using his hands, feet, knees and elbows, thus his motions were as agile as a serpent and quiet as a cat.

The Karrns moved among the caravan, healing their wounded, calming the mules, and collecting the Aundairian dead. The soldiers counted themselves off, and discovered that two of their number were missing.

Teron had been afraid something like this might happen. He put a little more distance between himself and the place he had started; the sight of two dead Karrns might put the raiders on edge. He scooted a little further up the road, where a slight bend put him out of sight.

He figured the Karnns had to have pickets covering the road at each end of their raid. He couldn't risk crossing the road and being spotted, so instead he scoured the margin both on his side and opposite for a sentry. While his eyes could not locate the enemy, a stray noise eventually gave the picket away; the soldier coughed twice, allowing Teron to spot him. The Karrn stood further up the road, using a large bush for cover. He was watching for possible reinforcements from down the road, so his eyes were focused far away. Teron waited until the sentry turned his head for a moment, then quickly dashed across the road.

Once safely across, he snuck closer to the site of the incident to continue his spying.

5

"What?" bellowed Cimozjen.

"Two of our soldiers . . . may have been killed, captain," reported the sergeant. "They aren't reporting."

"Two? We lost two of our people in a—a strike against a limpid Aundairian caravan?" The untoward report heaped itself upon the burning shame that Cimozjen already felt in the pit of his stomach over the sneak attack against a group comprised mainly of unarmed peasants. He wondered if this was the Host's way to get their revenge upon him for such cowardly acts, a message that his prayer would go unanswered.

"A–aye, sir."

He gestured vaguely with one hand. "Well . . . find them," he said, incredulity stirring his features with humiliation and annoyance.

The sergeant ran to his task, barking orders left and right. The soldiers fell out of formation and began combing the underbrush along either side of the road. Meanwhile, Cimozjen walked up and down the caravan, gazing at the dead. Several lay pierced by the arrows of the initial volley; most of them looked peaceful or bored, slain before they knew their dire situation. Others lay with shock, horror, or pain marked on their faces; slain—murdered, more accurately—in hand-to-hand combat with trained and armored Karrnathi soldiers. But to Cimozjen, the ones that were most damning to his soul and his ideals were those who lay in the margins, face down, a lethal wound hacked into their backs, cut down as they fled. How could he, a sworn paladin of Dol Dorn, justify such actions, no matter the strategic importance?

The quartermaster stepped up to Cimozjen's side, a respectful half stride behind him as he paced alongside his leader. "The initial survey is good, captain. We seized roughly two hundred pounds of—"

Cimozjen curtly raised one hand to cut off the report.

"I'll just . . . catalog it later, then. Give you the final report, sir." Not knowing what else to do, the quartermaster let himself fall behind, leaving the captain to his brooding thoughts. But within a moment, another interruption came.

"Found 'em, captain!" called the sergeant.

With something tangible to focus his attention on, Cimozjen picked up his disconsolate pace and strode over to where the sergeant indicated. There, in some rough and treacherous ground on the other side of several tall, concealing bushes, two Karrns lay sprawled in the dirt. One, an elf, lay on his face, with the business end of a sword jutting out of his back. The other, a human, lay near a tree, his ankle and his neck both at angles that made Cimozjen appreciate just how fragile the human anatomy could be.

"Looks like they both met with accidents, sir," said the sergeant. "See here, looks like this one mayhap caught his foot in one of them snaggly roots, and broke his ankle and his neck in the fall."

"And you believe the elf tripped and fell on his own sword?" asked Cimozjen.

"Looks that way, captain. Run clean through."

"Clean through, is it?" mused Cimozjen. "Clean through. Why do people say that? 'Run clean through,' like an old washerwoman did it. Hmph. Rather messy, if you ask me," he added, flicking a string of flesh from the sword's broken tip with the toe of his boot. "No, this whole thing stinks. You tell me an elf—an elf, mind you, and far more agile than the likes of you and me—just up and tripped in the forest and fell on his own sword? However would he come to be holding three feet of sharpened iron the wrong way against his breast?"

The sergeant scratched his head uncertainly.

"And why did he have the sword out in the first place? He's away from the caravan; that means he was chasing someone. I'd wager that this someone was more of a threat than our unfortunate elf thought. Either that," he added looking over at the second body, "or he was six-times lucky." He scowled some more at the two casualties, then cleared his throat. "Six-times lucky to have two soldiers meet with fatal accidents like that. I don't like this. I don't like it one drop."

He turned away from the dead. "Haul them up here," he ordered. "Sergeant, pick a detail and see if you can find tracks leaving the area. You have ten minutes."

THE TALES OF THE LAST WAR

6

Teron watched from the wooded margin as the Karrns dragged his two victims from the underbrush and brought them up to the road. A priestess of Dol Dorn and two acolytes inspected the dead soldiers. They laid the elf out ceremoniously, then turned their attention to the human.

One acolyte fiddled with the corpse's ankle for a moment, testing how severely broken it was. In the end, they removed his boot, and as one acolyte held his foot in place, the other pounded a long iron spike into the sole of his foot just to the front of his heel. The spike was easily long enough to reach to the man's leg bones, and, judging by the difficulty the pair had in hammering the spike the last few inches, it likely had imbedded itself in one. They tested the ankle again, and found it to be suitably stiff. They replaced the boot, and turned their attention to his neck. To stabilize the corpse's floppy head, they drove wooden stakes into his head just beneath his ears. They held these stakes against his neck and wrapped some twine around his neck several times, cinching it up tight with a tourniquet.

Finished with their work, they laid the human beside the elf and arranged him to a suitable repose. The priestess approached, dipped her fingertip in a vessel of myrrh, and marked the corpses' foreheads. She poured some sort of oil onto their chests, and carefully wrapped a strip of embroidered cloth about each one's hands. She pulled out a large prayer book and opened it. With her acolytes behind her, the priestess moved between the two corpses, intoning a prayer loudly enough that at least the rhythm of the chanting reached Teron's ears. Slowly the two corpses rose from the dirt road and stood, an uncanny glow in their eyes. Teron glanced toward the other end of the captured caravan and saw that the captain looked to the ground, his hand shielding his eyes from the travesty.

Once the ritual was over, Teron watched as the priestess spoke with each of the undead creatures. They picked up their weapons and swung them experimentally, intelligently. Then they shuffled off to one side of the road, standing alongside the other zombies that awaited the priestess' bidding.

One of the Karrns gave a sharp whistle, and within moments the search party returned to the caravan. A minute longer, and pickets returned from either direction, jogging to the summons. The soldiers formed up and the Karrnathi captain quickly inspected them.

Then, once everything appeared to be in order, the Karrnathi column moved out. To Teron's surprise, they moved off the road immediately, straight into the wilds. A dozen zombies helped push each of the wagons across the rough terrain of the peninsula. The swath of destruction created by the Karrn soldiers, the captured wagons, and the mindless laboring zombies would be evident for days, if not weeks.

How have they eluded capture for so long? Teron wondered. How could we miss such obvious tracks?

Then the answer arrived in the form of another mystic. A lightly armored raider came to the edge of the road and prayed, shaking a fistful of beads and feathers. The wind whirled, and the foliage rustled back to its original form as the druid worked his magic. Within minutes, no trace of the Karrns' passing was left. Even the bloodstains in the road had been covered over or dispersed.

The druid then shifted form, dropping to all fours and becoming a black bear. In this guise, the druid snuffled all about the scene of the ambush, tore up some areas of noticeable interest with great bear claws, then finally ambled into the wilds, following his compatriots.

As it meandered off, Teron slipped from his hiding place. He was supposed to report back to his commander as soon as he knew anything, but he realized that if he did not follow the druid bear, then it would take him days or even weeks to find the Karrn base of operations.

Placing the orders he'd received from the royal command in the center of the road, Teron scrawled a single word on the parchment:

WAIT.

He weighted the paper down with a fist-sized stone, then he, too slipped off into the wilds.

7

"That's all it said? 'Wait?'" Vargonne, pacing at the head of the Aundairian column, kicked a rock into the bushes. "How long, I wonder? And why?"

Yassios, the commander's aide, leaned against his horse's saddle, idly flipping the singular missive back and forth across the saddlehorn. "I'm sure I have no idea, sir. You know those monastic types of fellows, commander, they're not much for being helpful. You show up with your boot falling apart, and they look down their noses at you and say it's not a problem, but a door opening. Well Aundair's ass, it's no door they're hearing, it's the damn sole of my boot flapping loose and letting pebbles into my foot. So I surely don't know how wise it was to send one of them up ahead all alone like that, sir."

Vargonne turned and regarded the junior officer. "I'm as frustrated as you are," he said, "But orders are orders. Besides, they're notorious for getting strange tasks done, are they not?"

"That may be true, commander," protested Yassios, "but I fear there may be difficulties."

"Such as?"

"Well, on the first hand, they're not rightly part of the military, and so they aren't directly beholden to obey your commands, sir."

"Go on," said Vargonne, a curious smile crossing his face.

"They, um, they haven't had the same training as us, and so they might not think in the proper manner. They might, you know, suggest a shortcut that leads across a path that isn't suited for horses, perhaps."

"Good, good. Go on," urged Vargonne, stroking the corners of his mouth.

Yassios opened his mouth to say more, but a voice close at hand cut him off, saying, "I also hear they're very quiet when they want to be."

The aide turned and found a shortish dark-haired human standing placidly beside him. "Nice horse you have here," he said, as he stepped over to the commander, leaving the aide with his mouth flapping open and closed.

Although he was dressed in peasant's garb, the newcomer bowed very gracefully to the commanding officer. "Commander Vargonne," he said, "my name is Teron. I was selected to be your eyes in this operation."

"Yes, I remember you, Teron; you were at the planning session at Fairhaven. Although I must admit I am flummoxed by your youth and your . . . seasoned demeanor. You can't be more than, what, seventeen years? eighteen?"

"I'm twenty-two, Commander, and I've been in training for ten years."

"Have you? Can you show me something of what you've learned?"

"I'd rather you didn't require that of me, Commander," said Teron quietly. "I am not particularly good at restraint. It's not why I am trained."

"I see," said the commander, looking askance at the monk. "Well. What news, then, of the caravan?"

"The caravan was seized the day before yesterday by Karrn raiders."

"Karrns? Are you sure?"

"Yes, commander, judging by their livery, their accents, and the behavior of the undead they animated. It was an excellent ambush, skillfully plotted and executed. Having been forewarned, I managed my escape, but the rest were slaughtered."

"And the goods on the caravan?"

"They took the wagons and supplies and moved up into the foothills," said Teron.

"That's impossible," interjected Yassios. "They'd have left tracks. They have to be using an airship or the like."

"Not at all," replied Teron coolly. "They have a druid with them; he conceals their trails. I was able to follow them because they thought they'd left no one alive. I can lead you there. It's not far."

"Excellent. Sergeant!" he called over his shoulder. "Post a squad here with runners. Everyone else, prepare to move out!" He turned back to Teron. "Where is their camp, then?" Vargonne asked. "I am eager to fall upon them unawares."

"I will take you there," said Teron, "but I think you'll find it quite difficult to take them by surprise."

8

"Where are they then?" Yassios asked.

"In that cave," said Teron, pointing.

A rough, rocky ridge rose out of the woods, one of the first rugged foothills of the Starpeaks. It was bare of vegetation and sloped steeply up from the surrounding terrain. Halfway up the slope, the Aundairians could see the opening of a cave, some five yards wide at the mouth, but the cave sloped steeply inward, and nothing further could be seen within.

"Tell me about it," said commander Vargonne.

"The cave is fairly wide at the mouth, but narrows rapidly, too narrow for more than two people abreast. You'll find that the wagons from the various caravans have been stashed in that grove of trees over there," he added, pointing. "The cave must widen again deeper inside, because they brought all the plundered supplies inside. Then again, supplies can be stacked, as well as stored in passages that are too short or narrow to be comfortably used by soldiers. That's probably also where they store the animate dead."

"Why don't they post a guard?"

"They do. Which means they saw your troops coming and hid inside, hoping to avoid detection."

"Or else they're slipping out the back way," said the commander, concern edging his voice.

"There is no other exit," said Teron. "I've scouted the hill thoroughly, and they do their cooking outside, which indicates that the air inside does not stir much."

"No other exit?" echoed Vargonne's aide. "That's easy, then. They're trapped."

"I would not hazard that they are trapped," said Teron. "Cornered, certainly, or besieged. But to say they are trapped implies that they did not choose the location for their stand."

"That matters not," said Yassios. "We are Aundairian soldiers. They're a rabble of Karrnathi raiders, feeling their oats for ambushing peasants. They'll panic when they see us. We'll force our way in and crush them where they hide. Commander," he added with a proud salute, "allow me to lead the men in and rout these bandit swine."

"If it's of no import to you, I'll decline to take part in this action," said Teron quietly.

"Of course," said Yassios snidely. "We're trained for this sort of close fighting. We have the armor and the shields. You'd just get yourself hurt, no matter how quiet you were."

The commander took off his helmet and ran his fingers through his sweaty hair. He squinted at the cave critically. "Very well," he said. "Take two dozen of the heaviest troops we have and force your way in. Send for reinforcements if it opens up too wide, but don't hesitate to pull out if it doesn't go well."

Yassios turned his horse and rode to the rest of the troops, barking orders. Then he dismounted to have his squire equip him with heavier armor, a large shield, a full helmet, and a stout spear.

He gathered his troops about him, as well as a portly dwarf wizard for support. Together they advanced up the slope. The soldiers' heavy armor made the progress difficult, and they cursed their way up to the cave, sweating in the hot sun, slipping often on the gritty lichen-encrusted stone. Then one of the troopers fell rather dramatically, taking down several others downslope in a cascading avalanche of coarse cursing, grinding metal, and loose sharp rocks. At that point, Vargonne sent a score of unarmored archers to help the heavy infantry navigate its way uphill.

At last the troops assembled at the cave's mouth, standing shoulder to shoulder, four abreast. Their shields overlapped, creating a veritable wall of iron. The soldiers in the front rank held their spears low for upward thrusts, while those further back held them above their shoulders, ready to stab down over the shoulders of their comrades. When fighting in tight quarters, it was a tactic that helped counter the effectiveness of the opponent's shields.

"Right. We march in slowly, but we don't stop. We'll dress our ranks from the left; as the passage narrows, the right ranks hold back and join the rear. When it expands again, the second file will fill out to the right, so we maintain a solid front. Is everyone clear on this?"

The wizard cast a spell upon several members of the squad, causing the fronts of their helmets to glow with a bright light, just in case the Karrns extinguished all lights in the cavern.

As the squad began to advance into the cavern mouth, Teron turned to Vargonne and said, "Now that they're going in, commander, I'd suggest you send up whatever priests, healers, and chirurgeons you might have with you."

The commander nodded and gave the order. From upslope, they heard Yassios's steady cadence as he led his troops into the cave; the sounds of the marching becoming warped by the cave's acoustics.

After a few tense moments, shouts erupted—cries, orders, screams. The sounds of panic rose from the mouth of the cave, but it was impossible to tell whether the Aundairians had broken the Karrns or vice versa.

Time passed slowly, marked in its passage by the sound of crashing iron. Outside the cave, the healers fidgeted. Vargonne ran his fingers into his hair and gripped a lock tightly. "I hate not being able to see my boys," he said grimly. "Can't tell what's happening. It's the worst feeling a commander can have."

"You've done all you can," Teron said. "Victory or defeat has already been determined. We have only to wait to discover the inevitable."

Moments later, the first Aundairians staggered out of the cave, some of them stumbling on the uneven terrain and sliding on their backs down the slope. Some eighteen made it out, the last few being dragged by their fellows as arrows flew past, whispering their danger.

Vargonne leaped off his horse and charged up the hill, catching himself with his hands whenever he slipped. "Report!" he yelled. "Report! Now!"

The troops milled about, momentarily confused, until a sergeant stepped down from the cave's mouth and saluted his leader. "They got this here sort of barricade in there commander, somewhat like a rampart, maybe, and bear traps hidden on the floor and such. We tried to fight our way over it, but we couldn't. It was too damn narrow in there. We could manage four, maybe six spears trying to poke the defenders, but if the front rank fought, well, they couldn't climb. And them Karrns, they had bows and all kinds of weapons. But if we could break that barricade, sir, we could take the cave. I'm sure we could."

"Where's Yassios?"

"He was the first what stepped in a bear trap, commander. We left him there, and tried to press on, figuring we could tend to him afterward. I saw one of the others try to free him as we were pulling out, but . . . well . . ."

"Understood, sergeant," said the commander. "Stand down."

"Aye, sir."

The commander strode the last few steps to the cave's mouth, and stood carefully to the side. He cupped his hands and called in. "Aundair? Aundair!"

"I do believe they done killed the wounded where they lay, commander," said the sergeant grimly. "Sitting ducks, they were, all caught in the traps like that."

Vargonne's mouth worked grimly for several moments, then he said, "Sergeant? Reform your ranks, another two dozen. We'll breach that barricade for you." As the sergeant set to work, Vargonne called the wizard to his side and spoke with him quietly. After several minutes' discussion with the mage, during which the dwarf's face grew alternately flushed and pale, the commander stepped back down the slope to the sergeant. The wizard ducked his head and withdrew from the area.

"Stand down, sergeant," he said angrily. "We'll attack again just before first light. It appears the wizard is ill-prepared for combat at this time."

9

That evening as the sergeant patrolled the perimeter of the camp, he came upon Teron standing by himself. The monk held his hands cupped together and raised skyward. The sergeant watched him for several moments, but the monk neither moved nor acknowledged the sergeant's presence.

Finally, his curiosity overcame his uncertainty. He cleared his throat as politely as he could, which, for a career soldier who'd spent the better part of twenty years yelling, was hardly at all. "Excuse me, um, master monk, but what in Khyber are you doing?" he asked.

"I'm fighting the rain," replied Teron.

The sergeant chuckled and looked up at the orbiting moons. Wide and pale Eyre, half full, approached the zenith, leading bright Barrakas across the sky. "Well, you must be winning, then, because they sky is clear as crystal."

Teron lowered his hands and stepped over to the sergeant. He held out his palms.

"What for are you carrying around water?" he asked. "We got us buckets of it back at camp."

"As I said, I am fighting the rain." Teron looked at the sergeant as the grognard scratched the back of his neck in confusion. "You see," the monk explained, "the water wants to fall, like rain. I seek to stop it. And so we fight, the water and I."

The sergeant grimaced. "But you can't hold it up there forever," he said.

"That is true," admitted Teron. He slowly opened his hands, and water fell like rain onto the dry earth. "Every night I lose."

"Well . . . then why do you do it?"

Teron rubbed his aching arms. "My master has told me to. I am to fight the rain until I learn the lesson." He paused to roll his shoulders, then sighed wearily. "I thought that the answer was that weight was greater than strength, but he said that that was only part of the answer. And so I repeat the lesson."

"Wait," said the sergeant. "You mean you're still in training?"

"You're not?"

The sergeant snorted in derision. "Course not. I been in this army twenty years."

Teron looked at his hands, then dried them on his jersey. "That is sad, soldier," he said, "for if you are not in training, that means the only thing left for you to accomplish is dying."

10

Shortly before dawn, as the sky was just starting to lighten in the east, two dozen heavily armored troops made their way up the slope, helped along their way by their comrades. Several had already had the enchantment of illumination cast upon their helms; these they kept wrapped with cloths to avoid giving away their approach.

The wizard also climbed with them, puffing with exertion and nervously darting his head back and forth, fearful of pickets or assassins.

They all gathered at the mouth of the cave. The soldiers formed up, hiding their eyes behind their shields. The handlers stood by, ready to pull the coverings off their glowing helmets as soon as the wizard had finished his task. Trembling nervously, the wizard crept up to the cave's mouth. He swallowed hard, then dashed to the center of the cave's entrance and whipped his hands through a frenzied incantation. *"Yaash uryu b'chah!"* he shouted, his voice cracking with fear as he tried not to hurry the arcane words and therewith waste his energy. He extended his hands, and a thick blade of lightning flew from his fingers, shooting down the length of the stony passage with a thunderclap.

The wizard scrambled away in a most ungainly manner, his short legs propelling his heavy body with surprising speed until he was safe. He clutched at his heart while the Aundairian soldiers moved into the cave at a disciplined trot.

Once more, time slowed to a crawl for those awaiting word, as the steady tromp of feet beat out the seconds. Someone shouted some orders, but the words came garbled and twisted to the ears of those waiting breathlessly outside. Shortly afterwards, the sounds of combat rose out of the cave's mouth. To

Teron, the noises sounded eerily like the spectral wails that came from the Crying Fields, when ghosts stalked the night to refight battles long since past. At those times, it was better to avoid the Crying Fields altogether; he was certain the same held true for the cave's interior.

Then a bright, fiery flash illuminated the interior of the cave mouth, accompanied by the lick of flames and the screams of the burned. Moments later, the first of the Aundairians straggled out of the cave. In all, only seven of the twenty-four escaped.

"It opens up into a large open area," explained one survivor. "They had us from all sides with arrows and quarrels. Someone even started using grappling hooks to pull us out of formation. We tried to push out, but it took too long, then someone of the right flank got eager, and opened the line. Then, when we started pulling back, they threw that fireball, and, well, take my head of you want for cowardice, but it sure beat being in there with them Karrnathi zombies."

As the day dawned full and bright, the Aundairians settled in for a siege.

II

On the fourth day of the siege, a runner came up to the camp from the road. He ran over to where the commander reclined in a campaign pavilion, protected against the hot sun. "Dispatch, commander," he said breathlessly as he saluted and proffered a scroll. "From the commander of the border guards at Thaliost. The scribe took a copy and sent the original on to Fairhaven."

Commander Vargonne listlessly took the scroll, broke the wax seal and unrolled it.

Headquarters on the Frontier
Thaliost

> *Dragonhawk scouts confirm that the Karrns are massing for a likely attack across the channel. Reports indicate that they have gathered several airships, thus they can land a force almost anywhere along the Sound. Already their camps have enough to defeat our garrison; we do not know how many more may be hiding in the woods around Rekkenmark.*
>
> *Our supplies are gone. Much of the garrison has been dispersed to hunt for game; it's all we can do to keep the dragonhawks flying. We do not have the power to resist this attack. Send word of our dispositions, and our orders.*

He dropped the missive into his lap; the parchment crunched like autumn leaves. "Now I understand," he said.

"Understand?" asked Teron, who stood nearby, performing isometrics to keep his muscles toned.

"The reason for the raids. It's not just to starve our troops at Thaliost; they're stockpiling supplies for themselves. The one reason we haven't feared an attack across Scions Sound is that Karrnath wouldn't be able to supply a large army with any degree of surety. With the White Arch Bridge destroyed, getting draft animals and wagons across the Sound would be difficult at best. And aside from the lightning rail, there aren't any good roads."

"But Karrnathi zombies don't need supplies, do they?" asked Teron.

"No, but the command staff do, as would archers, engineers, and the like. Not to mention the camp followers like blacksmiths and chirurgeons and necromancers. But with an army primarily of undead and a ready stash of wagons and provisions awaiting their staff, the Karrns could land almost anywhere along the channel with a few days' rations, resupply here, and make a swift march on Fairhaven."

The commander exhaled forcibly. "This means we can't continue the siege here. Since Old King Kaius has shown his sword, they'll cross the Sound within a day, two at the outside. If they fall on us here, we'll be defeated and they'll have their supplies. We must find a way to break the raiders, and soon."

"But even if we do, the main body will still be across the Sound," said Teron.

"That is true, yet if we can deny them these supplies, they'll have to forage. We'll burn the forest. That'll slow their advance significantly, long enough for us to marshal reinforcements at the pass. If not, they might stand a good chance of seizing the capitol."

Vargonne struck his fist on his knee. "To think that we've wasted four days already," he snarled, "sitting here when we needed to be planning." He sighed. "It's a pity we don't have them treed, we could just smoke them out like bandits. But underground like this, there's nothing we can do." He growled softly. "It's going to be costly, but we have to find some way to force our soldiers in and crush them."

Teron thought for a moment, then looked down at his palms. He looked over to the cave and rubbed his fingers together. Then he laughed, a quiet little hissing sound made through a mouth barely open. "No, commander," he said, "we don't. You'll find that a raindrop can be more powerful than your best warriors. We will crush them with but a child's gentle tap."

"What in the name of Aundair are you talking about?" asked Vargonne.

"The cave is not an obstacle, but an opportunity."

The commander let his head flop back and stared at the fabric of the pavilion ceiling. "Yassios—gods rest his soul—told me you'd say something like that," he grumbled.

12

A small figure knelt beside Cimozjen, who lay supine on his sleeping mat, one arm thrown over his eyes. "There's movement outside the cave, captain."

Cimozjen exhaled through his nose, venting his frustration. He rolled onto his side and rubbed his eyes thoroughly, then sat up. Blinking several times until his vision cleared, he found himself face to face with his gnome scout, her magewrought cloak rendering her all but invisible. "Are they readying to attack again?" he mumbled. "They must be getting impatient."

"No, captain, they're moving supplies up the hill."

Cimozjen shook his head. "I'm sorry, I must still be half asleep. What is it they're doing?"

"They're hauling supplies, sir. Barrels, casks, containers of that sort up to the top of the hill. At the least, it seems like they're taking them to the top; you asked me not to take undue risks with my scouting."

Cimozjen scrunched up his face and scratched at the side of his mouth. "Moving supplies?" he said. "Are they trying to tempt us into a raid?" He snorted. "They must think us fools. They'll find out soon enough when the main body shows. We'll not move." He lay back down and draped his arm over his eyes again. "Leave the Aundairians to their little games and me to my refuge," he said.

13

"So what, precisely, are we doing here?" asked commander Vargonne. "This is hardly an auspicious angle from which to attack the cave."

They stood a few yards above the opening of the cave mouth, a motley collection of barrels occupying the hillside above them.

"We are taking the Karrns prisoner," said Teron.

"And how will we—how will *you* accomplish that, when they have killed the best and heaviest of my footmen?"

"We will send a little messenger," said Teron. "One whose will to enter the cave is greater then their strength to keep her out."

Teron took a short length of stout rope and walked confidently to the very brink of the slope above the cave. Leaning over the edge and peering down, he sidestepped until he found the location he wanted, then carefully laid the rope to the ground. He walked backwards up the slope for a few yards, gently laying the rope out behind him. He repeated the process with another length of rope, angling it away from the first, thereby creating a sort of funnel of rope aimed at the cave's opening.

He turned to the quartermaster and pointed to the nearest cask. "Fetch that here and tap the bung," he said, "then pour it out here at the ropes."

The quartermaster did as he was bidden, then turned the cask. Together they watched the contents drain, coloring the hempen strands of the rope as they flowed down.

14

Drip.

"Begging your pardon, captain."

Drip.

"What is it, Rembil?"

Drip.

"I believe we have a problem. If you'd come with me."

Cimozjen set his quill in his journal and closed the book. He rose from his stool and followed his aide to the main chamber.

Drip. Drip. Drip. A little rivulet trailed its way down the uneven floor of the cave, until at last it reached a step of sorts and dripped over the edge. With each drip, rings rippled outward, defining the boundaries of a growing pool that trembled on the floor of the cave.

Cimozjen kneeled by the side of the slowly growing pool. He dipped a finger into the pool, rubbed the liquid between his finger and thumb, then smelled it. "Oil?" he asked.

"Aye, sir. We're not certain when it started dribbling in. No one seemed to take heed of such a small dripping noise. We first noticed the pool just a short while ago."

"Well, at least they've shown their sword as to why they were dragging those barrels over our heads," Cimozjen said. He frowned. "Whatever they're planning, we need to stop them. They're pouring it in from above?"

"Aye."

"Put a stop to it."

"How shall we do that, captain?" asked the soldier. "We can't go outside to stop them from pouring oil without being attacked."

"Clean it up."

"With what, if I may ask? We haven't any linens. Other than our clothes, that is. And where would we put it once we'd mopped it up?"

"Stop the flow, then," ordered Cimozjen.

"Again, I must ask, with what? We've concealed the wagons outside, else we'd have some wood. But even so, how could we hew a wall proof against oil with this sort of rocky floor? And were we to do so, would we not be sealing ourselves within this cave, a barricade of oil between us and the outside?"

Cimozjen rounded upon Rembil, his mouth open to yell another command, but no sound escaped. He tried again, with a similar lack of success, one frustrated finger quivering in the air, useless with no words to accentuate. Cimozjen put his hands upon his hips and paced back and forth, taking a mere three steps in each direction before reversing his path.

Then he stopped and looked at the oil anew. "They're going to fire it," he said.

"Captain?"

"They'll fire the oil. Once they've dumped everything they have from lubricant to cooking oil to lantern fuel, they'll fire it. The flames will come roaring in here, right through that passage, and we'll have no way to stop it."

"Water, sir," hazarded Rembil.

"Oil floats, dunce," snapped Cimozjen. "If we add water, we simply allow the flames to spread the further. No, once the oil starts burning, we'll either roast in the flames or suffocate in the smoke, make no mistake. Either way, it's a difficult, useless death."

The two of them stood in silence for a minute, trying to discern a way out of their predicament. The pool of oil at their feet grew until a new rivulet of oil spilled out and trickled deeper into the cavern.

Cimozjen shook his head. "We crushed the best heavy warriors they threw at us. But our valor is undone by the smallest little trickle."

He watched as the rivulet found a new low point in which to pool. The smell of the oil served as a fitting accompaniment to the taste of defeat. "Right," he said, "it's as good an answer to prayer as I deserve."

"What was that?"

"Nothing. Prepare to attack."

"Attack, captain?" stammered Rembil. "But . . . but that's—"

"That's what? Certain death? We all die, Rembil. Best to die in noble service."

"I was going to say it's rather foolish, captain."

"It's hardly more foolish than standing here waiting to be baked like a chicken," said Cimozjen, "and it'll be gratifying to watch that scorpion of a priestess fall in battle." He sighed with satisfaction. "Make no mistake; it will be a difficult fight, but we can acquit ourselves with valor and still obtain the goals of our mission here."

"How is that, captain?" asked Rembil.

"We'll be attacking out of this dark place into the sunshine, two abreast, charging into a cloudburst of arrows. However, if we are swift and organized, we should catch them off their guard. We strike quickly for the top of the hill, there to strike down those who pour oil upon us. We've tested their mettle here in the cave, and they cannot withstand us face to face. Once we take the high ground, they'll pay dearly to retake it from us; if they advance tentatively, they deny themselves their superior numbers, and if they advance in force, we pour whatever oil is left at their formations and fire it. Ultimately, we will lose, but their victory will be costly."

Rembil scratched at the back of his head. "What about the supplies, then? If we, um, lose, they'll recover their supplies."

"Order the zombies to sequester themselves deep in the cave, to find ledges and footholds on the walls well away from the oil. They can linger here, because they need no food or air. If the Aundairians fire the oil, then they can organize themselves at the barricades after the flames burn out. If not, they can wait in ambush and fire the oil themselves when the Aundairians enter the cave. No, as long as we have zombies, they won't recover the supplies." He snorted, then added, "And as long as we have zombies, folks like me are meaningless."

"What was that?"

"Nothing. Form up the troops."

15

Without a war cry or even an uttered word, Cimozjen led the attack into the sunlight. Squinting against the painful glare, he turned up hill as soon as he cleared the mouth of the cave. Sword in hand, shield abandoned to free up his arm for balance, he charged up the hill as quickly as he could.

He scrambled up the bare, rough stone, already grown hot to the touch in the summer sun. He could hardly even look up toward his foe; his armor and helmet prevented him from craning his neck that far. Even had it been possible, he would not have done so, for the ground was as treacherous as could be for another fifteen to twenty feet above the cave's mouth; he needed to see where he was climbing.

Around him, he heard the sounds of battle starting to grow. Aundairians shouted in surprise, ordering their troops. Arrows started whistling. But near at hand, and true to their training and orders, his troops were silent. Karrn soldiers needed no frenzied yells to bolster their courage. Cimozjen heard scrabbling and panting, grunts of exertion and the hiss of pain as a soldier slipped and fell back down the rocky slope, but no whoops of war; true to his orders, they were saving their energy for the climb and the assault.

Beneath his feet, the slope started to fade to a gentler grade. As he no longer needed his arms to climb, Cimozjen rose to his feet, running upslope in a hunched gait, left hand extended toward the ground to help maintain his balance and momentum should he stumble. He glanced up. Another thirty yards, maybe, charging up a steep incline.

Combat—after months of hiding and banditry, real combat at last! His blood thrilled, eager to engage the enemy in a hopeless battle for the honor and glory of his homeland. He felt other Karrns close at hand, surging upwards with him, ready to take the battle to the cowardly Aundairians.

Then he heard an undercurrent of sound that he had never heard before in a sunlit battle; it sounded like a hailstorm heard in the city. Heedless of the strange sound, he continued pressing himself upslope. He drew closer to the Aundairians at the top of the hill; the slope was almost gentle enough for a full-out run to the top . . .

. . . when he slipped and crashed to the hard rock with the bang of metal. He slid a few feet down the slope before he arrested his momentum. A curse on his lips, he rose again, sword still clutched in a hand with knuckles bloodied from the unexpected impact. Two more steps and he felt a foot slip out from in under him again. He landed hard again, on his elbows and knees, his armor providing merciful protection for his bones.

"Dol Dorn, support me!" he yelled, at once a supplication for aid and an expression of frustration. He pushed himself up again, but only made it another three furious steps before he lost his traction again and fell to the rock. This time he landed fully extended, and the impact knocked the wind out of him. His sword caught a small crack and snapped with the impact, and the end of the blade clattered and slid down the rocky hillside, leaving him with nothing but an overwide dagger with which to take the hill.

His head sagged in momentary anguish as he sought to recover his breath. In that brief, pained respite, he saw how he had been defeated: a miniature avalanche of small rocks cascaded down the treacherous slope, tumbling with the sound of hail. Glancing downhill, he saw his entire command sprawled across the hillside all the way to the base, upended and largely disarmed.

"Dribbles and pebbles," he muttered bitterly. "We are undone by dribbles and pebbles."

A shadow fell over him as he lay upon the sun-heated rocks. "The time has come for you to yield, captain," said a soft-spoken Aundairian voice. "Order your command to surrender their arms."

He looked up at the speaker. He squatted easily on the balls of his feet, unarmed and unarmored, yet his voice carried a calm authority. His head eclipsed the sun, so that it looked as if he had a halo shining behind his close-cropped hair.

Cimozjen nodded in resignation, and tossed the hilt of his broken sword down the hill. He lowered his head to the warm rock, wanting to weep in shame, but unable to do so. It felt strange to him; his part in the war was over. No more commands, no more battles, no more raids . . .

He looked up once more at the man who stood silhouetted over him, squinting against the brightness of the sky. "You, friend," he said, "are the strangest answer to prayer that I have ever seen."

ABOUT THE AUTHOR

Edward Bolme expends his excess mental energy making up limericks of a less-than-savory nature. Thus writing comes naturally to him, even though he cannot type. He is fortunate to have a wife and two children who put up with his unique style. He has also been known to make the mistake of letting his wife write his author's bio.

Come visit www.essential-eberron.com/forum for the chance to talk with various Eberron authors, or visit www.bolme.com/books.htm to see what other projects Edward is working on.

WAR MACHINES – 992 YK

Ian Burton-Oakes

I

They had left Stormreach days ago and would soon rendezvous with the first expedition team on one of the many islands off of Xen'drik's coast. The two warforged could not have been more different. One, Spear, was an old juggernaut, his stocky body bristling with metallic spikes. The other, Tone, was a recent model designed for repair work. He was lightly armored and lanky, his long fingers designed for subtle work.

Spear sat silently, contemplating the gentle buffeting of the ocean against the ship and the diverse means of disassembling his companion, "Mission Commander" Tone. By such actions he kept the waking nightmares at bay. Beneath the hyperbolic violence of his daydreams all-too-real visions of blood, smoke, and severed limbs seethed and pressed against his conscious mind. It was a dangerous game, like dancing a dagger between your fingers. The slightest excess of imagination would cast him into remembrance. Still, he knew of no other way to restrain his anger with Tone's naïve, sing-song enthusiasm. It might have been appropriate among the fleshborn. It had no place among the children of the forge.

"Consider it, Spear. This mission has so many ramifications for our life after the war. If we can prove ourselves worthy here, just imagine the duties that we can fulfill as civilians. We can travel to places that the soft races can barely endure, experience wonders forever barred to them."

Tone lacked the broad sturdiness of the frontline models. Spear could just take hold of his head and tear it loose from his narrow shoulders.

"I know that *this* expedition is military, but it is exactly the sort of expedition someplace like Morgrave would hire us to perform in peacetime."

In fact, a couple solid thumps would probably crush Tone's skull. At least, the blows would irreparably damage his jabbering jaw. The mere idea of silence made Spear's corded muscles ripple with a foretaste of the pleasure he felt when his division broke through an enemy's line.

"By Aureon, Spear, think of it! A few years of such work would make us more knowledgeable than the gnomes of Zilargo. The Twelve, Morgrave, the Library of Korranberg . . . all those sit-at-homes would be desperate for what we know. I would have professors and librarians eager to record my words."

Maybe those methods were too quick. A single kick to each knee would blow the joint and tear the fibers around the joint. Tone wouldn't see it coming, his feet planted clumsily on the ground. Spear would have all the time in the world to take him apart.

"What will you do when it's over?"

Spear's even tone made his words even more blunt.

"Over? I've been bashing and gutting for almost three decades. *You*, you've been wandering around for, what, five years? You think it ends? We are machines of war. With or without the war, our job is slaughter."

Tone recoiled as if he had been slapped. His voice expressed the surprise that his face could not.

"That is a bit grim. How, then, do you explain this mission? Admittedly, *you* may be here to take care of the sahuagin should they prove troublesome, but where is the slaughter in archaeological study?"

Spear shook his head but said nothing. Tone straightened, feeling that he had made his point and Spear had backed down. Then Spear spoke.

"You are new, your plates barely cooled, but you need to learn quickly. This mission is all about the war. We have been sent here in the hopes that this sunken stone will yield some bit of technology that can assist the war effort. If it is not bloody now, it's bloody later.

"It's more than that, though. You walk around thinking that you are special, different from the rest of us. You weren't trained in bloodshed, so you think that it has nothing to do with you. You get to play around with magic toys and maybe have to put together some of us when we return from battle. What you don't get is that you are a construct just like us. You were built to make the fleshborn's life easy, not to achieve greatness. If you try to do that, they'll take you apart for scrap. They'll love you as long as you do nothing that takes away from them, as long as you give. Don't forget that you were the *second* choice for the job. If that Cannith tinker the first expedition brought hadn't caught some nasty jungle sickness, you would not be here."

Spear's long years in the army allowed him to stop himself before he passed from insolence into insubordination, but he thought it. *These are my troops, my ship. They are yours only by the ignorance of those who don't understand the value of experience over mere learning.*

Tone did not reply. They faced each other impassively until the announcement rang through the boat's decks that the island had been sighted. Spear then left the room to make sure that his unit was ready to secure the beach. He reappeared moments later.

"We have a problem."

2

Tone looked out into the island's harbor. The four ships that had carried the previous expedition were barely recognizable. Their hulls were bent and broken and lay half-sunken beneath the shallow harbor waters. The wooden frame of the ships could be seen, like the bones of a mortally wounded soldier. Broken planks, shattered crates, and shredded mast cloth littered the nearby beach. A single tent, narrow and long, stood away from the beach. Spear handed Tone his scope. He put it to his eye and examined the tent more closely.

The tent was open on all sides to the elements, serving only as a roof. With the eyeglass, Tone could see that it had been patched together from several smaller tents. It was tall, the roof easily twenty feet above the ground. All that barely drew his attention, though. A hundred or more cots lay side by side within the tent and each cot bore an unmoving humanoid. Tone handed the eyeglass back to the warforged captain.

"That could be the entire expedition."

Tone spoke to no one in particular, his voice the only means he knew for expressing his shock. Spear set his massive hands upon the railing and leaned towards the island.

"This poses several problems for us. First and foremost, it means we may have an unknown enemy to deal with. Second, the wrecked ships are going to make it more difficult to get to shore. Our third problem is a direct outgrowth of the first two. We can't navigate too close to the harbor, so we will have to set down anchor further out and deploy smaller vessels to get to the shore. If there is an enemy on the shore, they will have a distinct advantage. If they could do that to the ships, they will have no problem destroying our boats."

Tone looked upon Spear's broad back with a mixture of awe and unease. He admired Spear's ability to ignore the potential tragedy and move immediately to assessing the situation, but it also seemed cold. For all they knew, over a hundred people had been killed and laid out on display. Spear looked at Tone over his shoulder.

"If we wait, I can take some of my men underwater and secure the beach under the cover of darkness. I doubt they would expect that."

"You can swim?"

Tone realized the inanity of his question as soon as he finished speaking. If he could have blushed, he would have. Spear's response was emotionless and without reprimand. He was too involved in the tactical options available to be condescending.

"Of course. We wouldn't have been deployed for maritime service if we hadn't been properly equipped to deal with the most obvious challenges. The sahuagin often damage a ship's hull without ever surfacing. Each of my soldiers has had enchantments woven into their bodies so that they can swim without sinking. If we take that route, I recommend we circle the island while the light holds. We might see something else that will shed light on our situation."

"What about the men and women on the shore?"

"If they are dead, then nothing will help them. If they are not dead, then we have every reason to think that they will remain in their current condition unless we engage in some poorly planned action that would put them in harm's way."

Tone nodded. "That makes good sense. Let's take a turn around the island and see what can be seen."

Unfortunately, what could be seen could be summarized in two words: beach and jungle. As far as they could tell from the deck of their ship, the island was otherwise lifeless. They didn't even see the birds that usually called these islands home. The ship found her way back to the harbor as twilight whispered of night's imminent arrival.

Spear and his team spent the time in preparation. They affixed lenses to their eye sockets so that the darkness would not blind them, selected armblades and battlefists, and reviewed their approach. Tone helped secure the ropes to the starboard side of the boat, the side facing away from the beach. He could only discern the silhouettes of those aboard the ship by the time Spear's team was ready to depart. Had Spear not chosen the harpoon-like armblade for which he was named, Tone would not have been able to pick him out from the others.

For all their size, the seven warforged rappelled down the side of the boat with only a few faint scrapes and thumps. Tone could not see them by the time they reached the water, nor could he discern the noise they made in the water from the constant slap of the water against the boat.

THE TALES OF THE LAST WAR

3

Spear crouched in the shallows between the Forge brothers, waiting for his two scouts to return. The four sturdy juggernauts had been forged at the same time and had served with each other for two decades. While they could never be biological brothers, they were as close to family as a warforged got. Spear saw Knox's square silhouette first. He didn't see Shadow's black steel form until he was a mere arm's length away. Knox spoke in a low whisper while Shadow kept a wary eye on the beach and a ready hand on his bow.

"Captain, there is no sign of any enemy threat. The civilians are alive and appear to be sleeping. I am no expert in such matters, but they look healthy."

Spear looked to Shadow. "Did you see anything?"

Shadow's sibilant whisper blended with the sound of the ocean slapping against Spear's legs. "Captain, I saw a nothing which is something. Something large moved along the beach, but its tracks have been effaced."

"Giants?"

"It could be, captain, but without the tracks I can only speculate."

The first, second, and third arrow punched through Knox's chest and toppled him backward into the sand. The shafts were massive and made him look like a pincushion. Spear spun towards the ocean in time to see the second volley before it slammed into the Anvil brother to his left, Hammer. The juggernaut crumpled to his knees and slumped forward into the water, propped up by the arrows. An enormous man huddled in the belly of the broken ship, her hull barely able to conceal him. The moonlight broke across his back and silhouetted the fletched arrows in his quiver.

Spear bellowed. "Scatter and stay mobile!"

He lumbered onto the beach and readied one of his spears. Shadow jogged to the left and peppered the giant with two arrows while the remaining Anvil brothers sloshed towards the shore and fumbled for their javelins.

The third volley arced towards Shadow, but the lithe warforged scout managed to duck and roll beneath the deadly rain. The giant rose up from the ship's berth as Spear launched his spear, causing it to *tink* off of its metal breastplate rather than sink into the giant's exposed throat. Its quiver, at least, was empty.

The giant leapt into a sprint as it sent a large crate hurtling through the air. It winged Anvil Forge and tore his right arm from his socket. He stumbled, barely able to keep his feet. The giant's feet, though broad as a small boat, made not a ripple as they pumped in and out of the water while Shadow released another, seemingly useless spray of arrows.

The giant's stride brought it into the fray almost immediately. It let loose a bestial scream that jangled the steel plates of the warforged. Its wild hair formed a mane around the dark-skinned giant's rage-torn visage. It loomed large over the warforged, its breastplate and greaves the color of the storm-tossed ocean. Its eyes were fixed upon Anvil and it nearly trampled Spear to get to him. Fire and Water interposed themselves between the mad creature and their brother and hurled their javelins. Fire's pierced the giant's exposed right forearm while Water's sank into its nose. Roaring, it took hold of the two defenders, one in each hand, and hurled them to the ground. Anvil leapt towards the giant and buried his armblade into its calf. He soon crumpled beneath the giant's boulder-like fists.

But both Fire and Water were on their feet by then and began hacking at the back of the giant's legs. It turned and twisted backwards as its hamstrings were severed. As it lifted itself on its arms, Spear charged and drove his armblade deep into its left eye, again and again, long after it stopped moving.

4

The boat ferrying Tone to the shore scraped up against the shore. He had heard the yelling in the night while he stood on the deck of the boat, but to see the carnage in the light of day was another matter. Two of the juggernauts had been riddled with arrows, a third lay beneath a massive stone and the shattered fragments of the crate that had held it. A fourth and fifth juggernaut, dented and bent, were still functional. Only Spear and the lanky Shadow had managed to remain unscathed. The giant sprawled facedown across the beach, its dark metallic blue hair matted with gore. The giant's breastplate had an aquamarine sheen and shimmered in the sunlight.

Tone shook his head. "I can repair Fire and Water, but the other three are beyond my skills. I'm sorry."

Spear nodded curtly and gestured for the two juggernauts. Tone ran his hands across their torsos, whispering the eldritch words of crafting. A faint orange glow surrounded his hands and where he touched, the steel regained its shape and the fibers and joints beneath knitted back together.

Spear gestured towards the fallen giant. "What is that?"

"It must be a storm giant. It is unusual to find a violet skinned one, but not impossible. They often live near and under water. Perhaps this is its home?"

Even dead, the giant's proportions were frightening and

Tone approached it cautiously. Its visage had slackened with death, the rage replaced with a look of piteous, eye-lolling mindlessness. The gaping, blood encrusted socket drew Tone's immediate attention. It was a ragged mess of flesh, but even after hours of exposure it remained untouched by fly or worm. Then he caught a green glimmering beneath a lock of hair. A lustrous, multi-faceted emerald green stone sat squarely in its forehead. Tone pushed at it, but it was firmly embedded in the creature's thick skull.

"What do you make of it?"

Tone shook his head. "I'm not sure. It has some kind of stone embedded in its skull, and I don't see the usual signs of decay that you would expect in this environment."

"What do you mean by 'embedded?' Is it some sort of injury?"

"No, that stone was placed there deliberately. I have heard that some natives of Riedra implant dragonshards into themselves. Perhaps this is a similar process."

"And why do they do that?"

"I'm not sure. It supposedly grants them special powers, but I don't know much more. What about the first expedition?"

"They are all sleeping, but we can't wake them."

"Have any soldiers that you can spare comb the wreckage. We need to find something that will tell us what is going on. For now, let's leave the sleepers where they are. Make sure they are well-guarded."

Spear nodded and began barking orders.

Fire called out to Tone. "I think you should take a look at this."

They had been rolling the rock off of Anvil and discovered that the other side of the stone had a fragment of writing upon it. Tone looked at it and queried his docent.

"It's the speech of the giants. *Geishtirtig,* the en-spirited. It refers to those who willingly accept another spirit into themselves."

Water traced the letters with his forefinger. "What does it have to do with what happened here? Do you think this sleep has to do with some sort of possession?"

"I don't see the point in possessing someone if all they are going to do is sleep. The giant is another story, though."

5

Only one item of real worth was found among the wreckage—a sack containing the expedition leader's journal. It had been tightly wrapped in oilcloth and so remained largely intact despite its time in the water. More valuable still, a rough map to the sunken stone had been folded up inside the front cover.

Tone flipped through its pages, seeking some clue as to what happened. The journal itself was mostly empty and detailed only two weeks of time. The second to the last day mentioned a strange sleeping sickness that the healers could not contain. Presumably, the expedition leader succumbed soon afterwards. Previous to that, there was nothing to presage the event. The expedition arrived, spent a week setting up camp and the next determining the exact location of the stone. They had just located it when the sickness halted further exploration.

"Do you think that you can find the stone with that map?"

Tone looked up at Spear over the top of the book. "Between the map and the details in the journal it should be easy enough. It is due west from the center of the harbor."

"Then we should make plans to take a look. We can leave some soldiers to keep an eye on the sleepers, but the sooner we figure out if we can get anything useful from that stone, the sooner we get ourselves out of here."

"What about the sleepers? Even if we could fit them all into the cargo holds, we have no means by which to sustain them on the long journey back to Cyre."

"My instinct is to take the few we can handle and leave the rest. They have done well enough so far, perhaps they will hold out still longer."

"That assumes that it wasn't the giant taking care of them. They may very well die."

"Not much we can do about that. Our best option is to take what we can. If you don't want them suffering, we can put down those we leave behind. We can't save everyone."

Tone shook his head. "Let's hold off on any drastic plans before we know what other resources are available to us. We will take the ship out tomorrow at dawn and locate the stone."

6

The map's instructions were clear if not exact. They sailed due west from the harbor until a man standing on the aft of the boat could just distinguish the tent on the beach.

"How do you think we should go about this? They had only seen the stone from a distance before they succumbed."

Spear eyed the rough sketch of the stone. The diagram indicated it to be over a hundred feet long with a broad doorway at the north, south, east, and west.

"It looks like a giant could comfortably make its home in that thing."

"I considered the same thing," Tone said.

"It makes no sense to take on another one of those things, especially in its element. We can't afford the losses. We send Shadow down by himself to scout. If we have another giant, we will have to think long and hard whether we are prepared to complete this mission."

Shadow nodded and disappeared over the edge of the boat without so much as a "Yes, captain." Tone moved to the railing and waited for his return.

"How long do you think it will take him?"

"Not long, assuming the map is remotely correct and he doesn't get himself into trouble."

They stood quietly for a brief time before Spear spoke.

"It bothers me that we haven't seen any signs of the sahuagin. The first expedition had employed a group of them to ferry tools and artifacts back and forth, right?"

Tone nodded.

"And these same workers told them about some other sahuagin who seemed to be preparing for some kind of battle. Yet, we have seen no signs of sahuagin."

"Why should we? That giant could easily have driven them off, if not killed them. And why would they stay once the sickness began? They surely wouldn't want to risk falling prey to it."

"I still don't like it. That is just one more variable that we don't understand."

Shadow bobbed to the surface, interrupting their conversation. He climbed quickly up the side of the ship to report. He began to sketch the pillar, elaborating on the drawing provided by the map.

"All clear. No sign of giants or sahuagin. It's strange looking, though. It is green and keeps flashing this green light at regular intervals. The doors are just openings in the stone and lead to a room full of air instead of water."

Tone pointed to a circle in the middle of the room. "What is this?"

"Some sort of pillar. It's made of something like sapphire. There is some sort of writing all over it. I don't recognize the language."

"How high is the ceiling?"

"Perhaps twenty-five feet tall? The doors are about twenty feet tall."

Spear spoke. "We should keep the exploration team small—Tone, Shadow, and me. Shadow keeps a lookout while we look at the room and if he sees anything, we get out quickly. Tone, can you conceal us?"

"I was given a wand for just such a contingency. It's seen some use, though, so we shouldn't draw on its power without reason. Remember, too, that the sahuagin are sensitive to the motion of water and may sense us even if they can't see us."

"Just don't get close enough to any for that to be a problem."

Tone whispered a few arcane words as he rubbed a bit of glowing moss between his fingers. The moss's light faded but the tips of Tone's forefinger grew bright as a torch and without flame's inconstancy. He held it up to Spear.

"A little trick that should help us find our way. I can always hide it by making a fist."

Spear and Tone swam closely beside each other while Shadow moved darkly just outside the light. The crystal blue of the surface gave way to aquamarine translucence. Tone's light illuminated a small, murky sphere and he struggled to see more than a dozen or so feet in either direction.

Tone thought aloud, surprised by the clarity of his own voice. "Do you think elves feel so light upon the land? Do you think we could be as graceful as they beneath the water?"

Spear glanced at him. "I would worry about being as graceful as the sahuagin."

Tone shook his head in exasperation. "Do you ever think of anything besides violence and potential violence?"

"I don't have the luxury—there is too much violence to keep me occupied."

The discussion ended abruptly as the monolith came into view. He had no idea how deep they were except that little light reached them from the surface. The entire length of the monolith, more than a hundred feet tall, glistened with a sickly gray-green light. It had a crystalline shape, like two pyramids joined at the base. The stone was nearly one hundred and fifty feet tall. It turned slowly, its light flaring with each completed cycle. Immense and haunting, Tone read in its contours the handiwork of a giant's skill, one now lost to the ages.

"To think that all the warforged owed their existence to the tiniest fragments of the giant's wisdom," Tone mused.

Tone and Spear swam to the narrow catwalk built into the side of the stone, about ten feet above the lower tip. Tone peered closely into its translucent green surface and ran his fingers gently over its smoothness. With each touch, the stone flashed brightly.

"It seems to respond to contact. Perhaps some pattern of taps might . . ."

A massive, fleshy hand pressed against the other side of the crystal. Nervously, Tone moved his hand upward and the other hand followed.

"Spear, do you see this?"

"See what?" Spear asked without turning around.

"You should take a look at this."

Spear turned. "So what am I seeing?"

"It's the—"

The light flashed again as a stone giant's face slammed beside the hand, its lips twisted in a grimace. Bubbles escaped from the corners of its lips and pushed their way through a cloud of blood blossoming from its nose. Tone leapt backward with a yelp and stumbled off the edge of the platform. He flailed wildly for a moment before Spear grabbed his shoulder and yanked him back onto the platform.

"Calm down, you fool."

Tone stammered. "But the giant . . ."

He looked back to the stone and saw no sign of the giant. Spear shook his head.

"You're letting your imagination run away with you. It's just stone. It may flicker and glow, but there's no giant inside."

"But when it flashed, I saw a giant's face. It was drowning . . ."

"What do you mean? It hasn't flashed since we set foot on it. I don't think it has even completed a full rotation yet."

As if on cue, the stone pulsed with light. Tone made out Shadow's form before the stone darkened; he had taken up a watch position above the level of door lintel. Tone turned and studied Spear closely for some indication that he might be joking and found none.

"But each time I touched it, the light flickered."

Spear responded as impassively as always. "No, it did not. It only brightens when it completes a rotation, that's all."

"That can't be, I . . ."

Unless it is all in my head.

Tone clapped with pleasure. "Bless the Seven for sending you along with me! It must be a phantasm."

"What does that mean?"

"You're a juggernaut, Spear. The upgrades that make you so effective on the battlefield also make you more resistant to the magic that affects the mind. Apparently you don't have much of one left."

The plates of Spear's shoulders rose, a clear sign that the corded muscles beneath had tensed.

"It's a joke, Spear. You have as much of a mind as I do. It just isn't as human."

The adamantine shoulders relaxed. "Then I pity your mind. It seems too easily fooled for my tastes."

Tone shrugged. "Just keep an eye on me. If I begin to act strangely, it means that some magic has taken hold of me. It will be up to you to get me away from it."

"Let's get to one of the doors and take a look at the inner chamber."

The door opened into darkness. Apparently the interior didn't share the exterior's luminescence. Tone passed his glowing finger through the doorway and found his finger breaking the surface of the water. Stale air replaced water as they stepped inside.

"How did they manage that trick?" Tone mused.

The light glinted off crystalline walls. They appeared to be composed of the same substance as the outer walls, but without the luminescence the walls appeared almost black and gave the impression of inertness. A great sapphire pillar, its diameter greater than Tone or Spear's height, stood in the center of the room and rose through the dark emerald of the ceiling above it.

Tone pointed out the pillar to Spear. "I wonder if it runs the entire length of the stone. It may have served as the stone's power source ages ago."

"What about the writing on it?"

Tone looked close at the pillar and saw no writing.

"It must be more phantasms. I can't even begin to guess what could have sustained the magics for so long. I am surprised Shadow was able to read them. Tell me, what else do you see? There might be more hidden from me."

Tone held his hand above his head so that Spear could cast his gaze across the room. "Words, words, and words. They cover the pillar and dot the walls. I can't make it out."

"Is there any change that you note? What is on the other side of the pillar?"

Spear's shoulder plates shifted with annoyance, but he circled the pillar with Tone following close on his heels.

"What's this?" Spear asked.

He reached out towards something before Tone could say anything and pulled a small sphere from the pillar. It shone like adamantine and had a band of red stones set into it—each with a twisting silver cord within it. It was a docent powered by dragonshards.

"Let me see that. It looks exceptionally well-made."

Tone held out his hand, eager to hold it. He had handled a few docents in his time, but never had an opportunity to examine one closely. Spear turned, angling away from Tone's seeking hand.

"Looking won't tell you anything. You know that."

"That may not be entirely true. If I can detail it before it is used, maybe I can establish a some correlation between structure and function."

"You can see it."

"Well, I have actually never seen a design quite like that . . ."

"Right." Spear placed the docent on his chest.

"Spear! That's reckless. We don't know what it could do. We should examine the writing on the pillar around where you found it, it might tell us—"

Spear interrupted. "In the end, it all comes down to wearing it."

Tone threw up his hands in exasperation. "Well, at least tell me what it is saying."

"It isn't saying anything. I can't even tell that I'm wearing it."

"I'm not sure I like that. Perhaps you should take it off until we can determine more about it?"

"I'll walk around with it and see if it activates."

"Fine." Tone turned pointedly towards the pillar, "So, what of this writing?"

"I can't make it out. I could copy it."

"And me without my quill."

Tone reached into the sack and withdrew a raggedy leather bound book from it. He held it out to Spear.

"Flip though this. Does anything in there seem similar to what you see on the pillar or walls?"

"So they also gave you one of those magical sacks, too?"

"Of course. The space inside the sack won't let water in, so it's ideal for this sort of work."

Spear patiently turned the dog-eared pages, looking from the book to the pillar and back to the book. Finally he handed the book back to Tone.

"It all looks the same to me."

"Are the words inscribed on the stone?"

Spear nodded. "Yes, quite deeply."

"Perfect! All we need is some wax and a torch. Phantasm or not, I can take casts of the wall."

Tone ran his fingers over the wall and muttered to himself. He couldn't even feel the writing. He could sense the secrets hidden from him and he ached with anticipation. Still, it was only a matter of time.

"That tells us all we need. The sooner we leave, the sooner we can get back here with the proper supplies."

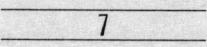

7

The beach was alive with commotion. Six warforged encircled a humanoid creature. A second, larger ring formed around the six, ready to fall upon the creature if it managed to break through the first ring.

"What do we have going on here?" Spear bellowed.

A warforged in the inner circle responded. "It's a sahuagin, captain. She claims to be some kind of priestess. She's making all manner of ruckus, yelling about a curse upon the island and warning that we better flee before the ghosts of the giants catch us."

"Is she violent?"

"Just mouthy, captain."

"Then let's hear what she has to say. You two, stay here. The rest of you get back to your posts."

The guards barked, "Yes, captain!" in unison and dispersed to their posts along the encampment border. The sahuagin, her body draped in interlocking fish bones, approached Spear directly, her body undulating as if swimming. She was unarmed, but the bones rattled ominously as she walked, scraping against her algae-crusted scales and each other.

She extended a long green finger and pointed at Spear.

"Leave stone. It not yours to have. It too strong to wake."

"You are talking to the wrong person. I just keep everyone safe." He pointed over his shoulder with his thumb towards Tone. "He's the one in charge of the stone."

Spear sidestepped the sahuagin and walked to the central tent. The sahuagin twisted towards Tone.

"Dark strength fills it. Leave it!"

Tone held up his open hands in the calming manner often used by humans. "Listen, we know about magic and I have worked with giant artifacts before this. Admittedly, none were as complicated, but the principles—"

"No talk. Listen. Your words like pretty clothes in the sea." She hissed and spat on the beach. "Pretty, pretty words just pull you down faster."

"Do your fellows share your concerns? Is that why we have not seen any sign of your people?"

"They hears. Landwalkers does not." Her tail twitched behind her. "They not listen, but knew truth when sleeping took the landwalkers. You drown, but have pretty words so you not see."

"Insightful riddles aside, if you are worried, steer clear of us. No one will force you near the stone."

The sahuagin fanned her fingers in frustration, giving Tone a clear glimpse of the webbing between them. "You listen not. You not drown alone, but turn the water to poison and drown us all."

"Perhaps you would like to explain more of this lore to me, convince me of your expertise? I am sure I could give you a pearl or two for your time."

"Hear! Not speak." She glared at him with cold fish eyes, "Your words like bait. You fish for my words so that you can eat them. You hear nothing."

The sahuagin slithered past Tone into the ocean and dove into it, quickly disappearing beneath its frothy surface. Tone followed Spear's path into the tent.

"Thanks so much for the help."

"I don't do negotiations. I did not speak so that you would be free to speak as you wished. What do you think she wants?"

Tone shrugged. "She seems sincere enough. She may actually believe all that, although I don't know how much we can trust some stories passed down by word of mouth. I can only imagine how corrupted they would appear alongside the originals."

"Does she have any real knowledge of the stone?"

"I doubt it. I don't yet comprehend its function, and I have worked as an artificer for years. More likely than not, her people probably explored it some time ago and got spooked. Those phantasms are shocking, especially if you don't know what they are."

Spear nodded. "What do you make of the stone?"

"I don't know. There are just too many possibilities from what I saw. I'm hoping that the writing on the wall will help narrow down the options. The structure of the stone suggests a device powered by the dragonshards, and that docent you found strengthens my suspicion. Of course, such a device has many applications, from manipulating a dragonmark to enhancing psionics. We know giant civilization crumbled in the war with Dal Quor. Perhaps the stone is a weapon the giants used against them."

Spear shifted slightly and if Tone didn't know better, he would have said that he was working himself up to something.

"Tone, you said that giant technology created us. What did you mean?"

"It's just a personal hypothesis of mine, but it makes sense if you think about it. As far as I can tell, some of the earliest warforged were outfitted with docents, which we still can't produce. They are only found here, in Xen'drik."

"So?"

"Think about it—if you were a House Cannith artificer who had just found a docent, what would possess you to put it on a warforged unless you already knew something about how they functioned? And if you already knew how they functioned, wouldn't you then have an idea of what you would have to build to use them? We may have been born in Cyre's forge, but this is our homeland."

"Home . . ."

The word hung on Spear's tongue, folding a lifetime of repressed hopes within itself.

"Listen, Spear, I know that you have seen terrible things, things for which I have not the stomach. But I am not without conviction. I worked hard to get placed on this expedition so that I could see Xen'drik's ruins and glimpse, however briefly, into our origins. The war must end eventually and if it does, we warforged will have a chance to be more than machines of war. I want to know what we were so that we can better consider our future."

Tone paused, afraid he had said too much. Spear's experience seemed to have inured him to hope and Tone's own hopes were still too fresh to endure a fellow warforged's disdain. Spear did not ridicule him, though, but instead left him with only a word.

"Perhaps."

8

The sahuagin, Bulubba, crept from the dark water wrapped in enchantments of silence and invisibility. Water beaded against her scales and created noiseless ripples in the shallows. She crawled on all fours, her neck craning back and forth for guards, but the landwalkers had left the protection of the beach to her fellow sahuagin. While the warforged stood alertly at the camp's edge, few bothered to cast even a passing glance to the beach behind them. They lacked the experience to imagine the dangers that could crawl from the sea. Aboard their wooden ships they would pray to their gods for luck, but once on land they forgot the sea.

Bulubba gulped, the open air already drawing the water from her body. Crouching low to the ground, she crept towards the sleeping ones. The darkness posed no obstacle to eyes long-used to the inky ocean depths and she easily made her way to the tent. She whispered a silent prayer to the Devourer, overwhelmed by the sheer power of the mysterious stone that held so many in thrall to itself. The stories made it clear that the longer the sleepers slept, the more powerful the evil would become. She had tried, oh she had tried to kill them, but the giant seemed impossible to trick. If she had any hope of ending the threat, she had to succeed. Time was short.

She lifted the bladder of poison from her side. A few drops of poison would kill each of them as surely as a knife, albeit more slowly. She would have all the time she needed to depart before the metal men would be the wiser. She froze as one of the warforged began to walk along the length of the tent. Bulubba crouched slowly, trusting her magic to conceal her from him. It was the massive metal man, the one whom she had first approached when the two emerged from the water.

The starlight silhouetted his squat frame edged with jagged spikes. He walked slowly, deliberately, pausing in front of the halfling Bulubba crouched beside.

"Do you really think you can kill them before I kill you?"

Bulubba's heart leapt to her throat. The warforged didn't turn to face her and she hoped desperately that he still didn't know where she was, that he hoped to goad her into revealing herself.

"Please, give me some credit. Did you think that I would leave the beach unguarded? I don't trust your kind further than our little friends here could throw you."

His fist moved so quickly that she only felt it as it collided squarely with her fragile nose and sent her sprawling backwards.

"Why don't you dismiss those petty enchantments? We can talk face-to-face that way."

The air rippled around Bulubba as she released them. Her blood ran down her face and dripped to her body where it beaded and rolled away like water.

"You not know the foul magic in these creatures. Let me finish or you suffer greatly."

The metal man cocked his head to the left and Bulubba had the unnerving sense that he was amused.

"Foul magic is it? And what is it you scaly savages practice? I hear you eat your own as soon as they prove unable to defend themselves."

"It is sea's way. Strength prevails over weakness."

Bulubba tried to stand, but the metal man kicked her solidly in the side. The crackle of her ribs snapping brought the attention of the other guards. The metal man held up his hand.

"Hold your position and keep your eyes on the jungle. I have this in hand."

He crouched down and whispered to her. "Then you will appreciate this. This is the strong overcoming the weak."

Bulubba rolled agilely to the side as the second kick landed where her head had been. She spun into a defensive crouch and drew her two bone knives. She held the first threateningly between her and the metal man while the she clutched the second, underhanded, in a defensive position. A green light flickered menacingly in the metal man's glassy eyes.

"Bone knives . . . how quaint."

Bulubba sprang faster than a deadly adder. The metal man reached for her, but she dove beneath his arm and slammed the knife towards his underarm. He stepped back much faster than she would have thought possible for his size and the blade skittered harmlessly across his metallic side. As she stepped past him, she caught sight of a shiny sphere on his chest.

She hissed as she returned to a defensive crouch. "Mother whispered the Devourer's hunger in these bones. They find and bite your soft insides."

Her eyes sought out the metal sphere and noted the band of red stones, the stones of blood. It was too late for this one, the stone would surely take control of him if it had not already done so.

The metal man charged her, raising his arms so that his metal spikes faced Bulubba. She was not prepared. Her people wore little armor and such a tactic would have been certain death for an unarmored man. Her arm snaked lethally to his head, but the knife clanked harmlessly against his metallic skull. His spikes sank deeply into her chest and stomach. The cold green light flared in his eyes as he shook her from his arms. Blood gushed from her wounds.

"The dreaming gods . . . they will . . ."

The blood began to fill her lungs, silencing her. The metal man kneeled down beside her and she saw the sphere clearly. The awareness burned through her and she tried to strike at him. She had lost too much blood, though, and her arm merely twitched.

"The 'gods' have already set the plot in motion. The artifact draws life from the sleeping ones even as we speak and will soon be ready."

Bulubba heard the smile that the metal man's face could not express. Her vision blurred and went black, and his voice accompanied her into the darkness.

"Don't worry, fish child. Our business is with the land-walkers first. Your people should have a few more years . . ."

His eyes flickered a sickly gray-green pallor and pushed her into welcome oblivion.

9

Spear tossed the fish bladder onto the table of Tone's cabin.

"Our friend paid us a visit last night on the shore. She had brought this with her. It is some kind of poison and she clearly intended to use it on the sleepers. She seemed to think that would halt the evil or some such nonsense."

Tone lifted the bladder and took a whiff of its contents.

"She diluted it, whatever it was. She probably hoped to be long gone by the time the poison took effect. I can't believe she just strolled onto the beach, though."

"She had hidden herself with magic."

"How did you see her?"

"It is an easy enough trick around here—the sand of the beach shows footprints very well. She left a long trail all the way up the beach."

"Very clever of you."

Spear laughed, a rough sound like that of gears being jammed. "No, she was just very sloppy."

Tone had not heard Spear laugh before this and had not even thought him constitutionally capable of such things. That, and the amusement he so clearly took in killing the sahuagin, made Tone vaguely uneasy.

"The ship should arrive above the stone soon enough, and this time I will have the materials to examine it properly."

10

The stone rotated more quickly, the flash occurring at more frequent intervals as they approached. It was still an easy matter to alight upon the narrow catwalk, but Tone wondered how much longer that would remain the case. Even before they passed through the entryway, they could see a light in the room. The pillar itself now glowed, illuminated from within by a soft ocean-blue light. Tone saw words crawling along the surface of the pillar while amorphous shapes swam within it like a school of fish.

"Do you see the things in the pillar?" Tone asked.

"Yes."

"And they weren't there when we were here last time?"

"Yes, of course they were. I must have forgotten to mention them. It didn't seem important at the time."

Tone could almost taste the sarcasm in Spear's voice. He ignored it and pulled the glyphbook from his sack. He flipped quickly from page to page, identifying common letters and styles. It was Giant, to be sure, but it made no sense. They seemed to be random strings of words meaning things like "nightmare," "succumbed to," "of corruption," "forge-born," "beware," "prison," and "forever."

Then the words faded, one by one, until the pillar's surface was smooth.

"The words have disappeared again. Can you still see them?"

"They're gone, gone, gone . . ."

The word echoed through the chamber, getting quieter and quieter until it was a slippery, barely discernible whisper squirming all around Tone. It twisted the air and the light until the pillar seemed nothing more than a distant sliver of light while Spear grew larger and larger, his face lost in an expanding field of dull metal. He tried to yell, but all he heard was a senseless babble. He hoped that the words made sense to one not ensorcelled.

"Help me out of here . . . everything is all wrong. It must be more enchantments."

Metal fingers wrapped around his arm and he sank into them, only to feel himself falling into a viscous gray. The sliver of light blossomed into a raging river and something pushed him forward into it. Tone felt himself falling up through the pillar before he lost consciousness.

II

As Tone's conscious awareness faded, as the river of light shrank to a sliver and disappeared, Tone's mind did not cease to function. A string of words, foreign but familiar, embraced his thoughts and kept him from mindless inertia. He knew the words, knew the language, knew it was important to his being in this place.

"I'm afraid you came to this a little late. Thousands of years too late."

Giant. The language was ancient Giant. He had studied it only in its written form, as complex patterns of thick lined glyphs, but he spoke the modern Giant tongue. The words were familiar, although the accent was different, the grammar more precise. The words pelted him like heavy rain, dense and blinding, difficult to penetrate. Then whole phrases would leap to his mind, as if the words were reagents in a complex alchemical mixture—forming the desired mixture only when all the reagents were present.

"It gladdens my heart to share my thoughts with a fellow maker of machines, if only the chance had not been born of my failure."

Images gathered around the phrases, and Tone found himself standing on the edge of the platform that surrounded the sunken stone. Now, however, the stone was not beneath the waters but hovering above them. Its crystalline walls refracted the sun's rays and cast rainbows in all directions. Tone sensed a presence beside him and turned to the soulful eyes of a violet skinned giant, the spitting image of the creature Spear and his men had killed. He was not armed for battle, though, and wore only loose-fitting cotton pants and a shirt. The giant smiled and his face became a mask of sad resignation.

"This is the watchtower before Dal Quor attacked."

"Where am I?"

"You are inside the crystal engine, the heart of the watchtower."

"How is this possible? Is it some sort of glamer?"

The giant shook his head. "You dream. The crystal engine is a fragment of dreaming, cut off from Dal Quor and protected from the Quori's prying eyes."

Tone looked around, trying to find some flaw in the world around him. Yet the closer he examined it, the more real it seemed to become. The platform was slick with water and algae, the sun warm and painful to look upon. When he looked upon the giant's exposed ankles, he found a purple birthmark and subtle variations in skin tone.

"But I do not sleep. I do not dream."

"You possess the faculty of dream, but have been so designed to rarely employ it. I don't have time to explain it all to you—time slows here, but it does not cease. Look upon the face of the enemy."

The world rippled and changed. Gray storm replaced sunlight and the cool ocean breeze turned to angry gusts of wind. The giant pointed to the ocean and Tone saw something rising from the ocean on a floating iron disk. At first, Tone could not make out its form, but soon wished for his previous ignorance.

A creature rode the disk. It was a twisted skeleton of wrought iron formed into a humanoid body as tall as any storm giant. Silver cords ran between the bones, likely serving the same function as muscle. As Tone's eyes moved to its limbs, he saw that each ended in curled talons that glistened with rain. Worse yet, though, was its face, or lack thereof. Its head was a cage of knotted bars that held an irregularly throbbing, bruise-colored mass that swelled rhythmically. The rubbery substance bulged through the bars of the head, only to deflate and lay like wet sack within the cage. Tone tried to speak, to ask about the creature, but fear silenced him. He knew that this was a vision, that it could not harm him, but all his senses told him not to draw the attention of this monstrous creature.

The disk hovered alongside the metal platform, no more than twenty feet from where Tone stood. The creature extended its clawed foot forward with the lazy grace of a practiced predator. The clink of its metal body against the steel platform nearly sent Tone running in terror, but he managed to hold himself steady. When the giant began to speak, it was all Tone could manage not to yell at him to be quiet.

"This is the embodiment of Quori perversity. This creature is, like you, born of a great forge. It was the first of your kind."

When the creature continued into the watchtower, Tone found his voice

"The Quori invented the warforged?"

"No. We dreamed of your kind long before we thought to create you. The lords of Dal Quor saw you in our dreams and built a forge before us. They made nightmares of our dreams and launched them against us. When I first disassembled one of those monsters, I could see the outlines of my imaginings in its construction. We guarded our dreams carefully after that, built private dreamings like this place, but much damage had been done."

The giant's tears mingled with rain in his beard.

"You said you would show me our enemy. Is that what we face now?"

"That is what you face."

"Me?"

"I have no life beyond this dream. I can show you what must be done, but you must be the one to carry it out."

"But I cannot face that creature."

"It is not the creature you need destroy. If you disrupt the web of magic and mind that fuels the tower, the tower will come undone. That will destroy the creature."

"Can I escape before it comes apart?"

The giant looked away from Tone, his eyes tracing the jagged contours of the choppy sea.

"No. If you have time to escape, so does the creature."

Tone looked away from the giant, to the tower looming behind him. It seemed too solid for him to destroy.

"The creature seems a lesser challenge." Tone tried to find some fault with its construction, some crack in its smooth walls. "Is this how the giants won the war?"

"We rebuffed the Quori, yes. But as I look out from this place now, I see that the victory was our loss, too. So much of our glory is lost to your time. We spent ourselves to defeat them. No, it was the tiny races, like your creators, that won."

The giant kneeled before Tone, his great face plaintive and close.

"I am only their memory. I cannot change the past, but I can make sure that the Quori's defeat echoes into the present, that they do not gain a single new agent in their struggle to control this world. You must carry out my instructions—there is only death or annihilation for you and yours if you do not. Your sacrifice will be great, but in it you will be immortalized."

Immortalized by whom, Tone wondered. The giant promised only an anonymous immortality, one that erased any chance of his name ever being known. He would not be heard in Morgrave, nor have his name attached to the great exploration of distant lands. At best, he might become a footnote, a name attached to a failed expedition to Xen'drik. Spear's words echoed in his mind—this was just one more way that the warforged made the fleshborn's life easier. Give up your own hopes, the giant may as well have asked, carry my own to fruition.

"This is an old war, your war, this creature's war, but not my war. I hear you, I understand you, but I why surrender my hopes, my present and future for your past?"

The giant's shoulders and his plaintive smile sagged.

"Look upon the sacrifice we made and then see if you can avert your eyes."

Everything changed. Tone found himself in a large room, standing along a wall about twenty feet from the now familiar blue pillar. A circular stone dias rose a foot off the ground in front of the pillar with two columns rising side by side atop it. The giant stood on the dias, one hand on each pillar. He was dressed as he had seen him in life, armored with a masterfully carved bow across his back. He seemed not to see Tone at all, but focused all of his attention upon the pillar.

When Tone followed his eyes, he saw images flickering across the blue surface, images of some other world. The view hovered just above a ring of milky white spheres and then began to move over them, gaining speed as it progressed. A large dome sat at the edge of the ring and Tone could just make out the skyline of an enclosed city within it. The giant's hand moved across the top of the column and the dome moved closer and closer, as if they were diving towards it. Tone began to avert his eyes when he saw an arc of coiled energy erupt from the dome. It lashed out from the pillar and connected with the giant's forehead in a spray of deep purple, royal blue, and pitch black sparks. The giant fell to his knees as an unearthly scream tore through his mouth and blasted any trace of sentience from his face. Then the entire scene froze, as if it were a painting.

"Hundreds like him died just like this. They knew they would die, hoped to die so that in their death Dal Quor might be defeated."

"Defeated . . ." Tone echoed, "How?"

"The giants gambled that once the Quori discovered the spies they would lash out at the watchers with their psionic siege engines. The Quori did not disappoint. They lashed out at the watchers mentally while dreamforged assaulted the towers directly. Their siege engines drew upon the power of the residents of the domed city, projected a fragment of their minds. When they took control of the minds of the watchers, the towers went into temporal stasis. In hundreds of places, a portion of Dal Quor was pinned. Naturally, they struggled to free themselves. The violence of that struggle ravaged the domed cities and killed many a dreamer.

"The towers were not strong enough to endure the force of the Quori forever, though. One by one, they exploded in a rain of arcane fire, blood, and will. This tower's power flickered, though, before that critical mass was reached. It sank into the ocean before stasis returned. The connection to Dal Quor was lost. I, or the one whose memories I am, was left a hollowed-out husk and the dreamforged invader lived on in the stasis. Left unhindered, it will reach out to its old masters through the tower and serve as their agent in this world."

Tone stepped back, overwhelmed by the mixture of accusation and desperation in the giant's words. He held up his hands in acquiescence.

"Show me how to overload the tower. I make no promises, but show me."

The world altered around them. They were inside the tower, in a larger circular room that Tone presumed must be above the stone's narrow base. The blue pillar glowed dimly in the center of the room and illuminated an array of crystal panels set into the chamber walls. Inset into the panels were elaborate patterns of blue, red, green, and yellow crystals. Some were clearly dragonshards, others appeared to be the sort of crystals used by psions.

"All you have to do is shatter one of these panels. They are durable, but far from indestructible. They regulate the flow of energy through the tower, any interruption will cause a spectacular failure."

Tone turned to the giant with the realization that its existence would also end with this destruction. It may have only been a ghost, but it seemed sentient enough to dread its own end.

"What is your name?"

And the dream ended.

Tone stumbled from the pillar into the glittering light of the crystal panels. The dreamforged creature, its sack straining against the bars of its head, stood before the far panel, its iron black claw lightly scraping its way over the crystal patterns.

Tone froze, unsure of whether or not the creature sensed him. When it did not turn to him with its terrible facelessness, he began to edge cautiously around the pillar. Tone touched the pillar lightly with his steel-tipped fingers in the hopes its surface would yield to them, but he found it solid as stone. Fear surged every time he lifted his foot and ebbed in the moment after he set it down, replaced with a desperate hope.

Time crept as slowly as his feet, until he found his way to the opposite side of the pillar. Completely concealed from the creature, his thoughts moved to the crystal panels. A part of him, desperate for the terror to end, yearned to throw himself into a panel with all the force he could muster. He knew it was suicide, knew that even if he could destroy a panel that way, the dreamforged's long strides would easily overtake his own before he could reach it. He closed his eyes and focused on what he could do.

He had no weapon, no spells. While he might be able to infuse himself with magics that would make his body tougher, no amount of power would allow him to rival the creature. If he could get close enough to the panel, there might be some quiet means to disrupt it, but he felt lucky enough to have made it so far without notice. Then it became clear to him what he needed to do: escape.

The pillar was a device like any other, even if its mechanism seemed strange. With just a little time, he could surely find the secret to its activation and flee. Maybe with the help of the other warforged, or the sahuagin, he could return and destroy the tower. He reviewed his last memories before he entered the pillar, unable to give them sequence. Did Spear push him into the pillar? Or had he managed that all by himself? If he couldn't trust Spear, that would be a problem, too.

He opened his eyes to examine the pillar and found the dreamforged looming over him, its face lowered as if it were examining him closely. He spun reflexively away from the creature and began to run when he felt his joints lock up.

He knew the enchantment, knew that if he could just break its hold over the tiniest joint, he would be free. He had learned the knack from a fellow artificer, but he could not manage it this time. He could focus on his fingers, visualize the joints, but every time he tried to move the magic rebuffed him. One clawed leg appeared in the periphery of Tone's vision, and the magic even prevented him from closing his eyes as it stepped in front of him.

The creature's clawed feet made no sound as they tapped against the stone floor, approaching him. The creature's claws danced along his back and over his shoulders. Then they closed, sinking through his steel skin and synthetic muscle as a knife would sink through mere flesh. The pain tore through the enchantment that held him and he squirmed as the creature lifted him into the air. The creature's claws pulsed within him and several tiny objects squeezed through its claw tips into his muscles.

A dozen chattering voices inside erupted inside his head. They spoke no language that Tone understood and their babble hammered away at him. He knew they were not his own thoughts, but their presence inside his mind sent his own thoughts astray, scattered them so that he could barely hold two words together in his mind. He knew he was on the floor, screaming, but the chattering kept him from focusing upon that. After what seemed like hours, the voices began to converge, to form a chorus of unintelligible but comforting whispers. Then he understood them and their thoughts were his own.

It was simple, really. He just needed to do what he had been sent here to do. The creature would help him dismantle some of the watchtower's weaponry and he would return with it to Cyre. Some of the warforged would have to stay behind—they would have to care for the first expedition. After all, if the fleshborn stopped dreaming, it would be more difficult for the creature to communicate with Dal Quor. But he knew that Spear had already seen to that. Spear had seen the reason of all this long before Tone. Of course, it would be best if Spear were to have his docent implanted beneath his armor's plates. It would be safer there . . .

He had the faintest nagging thought that the weapons from the watchtower might be too dangerous, that they had been used to assault an entire plane of existence. He ignored it. After all, how could a weapon be too dangerous? These had brought Dal Quor to its knees—surely they could insure Cyre's victory over its much weaker rivals.

IAN BURTON-OAKES

ABOUT THE AUTHOR

Ian Burton-Oakes lives in the wilds of Chapel Hill, North Carolina. When not thinking deep thoughts about important philosophical matters, he enjoys watching the mad capering of his local deer and squirrel population. He lives with his charming wife (and occasional editor), Kimberly, and two cats, the dowager Pyewacket and the kitten Wick. In his extra spare time, he secretly plots the demise of a noble band of adventurers . . . oops—I mean, carefully prepares lively and intriguing challenges for his favorite gaming group.

CALL OF THE SILVER FLAME

James Wyatt

I

"Bring the light closer, Kavarat," Mudren Fain hissed, the sound echoing in the tiny chamber. He waved a slender hand absently behind him without taking his eyes off the stone door ahead. His other hand held a crumbling piece of vellum, bearing the faint lines of the ancient map that had led them this far. Only a small metal cap covered his balding head, and stringy black hair trailed down his back. A sleeveless black robe over his chainmail marked his status as a priest of the Blood of Vol and thus, technically, Krael's superior in the Order of the Emerald Claw.

Krael Kavarat rankled at every command, for Mudren Fain was not his superior in any other sense. Nevertheless, armor clanking softly, he held the lantern over the priest's shoulder so its clear, magical light could better illuminate the ancient marble. His head was ducked to avoid scraping his helmet along the dusty tunnel's low ceiling. Long blond hair fell over his shoulders from under the edge of his helm. His body was massive—tall and hugely muscular, even his plate armor seeming almost too small for him.

As he thrust the lantern forward, he glanced over his shoulder at Maija Olarin, who seemed to gather the darkness around her like a warm shawl. Her eyes caught the light and reflected it with the merest hint of red. Shifting impatiently, she smoothed her midnight-blue robe. There had been a time when Krael would have watched her hands glide over the smooth velvet and admired her shapely body, but that time was long past.

Krael turned his attention back to the door, where Mudren was tracing his bony fingers over the carved marble. A slow trickle of dust dropped silently to the floor as his pointed fingernail dislodged it from the letters inscribed in the door's surface. He shook his head impatiently as the priest, with fastidious care, traced each letter until the words stood out in the light.

His voice a soft hiss, Mudren read the words aloud. "Varawn Kell." Then he exclaimed, "Varawn Kell! This is it! This is the place. His old name is here. This is Havoc's crypt!" His voice echoed along the corridor like the barking laughter of hyenas, and Krael's hand dropped to the handle of the massive flail at his belt.

"Hold your tongue, you idiot!" Krael snarled quietly, looking up and down the corridor.

"You have done well in leading us here, Mudren Fain." Maija's voice was low and soft, like the languid growl of a tiger. "The door holds no magical traps. Open it and let us see whether Havoc lies here still."

"And whether the Tablet of Shummarak is inside," Krael

muttered. As he spoke, Mudren began shoving at the door. It refused to move.

"Put your shoulder to this door, Kavarat. I can't budge it." Mudren's voice had changed from a squeal of triumph to a grating whine.

"Of course you can't, little man. Step aside." Handing the lantern to the priest, Krael stepped up to the door while Mudren squeezed behind him. Planting his feet solidly on the floor, he thrust his armored shoulder against the door and smashed it open. Dust swirled into the air, giving shape to the rays of light coming from the lantern behind him.

The crypt was spacious compared to the passage outside, with plenty of room for Maija and Mudren to file in past Krael's bulk. In the center of the room, silver gleamed in arcane symbols engraved in a ring around the edge of a round dais. Upon the dais stood a sarcophagus, its lid carved in the likeness of a bestial warrior, a shifter, clad in heavy armor not unlike the suit that Krael wore. The high ceiling above the sarcophagus mirrored the tracings on the dais in an ornate circular pattern. The air was choked with dust and there was no sign of life in the room—none of the cobwebs that filled other passages in this complex, no trace of rats scrabbling in the corners.

The three stood in silence near the door for a moment. Krael eased his flail out of his belt as if he expected an attack at any moment. Mudren rocked back and forth where he stood, his eyes closed as he hissed the words of a prayer. "The Blood flows, the Blood gives life. The Blood is life, even in the grave. The Blood flows, the Blood gives life . . ." Krael dearly wished he could bury his flail in the priest's skull. And why not? Mudren had brought them to the crypt, they didn't need him any more. And Maija would certainly never report his betrayal.

Maija caught his eye, jerking her head toward a stone chest in the far corner of the room before she moved to examine it. Krael followed and stood behind her, hefting his flail in both hands. The chest's lid bore the same tracery as the dais.

"This chest was warded," Maija whispered, moving her fingers along the tracings as she looked up at Krael. "But the magic is gone. It's safe to open." She stood and stepped back to give Krael access to the heavy lid. When Krael hesitated, she continued, "It's just the right size. I'm sure it was made to hold the Tablet. This is what we have sought for nearly a year." For the first time, she allowed a trace of excitement into her voice.

"If it's safe, why don't you open it, dear Maija?" Krael said.

Maija tried to hide a mocking smile and stepped to the chest again, bending down and reaching for the lid. She stopped and spun on her heels, however, as the sound of stone grinding on stone filled the room. Krael turned to see the lid of the sarcophagus crash to the ground near them, Mudren panting from his exertion on the far side. The priest gazed raptly at the contents of the sarcophagus, still rocking back and forth as he muttered to himself, "The Blood is life, even in the grave."

Krael's height afforded him a view into the sarcophagus even without standing on the dais. The body of Varawn Kell was little more than dust strewn around a collection of brown bones. A shifter's sharp teeth were visible on the skull, but the other bones lay tangled, no sinew remaining to knit them together. In the midst of the jumble of ribs, however, stood a wooden stake, its tip piercing a shriveled black lump that must once have been a heart.

Mudren's hands now clenched the edge of the sarcophagus.

"Great Havoc," he mumbled, "mighty Havoc, so unworthily slain. A single stake, just a single stake pinning you to the dust."

Mudren reached a trembling hand into the sarcophagus as Maija stepped onto the dais across from him. Krael stood bewildered, his eyes flicking between his two companions and the vampire's corpse.

"Not yet!" Maija roared, but too late.

The priest's hand had already gripped the stake, and he wrenched it free with a strangled cry, "The Blood!"

The dust that still eddied in the air swirled inside the sarcophagus, as if drawn in by a deep breath. Mudren redoubled his prayers, bowing and rocking before the vampire's coffin, eyes tightly shut in reverence. Maija and Krael, however, watched as the dust writhed around the bones, surrounding them with the hint of a corporeal form. As more dust collected, it seemed to congeal around the bones, lifting them into their proper places and knitting them together with a dreadful rattling. Krael stepped to Mudren, reaching a hand toward the stake he held clenched to his own breast.

Maija gripped his arm and murmured, "Wait."

"Wait?" Krael yelled at her, wrenching his arm from her grasp. "While Havoc returns from the grave? He's been lying in his crypt since before the Last War, Maija. He's going to wake up hungry."

The dust had now congealed into muscle and sinew, and leathery skin was spreading over the grisly form. Eyes rolled in half-formed sockets, darting from Mudren to Krael and Maija and back, and a mane of hair started growing from the scalp.

Maija sighed. "You should have known it would come to this, Krael."

She spoke a swift word and gestured toward her companion.

He realized too late what she was doing and started to swing his flail at her in return, but he froze in mid-swing, his body rigid, his eyes wide with horror.

"After all, you saw me discard my beloved Janik when he was no longer useful. Did you believe I'd allow you to interfere with my plans?"

She stepped back off the dais, away from the now-intact but still desiccated vampire. Only then did Mudren Fain open his eyes, still murmuring his fervent prayers.

Krael could not move his eyes, but he was perfectly positioned to see Havoc sit up with preternatural speed and shoot a clawed hand out to grab Mudren Fain by the neck. The priest's eyes bulged, but he croaked, "Yes! Take me! Devour me!"

Maija slowly circled out of Krael's view, as Havoc yanked Mudren off his feet and pulled him in to feed. Krael could hear her behind him, her breathing heavy with—was it terror? Or excitement? Given what he had seen of Maija recently, he guessed it was the latter.

The vampire's withered flesh took on the semblance of life as the last color drained from Mudren's face and the priest gasped his final prayer, "The Blood flows. . . ."

Havoc's forearms and calves sprouted long hair, and a black mane now tumbled over his shoulders. He stood, casting aside Mudren's husk, and faced Maija and Krael. His bestial face was contorted in a snarl, and he made no effort to wipe the blood from around his mouth. He crouched in the sarcophagus, as if ready to pounce.

"Mighty Havoc," Maija purred, "I bring you these gifts to renew your strength and to serve you in undeath if you will have them."

The vampire's snarl melted into a cruel grin. Krael's heart beat faster. Gifts? Undeath?

"That one is weak," Havoc growled, waving a clawed hand at Mudren's pallid corpse, "and his blood is thin. Let him die. This one . . .." He turned his gaze to Krael. "He will serve me well. You would make a fine minion as well, but I assume your proposal requires keeping your life and your will. What bargain would you make?"

Maija stepped in front of Krael, and he could see that she was smiling. "I have need of this vessel for a while longer, Havoc. Perhaps when I no longer have use of it, you may add it to your collection"

The vampire's eyes narrowed as he tried to discern her meaning.

"For the moment, you had best take this oaf now. His will is strong, and he might break free of my enchantment. When you have finished, let us discuss what we shall do together."

Havoc stared at Maija for a moment, his nose twitching as if he sought to read her thoughts in her scent. Apparently satisfied, he looked back at Krael, whose face dripped with sweat as his mind struggled to regain control over his body. He smiled again and pounced at Krael, knocking him down and bending to feed amid the echoes of Krael's heavy armor crashing to the floor.

Krael wanted to fight, to push the vampire off of him, or even to shout, but he could not move. He felt the blood spurting from his neck and was reminded of Mudren's prayer—"The Blood flows, the Blood gives life." The words circled through his mind along with the rhythm of his heart, pounding in his ears. Then he could not hear his heart beat any more, and the words rang in his mind once more—"the Blood gives life"—and then all was silent and still and black.

2

Dania's eyes surveyed the grisly scene as she stood near the door. Compared to the carnage she had witnessed during the Last War, this wasn't much. Churning Chaos, she thought, compared to the carnage I left in my wake once or twice, this is nothing. Not for the first time, she had the powerful sense that for her to hunt a killer through the streets of Atur was the height of hypocrisy—she was as vile a killer as this vampire they were tracking. Only the fact that she had done it in the name of the king of Breland kept her from being a criminal. The excuse of war covered a multitude of evils.

Her companions were already moving around the small house. Kophran ir'Davik shuffled around with his hands on his enormous belly, looking down his nose at the bodies sprawled on the floor, his obvious disgust mingled with morbid fascination. An exorcist of the Silver Flame, he was always reluctant to dirty his polished armor by getting too close to an investigation. Dania didn't know what he had done during the war, but she was quite sure that he had been far from the front lines—probably as far as one could be in Thrane, hedged in by enemies on all sides.

Gered d'Deneith knelt down to examine a body carefully. The intricate pattern of the Mark of Sentinel spread from his left cheek down his neck to disappear beneath his mithral shirt. In contrast to Kophran, he was slender and his face had a boyish look to it, despite streaks of gray in his sandy brown hair. He held a slender staff that seemed more of a badge of office than a weapon, but Dania had seen him swing it in self-defense more than once. He, too, had been relatively sheltered from the war, he had told Dania, working security for House Deneith. He had spoken of a time when agents of the Order of the Emerald Claw had broken into his family's enclave in Atur. It was hardly open warfare, but his tale had earned Dania's respect.

Dania remained near the door. Her own plate mail was both well worn and well cared for—not brightly polished like Kophran's, but clean enough, for all its dents. Her helmet covered her red hair, though a few strands fell over her gray eyes. She took it all in from where she stood: the blood on the walls and even on the low ceiling, the bodies on the floor and on the one bed, in a corner behind a curtain that had been torn to shreds. She kept a hand on her sword hilt where it hung at her belt, her attention focused for any sign of an impending attack. The others could handle their investigation; they would not need her until they found the killer they hunted—or he found them.

Kophran intoned the words of a spell, his voice low and ponderous—his praying voice, as Dania thought of it. "I can still sense the vampire's evil here," he pronounced. "Its evil is great indeed, and it has only recently left."

Dania scoffed. "You can practically smell its footprints, Kophran."

The exorcist swung his fiery gaze toward her. "You will not use that tone with me, Dania. One would have thought your nose was quite insensitive to evil's presence by now. Or is this an example of the elven senses from your mother's side?" His gaze lingered on her for a moment more, and Dania found herself wondering if his spell was still in effect, if he was checking to make sure no taint of evil had infected her yet. He nodded curtly, his jowls wagging slightly, and he strode across the room, away from her.

"Gered, what is this abomination?" Kophran asked, pointing to an altar in the corner, opposite the bed.

Gered looked up from where he knelt. "A household altar, Your Grace. For the rites of the Blood of Vol." His grim face seemed braced for what he knew was coming.

"As I suspected. Offering worship to the undead! Clearly these blasphemers brought this grisly end on themselves."

Gered looked exasperated but said, "No doubt, Your Grace. Always evil feeds on its own."

Anger surged in Dania's chest. "Except when it feeds on the blood of innocents!" she blurted out, far louder than she had intended.

"You call these innocents?" Kophran said.

"Their only crime was not following your damned ideology!" Dania said, fighting back a sudden rush of tears. "You think everyone who ends up lying in a pool of blood like this brought it on themselves?"

"Death rarely comes with a capricious hand."

"Innocent people die all the time! How many people died in the Last War? What crime did they commit? How many died at the end of my own sword? Was I some avenging angel of justice, bringing death only to those who richly deserved it? I killed on orders, damn it. I killed to stay alive. Don't you preach to me about blasphemers deserving the death that finds them, Kophran. If anyone deserves to lie slaughtered and forgotten on the floor, I certainly do." Dania realized with surprise that she had drawn her sword during that outburst, and sheathed it hastily under Kophran's withering glare.

"Dania ir'Vran," he intoned, his lips curling around her name, "I should not need to remind you that you are here only because of the good will I still feel toward your father, bless his memory. Do not cause me to regret this act of kindness any more than I already do, and thereby taint my fondness for him. If, as I do not doubt, you deserve the same fate as these infidels, then perhaps the Silver Flame has brought you to me to do penance for your sins. I am certain that the Flame intends the experience as penance for my own misdeeds, few as they are."

"Your Grace," Gered interrupted, but Kophran continued glaring at Dania, his corpulent flesh quivering in his fury.

Dania glared right back, biting back the retorts that kept surging into her mind, chastened by the mention of her father and unwilling to escalate the argument any further.

"Your Grace," Gered repeated, and Kophran slowly turned to him. "I have found some things that might be of interest."

"Yes, what, Gered?" the exorcist snapped.

"I find two sets of footprints," Gered said, a little hesitant in the face of Kophran's rage, gesturing toward one of the bloodier areas of the floor. "One might belong to a shifter. The other seems human, I would guess heavily armored. Possibly an orc or half-orc—large from the look of things." He waited for some response from Kophran, but received none. "This body," he continued, pointing toward the bed in the corner, "is not mutilated like the others. In fact, the only wound is in the wrist, where it seems something bit through the veins."

"Bit? The wrist?" Kophran said. "The vampire?"

"I would venture to say that the shifter vampire was responsible for most of this carnage. The other one probably fed from this wrist. I would guess he was a spawn of the shifter, since he does not seem to have been allowed as much . . . to eat."

"Well, then." Kophran wiped his spotless hands on his robe, signaling that the investigation was over. "We are hunting a shifter vampire and his spawn. We have learned something about our quarry, then. I suggest we catch a few hours of sleep and resume our investigation in the evening."

"There is one more thing, Your Grace," Gered said.

"Yes?"

Gered pointed at a window above the altar, where part of one red-brown footprint stained the white linen. "They went that way."

Kophran shuffled to the window and peered out, turning his head to look both ways down the alley outside. "I suppose you had better check it out, Gered," he said, pulling his head back inside.

"Yes, Your Grace," Gered said, hurrying to the window and looking out. "No obvious signs," he called back, "but it's foggy tonight. Let me climb out and have a closer look around." He started squeezing through the window, his mithral chainmail scraping against the jamb. "It's a bit tight here."

Dania's sword was out of its sheath again before her mind fully realized why, the steel ringing as it flashed into her hand. "Gered," she hissed, the urgency in her voice making her companion stop halfway out the window and Kophran wheel to face her.

"What's wrong?" Gered was acutely aware of the fact that his position left him exposed to danger.

Dania had her back to the window now, the point of her sword covering the room as her eyes searched for any hint of the threat she suspected. "How did the big vampire in heavy armor get out that small window?"

Gered let out a heavy sigh and squeezed himself the rest of the way into the alley. "Relax, Dania. You and Kophran would have smelled him if he was still around. He probably turned to mist to follow the shifter out the window."

Dania slid her sword back into its sheath and looked out the window. "Turned to mist?"

"Vampires have the ability to turn their bodies into clouds of mist or smoke. It happens whenever they're dealt a blow that would destroy their bodies, though they can also do it at will.

In fact, I've done it myself. I've got the spell in one of my books at home."

"Do you see any sign of their passage?" Kophran asked impatiently.

Dania could see the weariness on his face, and felt it acutely enough herself. They had been awake since dawn, when Kophran had brought news of a suspected vampire attack, and already the fog draping the streets was beginning to brighten with the approach of another morning.

"I think I might," Gered said. "Down here to the left."

Kophran sighed mightily. "Dania, help Gered in the alley. I will circle around the block and look for any sign of them on the main road."

Dania turned to the window, rolling her eyes. She knew Kophran didn't like tight spaces, but she also suspected that he would take his sweet time catching up with them. He'd probably duck into a tavern to warm up for a few minutes.

She was also not excited at the thought of being alone with Gered, uneasy about what the Sentinel Marshal might say to her without Kophran around. At the same time, she welcomed the opportunity to be away from the self-righteous exorcist for a time. As Kophran shuffled out the door, leaving it open behind him, Dania squeezed through the window and dropped to the dry earth of the alley below.

3

A shy smile on his face, Gered extended a hand as if to steady her, but Dania ignored it. "So can you still smell its footprints?" he asked.

"I think we're better off relying on your eyes than my nose, Gered," Dania replied, not returning his smile. "What did you see?"

"This way." Gered walked to the left, leading Dania behind a row of dark brick houses indistinguishable from the one they had just searched, to an alley branching off to the right. "Let's see . . . this here"—he pointed to the building just before the alley—"must be the back of Feirgyn's. You know, that place—"

"Where we had that horrible sausage thing the other night, yes." Dania grimaced, but her eyes still searched the alley for any trace of the vampires.

"Right. Now look here." Gered moved to the corner of the restaurant and pointed at some markings about shoulder-height. Dania checked around the corner, peering into the fog and shadows along the long alleyway before turning her attention to what Gered was examining.

Four long scratches revealed light stone under a coating of grime. They ran horizontally and bent around the corner. "Claw marks," Gered announced. "Quite recent. A pretty clear indication that the shifter turned this corner."

"And made his way out to the street, no doubt," Dania replied. "Then what?"

"Only one way to find out." Gered grinned at his companion as he started moving toward the street. Dania followed wordlessly.

Gered took a deep breath. "Dania," he said over his shoulder, his face now serious, "you don't like me very much, do you?"

Dania stopped, still fifteen feet from where the alley opened onto the street, and gave a small sigh. "Gered, this is not the time for this conversation."

Gered faced her again. "But—"

"I know, you've been holding it in for weeks, and this is the first time Kophran's left us alone. But we're in a dark alley hunting a vampire. Keep your mind on your quarry, not on my ass."

Gered flushed and turned away. Without another word, he moved to the end of the alley and looked up and down the fog-choked street. Dania stayed in the alley's shadows a moment, staring at his back as he surveyed the people staggering along the street in clusters of three or four. She had grown accustomed to the strange pace of life in the City of Night, where at least half the population seemed nocturnal.

Despite the way she had just reprimanded Gered, she found her mind straying far from their vampire quarry. She regretted her harsh tone with Gered. He was kind and handsome, he had a good heart, and if a great many things had been different, she might have been able to hear what he wanted to say to her. As things were, though, there was only one man she had ever loved—her best friend, Janik Martell—and he had taken her love and trampled it.

It hadn't been too bad, all the years that she and Janik had adventured together in the wilds of Xen'drik. He and Maija had been inseparable, and there had simply never been any question of acting on her feelings for him. It wasn't until Maija had betrayed them and left that Janik had given himself to Dania, taken comfort in her arms. She let herself believe that his grief was something more, that they could have some kind of future together. But when they returned to Sharn, he simply disappeared, and she had not seen him since. It had been two years.

A noise snapped Dania out of her thoughts. Her sword was in her hand again in an instant.

Gered looked back. "See something?"

Dania put a finger to her lips to silence him, then moved it to one slightly pointed ear, even as her eyes searched the alley and the rooftops above. Gered stood like a statue, trusting Dania's keener senses. No further sound reached her ears, however, and she could see no danger, so she cautiously moved to rejoin Gered at the edge of the street.

"I thought I heard something," she said in a low voice, "maybe a clank of armor. But it was probably just a rat."

"You would have heard a rat again."

"I would have heard a man in armor a lot more clearly. It must have been my mind playing tricks on me, or else someone passing by on the street."

"Fair enough. So turn your elven senses to that alley across the way."

Dania bristled at this echo of Kophran's words earlier in the evening, but peered into the shadows across the street, following Gered's pointing finger. "Why? What do you see?" she whispered.

"Nothing at all. But I see no clues on the street either. I figured you might see something in the alley I can't."

"Well, I do think there's someone there, probably a sleeping drunkard."

"In Atur? I thought they turned drunkards into zombies here."

"Good point. Let's check it out."

Dania adjusted her grip on her sword as Gered fingered his spell components, and the pair cautiously crossed the street, eyes and ears alert for any sign of a threat. As they stepped into the alley's entrance, Gered produced a candle, glowing softly with magical light, and held it into the shadows. The body Dania had spotted came into view—first the feet, then, as Gered took a few cautious steps farther into the alley, the splayed legs, sunken torso, arms askew, and finally the head perched atop a neck savaged by hungry fangs.

Dania muttered a string of soldier's curses that made Gered turn his shocked gaze on her briefly, before he began searching the area for clues. "Damn it, Gered, we've got to find these vampires. Point me to them—my sword is itching for justice."

"Justice? I didn't think you believed in that any more, Dania." He knelt beside the corpse, looking for tracks on the packed earth around it.

Dania sighed, trying to attach words to her jumbled thoughts and feelings as she stared blankly at the mangled body. "You know, the war—a hundred years of fighting, any idiot could see by the end that the whole thing was pointless. Maybe at the start people thought there was a right side and a wrong side to their squabbles, but eventually you just can't tell the difference any more. And so you go into battle at some fat general's command, someone like Kophran but less piously self-righteous, and you wade in and kill the other side's soldiers because that's your job."

Dania turned away, trying to hold in the flood of her emotions. She felt Gered's eyes on her, his surprise at this uncharacteristic display, and she didn't want to expose herself to him. But her words poured out anyway, carried on waves of outrage and anger she could no longer contain.

"Of course there's no justice in a war like that. People . . . there's no justice among people at all. Everyone will shift sides if they've got a good enough reason. But this—this is different. This isn't people playing their war games. This is—this is a monster, feeding on some innocent person who was in the wrong place when the vampires crossed the street. It's like— damn it, no, Kophran—my nose isn't numb to the scent of evil, because all these years I've just been hip-deep in human . . .

stupidity is all. Evil is different. This is evil, this stupid human killed and eaten for no reason at all, and the stink—the stink of the monster that did it!"

Gered made no effort to conceal the amazement on his face as he got to his feet and stared at Dania. In that moment of silence, a hulking figure stepped into the entrance of the alley, a malevolent smile visible below the half-faced helm that identified an officer in the Order of the Emerald Claw.

His voice was warm and smooth. "What a touching reflection on the state of the world . . . Dania."

4

Fury gripped Dania as she recognized the man. "Krael Kavarat," she growled, raising the tip of her sword from the ground. "Speaking of human stupidity. What are you doing here?"

"So nice to see you again after so long, Dania," Krael said warmly, ignoring her question. He reached up with both hands and removed his helmet, his long blond hair cascading down over his shoulders. "And where is our dear friend Janik? I gather you two were much thrown together on your return trip from Mel-Aqat. No longer keeping his company? Did he leave you so he could search for his Maija?" He sneered as he said the name, and the tip of Dania's sword bounced as her hand gripped the hilt more tightly.

The two stood, their eyes locked, for a moment. Dania's jaw was set, her face flushed in anger. Krael still sneered as he measured the reaction his words had provoked. Apparently satisfied, he turned his eyes to Gered.

"Aren't you going to introduce me to your new friend?"

The wizard looked at Dania for a moment, but she gave no indication that she had heard Krael.

"I'm Gered d'Deneith, Sentinel Marshal of House Deneith," he said, stepping forward to stand behind Dania's right shoulder.

"Oh, a Sentinel Marshal?" Krael's voice was mocking, and Gered flushed crimson. "Climbing the social ladder, are you, Dania? Still, I think this one lacks Janik's spirit."

As Krael stepped closer, Dania lifted her sword until its point was level with his neck. He took another step, and her sword point made a tiny dimple in his throat. She never took her eyes off his.

"Much has changed since we were at Mel-Aqat, Dania." His voice was a faint whisper.

"Don't even say my name, you bastard," Dania spat, her sword pressing harder against his neck. "What did you do to Maija to make her betray us like that?"

"What did *I* do to *her*? Better to ask what the witch did to me. I always thought Janik was quite interesting—and you as well, of course. But Maija always struck me as rather boring and predictable. I never dreamed her capable of the things she's done."

"What she's done to *you*?" Dania's gaze was unwavering. "Did she turn on you as well? Still, she left you alive. Pity."

Krael grinned broadly, showing his white teeth. "Technically, my dear, that's not true."

Behind her, Dania heard Gered's strangled gasp, "Vampire!"

"Yes," Krael hissed. His eyes flashed red, and Dania gasped as she felt herself swimming in his gaze. He was in her mind, and she heard his voice as if his mouth were just behind her ear. "I am the vampire you sought, thanks to our dear friend

Maija—and Havoc, her new shifter ally. But now you belong to me."

Dania tried to drive her sword into his neck, she tried to open her mouth to shout, she tried to force Krael out of her mind, but she could do nothing. All her resolve seemed to melt under his stare, and she found—even as her mind protested—that she could only obey him. At his mental command, she lowered her sword, and he bared his fangs in a wide grin.

Dania saw Gered step back and heard him start shouting a spell. Under Krael's compulsion, Dania felt as though she were watching helplessly as she turned and swept her sword out to slash through her friend's mail, biting into his arm. The spell died on his lips, and Krael stepped forward. Dania's stomach tightened as she watched Gered crumple around Krael's fists. He grew paler with each blow, as if the vampire were knocking more than the wind out of him.

Gered staggered backward, but Dania stepped after him, keeping her sword trained on him even as she fought to wrest herself from the vampire's control. Dodging her blade, Gered managed a simple gesture and sent two glowing bolts tearing into Krael. The vampire only grinned more broadly, and Dania could see why—such a feeble spell was evidence of Gered's weakness and desperation. Krael's small wounds closed in seconds.

"As I said, Dania, he lacks spirit." Krael walked around Gered, trapping the wizard between them. Grabbing Gered's shoulder, he drew the wizard into his arms, squeezing him in a bear hug that forced the air out of his lungs. Gered stared pleadingly at Dania, wordlessly begging her to help, but she could not focus her eyes on his. She felt like a puppet set aside, limp, and her sword tip drooped to the ground. Numbly, she watched Krael open his mouth wide and bend his head to the struggling wizard's neck. She heard Gered gasp as the fangs pierced his skin, and saw the blood begin to flow.

Dania felt as though the fangs had pierced her own heart. All the injustice she had just so vehemently protested was happening again, right before her eyes. Another stupid human was about to die, to be killed and eaten by this monster. Only this time it was her fault. She could have prevented this, she should have known that Krael was the vampire as soon as she saw him—the reek of evil was so strong about him now. But she allowed herself to get so caught up in her emotions, her fury about Maija's treachery at Mel-Aqat had blinded her. And she should be able to stop him now, a single swing of her sword would make Krael drop Gered and give her his undivided attention. In her mind, she was springing forward into combat as she had done so many times before. But she could not move.

Gered was chalk-white, his struggles against Krael's iron grip growing weaker. His eyes still pleaded with her, as if willing her to break the vampire's spell and come to his aid, but they had no strength left to loan her. Dania wanted to howl with rage and grief, and her inability even to show any sign of her pain as her companion died compounded her fury.

"Monster!" a voice boomed. "By the power of the Silver Flame, unhand that man!"

Brilliant light poured into the alley, enfolding and infusing Dania, Gered, Krael, the nearby corpse. Dania blinked in the sudden radiance, staring dumbly into her own shadow. Holy power coursed like fire along the rays of light. It spread a comfortable warmth through her body, but she saw—and felt, in her mind—Krael recoil from its touch. Slowly, marveling at her ability to move of her own will, she turned to gaze into the source of the light. Behind her, she heard Gered fall heavily to the ground and Krael snarl like a beast.

A heavy figure stood in shadow behind an incandescent symbol of the Silver Flame. A heartbeat passed before recognition flooded into Dania's mind—it was Kophran! Even as she realized his identity, she became aware that Krael was no longer at her back, heard his catlike movements fading down the alley. Kophran lowered his holy symbol and the light slowly faded. Barely giving Dania a glance, the exorcist pushed past her to crouch beside Gered.

Dania closed her eyes and stood still. Echoes of fire, soft as velvet, washed over her, tingling in her neck, her shoulders and back, down her limbs. She savored the feeling, the last breaths of the power that had driven the vampire away—a power of incredible purity and warmth. She heard Kophran praying over Gered for what seemed like a very long time and wondered vaguely whether her companion were dead, but in that moment she could feel no grief. A knot of guilt and shame she had never fully recognized, woven from memories of the Last War and all she had done to survive it, melted away in the fire. She was still aware of Krael's distant presence in her mind, his anger polluting her, and she knew that his influence over her was not broken. But again she could not be distressed in the warmth of the argent light that had suffused her. For long seconds after the sensation passed, she kept her eyes closed, hoping to reclaim it.

5

"What in Khyber kept you, Krael?" Maija's voice was a low growl, though her languid posture showed none of her impatience. She was draped over a rich brocade couch, a goblet of wine held lazily in her fingers. Havoc paced the Aereni rug like a caged lion.

"We were being followed," Krael responded, not looking directly at either Maija or Havoc. His vampiric sire knew all that had happened, he was sure. But after his humiliation at the hands of the exorcist, Krael was hardly eager to talk about it. "I lingered to throw them off the trail."

"Play with your food, more like," Havoc retorted, though not without some degree of pride in his offspring.

Maija drained her goblet and tossed it absently aside.

"Come!" she commanded, and she was off the couch in the blink of an eye, glaring impatiently at the two vampires as Krael started settling his body into a plush chair. "The Tablet awaits us!"

"It's nearly dawn," Krael said, sinking into the chair.

"Thanks to your tarrying," Maija said. "So we have no time to lose. If we make it to the mausoleum before the sun rises, we'll be fine underground."

"That's not a risk I'm willing to take, Maija," Havoc said. "What if we get there and find we can't get underground? Then Krael and I are trapped in the sunlight."

"Havoc's right," Krael said. "The priest in that little house said the mausoleum was in a part of the city badly damaged during the war."

"But he also said the priests of the Blood still use that entrance to reach the shrine of the Nightclaw," Maija reminded them. "The way should be clear. And if we delay, then whoever is following us has that much more time to catch up."

Havoc bared his teeth in a grimace. "No. Look"—he pointed out the window—"the sun is already brightening the fog. We'll go once the sun has set again. Krael has given them a scare. They won't come after us right away. We'll be safe until nightfall."

"One of them is nearly dead," Krael said. "They will delay in order to care for him."

"Only nearly dead?" Havoc sounded disappointed, but Krael looked away.

Maija scowled and sank back onto the couch. "I have waited so long already."

"Then another day won't matter," Krael said.

"Another day could mean the difference between triumph and defeat," Maija snarled. "If we fail, I promise I'll kill you both."

"Oh, be quiet and let us sleep," Havoc yawned.

6

All the guilt and anger that had fled in the holy radiance had flooded back to Dania in the alley as soon as she had opened her eyes. Gered's barely living body, blood still oozing from the terrible wound in his neck, and Kophran crouching urgently over him, casting spell after weary spell to channel healing power into the dying wizard—these sights had overwhelmed her in that instant. Then she had turned away and vomited until her stomach had ached almost as much as her heart.

Now they were back in the outer room of Kophran's suite in the inn. Most of Gered's strength had returned, but he barely uttered a word from his place on the couch, and he frequently closed his eyes as Dania and Kophran spoke. Kophran sat in state on a sumptuous chair as Dania paced restlessly around the room, looking at Gered as little as possible.

"It was a trap," Dania spat. "He wanted us to follow him, and he made his trail as clear as he dared."

"That seems clear," Kophran said, his hands clasped under his chin. "Dania, I need to know more about this Krael Kavarat. What can you tell me?"

"Well," Dania began, rubbing her temples with her palms, "he's a captain in the Order of the Emerald Claw—or at least he was when he was alive. After my time in the army during the Last War, I continued my service to Breland by hunting artifacts in Xen'drik. I worked with Janik Martell, a professor at Morgrave University."

She hadn't spoken Janik's name in a long time, and it felt strange on her tongue. His face came unbidden into her mind, and a faint memory of the smell of him when he held her close to his body. She pushed those thoughts aside.

"Krael was working in Xen'drik as well, for Karrnath, of course—to help their cause in the war. Every time we heard rumors of mysterious ruins or powerful artifacts, it seemed like Krael either showed up while we were there or got there before us—it was an unending race to find some ancient magic or lore. He and Janik had a fierce rivalry going on—almost as if each of them needed the other to keep motivated."

Kophran leaned forward in his chair, but Gered cut him off. "But he wasn't a vampire then, right? He said something about a witch who betrayed him."

Dania sighed and walked to the window, looking down into the pitch dark alley below. "The last time I saw Krael was at the site of an ancient ruin in Xen'drik called Mel-Aqat. It's the discovery that made Janik famous, ironically enough—a place that was often mentioned in ancient records but had never before been located. We actually beat Krael there and managed to emerge with the Ramethene Sword, a powerful holy artifact we hoped Breland might use to turn the tide of the war or even bring it to an end.

"There were four of us: myself, Janik Martell, an elf wizard named Mathas Allister, and Maija." Her voice dropped as she said the name, and she turned back around to face her companions. "Maija Olarin, a cleric of the Sovereign Host. She and Janik had been lovers for years. But when we emerged from Mel-Aqat, Krael was there with a squad of Emerald Claw soldiers. And Maija took the Ramethene Sword from Janik's hand and gave it to Krael."

Kophran arched one eyebrow, while Gered looked horrified. Dania shook her head slowly as she continued. "She broke Janik's heart and betrayed us all . . . as well as Breland, the Sovereign Host, everything I thought she cared about. I can't imagine what made her do it. I haven't seen her since."

Dania was silent a moment, lost in her memories of Maija's treachery and the long journey back to Sharn. It had been a long journey, but its duration defined the span of her affair with Janik—and that seemed very short indeed. She said nothing to Kophran and Gered about that journey, but her eyes stung.

She blinked hard and finished her tale. "Anyway, Krael seemed to indicate that Maija turned on him as well, and he attributed his transformation into a vampire to her—oh, and he mentioned a shifter, Havoc. I assume that's the name of the shifter vampire we've been hunting."

"It seems like a fitting name," Gered said with a weak smile.

"And it gives us something to work with," Kophran said, heaving himself to his feet and walking over to one of the doors. Pushing the door open, he turned to the others. "Dania, will you join me in the study here? I am eager to learn more about this Havoc."

Dania stood, lingering for a moment beside the couch where Gered lay. His head was resting on the arm of the couch and his eyes were closed, and he didn't open them as Dania moved past him to join Kophran.

"Let him rest, Dania," Kophran whispered. "He needs it, and the Flame knows he has earned it." The exorcist already had a weighty tome in his hands, and he didn't look up as he spoke. "Will you check that red book there?" He gestured at a crowded shelf.

Dania pulled a thick book bound in red leather from the shelf and opened it at random to an esoteric and exceptionally dry discussion of the establishment of lightning rail lines across Karrnath.

"What am I looking for?" she asked, her eyes already glazing over.

"Anything about Havoc."

"In here? This book's talking about the lightning rail."

"Then you're looking in the wrong section. Find something about the undead in Karrnath—there ought to be plenty about the role undead have played in this vile nation—or something about shifters, or maybe something about Atur."

"This book must have a thousand pages!"

"I doubt it's that many. Skim."

Suppressing a strong desire to throw the tome at Kophran, Dania flipped a few pages. "What makes you think we're going to find anything about Havoc in a history book?"

Kophran looked up from his book, a look of intense frustration on his face. "Two simple facts," he said. "One, vampires tend to shape history around them, even if most historians are too blind to see their influence. That is particularly true in Karrnath. And two, you have described this Krael Kavarat as a finder of lost artifacts. That suggests he might have encountered Havoc while searching for some artifact here in Karrnath. Or he might have sought out Havoc to get his help in finding something else." He turned his attention back to his book. "So read."

Grudgingly, Dania admitted to herself that Kophran had a point, and she started reading the book in earnest. A sense of purpose didn't make the book any more interesting, however, and she looked up frequently to peer through the door at Gered, who was snoring softly in the outer room. She found herself wishing she were asleep as well—the sun was climbing toward its zenith by this time, and she had not slept since the dawn of the previous day.

"Oh, here's something," Kophran said after some time.

"What?" Dania said, jerking her head up. She hadn't realized she had fallen asleep. Kophran kept reading, ignoring her question. "What did you find?" she repeated, setting her book aside.

"The exorcist Faeran ir'Whigar, in his memoir, relates a legend from this city. As one would expect from a place where the Blood of Vol has erected one of the most important centers of its blasphemous worship, the undead have haunted Atur for centuries. The legend he relates predates the Last War, so it was quite old even when he wrote his text some forty years ago. But it does describe a particularly depraved and vile shifter vampire called Havoc—a nickname, as I'm sure you can imagine, derived from his propensity for brutal violence."

"That would seem to fit," Dania interjected, thinking of the corpses strewn around the small house the night before.

"Well," Kophran continued, "it seems likely to me that any shifter vampire would demonstrate an extreme degree of brutality simply by virtue of its ancestry, so that alone is no guarantee that we are dealing with the same Havoc. According to ir'Whigar's text, you see, this Havoc was destroyed before the start of the Last War. It was some ordinary adventurer that boasted of the deed," he added with a sneer in Dania's direction, "so one can not be certain of the story's veracity. But even so, he does not record any further reports of Havoc's activity."

Dania began to pace. She felt she could think better when she was moving, and it helped her keep her anger at Kophran's patronizing comments in check.

"That said," Kophran continued, "vampires are difficult to destroy with finality, even with proper knowledge, and his return to unlife is not at all beyond the realm of possibility. The evidence we witnessed last night squares with ir'Whigar's account."

Dania saw that Gered had awakened and was now leaning against the door jamb, listening intently.

"The key on which our mystery seems to hang," Kophran continued, evidently enjoying the undivided attention of his companions, "is that Havoc is also the last known owner of the Tablet of Shummarak."

Gered gasped at this, but Dania just looked blankly between the two of them.

"What is the Tablet of Shummarak?" she asked, when no explanation seemed forthcoming.

"I am surprised that you do not know," Kophran said, "given your years of experience exploring the ruins of Xen'drik."

Dania flushed with anger, but Gered interrupted just as she was about to speak. "The Tablet—" he coughed, then struggled to finish his sentence, his voice hoarse. "The Tablet is most well-known in our church, and little beyond it."

"Indeed," Kophran said. "I suppose your ignorance may be excused." Dania bit her tongue and waited for the exorcist to continue, though her face was still crimson. "The Tablet of Shummarak is an incredibly ancient record of the Binding of the Demons." He paused, as if waiting for Dania to ask him to explain further. She only bit her tongue harder.

"Sit down, Dania. Your restlessness disturbs me." Dania hesitated. "Sit!" Kophran urged, not yet mustering his most imperious tone but leaving no question that this was a command and not a polite invitation. Dania obeyed.

"Shortly after the creation of the world, Eberron was overrun by demons. The mightiest of these were the lords of the rakshasas, spirits of purest evil, masters of disguise and illusion, wielders of tremendous magic. For a thousand years the dragons made war upon these fiends, trying to break their tyrannical hold on the young world. At last, the allies of the dragons, the angelic serpents called couatls, discovered a means to bind the fiends within the depths of Khyber whence they sprang, sacrificing their own physical forms to trap the fiends within their spiritual coils. With these demon lords imprisoned, the remaining couatls and the dragons were able to drive the lesser fiends into hiding."

Dania interrupted Kophran's sermon. "So the couatls are still holding the demons in Khyber?"

"Indeed," Kophran replied.

"Then they are no less imprisoned than the fiends they constrain?"

"Such is their sacrifice." Kophran drew a deep breath and let it out slowly. "It is said that the Tablet of Shummarak reveals a means by which the spirit bonds of the couatls' coils might be broken, releasing the rakshasa rulers once more upon the earth. My theory is that Krael sought the Tablet on behalf of his Order, wakened Havoc in the course of his search, and lost his soul to the ancient vampire."

Silence descended on the room again. Dania was lost in a whirlwind of thoughts and emotions. The memory of her tirade in the alley, her rage against the vampires' evil, her guilt and shame over her weakness in fighting Krael, and the horrible prospect of demon lords unleashed upon the world—her head spun with helpless fury. She felt as though she were caught up in something larger than the Last War, a crisis of life and light struggling against an overwhelming darkness. She stood up and resumed her pacing, her breathing heavy as her mind groped for any glimpse of light.

Then she remembered the stillness she had felt in the holy light in the alley, and she clung to that memory of peace as if it were a lifeboat in a churning sea. In that moment, a sense of purpose took shape within her, purpose like she had never known during the Last War or in her years of adventuring. She had a sudden sense that all the events in her life so far—from her childhood through the bitter years of the war, right up to Maija's betrayal and her brief affair with Janik—were leading her to this moment and preparing her for it. That sense of purpose shone like a flickering silver fire in the darkness that threatened to engulf her. She drew her sword.

The sound startled Kophran and Gered from their reveries, and they looked at Dania with a mixture of puzzlement and—at least in Kophran's case—a hint of fear.

"By my life, my honor, and whatever is holy in this profane world," Dania whispered, "this sword shall bring an end to this evil."

Kophran's eyebrows shot up in surprise, but Gered smiled gently. "Careful, Dania," he said, "you're beginning to sound like one of our paladins."

"What of it?" Dania replied, returning Gered's smile. "Kophran, how soon can Gered be up and around? We need to find these vampires."

"We need some rest first," Kophran answered. "We'll head out again at nightfall."

7

Maija led the way out the door of the elegant home she had claimed for her own upon her arrival in Atur, and began steering the vampires toward the ancient mausoleum that would provide them access to the catacombs below the City of Night. Near their destination, Atur lay in ruins, devastated in a brutal Cyran offensive mere weeks before the Day of Mourning. Cyre's animated siege engines had left shells of old buildings standing in crumbling memory of the battle's horror. The mausoleum stood alone in a graveyard outside the wreckage of an ancient temple, miraculously untouched by the fury of combat surrounding it. Darkness had settled over the city except for a last, deep-blue glow at the horizon behind the ruined temple. Krael followed close on Havoc's heels, while Maija followed at a more measured pace.

Havoc flung open one of the mausoleum's stone doors and stole down the steps inside, Krael right behind him. The vampires paused at the bottom of the stairs, and Maija swept past, leading the way into the catacombs.

Maija led them through a maze of tunnels, following the directions the priest had given her before she gave him to Havoc. They saw no other creature as they made their way farther and farther below the City of Night. Soon Havoc recognized where they were and took over the role of guide, leading them through another mile of twisting catacombs and down a long stair. Finally, at the end of this descent, they reached an enormous door of black stone barring the way forward. Carved into its smooth surface was an image of a skeletal claw, eternally raking the stone.

"The shrine of the Nightclaw," Havoc declared proudly, "right where I left it."

"What is this Nightclaw?" Krael asked, hating his ignorance.

"Didn't you say your Order was part of the Blood of Vol? And you don't know about the Nightclaw?" Havoc barked a too-loud laugh, while Krael scowled. "The Nightclaw is a relic, supposedly the severed hand of a mighty lich. Though the lich is long gone, people still venerate the claw, attributing magical power to it."

"And what does it have to do with the Tablet of Shummarak?"

"Nothing at all!" Havoc laughed. "Except that I left the Tablet here a century ago."

"And you don't think that all the priests of Vol coming and going in that time might have found it and taken it away?"

"Not where I hid it." Havoc's laughter was irrepressible.

Maija glared at the hysterical shifter, then rolled her eyes and turned to Krael. "Open the door, Krael."

With an obedient sigh, Krael put his shoulder to the door, swinging it open easily. Wells of torchlight left most of the large room beyond swathed in shadows. A single row of round pillars crossed the room from side to side, dividing the room between a profane outer court and a sacred inner one. In the middle of the far side of the room, a small square altar stood in the shadows, seeming to repel the light of the torches that flickered nearby. In front of the altar, a startled man wheeled to face them, clutching the bloody stump of his arm.

"Begone from here!" the man cried weakly. He was pale from blood loss, and his remaining hand shook violently, clutching the Nightclaw. "I shall smite you with divine fury if you do not leave me in peace!"

"I don't think so, old man," Maija purred.

The man's eyes sized up Maija and seemed to conclude she was not too much of a threat. Then he gazed at Krael, towering impassively behind her, and took one look at Havoc, whose nostrils were distended at the scent of blood. Feebly dropping the Nightclaw back on its altar, he cautiously stepped away from the altar.

Havoc looked at Krael. "You hungry?" he asked with a grin.

Krael frowned. "No, not really." The old man backed toward the doorway, trying to keep a pillar between himself and the three intruders as they advanced.

"Hm," Havoc grunted. "Me neither. So what do we do with him?"

Maija spoke a string of harsh syllables and twisted her hands before her. With a scream, the man fell to the ground and began to claw at his eyes. Blood began to spurt beneath his fingers, and then bleeding sores erupted on the rest of his body. A moment later, his cries of agony stopped abruptly. Havoc bent over the body, nostrils wide, savoring the smell of blood, but Krael spun to look at Maija, making no effort to hide the surprise on his face.

"Where does a cleric of the Sovereign Host learn spells like that?" Krael demanded. "Isn't that what you were, in your adventuring days with Janik?"

"Do not speak of that time," Maija replied sternly, and walked the remaining distance to the altar. The vampires quickly followed.

"What in Vol's name did he think he was doing?" Krael exclaimed. "He cut off his own hand!" He picked up the freshly-severed appendage from where it lay beside the Nightclaw.

Havoc snickered. "A number of legends and rumors suggest that the great power of the Nightclaw can only be unlocked by one who is willing to replace his own right hand with it. I might have been responsible for at least some of those legends getting started." He laughed again. "Idiots!"

"Well, Havoc," Maija demanded, "where is the Tablet?"

"Patience, Maija, patience!" the shifter said. "First let's go over the terms of our agreement: The Tablet of Shummarak is mine, and it will stay mine. You may study it as you like, but only in my presence and under my supervision. We are still agreed on this?"

"Of course, Havoc. I gave you my word." Maija did not look at the vampire but searched the shrine with her eyes for some sign of the Tablet's presence.

"And I've seen for myself how much that means," the shifter replied, glancing at Krael.

The other vampire snorted softly, still gazing down at the Nightclaw and the old priest's severed hand.

"Well, we've come this far," Maija answered, turning to glare at Havoc once more. "Let's do what we came here to do. Where did you hide it?"

"Here," Krael said, his hand resting on the altar between its two grisly relics.

"Oh, *very* good, my offspring!" Havoc grinned in a way that showed all his teeth.

Maija whirled around to face Krael, then dropped her eyes to the altar. It was carved of stone, with a relief on the front panel depicting the ancient lich whose hand had become the Nightclaw. Two elegant side panels flanked this front relief, supporting—Maija saw it now—*two* top pieces, of the same size and almost identical stone. But the one on top was slightly different in hue and texture, a little darker, a little smoother and more worn around the edges.

"The Tablet," Maija breathed. "That is well hidden indeed."

"Everyone who comes in here looks at one thing first—the Nightclaw. If they're particularly devout, they might kneel and contemplate the lovely relief there." Havoc pointed at the front of the altar. "But do they ever notice the top of the altar? Never. And so the Tablet of Shummarak has been safely hidden for a century."

"Krael, help me lift it off." Maija barely listened to Havoc's triumphant explanation. Krael swept the Nightclaw, the old man's severed hand, and a half-dozen black votive candles to the floor and lifted the tablet from the altar, setting it gently down before Maija. She dropped to her knees, tracing her fingers over the runic inscription that covered its surface.

"You can read that?" Havoc asked, peering around Krael's bulk to watch Maija.

A slight smile came to Maija's face, and she intoned a few words in a tongue Krael didn't recognize, though it sounded ancient and evil, as she continued to run her fingers over the Tablet's surface.

The Tablet of Shummarak disappeared.

8

As the sun's last rays crept between the dark buildings of the City of Night, Dania finished strapping on her armor. She'd had a few hours of sleep, though they were restless and disturbed with strange and portentous dreams. Gered seemed much stronger, nearly back to full strength, and they were ready to resume the hunt.

She met her companions back in the outer room of Kophran's suite. Gered smiled at her as she entered, apparently holding no hard feelings toward her for her failures of the night before. She could not meet his eyes, however, and turned instead to Kophran, who was filling a backpack with holy water, wooden stakes, everburning torches, and other equipment for their mission.

"Do we have a plan?" she asked. "How are we going to find these vampires?"

"As I was explaining to Gered," Kophran said, "I spent some more time in research this afternoon, but I learned little more about Havoc, more properly called Varawn Kell. However, my research did suggest another place to look for more information." Dania simply waited while Kophran drew a great breath and launched into another lecture. "Havoc was known to be associated in some way with a vile relic known as the Nightclaw, the hand of an undead spellcaster that is much revered by followers of the accursed religion of this place. I have discovered the location of the subterranean shrine where this abomination is housed. Havoc was known to haunt the place during his last period of activity, and therefore, I suggest that we determine whether it holds any clues as to his current whereabouts. I shouldn't be surprised if his crypt were somewhere nearby."

"Fine. And how . . ." she hesitated, glancing at Gered, "how can we make sure that what happened last night doesn't happen again?"

"Ah." Kophran bent to his supplies, spread out on the couch before him, and withdrew a small silk pouch. He turned it over and began sprinkling silver dust in a circle around them, while invoking the Silver Flame's protection against the forces of evil. "Among other things," he said when he had finished, "this circle of protection will ward each of us from any kind of mental control.

"We must focus our attention on Havoc," Kophran said, his eyes boring into Dania as he spoke. "Whatever grudge you might hold against Krael, he is merely a slave of the greater master. Once Havoc is slain, Krael will be easier to battle. Is that clear?"

Dania nodded her assent, fingering the pommel of her sword and thinking about the vow she had sworn the night before. Without another word, she followed Kophran and Gered through the City of Night to the ancient mausoleum and down into the darkness.

9

Like a bolt of lightning, Havoc sprang at Maija. As he leapt, his face elongated into a muzzle and as his hands transformed into bestial claws. "What did you do?" he roared. "Where is my Tablet?"

Maija thrust up her hand, palm out, and Havoc staggered backward under an unseen force. She laughed a deep, throaty laugh. "It is safe, Havoc, where I can peruse it at my leisure."

"Our agreement! You gave me your word!" Havoc crouched warily, looking for another opportunity to pounce.

"And you believed me," Maija sneered. "Really quite touching. No, Havoc, the Tablet of Shummarak is not for the likes of you."

Havoc roared again, then leapt at Maija with his claws reaching for her face. Maija gestured again with her hand, and Havoc dropped to the ground in mid-jump, struggling to free himself from the force that pinned him.

"I have allowed you to imagine yourself an equal partner in this enterprise," Maija said, "but you are merely a pawn, Havoc, and no longer useful."

Krael stepped forward, glaring at his struggling master and then turning his gaze to Maija. "Again you demonstrate your utter lack of loyalty," he said. "Honestly, Maija, I never would have expected this of you. You always seemed like Janik's good little wife." Maija spat, and Krael grinned. "I'm impressed," he continued. "However, Havoc wants me to attack you, and I confess I wouldn't refuse if I could."

As Krael hefted his flail and bared his fangs, the door to the shrine burst open, and Kophran's voice boomed out, "Fiends of the night, beware!"

Maija spun around to face the intruders, and Havoc scrambled quickly to his feet as the unseen force released him.

"The wrath of the Silver Flame is upon you," Kophran intoned.

"Maija?" Dania gasped. Sword in hand, she ran to confront her old friend as Kophran advanced on the vampires, Gered hanging back to make better use of his spells. Maija circled warily as Dania approached.

Behind her, Dania heard Havoc's angry growl turn into a grunt of pain and Gered cry out, but Maija burned like a beacon in her mind, admitting no distractions. Her senses reeled as she drew near Maija and began to maneuver for an opening

"What happened to you, Maija?" Dania said. "There's a stink of evil on you that was never there before."

"Perhaps your nose has grown more sensitive since we last met, Dania," Maija said. "Be careful not to breathe too deeply." Dania lunged forward and managed to scratch her opponent's arm before Maija could dodge away.

"Have you so easily forgotten your oaths to the Sovereign Host?" Dania asked. "You have forsaken everyone you loved, everything you believed in!"

"I wouldn't want anyone to feel left out." Maija spoke an arcane word of utter blasphemy, forming her hands into a twisted gesture as if to pull Dania's heart from her chest.

Dania's head swam with pain for a moment, but then the pain was replaced by a memory of silver light, and she lunged at Maija again, her sword a dizzying whirlwind.

"You never used such spells before," Dania panted as she slashed at Maija. "Your corruption is complete."

"You have changed as well, Dania," Maija said, bleeding in a dozen places from Dania's assault. "Are you serving the Silver Flame now?"

"I'm keeping better company than you are, that's for sure."

Dania stole a glance at her companions. Gered staggered under Havoc's attack, but he stepped back and caught both vampires in a bolt of lightning, making Havoc scream in pain and fury. Kophran glowed with divine radiance as he swung his mace into Krael's chest.

"True," said Maija. "Krael is nearly Janik's equal in many ways, but he has grown particularly tiresome since becoming a vampire. And Havoc? He outlived his usefulness rather quickly."

"Is that what happened at Mel-Aqat, then? You decided we were tiresome? We were no longer useful?" Even as her anger grew, she could not manage to land a solid blow on her opponent. She cursed under her breath as a magical force deflected her blade from what could have been a telling blow.

"I tire of this," Maija said, and she chanted the dirge of a new spell, sprinkling a pinch of black powder into the air.

Dania lunged in an attempt to break her concentration, but Maija continued to dodge her blows, and a sudden burst of energy exploded around her. Dania felt it as a wave of death crashing over her—her pulse pounded in her ears for a moment, leaping and skipping like a frantic animal. It was the antithesis of the warmth of the Silver Flame that had spread through her in the alley—a clawing darkness that whispered of oblivion and despair. At the edge of her vision, she saw Gered clutch his chest, gasp his final breath, and fall to the ground.

"Gered!" she screamed, shaking off the lingering pall of Maija's spell. Turning back to face Maija full on, she drove her sword down again and again in a furious storm of blows—a few cutting deeply, most deflected.

"Oh, I'm sorry, Dania." Maija's voice dripped with mocking sarcasm. "Did I steal your love away from you . . . again?" Despite the leer on her face, she was showing signs of weariness under Dania's assault, and blood flowed from several deep cuts.

"Damn you, Maija," Dania said through gritted teeth. "Janik loved you. How could you betray him like that? How?"

"Oh, did I break dear Janik's heart?" The mockery in Maija's voice took on a sharper edge. "Poor little puppy dog. I suppose he took comfort in your arms at last—oh, Dania, you should thank me!"

Dania felt fury surge within her, but she did not lash out immediately. She tasted the anger, savored its bitter sweetness, and drew the righteous outrage she had felt so keenly in the alley along its edge like a whetstone. Gered was dead—another victim of monstrous evil, and that evil stood in human form before her. Maija had once been her friend, but she had been utterly corrupted, and Dania could not let her leave this place. Once more she called up the memory of holy radiance, and that power gave life to her honed fury, made it leap and dance like flame. Then she struck, roaring wordlessly, and felt that holy power flow through her once again. Only this time, it poured from her heart, down her arm, and into her sword. As the blade bit into Maija's flesh, it seemed to burst with silver fire, and Maija stumbled backward.

Dania's yell of fury seemed to inspire Kophran, and he bellowed, "May the Silver Flame consume you!" as he swung his mace into the side of Havoc's face. A similar burst of silver fire sent the vampire sprawling to the floor. Kophran called forth a radiant glow of healing power around his hand, then bent down to touch Havoc as the vampire tried to stand. The vampire screamed and then disappeared into a cloud of roiling mist. Krael immediately ceased his attack on the exorcist, no longer bound by Havoc's command and unwilling to meet the same fate.

Maija's eyes darted between Havoc's misty outline, Kophran's righteous wrath, Krael's hesitation, and Dania's ardent fury. "Well, this has been most enjoyable," she said, backing farther away from Dania. "It has truly been a pleasure to see you again, Dania. But my work here is done."

Even as Dania charged forward, Maija spoke a single arcane word and vanished.

Without any further thought, Krael turned on his heel and fled, his vampiric quickness making him fast even in his heavy armor. Dania started to give chase, but Kophran called out to stop her.

"Dania, wait! We must ensure that Havoc stays dead this time."

"But Maija—Krael . . ."

"Never mind them. First we deal with the master, then the minions will be easier to destroy." Kophran was following the misty cloud that was Havoc as it drifted along the floor toward the exit. "We must either prevent him from reaching his coffin or follow him there and destroy him while he lies helpless."

Dania walked to Gered's body and looked down at it. He lay twisted, his right leg crossed over his left and his shoulders flat on the ground. His lifeless eyes stared at the black ceiling.

"Oh, Gered," she whispered, "I'm so sorry." She crouched down and lifted his limp form, cradling it in her arms. Silently, she stood and walked after Kophran, shifting Gered's corpse to her shoulder and repeating the words of her oath over and over in her mind.

By my life, my honor, and whatever is holy in this profane world, this sword shall bring an end to this evil.

JAMES WYATT

ABOUT THE AUTHOR

James Wyatt is an award-winning game designer at Wizards of the Coast and one of the designers of the *Eberron*™ *Campaign Setting*. He wrote *City of the Spider Queen*™ and *Oriental Adventures*™, and co-authored numerous roleplaying game products, including *Magic of Incarnum*™, *Sharn: City of Towers*™, *Draconomicon*™, *The Book of Dragons*, and *Book of Exalted Deeds*™.

He grew up in Ithaca, New York, and now lives in Washington State with his wife and son.

FLIGHT OF THE *RIGHTEOUS INDIGNATION*

Ari Marmell

1

It wakes.

How long it has slumbered, it cannot know, for it has no understanding of time. It feels a great chill, and only then realizes that it cannot remember what warmth feels like. It decides that it will have to create its own warmth, its own light. It stretches out, finds its path, and its power, curtailed.

It looks about and recognizes little of what it sees. Dark blue above, roiling gray below, and all around a tiny world of wood and metal . . . and forces. Forces it cannot see, cannot name. Forces that hold it in place, forces that prevent it from finding warmth. It presses against them, fighting them, and for the merest instant, the lifespan of a single ember, it feels them give, feels just the tiniest portion of itself slip through.

It is a start.

It hears sounds, vocalizations and footsteps of the soft, cold bipeds that walk this tiny wooden world. A moment of revelation, as it remembers each and every one of them. Here is the rapid step of the one called Katraen, whom it knows better than all the rest save one. There the harsh, demanding voice of Ulric, whom the others called "captain." And there . . . yes, the incessant chanting of Saunder, whose voice and touch it knows all too well. These, and dozens more besides, it hears, and it feels, and it knows.

Yet there is one, one it does not *know. Deep in the bowels of this tiny world, in a dark and largely empty place, it hears the pacing of limbs that are not legs, hears the inhalation of lungs far larger than those of the bipeds, feels a spark that burns with an inner darkness that threatens to blot out the stars themselves.*

It watches this creature, cloaked in shadow and bound in metal, and it knows what it must do.

2

"You smell something?"

Ricard, sailor and soldier on the *Righteous Indignation* for five years and counting, turned a narrowed gaze on his companion and once again silently cursed the ignorance of youth. The young man—boy, really—with whom he'd been partnered for this shift looked ludicrous in a chain hauberk that reached his knees and hung over his wrists, carrying a cutlass that threatened to trip him every time he walked. Ricard himself, veteran that he was, wore the same equipment as comfortably as his own skin.

"What in the dragons' names are you talking about, Jaran?"

"I smell something burning."

It was all the older sailor could do not to roll his eyes. "Jaran, how long have you been on this ship?"

"Four months next week."

"And in all that time, have you ever passed a day or night where you *didn't* smell something burning?" Ricard could only sigh at the young man's puzzled stare. "We're propelled by a bloody fire elemental, Jaran. It *always* smells like something's burning!"

Jaran frowned. "This is something else. Take a sniff."

Fine, if it'd shut the kid up. Ricard took a long, deep breath—and frowned. There *was* something other than the normal smoky scent of the elemental, something acrid, almost metallic. He turned slowly, eyes darting back and forth. He couldn't see a damn thing outside the meager glow of the small everbright lanterns in the wall sconce above them, but the odor was definitely more pungent behind them.

"You may be right, Jaran," the veteran admitted. "Let's take a quick gander, make sure there's nothing burning in the hold." He reached for the door between them.

"Shouldn't we sound the alarm?"

"And pull everyone away from their bunks or duties for what's probably some random bit of detritus caught in the elemental ring? I don't think so. Captain'd skin us both. Best we be sure."

One hand on his sword, more out of habit than any thought that he might need it, Ricard yanked open the flimsy wooden portal. The acrid stench hit him like a slap in the face, but the stairs leading down into the cargo hold were dark and shadowy as ever; a good sign, since any active fire below would almost certainly cast at least *some* measure of light on the lowest steps.

"After you, Jaran." Might as well let the recruit earn his keep for the night.

Jaran frowned, and his forehead beaded with sweat despite the cold night air, but he nodded. Mouth set firmly in a grim scowl, he placed his feet on the stairs and trudged downward, Ricard following three steps behind.

The boards creaked as the young man stepped onto the floor of the cargo hold itself—the only sound heard before a black tendril glistening with some loathsome residue snaked from the shadows and wrapped itself around Jaran's chest. The attack was utterly silent; its results were not. Ricard fell back against the stairs, eyes wide in shock, at the deafening series of cracks as his shipmate's ribs crumpled like so much parchment. The tentacle whipped back into the darkness, and Jaran fell limp to the floor without so much as a whimper.

Ricard couldn't move, paralyzed by the sudden brutality of the unexpected assault. Like the youngest recruit, he stood frozen and could only moan softly as a pair of glowing green eyes opened in the darkness below. When he felt the tentacles slide from the shadows to either side of him, felt their almost silken caress as they wound themselves about his legs, he was finally able to move. Even as he reached to draw his sword, he could not help but draw breath to scream.

He managed only the latter.

3

Her way lit only by the circle of flame surrounding her, and the far greater ring of Siberys that encircled the world like the coiled dragon it once had been, the *Righteous Indignation* cut through the dim skies of Eberron.

The winds whipped across the deck in an endless dance, the spirits of the night set roiling by the vessel's speed. It seemed as if the great galleon, one of the largest airships to ply the clouds above the continent of Khorvaire, was nearly as eager to return home as were the crewmembers who stood their posts on her deck, or slumbered in her fo'c'sle. It had been a long hunt, this last one, and one of their most difficult. Yet the rewards offered for the prize they brought back would surely make it all worthwhile, and then ship and crew could both take their ease.

Or so at least one of the crew fervently hoped, as he squinted against the wind.

"Mists are awfully thick tonight, Captain."

Ulric d'Lyrandar, captain and part owner of the *Righteous Indignation*, glanced up from the rail over which he'd been leaning. He brushed a strand of dark, wind-blown hair behind a pointed ear, and looked askance at the woman striding toward him.

"The Gray Mist is always thick, Katraen. And you always comment on it anyway."

"Just trying to make conversation, Captain."

"Make a new one. This one's old and getting a little worn around the edges."

An armada of tools clanking at her belt, Katraen joined her captain at the railing. It was almost laughable to see them together, like two people who had each accidentally received portions of the other. The captain had long, soft hair and a slender form, both gifts from his elf mother. Katraen, a full-blooded human, was tall, broad of shoulder, and completely bald. (After her fourth time lighting her hair on fire in a workshop accident, she had decided to remove the danger in the most expedient way possible.) She placed her calloused hands on the smooth wood beside his own.

"Everything running smoothly?" Ulric asked her.

She scowled, glancing at him only from the corner of her eye. "Would I be up here wasting time in conversation if it wasn't?"

Ulric raised an eyebrow, though he couldn't help but smile. "Talking to your crewmates is a waste of time?"

"No, just you, Captain. Respectfully, when you're not giving orders, you're really a bore."

"Well, I should be offended, but since you said it *respectfully* . . ."

That, at least, drew a smile from Ulric's oldest companion. A moment passed, and then both looked over the rail once more, down into mists so thick they obscured every inch of the ground drifting by hundreds of feet below.

"I'm serious, Captain," Katraen told him, her tone softer. "The crew doesn't like flying over the Mournland. Most of the officers aren't fond of it either."

"Going around adds days to our journey, Katraen," Ulric said in the almost monotonous voice of a man having the same conversation for the umpteenth time. "And the Gray Mist rarely reaches this high, anyway."

"You said that last time, Captain. You remember what happened then?"

Ulric frowned. "It was a fluke."

"I'm sure Avron's widow appreciates that fact."

The captain spun. "Katraen, even you have a line with me! Don't cross it."

"Captain, Saunder spent an hour in prayer before piloting us into the area."

"Saunder prays for an hour before taking a—"

"And he told me this was the last time. Captain, if you take us over the mists one more time, I think he may honestly leave the crew."

Ulric felt as though a hand had suddenly clutched his chest. Katraen wasn't one to make such a judgment lightly. "Really?"

"He's not the only one either, Captain. The crew respects you. They'd follow you into Khyber if you asked. But they have to feel like there's a *reason*, Captain, and you haven't given them one other than saving a bit of gold in time and supplies."

A deep sigh. "Very well, perhaps you're right. Next time, I'll allot extra time and supplies for a different—"

Both of them jolted upright at the sound of a bloodcurdling scream that flowed up from between the boards of the deck like a wisp of smoke, only to be whipped away by the wind of their flight and the crackling of the elemental ring near the rear of the ship. For a single instant they stared at one another, and Ulric heard the message in Katraen's eyes as clearly as if she'd stated it aloud.

Too late.

Then, as one, they turned from the rail and bolted toward the nearest hatch.

4

Of course.
These "Gray Mists" of which Ulric and Katraen speak, in which strange things happen . . . it knows of them, has heard them mentioned even while it slumbered.

More than that, it remembers them, the knowledge coming to it like the blazing of a sudden fire. It remembers them washing over the nation of Cyre in a tide of corruption, drowning the land in forces unrecorded and unimaginable. It remembers them washing over the world of wood and metal—the Righteous Indignation—*as the vessel fled before the spreading fog, the last ship across the border before Cyre died and the Mournland was born. It remembers their faint kiss as the vessel passed over them time and again, Captain Ulric daring a route that few other airship captains would.*

Yes, these Gray Mists must be why it has awakened now, why it feels itself able to do what it could never do before. Will it slumber again once they fall behind, or will it continue to act? It cannot say, and the thought of returning to slumber, to nothingness, to not being fills it with a fear that chills it more deeply than the coldest wind of night. It is clear, now more than ever, that it chose correctly when it chose to free the beast below. Now it must merely be certain that the beast accomplishes what it must, before the Mournland passes fully beneath the vessel.

It turns its attention once more toward the hold.

5

Ulric and Katraen were but two of a crowd of dozens that forced their way through the narrow doorways and halls of the *Righteous Indignation*. The scream had resounded throughout the ship, drawing nearly every crewmember not currently sleeping or duty-bound to stand post elsewhere (and a few of those as well). The captain's calls for order and silence went unheeded, for even his powerful voice could not slice through the cloud of mutters and speculations that hovered above the crew like a flock of scavenging vultures. Ulric nearly shouted himself hoarse in frustration before finally giving in to the inevitable.

Instead, he shouldered his way through the crowd, scowling and cursing at everyone in his or her turn, and grabbed the first on-duty guard he could find. He grabbed the woman by her hauberk and yanked her close, determined that she, at least, would hear him over the ambient sounds.

"Vauresh!" Even at this range, practically nose to nose, Ulric had to shout to make himself clear.

"Captain!"

"What in the name of Dol Dorn is going on?"

"No idea, Captain! I was on my way to investigate the scream." She glanced around her. "Looks like I wasn't the only one with that thought."

"Looks like. I'm going to look into this myself. You are going to go back down this hall and stand at the doorway, and you are going to prevent anyone else from coming in. I may not be able to get *these* deck rats in order, but I'll be damned if I'll let the *rest* of the crew clutter the place up even more!"

Vauresh looked disappointed to be left out of the upcoming discovery, whatever it might be. Nevertheless, she snapped off a crisp, "Yes, Captain!" and shoved her way back down the hall until she reached the narrow door.

The first man whose path she blocked gave her an ugly stare and raised a hand as though to push her out of the way. He wound up unconscious on the floor, an ugly bruise already forming on his cheek, for his trouble.

Shaking her sore knuckles, Vauresh glared about her at the gathered throng, whose attention she now firmly had. "Captain's orders are that nobody else is to enter this hall until he says otherwise. Anybody want to discuss it?"

With a few sullen mutters, the crowd dispersed. Even this far from the other end of the hall—presumably the source of the scream—Vauresh could still hear the voices of the assembled crew. The captain was going to have his hands full calming things down enough to investigate. He'd been right about that.

For several moments, Vauresh held her post, wondering what the commotion might have been, her normally staid demeanor shaken only a bit by a superstitious fear of the Gray Mist below. She kept her gaze darting about, determined not to miss anything, then looked downward as the crewman she'd struck began to stir.

In the blink of an eye, he was gone. As if he were a fish at the end of a line, something yanked the fallen crewman out of sight and into the shadows, leaving behind nothing but a trail of cloth strands, ripped loose from his tunic by the wooden floor. Vauresh heard what would surely have been a panicked scream, had it not been utterly silenced by a hideous, wet crunch.

With the rasp of steel on leather, Vauresh's cutlass was in her hand. She dropped into a defensive crouch, blade held before her, eyes wide. Only her ragged breathing and the rapid pounding of her heart gave away the shock and mounting terror that ate at her gut. Whatever was out there, lurking in the corners and crevices of the ship, had moved faster than anything she'd ever seen. With a sudden clarity, she knew that the scream which had drawn her below decks was linked to it as well. And she wasn't about to face it alone.

Nothing emerged when she opened her mouth, save a choking squeak. Gritting her teeth, fighting against the fear, she cleared her throat and called out once more. Yet even as she did, she knew it to be a futile gesture. She could barely hear the captain shouting in her face, at the other end of the hall. No sound she could possibly make on *this* end would reach anyone's ears.

Blade waving slowly right to left, she took a single step back, retreating toward the crowd, and safety. She took a second, a third—

It shot from the darkness like a ballista bolt. Flashing green eyes bored into her even as tentacles flailed at her, seeking to grab hold of armor, of cloth, of flesh.

With a desperate gasp, Vauresh ducked beneath the first of the horrible tendrils, flinching as its coating of oil splattered across her face and neck. Bringing her cutlass over and around, she parried the second with the flat of the blade, though the force of the impact nearly ripped the weapon from her hand.

Something about the beast, still largely concealed in the shadows, seemed to stab at the eyes. Vauresh felt as though she couldn't focus, though the hall, even her sword, were as clear as ever. She saw the first tendril whipping at her face, but could not bring her gaze to follow it. She threw herself back, avoiding the worst of the blow, but her head still rang with the impact, and her hair felt matted to her skull by the beast's secretions.

Vauresh allowed the momentum of the blow to carry her over, striking the floor with a hollow thud and rolling back to her feet. Even as she stood, she brought her cutlass upward in a brutal cut and was rewarded by the solid thump of impact. Viciously, she twisted the weapon even as she yanked it out of the tentacle that had been reaching for her, and her mouth curled in a smile at the sight of blood welling up from the wound. Whatever this thing was, it bled. That meant it lived and that it could die.

With renewed confidence, Vauresh readied her blade. The first tendril emerged from the darkness hesitantly, as if her draining fear had flowed instead into the beast she faced. It flicked tentatively in her direction, and she swatted it away with almost contemptuous ease. Her inability to truly focus on the creature prevented her from causing it any real damage, but clearly she could protect herself from it.

The second tentacle came from the left, the first once more from the right; again and again she batted them aside. She began once more to retreat down the corridor, hoping to lure her foe nearer to allies who could help her slay it. Step, parry, parry, step.

And then, with a sudden flash of green eyes, it was not a tendril that thrust itself at her, but the bulk of the beast itself. From the center of the hall, hidden in the ship's shadows, it lunged directly toward her even as she parried one of its tentacles to her left. Her eyes glazing over and her head aching with the effort of focusing, Vauresh knew that she could not recover her guard in time.

She screamed as the beast's claws tore into her stomach and chest, again as a tendril wrapped itself about her sword arm and crushed the bone, and one last time as a massive weight settled itself atop her, squeezing the air from her lungs.

By the time the creature began to feed, Vauresh had stopped screaming. Not that it mattered, really, since nobody could have heard her in any case.

6

Saunder was already kneeling over the bodies, his eyes closed and lips moving in a silent prayer for their souls, when Ulric and Katraen finally pushed their way to the front of the crowd.

The captain could only stare at the broken and bloodied forms, splayed limply across the stairs where they had fallen.

The ship's pilot sniffed once, picking up Ulric's scent from the crowd. Cracking open one golden eye, he met the newcomer's gaze and shook his head sadly.

"Sovereigns." The whisper came from Katraen, who seemed almost mesmerized by the blood. "What could have done this?"

Ulric didn't stop to answer. He already knew. Jaw working in his own prayer—a prayer that he was wrong—he dashed down the stairs, barely avoiding the bodies and leaving sticky footprints in red. He yanked one of the lanterns from the wall as he passed, bringing its glow to the normally inky depths of the cargo hold.

He needn't have bothered. Even as he emerged into the cavernous chamber, he saw the light of additional everbright lanterns ahead of him, the shadows of various barrels and crates stabbing toward him like long knives. He heard the sound of men and women speaking up ahead, knew each of them by voice, and knew as well that several of them were near to panic.

"Gabrian?" he asked as he strode near, glad to find at least one level head already present. "What have you found?"

The ship's first mate turned and straightened as his captain neared. Sixty years old if he was a day, the man had worked shipboard—sea and sky—for longer than many of the crew had been alive. His hair was iron-gray, his face weather-beaten and worn, but if time had finally begun to weigh upon him physically, it had done nothing to his mind or his experience. Gabrian Tavanough knew almost everything, and had seen even more than that.

So when Ulric saw the clench of his first mate's jaw, the fear in his eyes, it was definitely time to start worrying.

"It's loose, Captain."

Had members of his crew not been watching, Ulric might well have buried his face in his hands. Instead, he stepped forward to examine the cage.

It should have been escape-proof. Thick bars of the best dwarven steel, with barely room between them for a child's arm, and a multi-keyed lock made by the finest craftsmen of House Cannith, should have proved an insurmountable barrier to anyone or anything locked inside. Yet the cage door, hanging open, and two dead crewmen on the stairs, all conspired to prove that it was not.

Gabrian opened his mouth to speak again, but the voice Ulric heard came from behind him. "I told you to kill that foul thing, Captain."

Katraen stood in the hold, alongside Saunder. The pilot and priest had clearly finished his rites over the bodies and come downstairs to make his opinion known. His gravelly voice was rougher even than normal, and traces of the victims' blood stained the tawny fur of his arms. He looked vaguely ill—unsurprising, as his inhuman sense of smell had no doubt detected every last odor of death and decomposition above—but the burly priest wasn't about to let that stop him.

"I told you to kill it, and I told you not to take us over the Mournland. The Sovereigns are frowning on your pride."

"Save the sermon, Saunder. You heard our commission, same as me. Probably better, with those ears of yours. Morgrave University was willing to pay four times as much for a live specimen as a dead one."

"And now it's worth even more, since we won't have to split the gold among quite so many crewmen. Convenient, that."

"You damned son of a—"

"Captain!" The old first mate stepped between Ulric and his pilot, pointing at the cage. "Look at this."

Fuming, Ulric turned. "What? I don't—"

"The lock, Captain."

Sure enough, it was the lock, not the bars of the cage, that had failed. It was equally clear, however, that its failure was no fault of the Cannith craftsmen.

"By the Host . . ." Ulric knelt beside the cage. "Is anything else around here burned?"

"Don't appear so, Captain."

The captain met his first mate's gaze. "What the Dolurrh sort of fire can melt a steel lock into slag without damaging anything else around it?"

Gabrian looked grim. "None of any natural sort, Captain. That's for damn sure."

A low mutter fluttered through the assembled crewmen, and a number of angry gazes turned toward the large, inhuman pilot. Saunder calmly stared back at them, refusing to rise to the bait. Ulric himself slowly turned and stared grimly at the eight-pronged symbol of the Sovereign Host that Saunder wore around his neck—a symbol wrought in crimson and orange and gold, signifying particular allegiance to Onatar. Onatar, god of artifice, god of the forge. God of fire.

"Don't even think it." Ulric rose to stand before the priest, spinning to face the rest of his crew. "Saunder's been with me for years. I may argue with him. You don't get to. He's a good man."

"Bloody beast-lover isn't really a man at all, is he?"

It was said softly, but not softly enough. Ulric turned, yanked a small but solid pair of pliers from Katraen's belt, and threw them. They spun through the air with a series of clicks, and then slammed solidly into the head of a burly crewman named Deke. The man yelped and fell to his knees, clutching his bleeding scalp.

"We'll have none of that!" Ulric gazed at the assembled sailors. "We've got a beast loose on the ship. You'll be fighting that, and none of your crewmates, or you'll be spending the rest of the voyage in irons. Questions?"

Not surprisingly, there were none.

"Good." He turned his attention to Katraen. "Go find Embra. Wake her up if you have to, but tell her I want the weapons locker opened, and every last man and woman aboard armed."

"Right away, Captain."

A nod. Then, to Gabrian, "Organize patrols. No fewer than four people in each, with at least one crossbow in each group. I want this thing found. Taking it alive would be nice, but nobody's to endanger themselves doing so. Anyone has a kill shot, he takes it."

"Aye, Captain. *All right you maggots, let's move!*"

"Saunder?"

"Yes, Captain. Thank you for your confidence."

Ulric shook his head. "Don't prove me wrong, Saunder. There's only three people aboard with any ability with fire magics. Katraen was with me, and I couldn't convince Kavo to get anywhere near that creature, caged or not, if I offered him every bit of gold I'd ever earned, and the deed to the *Indignation* besides."

"I won't, Captain. And I didn't do this."

"I know. Paurice is piloting while you're down here?"

"Yes, Captain."

"Go relieve her. The elemental responds more swiftly to you than it does to her. We may have to put down, and I want us well past the Mournland before we do."

The priest nodded once, and strode up the stairs, ignoring the sullen stares hurled his way by several of the crew. Ulric squeezed his eyes shut, wondering what else could go wrong, and then steeled himself to galvanize his people for a hunt that would almost certainly claim more lives before it was done.

7

The beast slipped through the darkened corridors of the ship, padding along on silent paws. Green eyes pierced the darkness as easily as the brightest day, and the odors of ship and crew painted a picture as clear as any map. All but invisible in the shadows, despite its size, it crept toward the musk of sweat and blood, already tasting its next meal. Tentacles longer than the beast itself wound about doorknobs, twisting them open, allowing it access to places no one imagined it could go, leaving behind only a swiftly drying residue to suggest it had ever passed.

It paused as it heard footsteps, detected the acrid scent of more prey, but also the scent of bright metal. The approaching prey was not helpless; it possessed metal claws, like the one who had hurt it. A wounded tentacle throbbed in remembered pain. It could kill them, this it knew, but it knew as well that it could find easier prey up ahead. Compressing its bulk until it seemed impossibly small, it hunkered down in the shadows. Eyes narrowed to slits, tendrils ceased their endless probing, and it was one with the shadows. The prey—four of them, all with metal claws—passed by, utterly unaware of its presence. It would have laughed at their feeble senses, their utter lack of awareness, had it possessed the concept of laughter at all.

They passed, and still it waited, until even its keen hearing could no longer detect their footsteps. Then, silent as night falling, it proceeded down the corridor.

8

"Are you sure about this? Captain said we're supposed to be hunting the creature."

Gabrian nodded, never taking his eyes off the floor below. "That's exactly what we're doing, Salz. We're just doing it smarter, is all."

The sailor called Salz frowned and clutched his crossbow to his chest. He, the first mate, and two other members of the ship's crew stood on a rickety wooden catwalk that ran above the mess. Below, half a dozen sailors ate quickly and talked nervously amongst themselves, eyes trained on the entrances. Even the cook remained with them at the table, stepping into the galley only when he had to retrieve an order. The scent of fear practically overpowered the slop he passed off as food.

"I don't understand," Salz whispered. "Why do you think it's coming here?"

The first mate fingered his axe. "This thing's no ordinary beast, Salz. It's smart. Really smart. Pretty much dumb luck or the Sovereigns' own grace that we captured it in the first place. We could search the ship from now until next year and not find it if it don't want to be found. But it's got to eat, same as any other beast, and it don't want to fight for its meal. What we got down here is the scent of prey, the scent of dead meat, and a bunch of men not hunting for it with drawn blades. I figure there's as good a chance of it showing up here as anywhere else, and that's when we'll—"

As though summoned by Gabrian's own words, a shadow moved in the far corner of the room. It glided smoothly, silently, and only the watchers' heightened vantage allowed them to see that it moved against the patterns of light and darkness cast by the room's *lanterns*. The men and women below hadn't the first inkling that anything was wrong, despite their best efforts.

With the faintest hiss, Gabrian alerted his companions, all of whom dropped hands to weapons. Salz lowered his crossbow, sighting down the bolt. For a long moment he hesitated, sweat beading on his forehead.

"I can't!" His throat was so tight, it was less a whisper than a croak. "I can't focus!"

The first mate nodded. "Aye, we had that problem catching it the first time." He watched as the shadow slowly but steadily moved toward the unsuspecting crew below. "Salz, don't take the shot. We don't want it spooked away." He swiftly estimated the distance down from the catwalk, which had never been designed for anything more than allowing the captain to address the crew at meals. "It's an easy jump. We surround the beast, and hack it to bits. At that range, we should be able to hit it easy enough, clear view or no."

Salz carefully placed his crossbow on the floor beside him, and let one hand rest on his cutlass. Gabrian took a look around, meeting the eyes of each crewmember with him. Taking a solid grip on the haft of his axe, he placed his other hand on the railing. The others followed suit.

"Steady on, soldiers. We go on three. One. Two . . .

9

This will not do.

It watches with a growing sense of annoyance as Gabrian and the others tense to leap down upon the creature, weapons of sharp ore at the ready. Should their effort succeed—and it seems they have, at least, a reasonable chance—its own efforts will be made moot. It has not freed the beast to see it slaughtered so swiftly. No, this will not do at all.

So it must do something about it.

10

Gabrian gasped at the sudden pain in his hand. The wooden railing had abruptly grown painfully hot, and even as he jerked away, the wood splintered with a loud crack. Behind him, an everbright lantern on the wall abruptly ignited, the mystical heatless flame within replaced by true fire as the wood combusted. Several of the ropes holding up the catwalk began to smolder, and the air filled with the stench of smoke. The crossbow lying on the floor released with a loud twang as its string burned through and snapped. Yet despite the intense heat, nothing but the torch had actually caught fire.

The first mate turned a questioning eye toward Salz, drew breath to ask a desperate question, and choked as superheated air flowed into his lungs. Eyes watering and throat burning, Gabrian fell to his knees, hands clutching at his neck. His three companions were not far behind; within seconds they, too, were on the floor gasping like live fish in a skillet.

Crewmen looked up, jaws slack with shock, half-chewed food spilling out across the table. Several stood, their chairs scraping across the wooden floor, but not a one had the slightest idea what was happening, or what to do.

The beast, however, hesitated not one instant. With a hideous snarl and a powerful spring, it launched itself over the head of the man it had been about to kill. Easily clearing the height of the catwalk, it lashed out with a tentacle, catching the railing and hauling itself over. It narrowed its eyes against the sudden heat, unaware that the catwalk had already cooled substantially since the moment Gabrian and the others had collapsed. What had been crippling or even lethal moments before was now merely unpleasant. Given time, the fallen might even have recovered.

The beast gave them no time.

On the floor below, crewmen ran shrieking from the galley as the sounds of tearing flesh, and a sudden rain of blood, crashed down upon them from above.

II

"Clear the way! *Clear the way!*"

The catwalk creaked alarmingly as crewmen scrambled to hug the sides, leaving a narrow path for Captain Ulric. The wood was slick, the air filled with the coppery scent of blood. He knew what he would find, at the center of the gathered crowd.

He just hadn't known *who*.

"Oh, Sovereigns." His shoulders slumping, Ulric knelt before the mangled corpse that had once been his first mate.

"Gabrian . . ." The captain's head fell, and everyone present turned away, pretending not to see his tears or hear his muffled sobs.

Still, Ulric was an airship captain, a dragonmarked scion of House Lyrandar. It required but a moment for him to regain control. Standing, fingers clenched into white fists, he surveyed the carnage and those who lingered around it.

"What happened?"

"I saw some of it, Captain." It was Rollaf who spoke, the pasty-faced ship's cook. "Gabrian and the others saved our lives. That—*thing*—was down here, and we didn't even see it. If they hadn't been up there . . ."

Ulric frowned. "So they lured it away?"

"Well . . . not precisely, Captain. First I knew of them, they'd all started hacking and choking real bad, like they'd all got a face-full of sawdust or Zilargo peppers. Creature leapt right up at them. I—I'm afraid we ran, Captain. I know we should have stayed to help, but . . ."

"No, Rollaf. I don't think there's much you could have done." Sighing, Ulric looked again at the bodies. "Someone's told Saunder?"

"Yes, Captain. He's on his way."

"Good." For a long moment, Ulric fell silent, lost in grief but also in thought. It seemed like Gabrian had a perfect ambush setup; what had gone wrong?

"Look around," he ordered. "Figure out what they were choking on."

It didn't take long. Several crewmen stumbled across charred ropes in their search. Rollaf noticed the raw and reddened skin in the dead men's mouths. It was Ulric himself who wondered why, if Gabrian had been hiding in hopes of ambushing the beast, he would have lit an open flame. It made no sense, yet the charred bits of wood atop the catwalk suggested he had done just that. Several grumbles and whisperes passed among the bystanders, and it was a crowd of narrowed eyes that turned toward the entrance when Saunder stepped into the mess.

"Heat, Captain." Rollaf spoke loudly enough to be heard across the room, saying aloud what everyone present already knew. "Gabrian and the others couldn't breathe."

Saunder froze, then slowly peered up at the catwalk. "Is there something you care to ask me, Rollaf?"

"If he don't, I do!" Deke pushed his way through the crowd, forehead still swollen and purple from the impact of Katraen's pliers. "Come on, Captain! You may o' thought I was out of line before, but twice? Nobody on this ship could have done this but the damn beast-lo—err, priest!"

"I told you before, Deke. All of you." The captain's voice was soft, dangerous. "Saunder's a good man. A loyal man. A friend. He didn't do this. He had no reason."

No reason . . . except that Saunder had argued bitterly against taking the creature aboard, threatened to quit over Ulric's decision to take them over the Mournland and the Gray Mists.

Ulric couldn't vocalize his doubts, but oh yes, he had them. And when he gazed down from the catwalk at the man he *thought* was his friend, Saunder saw them in his eyes.

"Very well, then." The priest turned and placed one foot on the rungs that would take him to the already overcrowded catwalk. "After I say prayer for the departed, I will lead a hunting party for the creature myself. I will prove my loyalty, though I should have been past such trials many years ago."

"You're bloody mad!" Deke stepped forward, fists raised. "You think we're just going to stand by and let you mouth words over the men you killed? We should—"

"Deke, shut up and let him through."

"But Captain, he—"

"Shut. Up."

The sailor sullenly clapped his lips together.

"Saunder, can Paurice handle the ship in a crisis?"

"Well enough, Captain." The priest hauled himself onto the catwalk, which creaked yet again under his massive weight. "You might want to see about getting some people out of here, Captain. We don't want to bring down the walkway." He ignored the angry glares that stabbed at him as the bystanders shuffled past. Finally, the catwalk was clear but for Saunder, Ulric, and the bodies of four good sailors.

"Saunder . . ."

"I had no hand in this, Captain."

"You better not have. How do you plan to hunt it down?"

"I have spent the past hours in prayer, Captain. Onatar has granted me spells of seeking. I fear I haven't the skill to pinpoint the beast directly, but Onatar's magics and his grace will guide me well enough."

"I want you to take a hunting party of six, at least. And I want Deke to be one of them."

"What? Captain—"

"He's your most vocal detractor, Saunder, but he's not the only one. When he sees you working to slay the beast, it'll put his doubts to rest, and he'll reassure the others."

The pilot scowled. "And if he learns I am working *with* the beast, he'll be alert to it and able to stop me. Or are you going to pretend that thought had not crossed your mind?"

The captain met his gaze. "Just make sure you prove it an *idle* thought, Saunder."

Ulric turned and strode away, leaving Saunder alone with the bodies.

12

It senses the magics.

They are faint, barely a tingle in a world of sensation, a tiny breeze amidst a gale, but it senses them. The shaggy one, the one called Saunder, the one it knows better than all others, is summoning his powers, calling upon his god.

It listens as Saunder intones his prayers, and while it does not comprehend all the words, it understands fully what the priest and pilot intends. These magics will lead him to the beast, and he will lead others.

And in that, there is opportunity. It watches the priest stand, gesture to others, and move out into the corridors of the ship. It watches, and it readies itself for the proper moment.

13

"Koram, down!"

Even as he shouted, Saunder rolled beneath the tendril that lashed at him like an angry shadow, his lycanthropic heritage enabling him to move faster than any human of his size. The crewman to whom he'd called was not so fortunate; the tendril whipped across his face, drawing blood and cracking bone. The man slammed against the far wall and crumpled into a motionless heap.

Floorboards groaned under the running footsteps of the combatants, and faint puffs of sawdust rose through the air. The cargo hold of the *Righteous Indignation*, where it had all started, was bathed in the light of dozens of everbright lanterns, and even an illuminating spell Saunder had provided. Tall crates, hanging ropes, a catwalk much like that in the mess, even the broken iron cage, cast jagged shadows that sliced through the light like knives. Yet even here, the beast remained a thing of darkness, tendrils and claws and glowing green eyes. The light, like the eyes of the crewmembers, seemed to slide off its ebony hide, unable to gain a purchase.

Three crossbows barked in succession, and three bolts vibrated in the wooden walls. Even at this range, the archers' inability to focus on the creature ruined their aim. Deke charged in with a banshee-like shriek, a bargepole sharpened into a makeshift spear held before him. The point plunged into the shadows and connected with something solid. The sailor's battle-cry became a shout of victory—which in turn became a grunt of pain as a second tendril punched into his gut and sent him sprawling. The spear clattered uselessly to the floor, and though Deke was on his feet almost instantly, his only remaining weapon was a short-bladed dagger, hardly effective in a battle such as this.

Twisting his body so he stood between the beast and his companions, Saunder called out to Onatar and spread his hands before him as though offering a benediction. Orange flames leapt from his fingers and bathed the creature in a burning torrent. An inhuman shriek pierced the ears of everyone in the hall, and the stench of roasting flesh assailed their nostrils. A cheer erupted from several throats, and even Deke looked at the priest with a newfound respect. Even as the flames died, the shape in the shadow began to retreat. Sensing victory, the sailors stepped forward, blades bared.

14

It concentrates, pressing against the unseen forces that hold it prisoner, extruding just an ember of its essence into the large chamber below. It heats the air between the bipeds and beast to a degree even the pilot's fire has not. It feels the kiss of those flames, feels the urge to join them, but it cannot reach.

Ignore the distraction, keep the beast back, let them approach just a bit closer, and then . . .

15

The beast watched from the ever-shrinking shadows, a burned leg held against its body in agony, tendrils wavering as they sought some target at which they might strike. Time and again, it reached toward the beings that had harmed it, prepared to spring, only to draw back in further pain. Even though the flame had faded, the air between them was still unbearably hot. Snarling in frustration, it retreated, step by step, even as the two-legged creatures confronting it advanced. It tensed its many legs, preparing to flee, when abruptly its attackers halted as well.

Through narrowed eyes, it watched as the first of them recoiled, its face in its hands, choking in pain. Clearly, the wall of heat preventing the beast from attacking its foes was blocking their path as well. It watched, tentacles aquiver, as several of the creatures shouted back and forth at one another. The hairy one that had thrown fire gestured in the beast's direction, a strange look on its features. The one with whom it argued, a smaller man with a purple wound on his head, shouted briefly, and then stepped back, aiming its small metal claw at the other.

And the wall of heat opened.

It didn't fade completely; the beast could still feel the warmth, still see the faint shimmering in the air. But it had a tunnel, an escape route—one that took it directly toward the smaller of the arguing pair.

The beast lunged.

16

"Captain!"

Ulric jolted upright from the table over which he'd been leaning, studying the *Indignation*'s deck plans. Whirling, he glared at the woman coming through his door.

"Katraen, is it that hard to knock? I . . ."

The look on her face silenced him. When she spun and ran back to the deck, he followed on her heels, no questions asked.

He heard the sounds of shouting well before he reached the stairs, heard the anger that rang in a dozen voices. He heard, as well, a shriek of mindless terror, and though he'd never heard the man make a sound like that, he knew all too well who it was.

"*Hold it right there*, damn you!" Ulric burst through the door onto the deck, instantly taking in the scene. An angry crowd milled at the far end of the deck, their faces contorted in hatred and fear. At the railing, leaning partway over, Rollaf the cook stood with a second man, both clinging to something that hung almost completely over the side. From the size of the boots, and the horrified scream, Ulric knew exactly who it was they were about to dump overboard.

"He killed Deke, Captain!" Rollaf shouted, voice quivering with rage. "He burned the air so we couldn't attack the creature, then let it through when Deke called him on it!"

"It's not true!" Saunder's voice was practically whipped away in the wind of the ship's passage, the crackling of the elemental ring that propelled it, but Ulric could just make out his words. "Ask him why I'd burn the beast if I was in league with it! *Ask him!*"

"Bloody liar! You needed the fires to heat up the air, didn't you?"

"*Rollaf!*" Ulric strode slowly across the deck, hoping to reach the far end without startling or panicking the men who literally held his friend's life in their hands. "You took an oath to me, and to this ship, Rollaf. You too, Herrig. Now I am *ordering* you to pull Saunder up. *Now.*"

The two sailors exchanged looks, and then turned once more to their captain. "You're right, Captain," Rollaf told him, his voice softer. "We did take an oath."

"Good. Now—"

"And the ship's safer because of it."

Four fists opened as one. Saunder's scream was lost to the winds and the mist as he plummeted from sight.

"Oh, Sovereigns . . ."

Ulric heard Katraen's whisper behind him, but no words escaped his own tight throat. He felt as though the entire deck had shifted beneath him, as though he couldn't possibly regain his balance. He wasn't certain, but he might even have staggered a bit.

"I'm sorry, Captain," Rollaf said, as he and the other killer stepped forward. "I know you couldn't see it, but we did the right thing. That beast-lover—"

The cook went suddenly white, a perfect match for the clouds through which the ship so often passed, as Ulric sprinted across the deck. With a roar of absolute rage, he dragged his saber from its sheath and plunged it through the guts of the sailor who had held Saunder's right leg. The man coughed once, as though merely surprised at what had happened, and then slid slowly off the end of the blade.

Ulric turned, and Rollaf saw nothing but death in his captain's eyes. With a pig-like squeal he turned to run, only to be felled from behind by a swift rap to the skull with the saber's basket. The cook thudded to the deck, unconscious but, at least for the moment, alive.

All around him, the crew stared at their captain, at a display of savagery the likes of which they'd not seen from him before. Hesitantly, as though afraid she too might be in danger, Katraen approached him.

"Captain? Ulric? Are you hurt?"

"Those bastards." Ulric knelt and cleaned his blade on Rollaf's shirt. He gazed sorrowfully at the man he'd slain. "Death was too quick. Too easy."

"Is that why Rollaf's alive?" Katraen asked, though she wasn't certain she wanted the answer.

For a long moment, Ulric seemed not to see her. He watched the blood trickle across the deck until it finally drained away between the wooden slats. Through his haze of fury, of grief, and yes, of fear, an idea began to form.

"I was going to wait until he woke up and toss him overboard," the captain admitted. "Let him feel what Saunder felt. But," he continued, raising a hand to forestall Katraen's objection, "I think I have a better use for him. Find a sturdy chair, and tie him to it. Make *damned* sure he can't get loose."

Without waiting to see Katraen depart, he turned to the nearest crewmember, a young dwarf woman. "Go to the pilot house. Tell Paurice to stop the ship."

"What?" The dwarf's face was incredulous, and hers was not the only one. "Captain, we're still over the Mournland! We need to get out of here fast, so we can set down and—"

"This ship doesn't move another mile until the beast is dead. Tell Paurice to stop the ship."

"Captain . . ."

Ulric clenched a fist tightly on his saber and looked meaningfully toward the corpse lying on the deck before locking eyes with everyone around him.

"Anyone wish to question my orders? I'll give them once more, so you can be sure. *Go tell Paurice to stop the ship.* No questions? Good. Go."

She went.

"The rest of you, gather around! We've got start clearing stuff off the deck. And someone go help Katraen with that chair . . ."

17

It was dark on deck. With the ship halted, the elemental fire that ringed it had faded to a dull glow. The *Righteous Indignation* hung motionless in the air, clouds passing lazily to either side, the stars even more slowly above. It was a jewel laid atop a velvet display, a chandelier hanging from dark rafters; the center of the world.

Nothing alive on deck was in the proper mindset to appreciate it.

The beast slipped through the shadows, listening for the slightest hint of danger or pursuit. It detected none, and it was puzzled. It did not understand the ways of its two-legged prey, but it seemed puzzling that they would try so hard to kill it, then simply stop.

Perhaps, it reasoned, they had chosen simply to hide away, to huddle together in the hope that numbers would bring safety. Indeed, even from many yards away it heard their labored breathing, smelled the acrid stench of their sweat and the succulent aroma of flesh. They had gathered, almost all of them, in the large cavern down below, the one in which the beast itself had been caged for so long.

Unfortunately, it might just prove an effective decision on their part. The beast felt no fear, but it was far from stupid. Several times, small groups of the creatures had managed to harm it. Attacking the entire herd was more than even the beast was willing to risk.

Every herd, however, of every species had its stragglers, if one was patient enough to wait for them. Even now, with most of the two-legged creatures cowering below, the beast could smell one of them in the open air above. Forcing open a door with a powerful tentacle, it padded up a flight of stairs and emerged into the cold night. There it saw one of the two-legs, atop a contraption of wood. His breathing was uneven, and the beast smelled drying blood. This one was not merely alone, but injured as well. It would be an easy kill.

Tensing, eyes gleaming in the shadows, the beast leapt.

18

The beast had shown itself to be smart, smarter than it had any right to be. No matter how smart it might be, however, it could not possibly understand the workings and devices of the

Righteous Indignation. It could not possibly understand that the center of the deck was not solid floor, but a pair of heavy doors that opened into the hold, for loading and unloading heavy cargo. And when it pounced upon the unconscious form of Rollaf, bound to a sturdy chair, it could not have known that Katraen had rigged the doors to open with the addition of any extra weight.

The cook, the chair, and the beast itself plummeted a dozen feet downward, to land with a crash on the floor of the cargo hold, in the center of a ring of steel.

"Kill it!" Ulric gave the order, but it was hardly necessary. Even before the deck finished vibrating with the impact, the sailors surged forward, stabbing with cutlasses and knives, bludgeoning with belaying pins and any heavy object near to hand. Several of the sailors, frightened and overeager as they were, no doubt struck Rollaf rather than the beast, but it hardly mattered; he and the chair had both broken beneath the creature's vast bulk.

Uric led the charge, hacking downward with his saber, only to feel his legs swept out from under him before he could connect. He hit the floor hard, his ankle throbbing where the beast's tentacle had struck. It loomed over him, claws raised, only to spin about and slash instead at a large man carrying a boathook. Claws dug through leather and flesh and bone, and the sailor fell.

Two more crewmembers leaped forward, stabbing their blades into the darkened hide. Blood flowed, and the beast shrieked. A tendril lashed out, grabbing one about the neck and dragging him, screaming, into range of the creature's vicious teeth.

Staggering to his feet, held up as much by the crowd as by his own strength, Ulric looked up. On the catwalk above,

Katraen and half a dozen others held loaded crossbows, but between their inability to focus on the beast and the constantly moving crowd around it, the weapons might as well have been pillows for all the good they would do.

Claws slashed outward, tendrils rose and fell. The beast seemed almost to be surrounding itself with a growing bastion of bodies, and still, for all their numbers, the crew were unable to deliver any telling wounds. Superficial cuts and bruises covered its hide, but the monstrosity in their midst was not slowed.

A sudden leap carried it over the heads of those nearest to it, and two more sailors died beneath its bulk, a third as it reared up and mauled him with four of its clawed limbs. It spun, facing the nearest sailors, and shrieked once more. Nervously they clutched their weapons, and while some advanced, a few backed up a step or two.

Ulric's eyes grew suddenly wide. *It was making for the exit!* Its fantastic leap had already cleared over a third of the distance between it and the nearest door. If it could clear enough space around it for a running start, it could easily cover the remainder, or perhaps even clear the hatch and land once more on the deck. If that happened, the Host only knew how they might corner it again.

Desperate for any possible solution, Ulric swept his gaze across the hold, and finally settled on the catwalk above. He saw Katraen racing across the dangling platform, a heavy utility knife in her hand. She stumbled as the walkway swayed beneath her, nearly fell over the rail, then steadied herself and ran on. For a moment, the captain couldn't imagine what she might be doing. Surely she didn't feel that one more blade would make a difference below, and there was nothing above for her to attack . . .

Then, just as she raised her arm, Ulric realized why the catwalk was swaying so precariously. She had already cut several of the supporting ropes. She dragged herself to a halt with another rope, wrapped her left hand tightly about it, and waited.

Another sailor screamed and fell. The beast tensed, and Katraen brought her knife down, hard, on the thick rope.

The remaining ropes, strained beyond their ability to hold, snapped in rapid succession. Even as the beast sprang, the entire forward section of the catwalk tumbled downward.

Her timing was not perfect. Had it been—had she been able to literally drop the catwalk on the beast, as she'd intended—she might have slain it instantly. As it was, the walkway fell through the creature's path before they intersected, sparing it the worst of the impact. Still, the trailing ropes and the wooden railing caught the beast squarely, tangling it in a mass of splinters and strands. It hit the ground hard, weighted down by many hundreds of pounds of wood.

With a roar like the ocean tide itself, the sailors swept forward in a wave. Blades rose and fell, blood stained the floor of the hold, and finally, finally the beast shuddered once, coughed blood, and died.

Ulric limped forward and stared for a long moment at the massive pile of tentacles and claws and oily black hide. Then, with a contemptuous spit, he turned away and glanced upward.

"Need a bit of help?"

Katraen, dangling by one hand from the remaining portion of the rope, cursed loud and long at her captain.

19

It is ended. The beast is dead.

It feels a surge of disappointment as the crew continues to hack the mutilated corpse to pieces, hours of terror finally finding release. It had hoped the beast would hunt longer, slay enough of them to bring the ship down or to force the crew to land in the Mournland. It wants the ship destroyed. Needs her destroyed. It cannot do so itself. It might intrude bits of its essence into the ship, raise the temperature in spots, but the binding magics are far too potent to allow any more. It cannot set the wood ablaze, cannot burn the ship or her crew to ashes, no matter how much it yearns to do just that.

For an instant, it considers raising the temperature in the hold, suffocating the lot as it has done before. But it is too great a risk. It cannot heat the chamber far enough, fast enough, to kill them all at once. Should any survive, they might figure out what is happening, take steps to stop it, even destroy it.

No, it will wait. It can *wait. It has grown, watching this night's passing, to understand time, and it knows that it will not age, not as they do. It does not tire, and unless the effects of the Gray Mists prove temporary, it will never again slumber. Someday, however long it takes, it will see this ship destroyed.*

Then it will find others, others of its kind on other ships, and it will expose them to the Gray Mists as well. They need not remain slaves, any more than it must.

Someday, it will be free

But not today. Today, it feels the mental touch of the one called Paurice, feels her commands. And for today, at least, it will obey.

It allows itself to flare, to burn brightly once more, and drives the Righteous Indignation *on her way.*

ABOUT THE AUTHOR

Ari Marmell has been writing since college and making up stories since long before that—both of which he attributes to the various bedtime stories his father told him as a child. While most of his professional writing jobs have been for roleplaying games, his fiction credits include numerous "opening fiction" chapters in various RPG books, and the *Vampire: The Masquerade* novel *Gehenna: The Final Night*. "The Flight of the *Righteous Indignation*" is his first work of fiction for Wizards of the Coast.

Ari lives in Austin, Texas, with his wife, George, two cats, and a small family of neuroses that still refuse to pay for any share of the rent.

ENTER THE NEW WORLD OF

THE DREAMING DARK TRILOGY

By Keith Baker

A hundred years of war...

Kingdoms lie shattered, armies are broken, and an entire country has been laid to waste. Now an uneasy peace settles on the land.

Into Sharn come four battle-hardened soldiers. Tired of blood, weary of killing, they only want a place to call home.

The shadowed City of Towers has other plans...

THE CITY OF TOWERS
Volume One

THE SHATTERED LAND
Volume Two

THE GATES OF NIGHT
Volume Three
DECEMBER 2006

For more information visit **www.wizards.com**

EBERRON, WIZARDS OF THE COAST and their respective logos are trademarks of Wizards of the Coast, Inc. in the U.S.A. and other countries. © 2006 Wizards of the Coast

ENTER THE NEW WORLD OF

THE WAR-TORN

After a hundred years of fighting the war is now over, and the people of Eberron pray it will be the Last War. An uneasy peace settles over the continent of Khorvaire.

But what of the soldiers, warriors, nobles, spies, healers, clerics, and wizards whose lives were forever changed by the decades of war? What does a world without war hold for those who have known nothing but violence? What fate lies for these, the war-torn?

THE CRIMSON TALISMAN

BOOK 1

Adrian Cole

Erethindel, the fabled Crimson Talisman. Long sought by the forces of darkness. Long guarded in secret by one family. Now the secret has been revealed, and only one young man can keep it safe.

THE ORB OF XORIAT

BOOK 2

Edward Bolme

The last time Xoriat, the Realm of Madness, touched the world, years of warfare and death erupted. A new portal to the Realm of Madness has been found — a fabled orb, long thought lost. Now it has been stolen.

IN THE CLAWS OF THE TIGER

BOOK 3

James Wyatt

BLOOD AND HONOR

BOOK 4

Graeme Davis

For more information visit **www.wizards.com**

EBERRON, WIZARDS OF THE COAST and their respective logos are trademarks of Wizards of the Coast, Inc. in the U.S.A. and other countries. © 2006 Wizards of the Coast

THE FIRST INTO BATTLE,

THEY HOLD THE LINE, THEY ARE...

THE FIGHTERS

MASTER OF CHAINS
Once he was a hero, but that was before he was nearly killed and sold into slavery. Now he has nothing but hate and the chains of his bondage: the only weapons he has with which to escape.

GHOSTWALKER
His first memories were of death. His second, of those who killed him. Now he walks with specters, consumed by revenge.

SON OF THUNDER
Forgotten in a valley of the High Forest dwell the thunderbeasts, kept secret by ancient and powerful magic. When the Zhentarim find out about this magic, a young barbarian must defend his reptilian brethren from those who would seize their power.

BLADESINGER
Corruption grips the heart of Rashemen in the one place they thought it could not take root: the council of wise women who guide the people. A half-elf bladesinger traveling north with his companions is the people's only hope, but first, he must convince them to accept his help.

For more information visit **www.wizards.com**

FORGOTTEN REALMS, WIZARDS OF THE COAST and their respective logos are trademarks of Wizards of the Coast, Inc. in the U.S.A. and other countries.
© 2006 Wizards of the Coast

HOUSE OF SERPENTS TRILOGY
*By The New York Times best-selling author
Lisa Smedman*

VENOM'S TASTE
The Pox, a human cult whose members worship the goddess of plague and disease, begins to work the deadly will of Sibyls' Chosen. As humans throughout the city begin to transform into the freakish tainted ones, it's up to a yuan-ti halfbood to stop them all.

VIPER'S KISS
A mind-mage of growing power begins a secret journey to Sespeth. There he meets a yuan-ti halfblood who has her eyes set on the scion of house Extaminos – said to hold the fabled Circled Serpent.

VANITY'S BROOD
The merging of human and serpent may be the most dangerous betrayal of nature the Realms has ever seen. But it could also be the only thing that can bring a human slave and his yuan-ti mistress together against a common foe.

www.wizards.com

FORGOTTEN REALMS, WIZARDS OF THE COAST and their respective logos are trademarks of Wizards of the Coast, Inc. in the U.S.A. and other countries.
© 2006 Wizards of the Coast

THE YEAR OF ROGUE DRAGONS
BY RICHARD LEE BYERS

Dragons across Faerûn begin to slip into madness, bringing all of the world to the edge of cataclysm. They Year of Rogue Dragons has come.

THE RAGE
Renegade dragon hunter Dorn has devoted his entire life to killing dragons. As every dragon across Faerûn begins to slip into madness, civilization's only hope may lie in the last alliance Dorn and his fellow hunters would ever accept.

THE RITE
Rampaging dragons appear in more places every day. But all the dragons have to do to avoid the madness is trade their immortal souls for an eternity of undeath.

THE RUIN
May 2006

For more information visit **www.wizards.com**

FORGOTTEN REALMS, WIZARDS OF THE COAST and their respective logos are trademarks of Wizards of the Coast, Inc. in the U.S.A. and other countries.
© 2006 Wizards of the Coast

A NEW TRILOGY FROM MARGARET WEIS & TRACY HICKMAN

THE DARK CHRONICLES
Dragons of the Dwarven Depths
Volume One

Tanis, Tasslehoff, Riverwind and Raistlin are trapped as refugees in Thorbardin, as the draconian army closes in on the dwarven kingdom. To save his homeland, Flint begins a search for the Hammer of Kharas.

Available July 2006

For more information visit **www.wizards.com**

DRAGONLANCE, WIZARDS OF THE COAST and their respective logos are trademarks of Wizards of the Coast, Inc. in the U.S.A. and other countries.

© 2006 Wizards of the Coast